TIFFANY REISZ

The QUEEN

Recycling programs
for this product may
not exist in your area.

ISBN-13: 978-0-7783-1843-9

The Queen

www.MIRABooks.com

Printed in U.S.A.

First printing: November 2015
10 9 8 7 6 5 4 3 2 1

Dedicated to...
The Author of the Universe

"Love is merely a madness; and, I tell you, deserves as well a dark house and a whip as madmen do; and the reason why they are not so punish'd and cured is that the lunacy is so ordinary that the whippers are in love too."

—William Shakespeare, *As You Like It*

"God creates out of nothing. Wonderful you say. Yes, to be sure, but he does what is still more wonderful: he makes saints out of sinners."

—Søren Kierkegaard,
The Journals of Kierkegaard

1

The First Wedding

NOW, THIS WAS A HAPPY ENDING.

It was all Nora had hoped for, all she had prayed for, and she couldn't stop grinning as the music began—Jeremiah Clarke's *Trumpet Voluntary*.

She smiled even wider when two elderly gentlemen in traditional servant's livery opened the great oak double doors with a flourish befitting the exalted occasion.

After one deep breath, Nora stepped through the open doors and did the one thing she'd sworn she would never do—she walked down the aisle of a church in a wedding dress toward Søren, who waited for her at the altar.

He hadn't seen her for hours and this moment was Søren's first look at her in her wedding dress. It had been twenty years since she'd walked down an aisle toward Søren as a bridesmaid in a wedding he'd performed. Even now, halfway down the aisle, she could see the look in his eyes, a look that said the twenty years had been worth the wait.

As Nora took her place at Søren's right hand, she leaned in close and whispered, "Stop looking at me like that."

"Why?" he asked as the two hundred assembled guests rose to their feet when the groom made his entrance into the Great Hall that had been converted into a church for the wedding.

"You're on duty," she reminded him. "*Father* Stearns."

"Can I look at you like that after the wedding?"

She smiled at him as the two grooms joined hands in front of Søren.

"Today you can do anything you want."

"Watch out. I'll hold you to that promise," he said as the music faded into silence leaving her unable to retort. She swallowed her words, composed her face and tried not to cry when Søren began to speak.

"Dearly beloved, we are gathered here today to join this man, Michael Luka Dimir, and this man, Griffin Randolfe Fiske, in holy matrimony. May your love be blessed by the sacrament of marriage and may we all who are gathered as witnesses rejoice together in the beauty of your commitment to each other as we would bask in the warmth of the sun..."

Nora made it three whole minutes into the ceremony before the tears started flowing. Luckily all eyes were on Michael and Griffin as they spoke their vows and made their promises. Once upon a time in a very different setting, Nora and Søren had made promises to each other and she wore those promises around her neck in the form of wedding bands engraved with two words—*Forever* and *Everything*. They weren't wedding vows but they had bound them together nonetheless. What was a sacrament but the outward sign of inner grace? If she and Søren loving each other and staying together despite all they'd been through, all they'd put each other through for twenty-three years, wasn't a miracle, she didn't know what was.

"Therefore," Søren said as the service drew to its conclusion, "now they are not two, but one flesh. What therefore God hath joined together, let no man put asunder."

Søren spoke with authority and power, as if the words themselves could bind hearts together.

"I now pronounce you husband…and husband."

Griffin took Michael's face in his hands and kissed him.

And kissed him.

And kissed him.

A kiss of love and of lust and of complete and utter devotion, it went on so long the assembled witnesses started to titter, then giggle, then laugh. They kissed until Søren cleared his throat not once, but twice, louder the second time than the first. When even that didn't put a stop to their rather protracted display of public affection, Søren uttered a low "For heaven's sake, Griffin, people have places to be. Can't you save the consummation until later?"

Griffin paused long enough to look at Søren and answer, "Nope," before returning to the kiss with gusto.

Nora applauded him. Good man. Don't let anyone tell you to stop kissing for such a silly reason as two hundred people watching. What better place in the world was there to be than here, watching true lovers kiss? One didn't see such a thing every day. When witnessing a miracle, one should never hurry it along, for it'll be gone all too soon and who knows when one will see another miracle in one's lifetime?

Time stopped with that kiss. The image imprinted itself upon Nora's mind like a tintype photograph… She stood at Søren's right as Michael's mistress of honor—no one would have believed her a maid or a matron, so mistress it was—and Kingsley stood to the left of Søren as Griffin's best man. The wedding was held in the Great Hall of the thousand-year-old castle. The vibrant blue walls gleamed like polished azurite in the glow of a dozen brass-and-crystal chandeliers. Candles and flowers stationed on the ebony oak floors encircled the wedding party. Kingsley, Griffin and Søren all wore kilts. Griffin's and Kingsley's were red, white and green, the tartan of his mother's ancestors. Søren's kilt was black and blue, the traditional clergy tartan of Scotland and bruises. Upon request and because she couldn't tell Griffin no when he'd asked so nicely, she'd worn a Scottish wedding dress, tiered white silk and lace peeking out from under a corseted red-and-green tartan overlay. Michael had forgone the kilt—not his style, he said—and chosen a hip Rat Pack–era tuxedo with a black shirt and black jacket. A better-looking married couple she'd never seen in her life and not because they were so beautiful, although they were, but because their love was true and pure and hard-won. Every act of love was an act of courage, but for Michael and Griffin it was especially so. The world didn't often reward those who loved outside the lines. Nora had learned this lesson the hard way.

The kiss went on so long the guests rose to their feet and applauded.

Griffin turned to the masses and issued an order.

"Less applauding," he yelled at his guests. "More kissing!"

"No one has to tell me twice," Kingsley said, holding out his hand to Juliette, the mother of his daughter with another one on the way, and the most beautiful woman in attendance by far. Laughing, Juliette rose to her feet and put her hand in Kingsley's. He dipped her back and gave her an old Hollywood kiss.

"Shall we?" Søren asked.

"In front of two hundred people?"

"Why not?"

"Is that a rhetorical question or do you really want me to list all eight hundred reasons why not?"

Søren answered by taking her face in his hands and kissing her—a kiss like Communion, like wine on her tongue. She heard a few gasps of shock from the assembly followed by laughter and applause. Apparently this was the first time they'd seen a Catholic priest kissing a woman. It was a first for Nora as well, being kissed by Søren in front of so many people they didn't know. Yes, Kingsley had forced all the staff and the guests to sign non-disclosure agreements, but that was no guarantee word wouldn't leak that a certain well-respected Jesuit priest passionately kissed a fairly notorious dominatrix at a wedding in Scotland. And not just any wedding—a same-sex wedding. Søren could be laicized for performing a same-sex marriage. He'd get in less trouble if he were caught by the Pope himself sodomizing her in the Tomb of Saint Peter. Not that she'd ever had that fantasy—not very often anyway. Officiating the service had been Søren's gift to Michael, whom he loved like a son. When Nora had reminded him of the very real danger of excommunication if caught, Søren had replied, *Michael asked me. It's my honor to do it.* Since Søren was a man of honor that had been the end of it.

But it wouldn't be the end of it.

Søren was a Jesuit priest who had kissed a woman in front of two hundred people and performed a same-sex wedding. A kiss plus a wedding plus what would happen tonight at nine o'clock added up to one very simple conclusion.

Søren's days as a priest were numbered.

2

NORA PULLED BACK FROM THE KISS AND SAW A DOZEN or more couples kissing, including Griffin and Michael, who were still kissing.

And.

Still.

Kissing.

"Oh, for fuck's sake, Griffin," Nora said, reaching in front of Søren for Kingsley's hand. "You two make out as long as you want. The King and I are going to get a drink."

Nora gave Kingsley the end of the long plaid ribbon she'd tied around her bouquet. As they walked on either side of the happy couple—still kissing, of course—they lifted their hands and passed the sash over their heads like a wedding bower. Behind her she heard Søren speaking to the crowd of guests.

"I'd suggest everyone retreat to the banquet hall," he said in his most authoritarian clergy voice. "It seems the groom and groom might be a while."

Kingsley took her arm in his to escort her down the long aisle to the door.

"I heard we have you to thank for the wedding," Kingsley said, kissing the back of her hand.

Nora winced. "Michael had a little case of cold feet. I beat it out of him."

"Literally?"

"It took a solid hour of flogging followed by an hour of wax-play. Kid came so hard he almost passed out. Two-hour nap, and he was ready to get married. I love saving the day," she said. "I'm so good at it."

They waited in the foyer and soon they were joined by Michael's mother and sister, Griffin's parents and three brothers, and Søren. Juliette, wearing a red gown to match Kingsley's kilt, passed Céleste into his arms. And when Michael and Griffin finally emerged from the Great Hall it was to a hail of applause and a shower of rice. Céleste was the best rice thrower of them all, Kingsley assured his little girl. Michael's lips appeared swollen from so much passionate kissing and his pale cheeks were flushed, but Nora had to admit, she'd never seen him or Griffin ever look happier. Today was a beautiful day to be in love.

The guests who greeted the couple with hugs and kisses were a hodgepodge of friends and family, or as Kingsley called them, "the freaks and the straights." Mistress Irina, the first dominatrix Kingsley had trained for The 8th Circle, had sat next to Michael's aunt and uncle during the ceremony. Michael's sister Erin had borrowed a tissue from Alfred, Griffin's white-haired butler, who'd had to surreptitiously wipe his own eyes a time or two during the ceremony. Nora'd been a little surprised he'd come all the way to Scotland for Griffin's wedding. When she had asked him why he'd made the long trip from upstate New York, he'd answered, "He's a man-child and a deviant, and he has more money than sense, young lady. So of course I'm here for his wedding to his shamefully younger boy toy. It's the only sensible thing he's ever done in his life." Then he'd stalked off before Nora could hug him or worse, cry in his arms, which would have been an unforgivable affront to his dignity.

"Good ceremony, Father," she said, smiling up at Søren. "I loved the homily."

"Thank you. The Lord gives me good material to work with. I suppose He deserves most of the credit." Leave it to a Jesuit to be simultaneously pious and smug.

"Oops, picture time," she said. "I should go."

The photographer was already attempting to corral the wedding party back into the Great Hall. Søren started back into the hall with her.

"You can't be in the pictures," she reminded him.

"Michael expects me to be in at least one of the photographs for him and Griffin."

"Søren...this is not a good idea."

"Michael's like a son to me," he said. "When you have a child, you make sacrifices for them."

"All right. Pictures it is. In for a penny, in for a pounding, right?" She took his hand in hers. His fingers trembled, and she met his eyes with a question.

"I'm fine," he said before she had the chance to ask.

"It's fine if you aren't fine."

"I am fine."

"Your hand is shaking."

"This kilt is...*breezy*."

"It's like a hundred feet of wool."

"This castle has an updraft. I'm not used to inclement weather in that region."

"It's your own fault for going regimental."

"Kingsley was. And when in Rome..."

"How do you know Kingsley's going full Scotsman?" She narrowed her eyes at him. "Did you actually go running this morning or did you two play a game of hide the claymore?"

"I ran," he said. "Before."

"I knew it." She took both of his hands in hers now and interlocked their fingers.

Søren glanced at a grandfather clock and back at her.

"Five thirty," he said. "Three and a half more hours."

"It'll go fast," she said, smiling a hopeful smile. "Won't it?"

"It will be the longest three and a half hours of my life."

For Nora, too.

"They won't need me at the reception which isn't a reception. I can wait with you," she said.

"Thank you." He kissed her on the forehead. "What would I ever do without my Little One?"

Nora swallowed an unexpected lump in her throat.

"I promise, you won't ever have to find out."

Reluctantly she let go of Søren's hands as the photographer led her and Kingsley toward Michael and Griffin. The first pictures were of the groom and groom, best man and mistress of honor.

Kingsley held out his arm for her and she took it, grateful for his company in the secret they shared.

"How is he?" Kingsley asked.

"He is exactly how you think he is," she said.

"Never so scared in his life?"

"White-knuckle petrified."

Kingsley kissed her cheek. "I know how he feels."

Pictures took half an hour. Kingsley promised to make her and Søren's excuses to anyone who asked where they were. Michael and Griffin could be told the truth, of course. They would understand. Michael had agreed to a big wedding with one stipulation—no official wedding reception. A party? Sure. Fine. Michael, young artist that he was, found manufactured moments like the ceremonial cake-cutting offensive. The reception was only for people to eat and drink and dance. Once the wedding was over, the wedding party was free to get up to whatever depraved shenanigans they wanted to. And as she and Kingsley were the wedding party, depraved shenanigans were a given.

Nora went looking for Søren and wasn't the least surprised to find him in the castle's small stone-and-wood chapel. She stepped inside and strode toward him.

The sun streamed through an octagonal window and cast eight-sided light onto Søren, turning his blond hair into gold in a moment of pure alchemy. In a breath, in an instant, she was fifteen years old again, and he twenty-nine, and he looked exactly like he did the first time she'd laid eyes on him. The sunlight melted the years between then and now. Her hand trembled so it was a miracle she didn't drop her glass of red wine.

Her footsteps on the stone floor alerted Søren to her presence. He lifted his head and turned back to her. The mask of composure had fallen, and she saw anguish in his eyes. She set her glass of wine on the altar and went to him, gathering him in her arms, holding him to her heart and resting her chin on the top of his head.

"How are you, my sir?"

"I don't know," he admitted, looking up at her. "There have been days in my life where I've woken up not knowing that later on that very day, my entire life would change. The day I met Kingsley, the day I met you. Usually you don't know the day or the hour. Today I do."

"Remember that story I wrote about Queen Esther when I was in high school?"

"How could I forget it? I must have read it a thousand times."

"You did?"

"An erotic story written by a beautiful sixteen-year-old girl I was desperately and unrepentantly in love with and featuring a hero who looked suspiciously like me? I read it until the ink faded and the pages crumbled."

It embarrassed Nora how much it pleased her that Søren had loved her story that much.

"I'll have you know I did not base King Xerxes on you."

"He was blond. A blond Persian."

"Poetic license." She sat at his side in the pew. "Queen Esther looked suspiciously like me, as well. Anyway...writing that story changed my life. I'd never written anything like that before. All I was trying to do was flirt with you and now twenty-two years later I've made an entire career from writing. I didn't know my life would change that day by writing one little story. And yet...here we are. All thanks to you."

"And Queen Esther. And Queen Eleanor."

"I'm not really a queen."

"You've always been a queen in my eyes. Especially now."

"I can't believe I'm wearing a wedding dress. How do I let Griffin talk me into these things?"

"It's exquisite. You're exquisite."

Søren kissed her lightly on the lips. His mouth shivered against hers. Søren was a man of quiet depth, as if he kept a secret second heart locked away in a glass case. It would explain how much he felt and how strongly and yet how rarely such feelings were allowed to escape from captivity. Sometimes before they made love he would cut her skin with a sharp paper-thin blade and the act was so intimate and harrowing it would leave him shaking. It scared him to take her life in his hands, and yet it was at such times they felt closest to each other. She knew his trembling now was for a similar reason.

"Do you forgive me, Little One?" Søren asked.

"What mortal sin have you committed recently?"

"You know my sins better than I do."

"Yes. Which is why I tell you there is no need to beg my forgiveness for anything."

"You have a forgiving heart," Søren said. "I have always admired that about you."

"I know myself. I know my own weaknesses and failures. Jesus was always so kind to sinners and so cruel to hypocrites."

"Am I a hypocrite?" Søren asked.

"You're human."

"You don't have to be insulting, Eleanor."

She laughed and rested her head on his shoulder. He sighed so her whole body moved with his. Somewhere behind and above them a bell rang. Six times the bell chimed. Six o'clock and all was well.

Three hours and counting.

"It's strange, isn't it?" Søren said.

"What is?"

"Just yesterday Michael was fifteen years old and had barely healed scars on his wrists from when he tried to kill himself in my church. And today...today he's twenty-one and married. Michael. Married." He looked at her and half laughed.

"I know. Crazy, isn't it? I swear yesterday *I* was fifteen, and I saw my new priest for the very first time, and loved him from the moment I saw him, and knew I'd love him until I died. Today I'm thirty-eight, and I still love him and know I'll love him forever." The days danced and flashed around her like fireflies on a summer's night. "Where is the time going?" she asked him. "How did it all go by so fast? And what if it's all gone tomorrow?"

"We live each day like it's our last. But not by running about wildly, attempting to cram every possible experience into one day. Instead…every day we should make our peace with God and each other. Say what needs to be said and not leave it for another time. If I knew I would die tomorrow I'd spend all night telling you and Kingsley how much I love you both, and I wouldn't let God take me until I was certain you knew I meant every word. I would sing it to you like the angels sing praise to God in heaven—unceasingly."

"We know. Kingsley and I, we already know."

"But I would still tell you," he said softly. "Even if you didn't need to hear it, I would have to tell you."

She held him close again, kissed his cheek, his forehead, like a mother kissing a scared child. And he was scared. She could feel it in every touch.

"Talk to me. Distract me. Help me get through these hours."

"Will you hear my confession?" Nora asked. She turned and met his eyes. How she loved those eyes, the strength and color of steel. "This could be my last chance to confess to you, after all."

"I won't leave the priesthood. I promised you I wouldn't."

"You were in the wedding pictures. You performed a same-sex marriage. You kissed me in front of two hundred wedding guests, half of them we don't know. You can tell me all you want that it's fine, that it won't matter, but we both know those are not the actions of a man who is planning on being a priest for much longer."

"I have to tell them. Some things shouldn't be secrets."

"You tell them the truth, and they will kick you out."

"Possibly. I've made choices, difficult ones, but I did it in full knowledge of the consequences. Nothing stays the same forever, after all."

"That's not true. My love for you is forever. I made that promise, and I will keep it. But tomorrow or next week or next month you might not be a priest anymore. So please… hear my confession and absolve me? One last time?"

He rose from the pew and moved a chair from the side of the chapel and set it in front of her. From the leather sporran of his kilt, he pulled a leather case, unzipped it and unfurled a purple sash. He kissed it and draped it around his neck and over his shoulders. He sat in the chair and pressed his palms together. Nora looked at his hands and saw they were now steady and still.

She smiled and looked up to the octagonal window. The sun would set in under three hours. By nightfall everything could change.

"First of all," she began, "I'm confessing these sins to you because I committed them against you and only you can absolve me of them."

"What are your sins?"

Nora loved Søren. This was an incontrovertible fact of the universe, strong as gravity, inevitable as sunrise. She'd told him almost everything there was to tell him about their years apart, everything but this. She hadn't wanted to hurt him but she didn't want to keep the truth from him anymore. No more secrets. No more lies. Nothing between them anymore and never again.

"Forgive me, Father, for I have sinned," she began her confession. "When we were apart there were two times I almost came back to you and didn't."

"Two?" Søren looked at her, wide-eyed and stunned. Usually she loved shocking him, it was such a feat. Not today. "Why didn't you?"

"Are you sure you want to know?"

Then Søren said to her the two words she'd once said to him that had changed her life.

"Tell me."

3

Power Games

New York City
2005

ELLE HAD NEVER FELT MORE POWERLESS IN HER LIFE.

A strong statement from a woman who'd been the property of a sadist and dominant for her entire adult life. She'd knelt at his feet, called him "sir," obeyed his every order, submitted to his every desire, sexual and sadistic. Not even with her forehead on his bedroom floor, a collar around her neck and a flogger on her back had Elle felt this trapped and impotent. With Søren she could have stopped it all with her safe word. What would she have to say to stop it now?

Elle was broke and homeless, had no job and no idea where to go if Kingsley kicked her out of his house. There was no safe word that could save her tonight. So when Kingsley sat on his desk in front of her in the middle of a cool spring night and said to her, "I want you to become a dominatrix," she didn't laugh in his face. She didn't have the luxury anymore of laughing in Kingsley's face about anything. He had all the power, and she had none. An unusual and unpleasant sensation. She resolved never to feel it again.

"A dominatrix?" Elle repeated after Kingsley had made his royal proclamation. "Me?"

"A dominatrix." Kingsley pointed at her chest. "You."

"So...you want me...to beat people up...for money?"

"*Non*. Not for money." Kingsley waved his pointing finger in front of her face in that annoying French way he had of tsk-tsking her. She almost bit that finger off. Instead she behaved herself because she was too scared not to. "For a lot of fucking money, Elle."

"How much fucking money?" she asked.

"When I'm done training you, you'll be making one to five thousand dollars an hour."

If Elle had water in her mouth at that moment she would have spit it all over the front of Kingsley's barely buttoned white shirt.

"A thousand dollars an hour?"

"Minimum," Kingsley said.

"Dominatrixes don't usually make that kind of money."

Mistress Irina, Kingsley's Russian sadist, worked the top end of the scale. And she made five hundred dollars an hour—a thousand an hour when the client demanded very special and intimate attention that would likely lead to hospitalization. The extra fee was for all the paperwork involved.

"But you will. You will be offering a service others will not."

"Sex?"

"Sex would hardly warrant five thousand an hour. Almost anyone can lie on their back, close their eyes and think of France."

"It's England."

"Why would anyone think of England during sex?"

"Forget it. Tell me what I'm doing."

"You know what you're doing," Kingsley said. "Exactly what you want to be doing except you'll be doing it for money."

"A lot of fucking money," she said, looking up at Kingsley. He sat on the edge of his desk with one foot on the arm of the chair, gazing down at her waiting for her answer.

"This is not a good idea, King," she said, keeping her voice even, not saying yes or no to his offer.

"It is not a good idea, no. It is the best idea. *Chérie*...you could buy anything you want," Kingsley whispered. She knew that tone. He was seducing her. "In a year you'll be rich. You remember Mistress Felicia? You should have seen her house in Bedford. I've known minor royalty who didn't live as well as she did. Rich men gave her diamonds the way poor men give girls daisies—by the dozens."

A house. That would be nice. A home of her own. Not a room in someone else's life. Her own home that was in her name that no one could take away from her.

"I still don't know why you think men will pay me so much money," she said.

"Mistress Irina works from her dungeon, sometimes from the town house. They come to her, her clients do. But you... you will go where the money is. Clients who wouldn't dare set foot into a club or a dungeon? You will go to them."

"Is that safe?"

"Is life safe?"

"I'll take that as a no."

Kingsley smiled. "Is there anything worth doing that is safe?" he asked.

"I don't know. I've read a lot of books worth reading. Never gotten hurt doing that before."

"You've never gotten rich doing it, either."

"King, I can't... No. This is absurd. My entire adult life—and most of my teenage life—I've been a submissive."

"You know what is more absurd? You sitting there and pretending you haven't wanted this for your entire adult life. And most of your teenage life, too. I knew you then. I remember..."

"What? What do you remember?"

"The first time I saw you, you nearly gave a boy a concussion, because he committed the unforgivable sin of annoying you when you weren't in the mood to be annoyed. He was talking back to a priest and stood up. I saw you stretch out your leg and hook your boot under his chair and slide it aside right at the moment he tried to sit back down. He landed on the floor so hard I heard a crack and thought it was either a rib or his skull. And you..."

"I put my feet on his chest."

"No, you put your *boots* on his chest and told him to shut the fuck up. That instant, I knew you were either going to grow up to be a dominatrix...or a sociopath. I was hard as a rock watching you and you were barely sixteen years old. I could come right now thinking of it."

"You don't really think I'm a sociopath, do you?"

"You have a conscience. But you know what they call a sociopath with a conscience?"

It sounded like the setup to a joke so Elle took the bait.

"No, what do they call a sociopath with a conscience?"

"They call her 'Mistress.'"

Elle stood up from her chair and walked to the window behind Kingsley's desk. She pushed back the curtains and gazed onto the dark streets. Even during the dead of night, New York still felt awake and alive. Last night she'd been in a convent in rural upstate New York where the world went to bed at seven and woke up at four and slept like a corpse in the hours between. And not a man in sight. Now she was alone in a room with a man she'd beaten last year, a man she'd burned and bruised and brutalized. And God, it had been fun, hadn't it? More than fun, it had been her. For years, ever since she was a teenager, her sexual fantasies had involved dominating men, tying them up, tying them down and fucking them half to death. When she'd finally gotten her chance to try it with Kingsley, she'd been scared. She'd even cried at first from fear and confusion. But the moment she let go and let it happen, she felt like...

"I've seen her, Elle," Kingsley said as he came to stand behind her. She was acutely aware of his body so close to hers. She hadn't had sex with a man for over a year, since she ran away and hid out at the convent. Any other man might not have made her feel so much in such close quarters, but it was this man who'd put a riding crop in her hand, given her permission to destroy him. Oh, and she had destroyed him, and in the process, she'd destroyed herself. Her old self. She still hadn't found her new self yet.

"Who have you seen?"

"You. The real you. I've seen her."

"What does she look like?"

Kingsley sighed and smiled. "She's beautiful. Dangerous. All eyes are on her when she walks into a room. Men fear her but not because she's the enemy. They fear her because she alone can show them who they really are. They fear this knowledge but will pay any price for it."

"Is she happy?" Elle asked.

"She's powerful. She can make her own happiness when she wants it."

Elle turned and looked up at him.

"Is she with someone?"

"She isn't lonely," Kingsley said. "Not this woman. This is a woman who can walk into any room, find the most handsome face in the crowd, look him in the eyes and know she will take him home with her on a leash."

Elle laughed at the idea. Sounded good to her.

Kingsley caressed her cheek with the back of his fingers.

He narrowed his eyes at her, his expression inscrutable.

"What? What is it?" she asked.

"I missed you," he said, blinking as if attempting to clear a fog. "Forgive me. I just realized that."

"I missed you, too. I thought about writing you but I didn't know what to say."

Kingsley turned his head, didn't look at her.

"It didn't matter. I was gone, too. I came home two months ago."

"You left, too? Why? When?"

He paused before answering. "The day after you left, I left. And you know why. If I stayed…"

If he'd stayed, they—Kingsley and Søren—would have found her and brought her home, and no door, even one that said "No Men Beyond This Point," could have kept them from taking her back.

"Thank you," she whispered.

"For what?"

She wanted to thank him for forgiving her even though she didn't regret it. But instead she said, "Thanks for not kicking me out. Tonight, I mean. I wouldn't have blamed you if you did."

Briefly she met his eyes. She'd didn't say what she wanted to say, couldn't say it. Last year she'd accidentally gotten pregnant and it had been Kingsley's. As much as he wanted children, she wouldn't have blamed him for rejecting her pleas for help, sending her out into the night again, banishing her from his life. She was in debt now and hated it, hated owing him for something as simple as letting her back in the house she'd once shared with him.

"Elle…" He took her by the shoulders and met her eyes. "When Søren first told me about you, I called you his princess. And he said, no, you were a queen. And I laughed. But last year when you and I were together, when you cut me and burned me and you did it all with a smile on your face… I was wrong. He was right. You are a queen. At least…you could be one. Is that what you want?"

"I don't know."

"Tell me what you want."

"I want a job."

"This is a job."

"I want money so I can support myself."

"These are all very boring answers. Tell me the truth. What do you really want?"

"I don't want to feel like this anymore. That's what I want."

He furrowed his brow at her. "How do you feel?"

"Powerless," she said. "I'm afraid to say no to your 'job offer.' What would I do if you kicked me out? Where would I go?"

"Back to him?"

"No. I can't. That's the last place I could go."

Kingsley nodded, seeming to understand her predicament.

"I can't turn down your offer, can I?" she asked.

"Do you want to? Truly?"

The question seemed sincere, not teasing as it might have been. He meant it—did she want to turn down his offer?

"What's the alternative if I say no?" she asked.

Kingsley opened a desk drawer and in the desk drawer was his locked cashbox.

"There's one hundred thousand dollars in there. It's yours

if you want it. Take it and walk out the door." He held up the key to the cashbox. "You can live on that much money for five years if you're careful. Go south where the winters are warm and rents are cheap. Get a job. Go back to school. Be a lawyer or a therapist or a schoolteacher. Marry a rich old man for all I care. Start your life over away from here, away from me."

"I don't want your charity."

"It's not charity. After Sam left, you worked as my assistant for years without any pay other than room and board. I give it to you free and clear with no strings attached. You've earned it. All I ask is that you never contact me again. I spent an entire year worrying over you, feeling like you were my responsibility and I'd failed you. I won't do that again. I can't. Take the money and go, and I will absolve myself of all responsibility. My conscience will be clear. At least where you're concerned. Or..."

"Or I can work for you. Here. As a domme."

"*Oui*. And working for me here as a domme you will have a job, you will have money and you will have power."

"Power? Working for you? If I work for you, you'd have all the power."

"You won't be my employee. You'll be my queen. You will be my queen and in a year you will have all the money and power you could possibly desire. One hundred thousand dollars and you go tonight and you never come back. Or you stay and work for me and one hundred thousand will seem like spare change to you in a year. Think about it. I'll give you five minutes."

Kingsley turned and walked out of the office just like that, leaving her all alone.

Once alone Elle sagged against the wall, the choice before her dizzying. A hundred grand and she could start a brand-new life far away from here. Her passport was in her bedroom. If

Kingsley hadn't thrown everything out, she could get it and leave the country. Money was power. Money was freedom.

But…it was a game, wasn't it? she thought as she sat in Kingsley's antique leather swivel chair behind the grand old Art Deco-era desk. Take the money and run? Or stay and work and make two, three, four times that amount?

And yet…it wasn't really the money she cared about. Money was a means to an end and that end was power. She never wanted to feel the way she felt half an hour ago when she'd knocked on the front door of Kingsley's town house knowing that if he shut the door in her face, she had nowhere else to go.

On Kingsley's desk sat a chessboard with red pieces and white pieces. When she and Søren played, he took red and she took white. When she and Kingsley played, she took red and Kingsley took white. Chess…a strange old game. She wasn't very good at it and neither was Kingsley. Søren alone had the gift for it. She'd asked him once why he made her play chess with him when she wasn't good at it. He'd answered, "Chess teaches that actions have consequences and the wise man—or woman—will always look to the endgame…"

Elle picked up the red bishop. The bishop moved diagonally along a straight line. The poor pawn could move only a square at a time. Although if it were played well, it could become a queen. She put the bishop back on the board and picked up the red queen and the white king. The king was a strong piece, of course. The most important chess piece and the most vulnerable to attack. But the queen…the queen was the most powerful chess piece. More powerful than the king. And the queen could move any way she wanted…

Kingsley opened the door to his office.

"What's your decision?" he asked standing on the threshold.

Elle placed the king and queen side by side on the chess-board and looked up at Kingsley.

"Let's play."

4

Three Ways to Be a Queen

"GOOD ANSWER," KINGSLEY SAID, SNAPPING HIS FIN-gers at her to indicate she was to follow him. Elle stood up and followed him out of his office.

"Did you really think I'd take the money and run?" she asked as they walked down the hall side by side.

"In your shoes, I might have," he admitted.

"I was tempted."

"What made your decision? Him?"

"You," she said. "I'm not done beating the shit out of you yet."

Kingsley laughed and it was a sight to behold. His face was handsome, striking, even in repose, but when Kingsley Edge laughed it could drop a girl to her knees for more reasons than simple obeisance.

"Plus, being a queen sounds more fun than being the wife of some rich old man."

"When I'm done with you, you will be the domme of many rich old men. Instead of you cooking and cleaning for them for free, you will beat them and use them and they'll pay you for the privilege."

"Sign me up for queenship, then."

"It's not that easy," Kingsley said as they headed down the steps and to his private sitting room. "There are, in fact, only three ways to become a queen. Signing up isn't one of them."

"What are the three ways?" she asked. "Marry a king, I guess."

"Will you marry me?" Kingsley asked.

"No offense, King, but I'd go back to the convent first."

"And I'd join the priesthood before marrying you, as well. You and I are not husband-and-wife material. For each other or anyone else."

Kingsley opened the door to the sitting room and Elle followed him inside. When she turned on the Tiffany lamp she saw nothing had changed in the room while she was at the convent. Same bookshelves filled with leather-bound classics in French and English. Same red velvet fainting couch. Same gilt-framed portraits of naked nymphs at play. Same everything and on a night of upheaval and change, the sameness comforted her.

"Sit," Kingsley ordered.

Elle sat.

"Where was I?" he asked, stalking about the room like a caged wolf, more rather than less dangerous because of the cage. Energy contained is energy focused and she felt almost afraid to be alone in the room with someone this dangerous. She had been at the convent so long she didn't know how to be alone with a man again.

"Three ways to be a queen."

"Yes. First, you can marry a king. That won't work in this instance. Mainly because I already have a consort, and she might not like it if I took on another."

"Wait. What? You have a new girlfriend?" He'd been so heartbroken over his ex-girlfriend Charlie's defection she never dreamed he'd take on another 24/7 submissive again.

"Not a girlfriend. Consort. Her name is Juliette, and she is the perfect submissive. She's also currently chained by her ankle to my bed so I wouldn't go in my bedroom for at least a week."

"Chained to your bed? King, you can't leave her alone chained to your bed. What if something happens to her?"

"I left a bell by the bed to ring if she needs me, and the phone, of course. And the key if she wants to unlock herself. She can get out the second she wants to get out. But I know her—she'll stay there until I unlock her."

"Can't wait to meet her."

"You'll love her. I met her in Haiti."

"Special, is she?" Elle asked.

Kingsley grinned ear to ear, a rare sight and a breathtaking one.

"I'm in love with her. I think she will be with me all my life."

"It's good to see you happy. You deserve that."

"I most certainly do. Now, the second way to become a queen," Kingsley said, taking a book down off the shelf and flipping through the pages, "is how I became a king. I claimed a territory, called myself a king, acted like a king, and soon everyone simply accepted that I was. But you will become a queen the third way."

"Which is?"

"By deposing the current queen and taking her realm away from her."

"There's a queen? We have a queen? We never had a queen before. Jesus, how long have I been gone?"

"Too long," Kingsley said with real feeling. They were so

much alike, she and King. Too much alike. Impossible to be friends. Impossible to be enemies. But partners in crime? Yes, they could be that.

"Nature abhors a vacuum, they say. When I left and you left, it created a power vacuum. A dominatrix appeared on the scene and started scooping up the best and richest clients. Half of Irina's clients deserted her. So did Mistress Vee's."

"Ballsy woman. I wouldn't want to get on their bad sides."

"She's on my bad side. One of Irina's clients came back to her, begging forgiveness and asking to be hers again. His new domme sent pictures she'd taken during their sessions to his wife. Thankfully he'd already told his wife about his submissive side, and she'd given him permission to explore with a professional. But it was a petty, vile thing she did, and she won't get away with it. She keeps her clients in line through fear, not love and devotion. She abuses her power, and I won't stand for that in my city."

Elle winced. Kingsley had his reams of blackmail material on anyone in the city who mattered and many people who didn't, but he used it to protect the citizens of his kingdom, not humiliate and ruin them for their proclivities. And to destroy his enemies, of course. Sounded like he'd made a new enemy.

"Who is she?" Elle asked. "What's her name?"

Kingsley held the book in his hand out to her and pointed to an illustration of a beautiful woman in an eighteenth-century gown. Elle glanced at the title of the book and back at the page.

"Milady…" Elle said, studying the face of the woman on the page. The book was Alexandre Dumas's *The Three Musketeers*, and the woman in the illustration was the infamous Milady de Winter.

"That's what your rival calls herself. No first name. No last name. Milady. Nothing else."

"Do you know anything about her?"

"I know nothing about her and not for lack of trying. She claims to be the illegitimate daughter of a Japanese geisha and an English lord. She also claims she went to Harvard but didn't graduate because she was caught topping one of her professors. Oh, and she says she married an Italian knight—they do exist, by the way, I've met a few—but he was fifty years her senior and when he died, he left her a wealthy widow with a villa in Tuscany. And if any of that is true, I'll eat my vest."

"You think she's lying?"

"I do but I have no proof of it. She's careful. Even wears gloves all the time so no one can get her fingerprints. When in the city she stays in a hotel under an assumed name and pays in cash. That level of paranoia and fear makes me suspicious. But her story makes for wonderful marketing. Her English is flawless, not a trace of an accent, but she also speaks Japanese flawlessly with no trace of an accent. She's well educated and intelligent. She's also mysterious, seductive, painfully beautiful and terribly cruel. Men throw themselves at her. There are rumors she secretly tapes her sessions so that if a client wishes to leave her, he either pays her a huge sum of money for the tapes or he stays with her. Most of them stay."

Kingsley snapped the book shut and placed it back on his shelf.

"Have you tried sleeping with her?" Elle asked. Knowing Kingsley as she knew him, it wasn't an unreasonable question.

"No," he said. "I haven't met her yet."

"Is she good?"

"Very good from what I hear."

For Kingsley to call a domme good was quite a compliment. The man could take more pain and wanted more pain than anyone she'd ever known in the scene.

"But…"

"But what?" Elle asked. Kingsley took her chin in hand and tilted her face up to him. He smiled.

"You'll be better."

"Will I be better than him?"

"No one is better than he is at sadism," Kingsley said. "But..."

"But?"

"You'll be a close second. Considering you're untrained, and he's been studying pain since he was born, there's a very good chance you could put even him on his knees."

"I don't ever want to see him again, on his knees or off."

"You say that now."

"I'll say that tomorrow, too."

"Very well. I will respect that. For now. He's not my favorite person either, nor am I his. But ours is a small world. You can't avoid him forever."

"Have you seen him?"

"I have."

"How is he?" she asked.

"Not the question someone usually asks about someone she hates."

"I want to know he's hurting."

"Then you'll be happy to hear he is."

"Good," she said. That made her happy. So happy. So fucking happy she wanted to cry. "He's still a priest, isn't he?"

"He is."

"I was afraid he'd leave the church."

"He didn't."

"That's good then." She exhaled a breath she'd been holding for over a year. "He... Whatever his faults, he's a good priest, isn't he?"

Kingsley put his hands on her shoulders.

"Yes, he's a very good priest."

"I'm glad I left, then. He…he would have regretted leaving the Jesuits for me. I know him. It was good I left him if he's still a priest."

She knew she was speaking to convince herself, not Kingsley.

"This life I'm offering you isn't easy money, Elle. The things dominatrixes do with their clients? Not even the priest would dream of some of it. It will be hard work. You'll be tempted to return to him. Better to face that temptation head-on instead of running and hiding from it. *Tu comprends?*"

"*Je comprends.*" He was right although she hated to admit it. No way could she avoid Søren forever.

"Don't be afraid. You won't have to see him right away. He doesn't know you've returned. No one outside this house does, and Calliope and Juliette will keep the secret."

"What's the plan? How do we 'depose' this Milady of yours?"

"In six weeks' time, there will be a party at The 8th Circle. The summer solstice party—the Midsummer Night's Fling. Everyone will be there. I will let it be known that I have a new domina who will make her debut that night. I will warn the world that she is the most dangerous, most sadistic and most beautiful domme they've ever seen. A domme who will put the great Milady in the shade. She will come, of course. If she doesn't, she'll be seen as a coward."

"Six weeks? You think I'll be ready in six weeks?"

"We'll start your training tomorrow. I'll work on a plan of attack, and we'll build your dungeon."

"I get my own dungeon? At the club? Seriously?"

"You will have the best dungeon in the house."

Elle couldn't repress a grin at that thought. Her own dungeon—she'd dreamed of such a thing but never spoke that fantasy aloud. That alone would be worth all the work Kingsley would demand of her.

"Okay. Six weeks. Milady shows up to this party. Everybody's there. I turn up. And then what?"

Kingsley looked at her without smiling and the look on his face both scared and excited her.

"Then you will do what you do best."

"What is that?" she asked.

"Hurt men."

Elle laughed, her first real laugh since she'd set foot in this house.

"Hurt men? With pleasure," she said. "Theirs and mine."

"And mine," Kingsley said and he knelt on the floor at her feet, sitting between her knees. He cupped her face with his hands and brought her mouth to his. A kiss... The very last thing she expected him to do was kiss her. And not a simple, benign, friendly kiss between ex-lovers greeting each other after a year living separate lives. No, this was a kiss that meant something. His lips pushed hers apart, his tongue slipped between her teeth, his thumbs brushed her cheeks. She returned the kiss, pushing close to him so that her legs wrapped around his back and her hands found their way to his hair. She dug her fingers into the soft dark waves and pulled, tilting his chin up, taking control of the kiss.

"I'm glad you came back," Kingsley said between kisses, his voice low and intimate, his French accent thick and his erection pressing against her thigh.

"Why is that?" she asked, aching for more than a kiss.

"Because," he said, kissing her neck under her ear and breathing the words so that she felt them brush across her skin like fingertips, "I'm your first client."

5

Flogging Lessons

"HARDER," KINGSLEY SAID. ELLE DID IT HARDER, HARD as she could. "You call that harder?"

She threw the flogger down and turned to Kingsley.

"How do you know how hard I'm hitting when I'm not hitting anyone?" She pointed at the towel on the wall. "That is a bath towel, not a person. No matter how hard I hit it, it's not going to scream."

"It's still hanging on the wall. And if it's still hanging on the wall—" Kingsley picked up the flogger, threw it once with a practiced snap, and the towel fell to the floor landing in a soft pile at their feet "—you aren't hitting it hard enough."

Elle exhaled heavily and scooped the towel off the floor to pin it back in place. They were in Kingsley's playroom. It boasted a red St. Andrew's Cross, a leather kneeling bench, two dozen floggers, canes and enough rope to truss up an entire herd of cattle. From the ceiling hung an elegant glass chandelier, which gave the playroom that touch of class everyone expected from the King of the Underground. For the past two weeks Kingsley had brought her here for four hours a day, training her in the various arts of pain. Caning was a breeze. Clamps were a blast. Flogging, however, had proven to be more difficult than it looked.

Once the towel was back in place, Elle held out her hand. Kingsley gave her the black-tailed elk-hide flogger, slapping the handle into her palm.

"I could knock it off with a whip," she said.

"No whips. No single-tails. You could kill someone with one of those. You get to touch the whip when you're ready and not a moment sooner."

"I like whips."

"Don't we all, but you'll use floggers more often than whips. No whipping until you've mastered flogging. Then I'll find you a whip master. Now do it again," he said, his voice calm and steady. "Make it hurt."

"I'll make it hurt." Elle narrowed her eyes at the towel. "I can make it hurt. Who knows more about pain than the submissive of a sadist?"

"You are not a submissive. You never were."

"Then what the hell was I doing the past decade of my life, King?"

"Wasting everyone's time?"

She glared at him. "Look, I want to do this right. I loved topping you. I loved hurting you. But that doesn't mean I didn't love submitting, too."

"You have to let that part of your life go. You aren't her anymore."

"I'm still Elle Schreiber. No matter which end of the whip I'm on, I'm still Elle Schreiber."

Kingsley narrowed his eyes at her.

"That's it."

"That's what?"

"You need a new name," he said.

"What?"

"A new name. A scene name. Everyone already knows you as Eleanor Schreiber. Everyone already knows you as his submissive, his property. But you aren't his anymore. You need a new name."

"Like what?"

"I don't know. I'll figure something out."

"You're going to give me a new name? Do I get any say in this?"

"You can pick out the font on your business cards after I decide on your new name. Now flog."

Elle took a few steadying breaths and focused her attention. She could do this. How many times had she been flogged in her life? First time when she was twenty, eight years ago. She'd spent at least one night a week in the company of the most infamous sadist in their vast kink community during all those years. Sometimes two. Two times fifty-two times seven equaled a lot of fucking floggings. And that didn't include all the ones Kingsley had given her.

With one more heavy breath she placed her feet in position and raised the flogger over her head. With her right hand she held the handle, with her left hand the tips of the tails.

She pulled the tails taut and then let it go with a flick. It was a good hit, a strike right down the middle. And yet, the towel stayed pinned in place.

"Fuck."

Kingsley gave a low chuckle, and she nearly flogged his French face.

"You're finding out that being a dominant is more work than you ever imagined, aren't you?" he asked.

"I need more practice. These floggers are heavier than they look."

"And you're a woman and you're five foot three, and you don't possess one-tenth of the upper body strength I do."

"I swim laps."

"Not enough."

"Fine. I'll join a gym."

"Yes, you will. But you'll never be as strong as I am, or as strong as he is or as strong as the average healthy man on the street is. This job isn't about muscle strength. The physical part of dominating someone is the smallest part of it. Your clients will be men, and they will be bigger and stronger than you are. You'll never outweigh them, and you'll never be able to beat them at arm wrestling."

"So...shoot them?" she asked.

Kingsley smiled.

"They want to submit to you. They want you to hurt them. They won't want to hurt you, because that's not their nature. They want to be dominated by a woman because they don't feel alive or sexual or aroused until they're beaten, used and treated like objects. But if you want that respect, if you want their lips on your boots and their souls at your feet, you have to earn their respect. And you earn it by showing them you aren't afraid to hurt them. Milady hurts them. You'll hurt them more. Now do it again."

She did it again. And again. And again. She did it until her back burned and her muscles screamed and she thought she'd die if she had to lift her arms over her head again. But she did it again, and she didn't die. She wanted to die, but unfortunately she didn't get her wish.

After half an hour Elle dropped her arms to her sides. Sweat poured from her forehead and down her back. Her heart pounded and she gulped down an entire bottle of water in a few swallows.

She pulled the towel down—she still hadn't managed to knock it off the wall—and raised it to her face.

"Why are you doing that?" Kingsley asked.

"Wiping my sweat off? Because I'm sweaty."

"You have a man in this room. Why not use his clothes to wipe your sweat off?"

"You want me to wipe my gross sweat on one of your Signore Vitale custom-made shirts? You'd kill me."

"Would I?" he asked.

"I would if someone did that to me."

Kingsley smiled at her and her stomach tightened in unwanted wanting. Every night she waited for Kingsley to come to her bedroom like he used to do, but not once had he slipped under her covers and whispered sexual orders to her like he had so many times in the past.

"When we were lovers in high school," he began and she knew who he meant by *we*, "it was my job to undress him many nights, but his clothes *must* be folded neatly, precisely, reverently, and then placed on a chair. No mess, no wrinkles. But he…he would strip me naked and drop all my clothes onto the floor. Then he'd walk on them. Not barefoot, either. With his shoes on most of the time. And you know what?" Kingsley asked as he stepped closer to her, close enough she could kiss him if she wanted to.

"What?"

"I worshipped him for it." Kingsley smiled at her, a Mona Lisa smile that hinted of secrets but didn't reveal them. "He would sometimes pretend I wasn't there when I spoke to him…and I worshipped him for it. He would tell me he didn't want me anymore and then at the moment I was ready to kill myself in despair, he'd smile to show it was all a joke…and I worshipped him for it. I mocked him once for what happened between him and his sister Elizabeth, and you know what he did?"

"I don't want to know."

"He blindfolded me, tied me to the cot and made me say my sister's name over and over again while he gave me the most intense erotic pleasure of my life with his hands and his mouth. When I stopped speaking he stopped pleasuring me. Then he made me say my own sister's name when I came. And you know what?"

"You worshipped him for it?"

Kingsley nodded.

Point taken. To show Kingsley how thoroughly she'd absorbed her lesson she walked over to where he stood by the St. Andrew's Cross, his arms folded over his chest. He wore camel-colored breeches and dark brown Hessian riding boots, a snow-white shirt held together at the throat with a gold pin and a dark brown vest with little gold fleurs-de-lis embroidered on it. Kingsley looked magnificent, like a Regency-era fever dream. If Jane Austen had set eyes on Kingsley, she would never have written her genteel comedies of manner.

She would have written porn.

Elle wiped her sweaty forehead off on his shoulder.

"See?" she asked, smiling up at him. "I can be taught."

He looked down at the wet smudge she'd left on his pristine shirt and back at her.

"I could have you flogged for that."

"I'm not a submissive anymore, remember?"

"I'm glad you're starting to realize that," he said and then lowered his voice to a whisper. "Finally."

"I know I'm a dominant. I know I am."

"Are you sure?"

"I think I'm sure."

"Then you aren't sure. Elle, what we're doing here... I need all of you for it. Your heart, your soul, your strength, your guts. All of you. If you can't give me all of you, then you are, yet again, wasting everyone's time. Now tell me…do you want this? Do you want to be my Queen?"

"I want it."

"It? What is it you want? Money?"

"Yes," she admitted without shame. She needed a good job that didn't take up all her time if she were going to do something with her writing.

"Power?"

"Definitely."

"Me?" he asked.

"You did say you'd be my first client," she reminded him.

"I will be."

"You said I won't be having sex with my clients."

"Are you asking me if we're going to have sex again?"

"Yes," she said without shame or apology. She wanted him. She knew he wanted her. Why hadn't they fucked yet?

"Would you like to?"

"Yes."

"Prove it."

"Prove it? How?"

"By acting like the domme I know you are. Once you are a domme, I will be your client, and you can do anything you want to me."

"Anything?"

Kingsley met her eyes and whispered, "Anything."

"You're going to regret that."

"I can't wait to regret it."

"This is a test, isn't it? You're testing me?"

"Of course I am."

"And if I pass this test, what do I win?"

"Me."

"Good prize."

"When I am done with you," he said, taking her face in his hands, "there will not be a man in the world who wouldn't take a bullet to lick your boots."

"It's not my boots that need licking right now."

Kingsley smiled at her, a sensual, mysterious smile. It did not bode well.

"I'll give you a hint about how to win your prize. Do you know a woman by the name of Theresa Berkley?" he asked.

"If I met her I don't remember."

"You've never met her. She died in the 1830s. But before she died she worked as a dominatrix. I doubt she used that term, but that's what she was. She invented a sort of standing table she called a chevelet. It was used to torture men on one side of their bodies while another woman could sexually stimulate them on the other side. We have the freestanding St. Andrew's Cross for that now, but it was quite an ingenious bit of furniture."

"Sounds like my kind of girl."

"A client coming to London wrote a letter to her once requesting a session on her chevelet. These were the conditions he offered. He would pay her 'a pound sterling for the first blood drawn, two pounds sterling if the blood runs down to my heels, three pounds sterling if my heels are bathed in blood, four pounds sterling if the blood reaches the floor, and five pounds sterling if you succeed in making me lose consciousness.' His words, *chérie*."

"Lose consciousness? Jesus."

"Don't be vanilla," he said. He lowered his voice to a whisper. "We masochists love our beatings. But that's not the moral of this story."

"Then what is the moral, King?"

"The moral is that if you want my pounds sterling or any other sort of pounds, you'll have to earn it."

Kingsley turned his back on her to leave and without thinking she raised the flogger over her head. She threw it across his back hoping to impress him with one hard hit. But Kingsley turned at the last second and caught the tails in his hand. She'd put the handle strap around her wrist thus making it all too easy for him to yank her to him and shove her back against the wall.

"What the fuck was that?" he demanded, squeezing her wrist to the point of pain. "Don't put the fucking cord of the fucking flogger on your fucking wrist. That's how you fucking hang the flogger on the fucking wall. And if you fucking put it on your fucking wrist, someone like me can fucking grab you and fucking fuck you up, you fucking rookie."

He ripped the flogger off her wrist and tossed it aside.

"King, sorry—"

Kingsley cut off her apology with a hand over her mouth. Elle started, heart racing in pure fear.

"Shut up," he said. "You fucked up, and you will be disciplined."

He dragged her bodily to the bed and threw her down onto it. No amount of pushing and fighting could force him off her.

With knees and feet and arms and hands, Kingsley pinned her down to the bed. He had sixty pounds on her at least and was unbelievably strong. Finally she gave up her struggle. She was flat on her back on the bed and going nowhere until Kingsley let her go.

"This is what is known as a reality check, Elle. Repeat after me," Kingsley said. "I am a bad dominant."

A furious growl rose in the back of her throat.

"Say it," Kingsley said.

"I am a bad dominant."

"Good dominants do not hit people without their permission. Say it."

"Good dominants do not hit people without their permission."

"Are you a good dominant?" he asked.

"I want to be."

"Let's find out," Kingsley said, his face a mask of steely resolve. He might be a masochist, he might be a switch, but right now he was all dom and all terrifying.

Kingsley released one wrist and unzipped her jeans.

"Safe out right now," he said. "Right fucking now."

"Or what? You'll fuck me? Go ahead."

"You'd like that too much," he said, pushing his hand into her jeans. "And you haven't even come close to earning my cock yet."

He shoved a finger inside her and Elle cried out, not in pain but in pleasure.

"Thought so," he said.

"What?" She tried squirming away from him but couldn't move. He had her riveted to the bed.

"You're dripping wet. So much for being a domme."

"I haven't gotten fucked in over a year."

"That's your problem, not mine."

He pulled his hand out of her pants and pushed her onto her stomach. With his mouth at her ear he whispered a warning.

"There's one man in the world who cares about you more than I do," Kingsley said. "Just imagine what a man who doesn't give a fuck about you would do if you fucked up during a session as badly as you fucked up with me."

"I fucked up," she said.

"You did."

"I won't do it again."

"We won't have to have this talk again, will we?"

"No."

"No what?"

"No, Kingsley."

"You aren't going to call me 'sir'?" he asked, his voice cold but teasing.

"No," she said.

"And why not?"

"Because I'm not a submissive anymore. I don't call anyone 'sir.'"

Kingsley leaned in even closer, pressed his lips to the back of her neck and kissed her.

"Glad you finally are realizing this," he said. "It's about fucking time."

6

A Special Delivery

ALONE IN HER BEDROOM ELLE STRIPPED OUT OF HER clothes—her favorite old Pearl Jam concert T-shirt she'd had since 1994 and a ratty pair of cutoff denim shorts. They'd been her comfort clothes, her lazy-day uniform, when she'd lived here at Kingsley's before she'd gone to the convent. There she'd had to wear black tights and long skirts and buttoned-up blouses. It had been like wearing a costume every day so it should have been nice to wear her own clothes again. Although they didn't feel like hers. They felt like a different sort of costume. They belonged to Eleanor. *His* Eleanor. But if she wasn't his anymore, was she even Eleanor? Kingsley said he would change her name. She almost didn't care what he changed it to as long as she could be someone who wasn't Eleanor anymore. Eleanor was tired. Eleanor was scared. Eleanor missed her priest.

For almost an hour she stood under the scalding water and let the heat seep into her sore muscles but no matter how long she stayed under the water, the pain remained. She dried off on plush white towels she wouldn't have to wash and dry and fold—Kingsley had a housekeeper. It should have felt like heaven, living in luxury again. And yet...

"You fucked up today."

Elle stepped out of her en suite bathroom to find Kingsley sitting on her bed, boots crossed at the ankle, looking smug and satiated. His collar was open and the vest unbuttoned. While she'd been in the shower he'd been in Juliette. His new lover received the lion's share of Kingsley's erotic attentions lately. Elle didn't blame him. Juliette was easily the most beautiful woman she'd ever seen in her life, and she'd seen her fair share of beautiful women come and go from Kingsley's bed. Juliette, however, seemed likely to stick around.

"Yes, you mentioned that earlier. I won't do it again."

"I know. You'll make me proud. Eventually."

Elle smiled at him and then dropped the towel. Kingsley didn't blink or say a word at her sudden nudity. He'd seen her naked before, but she noted his eyes narrowing as she walked past him. Not a look of ardor at all. He appraised her as she dressed in black panties, a black bra, a denim skirt that hugged her curves and a low-cut shirt.

"You've gained weight," he said.

"Six pounds since coming back from the convent. If you'd had to eat convent food for a year, you'd go a little nuts with New York–style pizza, too. I promise I won't gain any more."

"Don't lose the weight. We'll turn it into muscle."

"Don't lose the weight? Those are the sexiest four words anyone has ever said to me."

"Money money money money."

"Those are the other four sexiest words anyone's ever said to me."

"I didn't come to seduce you. I came to invite you to a party. Not quite an invitation. Attendance is mandatory."

"What sort of party?"

"The sort of party Milady will attend. We need to see her in action."

"You said nobody could know I was back yet."

"They won't know. You'll be in disguise. I don't want you leaving the house between now and then, either."

"Sure. Of course. Whatever you say, boss." She added the "boss" at the end more sarcastically than she meant.

"Don't get pissy at me because you fucked up," he said, wagging his finger at her.

"I'm not pissy because I fucked up."

"What is it?"

She sighed. "This is harder than I thought it would be."

"Being a domme?" he asked.

"Not being a sub."

"Not being his sub, you mean."

She nodded. Reluctantly.

"You need to face him," he said. "The longer you wait the harder it will be. You've been back two weeks. It's time."

"I'll go talk to him. Soon. I promise."

"Not today. I don't want anyone knowing you're back yet. No going out. Anywhere."

"Fine. I'll be good. Happy?"

"Good, *chérie*, is the last thing I want you to be."

He chucked her under the chin and left. A few minutes later Elle heard a soft knock on her bedroom door, which meant it wasn't Kingsley returning. He never bothered knocking.

Elle opened the door.

"Juliette," was all Elle could say. Beautiful, glorious, magnificent Juliette. Even Elle got a little tongue-tied around Kingsley's consort.

"Calliope brought in the mail. There's something for you."

"For me?" She held out her hand and Juliette passed her a thick manila envelope.

"*C'est pour toi.*"

"Thanks." She tossed it in a drawer.

"You aren't going to open it?" Juliette asked, her hands lifting gracefully in a question.

"I'll open it later."

"It's from a literary agency," Juliette said.

"Yeah, I know who it's from."

"I didn't tell monsieur you received any mail today."

Elle smiled, relieved. "Thank you for that."

"For years, I lived with a man who monitored any mail I received. I had no privacy. It was…unpleasant. You should have your privacy. But I think it's wonderful you're receiving mail from a literary agency if it means what I think it means."

"It means I wrote a book. But please don't tell."

"Something tells me the subject will not come up. I keep monsieur on other topics," she said with a sly smile.

Elle liked Juliette. It didn't take long for her to decide this was the perfect woman for Kingsley. She had a backbone of iron and a love of submission that made her the ideal consort for their king. Since Elle did like her so much she had to say what she said next or she wouldn't be able to look Juliette in the eyes much longer.

"Juliette, you do know Kingsley and I used to sleep together, right?"

"He told me, *oui.*" Juliette seemed entirely unperturbed by the fact.

"And we'll probably be sleeping together again in the near future."

"He keeps me abreast of these sorts of things."

These sorts of things? Probably the tamest euphemism Elle had yet heard for Kingsley's sex life.

"You're fine with that?"

She nodded her head regally. Everything Juliette did or said looked or sounded regal. If Elle wanted to be a queen she would do well to emulate Juliette.

"He told me what he was and what he needs. I would never deny him what he needs."

"Some people don't like the thought of sharing."

"It isn't sharing. Not to me. He is one man when he's with you. Another man when he's with me. It's clear you care for the man who he is with you. I care for the man who he is when he's with me."

"He loves pain when he's with me. I'll send him back to you covered in whip marks and bruises, cuts and welts. I left a lot of burns on him last year. You should be prepared for that. I mean that literally. Keep the medicine cabinet well stocked. He hates doctors. You'll have to handle first aid."

"I will be prepared. In truth, I couldn't watch while he's being hurt, but I admit I enjoy the thought of tending to his wounds after…"

"That's a kink, you know. Comforting someone after a hard scene. Usually it's the person who did the hurting who handles the cleanup, but I've known kinky people whose favorite thing to do was dress the wounds of masochists after a beating. Aftercare can be very intense, very intimate." Søren had always taken good care of her after the beatings. Washing her wounds, cleaning her cuts, kissing her boo-boos away. Those were her favorite moments, when he put her back together after tearing her apart. "It's like playing doctor or naughty nurse."

"I would look good in a nurse's costume, wouldn't I?"

"You would look good in a brown paper bag."

Juliette smiled, a smile so steamy it could have fogged the windows in a parked car.

"You break him down," Juliette said, pointing at Elle. "And

I—" she pointed at herself "—I will build him up so he'll be ready when you break him again. Between the two of us he should be a very happy man. It's a good plan, *non*?"

"A very good plan, yes. So you think we can be friends?" Elle asked. "No jealousy? No awkwardness?"

"Jealousy is a sign of insecurity. He adores me," Juliette said, sounding almost affronted by the very suggestion Kingsley would ever choose another woman over her. Veritable madness. "And I am never awkward."

"I can believe that. Thank you for this." Elle swallowed hard, suddenly on the verge of tears and not knowing why. A tiny kindness from a woman she barely knew and…tears? This wasn't like her. Not at all.

Juliette gave her a long searching look.

"You miss him," Juliette said. "Your lover?"

"I shouldn't," Elle said. "I left him."

"I miss mine, and I hated him."

"I hate my ex, too."

Juliette raised a finger, shook her head. "Elle, you do not know hate the way I know hate," and Elle believed her. "Starting a new life isn't easy. Not even for me and I have wanted this new life *all* my life."

"I hate crying," Elle said. "Seems…weak. I'm usually stronger than this."

"It's not weak. I cry, too, and I'm not weak. If I feel weak because I'm crying I remind myself of one true thing."

"What's that?" Elle asked.

"This is a new life I'm living. I am reborn. And all babies cry when they're born."

Elle smiled and knew she'd remember that one true thing all her life. Being born hurt. So did being reborn.

Juliette left her alone and the second she was gone, Elle locked her bedroom door and tore open the envelope. A handwritten note lay on top of a rubber-banded bundle of papers. Her book printed out with edit notes.

"Elle," the note read, "Loved it, loved it, loved it. I've made some notes in the margins. I found a couple scenes to cut but most changes are minor. I'd love to have it back by next Friday."

The note was signed by her new agent. Kingsley had ordered her to stay in the house. Elle did not follow men's orders anymore. So she stuffed the book into a backpack, threw on a hat and headed out into the city.

Coming back to Manhattan had been harder than Elle had anticipated. Even now, two weeks after she'd returned, the noise of the city had kept her on edge. Life in the convent had been so quiet. She'd fallen asleep at night to the sound of soft breezes and chirping crickets. With nothing but Kyrie to distract her, she'd been able to write her book quickly. Yet another reason to make as much money as she could as fast as she could. A quiet house of her own where she could write in peace. That was the dream...

But first, she'd need her own damn computer. Sneaking to the library to work on her book was hardly ideal. She didn't put it past Kingsley to chain her to the bed. He'd done it to Juliette, after all.

She reached the library but didn't go into the computer lab yet. First she walked through the stacks, as she always did, seeking inspiration. The convent library had "uplifting" or "religious" literature in its small library and not a single novel. But here she found Jane Austen, George Eliot, Henry Miller and her beloved Anaïs Nin. She walked the stacks and paused when a book in the *C*'s caught her eye. She pulled it from the shelf and held it in her hand.

Through the Looking-Glass, and What Alice Found There by Lewis Carroll.

Elle had her own copy of this book back at Kingsley's. Søren had given it to her when she was nineteen. He'd brought the book home with him from Rome. Back then she'd been too young to wonder how a priest under a vow of poverty had gotten the money to pay for such an expensive early edition of this book. When she'd gotten older and had learned to ask more questions, he'd told her that he had a wealthy friend in Rome, a madam of a brothel who'd worked all her life as a dominatrix to European businessmen, royalty and clergy. Whenever he returned to Rome he visited with her. And although Elle had never met his friend Magdalena, Magdalena seemed to know Elle.

Why me? Elle had asked him when Søren admitted the book had been given to him by Magdalena to give to Elle.

Søren had answered, *Because a long time ago she looked into my future and saw you. So she says, anyway.*

What's my future? I'll go through the looking glass?

She says you are like Alice in the Looking-Glass world. First a pawn and then a queen.

Was that what had happened? She'd stepped through a mirror into a world where everything was backward—where she was Kingsley's domme and not Søren's slave? Where she was a dominant and not a submissive? Where she was a queen and no longer a little girl?

Elle put the book back on the shelf. No reading right now. No remembering. Queen or not, she had work to do. She took the computer right next to the wall and started cutting. Today's project was her last project before her book went out on submission with editors. Her agent had told her that her book needed trimming. Less was more and Elle knew she was right. Elle highlighted a scene consigned to the chopping block and hit Delete.

It hurt, of course. She might have winced a little between

highlighting and deleting, but it was also empowering. She felt like a god of her own world in a way. She created their reality—what her characters ate and drank and how they lived and loved and fucked and if they did something she didn't want them to do then all she had to do was...poof...delete...gone...

Just. Like. That.

She wished real life came with a delete key. But if she could change her reality, would she? Maybe. She knew she'd never truly be free of Søren as long as she remembered everything that had happened between them, from their first meeting at Sacred Heart two weeks before her sixteenth birthday to that last awful night when he'd been so angry he'd scared her. But it wasn't that night that she wanted to be free of. The bad memories gave her the strength to keep following this path. It was all the good nights that held her hostage, her memories of beautiful kink, passionate sex, lying in bed after Søren had spent his pain and passion on her, talking about everything and nothing until she fell asleep against his chest and woke up with her collar locked away in the rosewood box until the next time he would make her his. Too many good memories. They were like links in a chain that bound her to the past.

Why couldn't she push Delete on those memories and make them go away like she did the scenes in her book that slowed the story down?

Maybe she could.

Elle opened a new blank document on her computer screen and stared at the blinking cursor.

What to write...what to write... What memory did she most want to rid herself of? Which night haunted her more than any other, weighed on her more than any other? Impossible to pick only one, but she had to start somewhere.

She thought of the book again—*Through the Looking-Glass*. Her favorite part of it had always been the "Jabberwocky" poem, especially when Søren read it to her at night in his poshest and most entertaining English accent. Some evenings he'd read to her before they adjourned to his bedroom for kink and sex and on those nights it was torture to have to sit and wait while he read when all she wanted from him was pain and fucking.

But there were other nights, special nights, private nights she would tell no one about even on pain of death...

A memory hit her so hard in the stomach she almost whimpered aloud. God, it hurt to remember. But wouldn't it feel good to forget? Not good, but powerful? She could show those memories who was boss. She was god of her own world.

She knew right where to start.

Elle put her fingers to the keys and started to type.

It was a winter's night in Ordinary Time, but this was no ordinary night.

7

Ordinary Time

IT WAS A WINTER'S NIGHT IN ORDINARY TIME, BUT THIS was no ordinary night.

First of all, He had summoned her to His home and no ordinary night began with such a summons.

Second, it had snowed last night and all the world for as far as she could see had turned white. She inhaled Him, for He smelled like snow and nighttime and chimney smoke in the distance. Only He smelled like both winter and fire at the same time. Only He was so cold and yet could make her burn.

The roads were safe to pass by late afternoon and when the winter evening turned inexorably into the winter night she drove to His home. The snow crunched under her boots as she walked to His door and she paused long enough to gaze up at the black sky, which was so white with stars it was as if the snow had fallen up as well as down.

When she walked through the kitchen door she found a box on the table and that's when she knew the third reason it would be no ordinary night.

On the box was a card with two words written on it.

"Wear me."

Elle took the box up the narrow wooden stairs to the bathroom. Inside it she found a nightgown, creamy off-white muslin with lace accents on the innocent puff sleeves. It was a child's nightgown, not a woman's.

No.

She closed her eyes as hot tears burned them, scalding her cheeks. Not this. She didn't want this.

But she did. She did want it but she didn't want to want it.

And that's why He'd summoned her here tonight. Because when she wanted something she didn't want to want, that was when He wanted her the most.

It was her own fault. Two weeks ago she'd been at a private party with Him and their king. A couple had entered the party, a couple she'd never met before—an older man with silver hair, a younger woman with skin fresh as March dew on rosebuds. She'd watched them with interest, watched the older man taking her short pink coat off her as if she were too young to unfasten her own buttons and instead of answering when he asked questions, the younger woman had nodded, wide-eyed and innocent. When they walked she held on to his hand with both of her hands as if she feared the crowd would separate them, and she would never see him again. In a room reserved for the private party they all attended, the older man did the talking and the younger woman clung to his side. When he sat in a chair she sat in his lap, her arms wound round his neck, his large hand absentmindedly rubbing her lower back as if soothing a fussy child. And once he kissed her on the cheek and told her she was being a very good girl. That's when the younger woman spoke the only three words anyone would hear her speak that night.

Thank you, Daddy.

The king warned her if she kept watching the couple so intently she would be punished for it. One of the rules of such gatherings was "Don't stare. We're all freaks here." But stare she did. The thirty-

something woman transformed herself into a little girl by simply making her face a mask of innocence, turning her lips into a pout, opening her eyes wide and clinging to her older lover with both hands. She found it fascinating that a woman would want to be treated like a child when she herself had fought so hard for so long to be treated like an adult.

"Is this a game you want to play?" the king whispered in her ear.

"No, of course not. It's…"

"What? Too naughty even for you?"

That stung. Nothing was too naughty for her.

But…still…would she like this? Playing like a little girl? Calling your lover "Daddy"? Disturbing. Troubling.

And so very arousing…

No. Absolutely not. She refused to even entertain the idea of playing that game. It would be humiliating to pretend to be a little girl, to call Him Daddy, to act like a child when she was twenty-five years old.

It was too late, however. Her interest in the couple had been noted. By Him.

Long ago, He'd warned her that He could become aroused in only one of two ways—by inflicting pain or inflicting humiliation. Some nights pain might not be enough for Him. Some nights He would humiliate her for His own pleasure. He then promised to refrain from that particular side of His sadism as much as possible. But now and again it appeared, unbidden. During a beating she'd realized she'd had a painfully full bladder and instead of excusing her to the bathroom He'd kicked a bucket into the center of the room and uttered the order, "Go." When her period had started a few days early and she'd woken up to blood on His white sheets, He'd stood over her at the bathtub while she'd had to scrub the stains out, crying with mortification the entire time.

But after…oh…after… He'd bent her over the bathroom counter and fucked her from behind so hard that if she hadn't been bleeding already, she would have started.

Those humiliations, however, paled in comparison to this new hell.

With trembling hands she dressed in the child's nightgown that fit her so well she knew it had been made for her. The club had a quartermaster of sorts whose sole job it was to provide the high-level members with anything they needed. A child's nightgown that would fit an adult woman likely numbered among the least strange of the requests she filled weekly.

There were ribbons, too. It took three tries for her to plait her untamable black hair into twin braids and to steady her fingers enough to tie the ribbons in little bows at the ends. She felt scared as a child, nervous as a child, excited as a child.

When she walked out of the bathroom, she wasn't twenty-five anymore, but seven. Seven and scared and miserable. If it had been a game she would have played it with pleasure but this wasn't a game to her, although it was to Him. She would never tell another soul of this night; it was far too private and personal and, of course, because that was the point...it was far too humiliating.

In His bedroom, the lights were all off but for the old brass lamp on His bedside table. He reclined on His side on the bed wearing jeans and a black long-sleeve T-shirt with the sleeves pushed up to reveal His sinewy forearms. His feet were naked, and His blond hair was slightly damp and slicked back as if He'd run His fingers through it a few times after coming in from the snow. Open on the bed in front of Him was a book, a book she hadn't seen before. The bed was the same bed but the covers looked different. Usually He slept on white sheets covered by a simple white quilt. But He'd changed them tonight. Once she'd told Him that as a little girl she'd loved visiting her grandparents because she had her own bed there—a twin bed with a pastel-blue-and-white-striped quilt and the sheets were covered in laughing white moons and smiling yellow stars. The sheets and the quilt on His bed weren't identical to the ones she remembered from her childhood days visiting her grandparents. But they were close enough to take her breath away.

He must have known she was standing there, but He didn't look at her and He wouldn't look at her until she spoke the word He wanted her to speak, the word that would begin the night's humiliations. The last word she wanted to say to Him.

"Daddy?" Standing in the open doorway to His bedroom, she felt more exposed in that child's nightgown than she would have been naked.

He looked up from the book in front of Him and smiled an indulgent fatherly smile at her.

"What's wrong, Little One?" He asked, and the name He'd called her for years now took on a darker connotation. "You look upset."

She nodded and held on to the bow of her nightgown with both hands, twisting the fabric nervously.

"Come here." He waved her over to Him and on her bare feet she walked to Him, slowly...slowly, drawn to Him and repelled in equal measure.

He closed the book and set it on the bedside table. She stood between His knees. Reaching out He tugged lightly on the tip of her braid.

"Are you tired?"

She shook her head.

"Then what's wrong?" His voice was so tender and fatherly she burst into tears. He pulled her into His arms and held her while she cried. Holding her on His lap, He gently rocked her and shushed her until her sobs subsided.

"I don't want you to be mad at me."

"I'm never mad at you."

"Then why are you making me do this?" she asked.

"Because I love you."

"You aren't mad at me?" She was certain He was punishing her for something by making her play this horrible game. But was it a punishment? Was it a horrible game? Or was it something she had wanted, something she had dreamed of, something she had desired and never told Him because she couldn't bring herself to tell Him?

"I could never be mad at you. Never ever."

"Promise?" she asked.

"Look at me," He said in such a tone she obeyed instantly. "You know that, don't you? You know you could never disappoint me? Yes?"

She nodded. "Yes, Daddy."

"Good girl." He tugged her braid again, then tickled her nose with the tip of it.

She wrinkled her nose.

"That tickles," she said. "Stop it."

"Stop it? Stop what? This?" He tickled her neck now with the tip of her braid.

"Yes, that. Stop." She tried to pull away from the tickling, but He grabbed her arms with both hands. Before she knew it, He had her flat on her back, His knees straddling her hips.

"You don't like being tickled?" He slipped His hand under her nightgown to lightly caress her stomach. She squirmed under His touch. He was only thirty-nine, but He seemed older tonight. Or maybe He only seemed older than thirty-nine because she felt so little and young and scared.

"No, Daddy." She tried to wriggle out from under Him but there was no escaping Him and His searching, finding fingers.

"Why not?"

She panted, breathless with laughter.

"Because..." She attempted to twist herself out of His grip and failed miserably.

"Because why?" He brushed His fingertips over her rib cage and the sensation was so acute it hurt.

"Because...it...tickles..." Finally she managed to slip out of the prison of His knees and tickling fingers. She made it to the other side of the bed before He caught her again and pulled her to Him.

"You aren't allowed to run away from me, Little One. You know it's your bedtime."

"But, Daddy—"

"And no talking back." With that He put her over His lap and gave her a vicious swat on her white cotton panties. The pain of it was equal to the shock, and she gasped and stiffened. He spanked her again. Once, twice. Five times total. Her body burned when He'd finished. All of it, not just where He'd struck her. She lay there across His lap and panted while He rubbed her scalding skin.

"Are you going to behave now?"

"Yes, Daddy."

"That's my good girl." He rubbed her bottom and thighs gently as He rocked her in His arms again. She felt peaceful, quiet inside, happy. She'd forgotten who she really was in His arms and that this was a game He'd made her play. She was His little girl. Now. Always. "You need to settle down. It's bedtime."

One finger traced the edge of her panties all the way between her thighs. He pushed the fabric to the side and found her clitoris. He stroked it carefully, steadily and it swelled under His fingertips, throbbing against them as little bursts of fluid coated her labia and vagina. When He inserted one finger into her, He smiled at how wet He found her.

"Very good girl," He whispered as He moved His finger in deeper. She buried her face in the crook of her arm while He fondled her. A second finger joined His first one and He spread them apart inside her to open her up.

"Thank you, Daddy," she said, the word rolling easier off her tongue now.

"Are you ready for bed now?"

"Ready."

He took His fingers out of her, and she scrambled back on her hands and knees. He tossed the quilt and top sheet back, and laid her on the bed. He fluffed the pillow under her head before reaching under her gown and sliding her panties off her legs. He stood at the side of the bed and she stared at the ceiling, but she knew He was unzipping His pants. She opened her legs for Him before He asked her to.

"That's my girl." He covered her body with His and when He pushed her legs open wider, she whimpered but didn't say a word.

As wet as she was, He entered her easily, filling her with His full length in a stroke. His hands were on either side of her shoulders, bracing Himself up and over her to keep His weight off her smaller form. In the low light He seemed enormous, as if He would crush her if He lay on top of her. His shadow on the wall looked like a giant's.

After a few minutes He paused but only long enough to pull her nightgown down her arms. Her nipples hardened as He uncovered them. When He bent His head to lick them, the deep muscles inside her twitched and throbbed and tightened to the breaking point. Not moving took more effort than moving. Her fingers clutched the sheets. He fed on her embarrassment like food. Tonight's humiliation was a banquet.

She closed her eyes and laid her head back on the pillow. An orgasm so strong she felt it all the way up the center of her back and in her thighs tore through her. When her body ceased its shuddering around Him, she closed her eyes. At last He came inside her, His lips pressed to her forehead.

"You were a very good girl," He said as His fingertips brushed her cheek, pushed a loose strand of hair behind her ear.

"I love you, Daddy."

"I love you, too, Little One."

He pulled out at last, straightened her nightgown and covered her with the quilt.

She opened her eyes. *"Can I have a glass of water, please?"*

"Of course." He kissed her on the forehead again and left the room. When He returned a few minutes later, all traces of His exertions were gone. Every button buttoned and every hair back in place. He passed her the glass of water. She took it with both hands and drank from it as He picked up the book off the table.

"This book is called Jabberwocky," He said, opening it to the inside cover. *"And it's yours."*

On the inside she silently read the words "Never forget the lesson of the Jabberwocky. And never forget I love you." It was signed with an elaborate S with a slash through the heart of it.

"What's the lesson of the Jabberwocky?" She looked up at Him with eyes as wide as Alice's lost in Wonderland.

"Let's find out." He opened the book and in His voice that belonged to a man from another time started to read to her. ""Twas brillig, and the slithy toves...'"

Meanwhile His semen dripped out of her body onto the laughing white moons and the smiling yellow stars.

Elle blinked and a tear landed on the keyboard.

She read through the story once. Then twice. She remembered the humiliation and the desire. She was aroused, painfully so, and would give anything for release. Her cheeks flushed hot with the sensory memories of her mortification. She could still feel Søren's semen slick on her thighs. When she wrote her scene, she hadn't been able to type his name. She could only write "Him," capital *H* as if he were God instead of a mere man. Maybe he was a god with a god's power and a god's wrath. She had seen both with her own eyes. And he had seen into her soul the way only a god could and had conjured a scene for her designed to touch the most tender spots on her heart, the parts of her that mourned for her lost childhood and the love she'd had for her real father as a little girl. The night her father died, the night she had condemned him to die, she'd declared to Kingsley, "My only father is a priest." Had Søren seen those words printed on her soul? Was that why he'd put her in the nightgown, made her call him "Daddy"? That wasn't his kink, his fantasy. It was hers and he used it like a knife. But not a knife like a weapon, a knife like a scalpel, and he'd cut the wounded spot out of her heart with it. Her father hadn't loved her. Her priest, that Father, did love her and always would. Her father had abandoned her. Her Father never would. Her father had never held her and rocked her and read her stories. But her Father had.

The memory of that night glowed in her mind like something radioactive; potent, powerful and dangerous. Such a memory could make her forget things she didn't want to forget, like the sound of an antique riding crop snapping into the three pieces, or ugly words like *you are mine*.

A memory such as this could make her crawl back to him. The day she'd first seen him when she'd been fifteen, she'd felt a golden cord tied around her heart pulling her toward him. Even now she felt the cord, felt the pull. The cord tightened around her heart leaving her breathless with pain and wanting.

She didn't want to go back to him.

She didn't want to go back to him.

God, she wanted to go back to him.

If she went back to him it would all be for nothing— leaving, the year at the convent, swallowing her pride to beg Kingsley for a job, the plan to turn her into the Queen of the Underground. She'd have to give it all up to go back to him. He'd ordered her to stay away from Kingsley. He'd ordered her not to top Kingsley. He'd ordered her to marry him.

Would he order her to do all that again if she went back to him?

She couldn't take that chance.

Elle highlighted every single word in the document, every word she'd just written.

She hit Delete.

Poof. It was gone.

Just like that.

Elle smiled although it had hurt.

Daddy's little girl was all grown-up now.

Slightly shaking, Elle got up out of her chair, logged off the computer and walked back to the stacks, searching for a book, any book, anything to take her mind off what she'd just written, what she'd just done. She felt freer now. Stronger. Lighter but emptier in a way. But that's what she wanted, wasn't it?

From the shelf in front of her she pulled out a book, an Agatha Christie mystery she'd always meant to read. She wasn't quite in the mood for a mystery right now. She needed something else...but what? When she put it back on the shelf she saw a pair of eyes staring at her from between the books.

Familiar eyes.

Without thinking, Elle shoved the books on the shelf to the side and there he was, staring at her like a goddamn creeping creeper.

"Griffin Randolfe Fiske, what the fuck—"

"Um...sorry. Also, hi, Nor." He put his hand through the gap in the shelves and waved, calling her Nor like he always had. He hated "Eleanor," thought it sounded too prissy and prim. Prissy? No wonder Søren had liked the name so much. "Missed you. Welcome home."

"Jesus H. Christ." She rolled her eyes, walked around the end of the stacks and found him in the next aisle over looking as sheepish and self-conscious as a six-foot-tall, two-hundred-pound weightlifter with a trust fund as well-endowed as he was could look. He was dressed in his usual uniform of stylishly ripped jeans and a heather-gray fitted T-shirt. He'd grown a beard since she'd last seen him. No, not quite a beard but more than a five-o'clock shadow. "What the hell are you doing here? Are you following me?" she whispered, but loudly.

"Um...maybe."

"No more ums. Use your words."

"Yes. I'm following you."

"Care to tell me why you're following me?"

"King told me to."

"King told you to follow me?"

"Yes, if you left the house, which you did. He's trying to keep you safe."

"Safe from who?"

"Yourself, I think."

Of course he was. Kingsley knew her, knew she'd be tempted to go back to Søren. Somehow he'd cajoled Griffin into saving her from herself. Well, as plans went it wasn't the worst one she'd heard.

"And you couldn't say, 'Hi, long time no see'? You had to follow me?"

"King told me not to tell you I was around."

"Why not?"

"Um…"

"What is it, Griffin Fiske?" She crossed her arms over her chest and glowered at him, domme-style.

"King said if you saw me, you'd probably jump me, and if we're fucking I won't be able to do my job of keeping an eye on you if we're having sex since I do most of my thinking with my cock."

"King thinks that although I haven't seen you in over a year, I will jump your bones the first chance I get and then you won't be able to follow me because I'll know you're there? That's the situation? That's why you're stalking me?"

"Well…yeah." Even with the beard, Griffin looked terribly young and innocent, and she had a feeling he'd grown the beard so he'd look less terribly young and innocent. Caught red-handed. Shamefaced. Slightly embarrassed. Utterly adorable. And Griffin looked at her as if Christmas came early this year, and he'd been a very good boy.

Merry Christmas.

"Well, you want to know something?" she asked.

"What?"

"King was right."

She dropped her backpack and crooked her finger. In an instant Griffin was in her arms, pressing her back into the bookcases. He kissed her hard, and she kissed him back harder. So hard. Everything was hard. The kiss and Griffin's cock and how much she wanted it inside her.

"Did you miss me?" she asked into his lips.

"So much," he breathed as his hands scored her back and clasped her tight to his chest.

"How much?" She raised her chin to give him access to her neck. She needed neck kisses. She needed all the kisses.

He pushed his erection against her.

"This much."

When he kissed her ear she could feel the scruff of not quite a beard but more than a five-o'clock shadow tickling her neck. She wanted this, didn't she? Wasn't this what she'd been waiting for, what she'd been aching for since she'd come back to Kingsley's? A male body, strong arms…power? Right? And Griffin kissed masterfully. He could dominate with a kiss alone by setting the pace, holding her where he wanted her, keeping her captive and mute with his tongue in her mouth so that she couldn't raise a word of objection.

But.

It wasn't quite right.

Something was missing, and she knew she needed it if this were to go further than one good kiss.

"Please…" Griffin growled in her ear. She loved to hear him beg.

"Please, what?"

"I have to fuck you."

"No one *has* to fuck me. You *want* to fuck me. Going without sex never killed anybody."

"But why take that chance?"

Elle reached down between their bodies and pressed her hand into his cock through his jeans. Already erect, Griffin stiffened even more in surprise and what must have been a modicum of discomfort.

Elle laughed softly and the sound of it surprised her. It was an arrogant, throaty laugh that sounded foreign to her own ears. Kingsley laughed like that while he mocked a trussed-up submissive when she squirmed or begged for mercy. It was a dominant's laugh. A queen's laugh.

She unbuttoned his jeans. Hidden in such a faraway corner of the stacks, she felt it was safe to touch him. If they got kicked out of the library for fooling around? Well, it wouldn't be the first time.

"You did miss me, didn't you?"

He put his mouth at her ear. "I still think about that night, your birthday. When we were in the Rolls and—"

"I remember."

"Fucking you…watching King and Søren fuck you… Jesus, I've known gay guys who didn't love cock as much as you do."

"They don't know what they're missing."

"But you do," Griffin said, tilting his pelvis forward to push his cock against her hand.

"I do want it. But on my terms."

"What are your terms?" Griffin asked. She had a feeling he'd agree to anything at this point, including but not limited to committing felonies. Or, at the very least, a series of misdemeanors.

Elle looked up and met his eyes. He was so much taller than her but she didn't care. She had his attention.

"I am not a submissive anymore, and I will not be treated like one. I kiss you. You do not kiss me. I top you. You do not top me. If you can play by these rules, we can play. If not? Game over."

Griffin closed his eyes. He'd grabbed on to the bookshelves on either side of her arms, and gripped them as hard as she gripped him.

She slid her hand down his cock and wrapped all five fingers around the base, squeezing, holding, waiting. Griffin's hips pulsed against her hand, fucking her fingers until he could fuck other parts of her.

"If you let me top you, we can fuck. Deal?" she asked.

The slightest cry or maybe it was a whimper escaped his lips. His eyes were shut tight as if he were in pain or in pleasure or in both. Didn't matter to her except he better make up his mind fast before he ejaculated all over *The Collected Novels of Willa Cather.*

"No pain?" he asked. Griffin was no coward, but he was a recovering drug abuser. When he was in pain he wanted drugs to ease the pain. Even one strong painkiller could send him backsliding into the hard stuff again.

"No pain. I promise. Only other sorts of torture."

"Fun torture?"

"There is no other kind of torture when you're with me."

Griffin took a shuddering breath as she ran her hand up and down his cock again.

"Deal."

A smile crossed Elle's face, and she wasn't sure if she'd ever smiled like that before, as if she were nothing but smile.

"Good boy."

8

Seven

THEY TOOK A CAB TO HIS NEW PLACE IN CHELSEA where Griffin had moved three months ago. Inside the apartment he tossed the keys into a silver bowl and locked the door behind them. He offered a tour of the new digs but she declined. All she wanted to see was the bedroom and the bedroom did not disappoint. His bed was a king-size, low to the ground and minimalist. Black frame—padded black leather headboard, metal slatted footboard. The headboard was for cushioning the head during rough sex. The footboard was for bondage. She gave Griffin credit—the kid could decorate like a motherfucker. The coverlet and sheets were black, red and white. Apart from the bed he had nothing much else in his room except for a black leather Chesterfield sofa, the sort of sofa one fucked on if one were the sort to fuck on sofas, which Griffin was.

Elle stood facing the bed. Behind her, Griffin locked the door and came up to her. He wrapped his arms around her and kissed the side of her neck.

"I'm all yours," he whispered.

"I have to tell you something."

"Anything."

"I haven't had sex with a man in over a year."

Griffin grabbed her by the shoulders and spun her around to face him. He looked at her as if she'd sprouted a second head.

"How are you even alive? Over a year without sex? How's that even possible?"

"I was in a convent, Griffin. No men in convents."

"Then order delivery. There are people who will bring the sex to your house."

Elle laughed. "It's okay. I said I hadn't had sex with a man in over a year. I have had sex."

His wide eyes widened even wider. If they got any wider, they'd fall out of his head.

"You fucked a girl."

"Shh…don't tell."

Griffin fell sideways, collapsing on the bed.

"Griff?"

He rose up on his elbows. "Was she hot?"

"She was a twenty-one-year-old virgin with small breasts and long legs. And yes, she was hot."

"She was a virgin until you?"

"Yes. I fisted her our first night together."

Griffin gasped and looked down at his crotch.

"Oh, my God," he said.

"What's wrong?"

"My cock twitched. I didn't know it could do that."

"Can you be serious for two seconds?"

"I am serious. It wiggled like one of those plastic flower toys that dance when you play music."

"I haven't had anyone or anything inside me for a long time. I might be a little…tight."

"I can handle tight. I buy lube in bulk. Can we fuck now please?"

"Not yet. You aren't ready."

Griffin looked down at his crotch.

"He just told me he's ready," Griffin said. "Telepathically."

Elle sighed. Heavily. She did want him, and his cock, but he'd agreed to bottom for her, and she wasn't about to rush this or waste her chance. But what to do to him...?

"You're bi—" she said.

"I am? Oh, yeah. I am. Sorry. I'm focused on your pussy right now. Almost forgot."

"You have a leather chest harness somewhere, don't you?"

"Maybe...somewhere..." He didn't sound excited about the prospect of wearing one.

"Will you wear it for me?"

"Must I?" he asked.

"I've masturbated to the thought of fucking you while you're naked but for a chest harness."

"It's in the closet, back wall, hanging on a hook next to the spreader bars."

She retrieved the harness and laid it on the bed next to Griffin.

"What's with the beard?" she asked as she ran her hand over the soft scruff on his cheeks and chin.

"I was roughing it. Went backpacking to Clingman's Dome with friends. Got back a couple days ago."

"How was the Dome?" She tugged his gray T-shirt off and threw it onto the floor.

"I didn't get to the top. I came home early."

"Why? Bored?" She slipped the harness on him and buckled it in place.

"I checked my messages. King said you were back."

Elle was silent a moment. She swallowed before speaking again.

"You came back from your trip early, because you heard I came back?"

"Told you," he said, shrugging. "I missed you."

"I didn't think anyone would miss me. I mean, anyone but him."

"Søren."

"Yeah, him."

"I know this might surprise you, but I'd gotten used to the idea of thinking we were friends. Almost best friends," he said. "I wanted us to be that and you acted like that's what you wanted, too. Then you disappeared and you didn't tell me where you went or why you left. So obviously we weren't best friends if you couldn't tell me where you were going, which is fine. That's cool. But knowing you didn't feel the same about me didn't make me feel any differently about you. When King said you were back in the city, I came back the same day. And when he said he wanted me to keep an eye on you since you were, you know, going through a rough adjustment period, I said I would. Because maybe if I keep an eye on you, next time you run off I'll know where you went."

Simple words and not very eloquent, yet they somehow slipped through the cracks in the hard shell she'd built around herself since leaving the convent. No, since leaving Søren.

"Do you want to be my best friend?"

"With benefits?" he asked.

"Abso-fucking-lutely."

"I'm in," he said grinning broadly. "Buddy."

"Good, old pal." She pushed him onto his back and straddled his hips. He looked utterly delectable in his black jeans, his leather harness. She ran her hands up and down his taut stomach, tracing the edges of the harness, caressing his chest and arms. She kissed his scruffy, handsome face and wondered at the change in him. He'd always been a charmer, a rogue, a wicked playboy trust-fund baby cracking dirty jokes and acting as the life of the party, every party. No one who knew him as Master Griffin would believe he was on his back for her. No one would believe he had this tenderness to him. Where had he been hiding it? Did it show itself with her because they were friends? Or was it something else? Or maybe it wasn't Griffin who'd changed at all. Maybe it was her. Maybe she'd changed. Maybe it was always there and now she finally noticed it.

Elle lowered her mouth to his ear and whispered, "Pick a number between one and ten."

"What?"

She pulled back and looked down at him.

"You heard me."

"What am I picking?"

"I'm not going to tell you until you've picked your number," she said.

"But how do I know what number to pick until I know what I'm picking?"

"Exactly."

Griffin narrowed his eyes at her. "You're evil."

"Still waiting on that number, Griff."

"Fine. I don't know. Seven?"

"Seven. Good."

"What's good? Why is seven good?" Griffin sounded slightly panicked.

"Because seven is the number of orgasms you're going to give me today. And when I've had seven you can fuck me. And you can't fuck me until I've had seven."

"Seven orgasms? You want me to get you off seven times? One-for-each-day-of-the-week seven?"

"Is that a problem?" She cocked her head at him.

"Yes, that's a problem. A big problem," Griffin said.

"Is it? And why so?" she asked.

Griffin grinned up at her, a grin she felt right in her belly.

"Because I should have picked ten."

Elle laughed and kissed him again.

"Ten might kill me," she said.

"But what a way to go."

Standing up, Elle crooked her finger at Griffin, who slipped his hands into her underwear and started to slide them down her legs.

"Fold them," she said.

"What?"

"Fold my underwear. Don't throw them."

"You threw my T-shirt."

"Who's in charge here? Hmm?"

"You are."

"Good. Now fold them."

Griffin gave her the classic "you've gotta be kidding me but if it'll get me laid…" look and obediently folded her black silk panties. Clearly he hadn't folded much women's underwear in his life as they resembled a pocket handkerchief when he'd finished with them. Someday they would go out in formalwear, and she'd make Griffin put her panties in his breast pocket.

"Any rules?" he asked.

"You can use your mouth, fingers and toys, but no cock." She crawled back onto the bed and lay back on the pillows.

"How many fingers?"

"Are you asking if you can fist me?"

"They don't call me Griffin Fist because I know how to box."

"If you can get your whole hand in there, then you're welcome to. But I'll be surprised."

"Have a little faith in me. I'm the David Copperfield of fisting."

"The Dickens character or the magician?"

"There's fisting in Dickens? I should have majored in English instead of art." Griffin winked at her as he grabbed a pillow from the head of his bed and pushed it under her hips. He kissed her again on the mouth and she sensed real affection in Griffin's kiss. He cared for her. It made it easier for her to relax and open her legs for him without any nervousness or self-consciousness.

With the tips of his fingers, Griffin found her clitoris and lightly rubbed it as he kissed her neck. Passionate kisses on a naked neck. No, she didn't miss her collar at all.

Griffin slid down her body and settled between her thighs. Carefully he parted her wet folds, touching her at first with his fingers. When he lowered his head and licked her clitoris she inhaled sharply. Such sudden pleasure, it was a gift.

"The clit." Elle sighed. "The only organ on the human body designed solely for pleasure. Proof God is a woman."

Griffin laughed and his warm breath brushed over her most sensitive parts. He worked his tongue over her again and again, lightly at first and then harder as she began to pant. What was better? What she felt or what she saw? Looking down and seeing Griffin's naked shoulders, the leather harness strapped on his back moving with every breath, the hard muscle, the tan, the prominent ridge of biceps as he held himself in place. Bare feet. Ripped black jeans. A willingness to submit to her.

"You were the right man to break my dry spell," Elle said.

"Welcome to a long, hard wet spell," Griffin said, a divine bit of poetry.

He pushed his tongue deep inside her before returning his attentions to her clitoris. He slipped a finger into her and pressed into the soft depression right under her pubic bone.

Elle let out a very un-domme-like gasp of pleasure. She was so close…so close… She hadn't been touched so intimately in so long she knew she would come any second now. Any second… Everything throbbed inside her, everything ached, and her hips rose off the bed and pulsed against Griffin's mouth. Between her thighs his head dipped and his tongue licked and his lips sucked and she came with a cry, clinging to the pillow Griffin had put underneath her.

He rose up as she panted to calm her racing heart.

Griffin wiped his mouth off with the back of his hand.

"One down," he said. "Six to go."

"I'm not going to survive it," she said, panting hard. "I should have made you pick a number between one and five."

"Too late. Don't give someone as competitive as I am a challenge if you don't want me to do it."

With that pronouncement, Griffin's head disappeared again. Not between her legs but under the bed.

"Griff?"

"Be right back," he said and she heard him rummaging under the bed for something. She put both her legs on his back to anchor him and because she really wanted to put her boots on his back.

"You make a very sexy ottoman, Mr. Fiske," she said.

"I'm not Turkish."

"I meant the furniture, you ridiculous slut."

When Griffin resurfaced from his under-the-bed diving expedition, he had a metal briefcase with him.

"What's that?" she asked, eyeing it as he clicked the locks.

He opened the lid and turned it to face her.

"Vibrator collection," he said. "Brand-new. Time to christen them. Your pussy is their maiden voyage."

"You're a man with a vibrator collection?"

"I was a Boy Scout a million years ago. Gotta be prepared."
He gave her a three-fingered salute.

Griffin set the open briefcase next to her on another pillow.
He sat back on his knees and unzipped his pants.

"No cock yet," she said wagging her finger in that way
Kingsley wagged his. Great, now she was doing it. Must be
a dom thing.

"I know, but I want to get closer to you. Is that okay?"
She smiled at him. "Very okay. But first—touch yourself."

His jeans were unzipped and open, hanging low on his
narrow hips. She wished she had a camera to take a picture
of this scene—Griffin running his hand up and down and all
over his erection, the look on his face as he stared directly in
her eyes while he did it, shameless, sensual, sexual, all in one.

She crooked her finger at him and he crawled over her kissing her on the mouth again.

"Can I take your clothes off?" he asked. "Please?"

"Of course."

She sat up to help him pull her shirt off. This time she didn't
have to tell him to fold it neatly and put it away like a good
boy. Fast learner. She liked that.

He unzipped her denim skirt and folded it. He slid her bra
off her arms and hung it from the knob on the nightstand
drawer. When he went for her boots she issued an order.

"Leave those on."

"With pleasure," Griffin said, dipping his head to kiss the
laces.

"For a dom, you're a very good sub."

Griffin grinned at her. "If I have to fold your underwear
and kiss your boots to get inside you, then I'm more than
happy to do that. But—for the record—King diagnosed me
as a born service top."

"You think I'm bottoming from the top?"

"Maybe I'm just topping from below." He kissed her right on the tip of her nose. Typical top. She'd show him who was boss. At least in this scene.

Elle laughed as Griffin yanked off his jeans and, naked, slid into bed next to her. He gathered her in his arms and put her on top of him, his chest to her back. With the padded headboard behind him, Griffin was half sitting up, which made her feel as if she were lying on a human chaise longue. A human chaise longue with a massive erection halfway up her ass. She ground her hips from side to side and in a slow undulating circle.

"Vicious wench," he said. "If you keep doing that I'm going to come on your back."

"No, you aren't."

"I'm not?"

"You aren't allowed to come until I'm done coming."

"You didn't say that earlier."

"New rule," she said. "I make the rules. You follow the rules."

"In that case, we better get to six fast before I break that rule all over the both of us."

From inside the briefcase he pulled out a medium-size vibrator, about six inches long and of average thickness. She was already wet from her previous orgasm so it slid into her easily. Griffin put it on its lowest setting and she turned her face to meet his. As he fucked her with the vibrator they kissed again, a long, slow, deep kiss. His one free hand cupped her right breast and squeezed it. He grasped her nipple between his thumb and forefinger, kneading it lightly. Her whole body felt his presence. Her thighs were draped over his thighs, her back rested against his stomach and chest, his arms wrapped around her and his mouth was on her mouth. When she came a second time it was against his lips. The mingling of their breaths as she climaxed was as erotic as the orgasm itself.

Griffin turned the vibrator up to a higher setting and fucked her with it again. The fingers of his free hand massaged her clitoris gently and it wasn't long before she came a third time with a deep shudder.

After number four he took the vibrator out of her and explored her with his bare hands.

"God, you're so wet," he said in her ear and she could hear the strain in his voice, the need. "I can't stop touching you."

He pulled her folds wide, spreading her out and pushing two, then three, then four of his fingers into her. With his four fingers inside her, he moved his hand in a spiraling motion, circling in and out, in and out, the spiral widening with every turn and his fingers finding soft spots and muscles inside her she'd forgotten she had.

She could hardly stand it, how good it felt, how open she was, and how much she wanted him. She could barely breathe for it, for the pleasure and the pressure and the slow building toward release. Underneath her Griffin's hips pushed against her. They were adrift together, moving and rocking and floating above the bed.

"Please come for me. Come on my hand so I can feel every muscle inside you," he said as he pushed the heel of his palm against her clitoris.

"Deeper," she said.

"Faster," she said.

"Harder," she said.

Griffin did all three and he did them all at once. When she came for her fifth time it was with a cry that sounded to her own ears like pain but her body told her differently. The muscles inside her contracted all around Griffin's fingers, hard enough he swore in her ear.

"Fuck," he said, slowly pulling his hand from inside her.

"Good idea."

"What?"

"Let's fuck."

"But that was only number five."

"What did I say about the rules?" she asked.

"You make the rules."

"Right. Now I'm changing the rules. I need to fuck you. I'll die if I don't."

"No one ever died from not fucking," he reminded her.

"Whoever said that was an idiot. Get on your back, head by the footboard. I want to tie you up and use your cock for my own selfish needs. Do you have any objection to that?"

"I—"

"Don't care. Just do it."

He just did it.

Her legs wobbled as she stood up and dug through Griffin's closet for bondage toys. Not in the mood to be fancy, she grabbed a pair of basic rope cuffs, wrapped them around the top bar of the footboard and slipped them onto Griffin's wrists.

"Condoms?" she asked.

"In the drawer. And between the mattresses. Also in a box under the sofa. There's some in the bathroom, too. And the kitchen."

"Is there anywhere in the house you don't have condoms?"

"The cookie jar. There are actual cookies in there. No. Wait. There are condoms in there, too. I ate all the cookies."

Elle laughed so hard she had to rest her head on his chest for a minute.

"You're ridiculous and sexy and ridiculously sexy," she said, meeting his eyes.

"I know."

"I'm going to fuck you now."

"Thank you."

She reached into the bedside table for a condom.

"Wait," Griffin said, lifting his head. "Not those. The ones under the mattress."

Elle raised her eyebrow and slid her hand between the mattress and the bed frame. She pulled out a sheaf of condoms.

"Your favorites?" she asked.

"Lambskin," he said. "Love them. I got tested last month, and you haven't been with a guy in a year and, you know, they're roomier. You can't use them for anal so I save them for only the most special pussies."

"My pussy and I are honored."

Elle straddled Griffin's hips, took his cock in her hand and guided it to the entrance of her body. She sunk down slowly onto it, relishing every inch. Already she was bathed in sweat but as Griffin entered her fully the temperature in the room rose ten degrees. Or maybe that was her body temperature rising. Didn't matter. They were both slick with sweat and burning up for each other. When she leaned closer to him, he lifted his head and captured a nipple in his mouth, sucking it deeply, and she felt the pull of pleasure all the way into her stomach. Elle gripped the bar of the footboard over Griffin's head and used it to steady herself as she rode him. She pushed against him and his back arched. She did it again. His eyes closed and his lips parted.

"You're enjoying this," she said, rocking into him again.

He nodded, biting his own lip, a gesture she found innocently erotic.

"I was afraid," he said.

"Of what?" She touched his face.

"Of never seeing you again."

"You don't have to be afraid. I'm not going anywhere. Not with you inside me."

"Thank you, Mistress."

Elle stopped moving.

"What?" Griffin looked at her, his eyes open again.

"You called me Mistress."

"I did. Did you like that?"

"Say it again."

"Yes, Mistress… Mistress… Mistress… My beautiful Mistress Nor."

And the more he said it, the more she wanted him to say it. And when he came it was with the word on his lips.

She laughed and Griffin whispered, "What? What is it?"

"Mistress Nor. I like the sound of that."

9

ELLE ATTEMPTED TO CREEP BACK INTO KINGSLEY'S town house under cover of night. A few years ago she might have succeeded in her sneaking but that was before Kingsley acquired his "children."

Four black Rottweilers—the children in question—bounded down the stairs, galloping toward her in a hail of paws and ears and tails and tongues. She ended up flat on her back beneath them with four wet noses in her face. Kingsley's dogs—Brutus, Dominic, Sadie and Max—were reportedly vicious attack dogs. Anyone who knew them, however, quickly discovered that although they, like their owner, were capable of killing if necessary, in general they were lovers, not fighters.

"Brutus, stop it," she said as Brutus, the alpha of the bunch, stuck his nose between her thighs. "Jabberwocky."

"They don't respond well to safe words," Kingsley said from the top of the stairs.

"Jesus Christ," she said, petting and pushing the dogs away at the same time. "Why couldn't you be a cat person?"

"There's enough pussy in this house as it is." Kingsley started down the steps toward her. He was dressed but disheveled, looking like a well-fucked rogue. Apparently she and Kingsley had both had a nice evening. Finally he whistled, calling the dogs off her. They whimpered but obeyed their master although it was obvious they were not done with the lickings and the pettings.

"Where's Calliope?" Elle pulled herself off the floor and brushed herself off. "I thought they slept with her."

"They do. But she's on a date."

Elle walked past him heading up to her room.

"Guess we're all getting lucky tonight," she said.

Kingsley grabbed her arm as she tried to pass him, stopping her on the stairs. "Griffin?"

"Yup."

"He wasn't supposed to tell you he was watching you," Kingsley said.

"He didn't tell me. I caught him in the act. He'd make a terrible CIA agent."

Kingsley sighed heavily. "I'll kill him."

"Don't kill him. I need him alive if I'm going to keep tying him up and fucking his brains out."

Kingsley narrowed his eyes at her. "But Griffin's a dominant."

"So?"

"You topped him?"

"I did."

"You topped a top."

"I've topped you," she said.

"I'm a masochist. Griffin isn't."

"Griffin's barely twenty-three and couldn't scare someone if he wore a suit made out of knives. He's a puppy, King. It's pretty easy to top a puppy when you've already topped a…" She looked down at Brutus sitting at Kingsley's heels. "A Rottweiler."

Kingsley cocked his eyebrow at that. Probably the first time in his life a woman had ever likened the inestimable Kingsley Edge to a dog.

"You enjoyed it with Griffin?"

"As much as he did. So…a lot."

"My office. Now."

"Now? I'm so tired," she said. "I came like eight times today. I need to put an ice pack on my pussy."

"Ice later. Talk now. Go."

Elle went. The fantasy of owning her own house was growing stronger every day. Wouldn't it be lovely to return home from a day of debauchery to an empty house? Or if not an empty house, a house devoid of her boss. She wouldn't have to answer questions about where she went and what she did and with whom she did it. Someday…once she got her money. Not money, she corrected. A lot of fucking money.

Since Kingsley would be the source of her getting "a lot of fucking money" she dutifully trudged up to his office and sat gingerly in the chair opposite his desk. Next time she took a year off cock, she'd pick a guy with a much smaller penis to help with her reentry into the world of PIV intercourse.

"I have good news," Kingsley said. He sat on the edge of his desk in front of her.

"I like good news."

"Milady will be at the party we're attending tomorrow night."

"Good," Elle said. "Can't wait for the beat and greet."

"You think you're ready to go out again? Be around our people?"

"He won't be there, will he?"

"No."

"Good."

"But eventually you will have to see him again. You need to prepare yourself for that. If you saw him right now, could you handle it?"

Elle paused before answering. Finally she spoke.

"While we were having sex, Griffin called me something. He called me Mistress. Mistress Nor."

"You liked that?" Kingsley asked.

"I loved it." She heard the heat in her own voice, the emotion betrayed, and she quickly worked to cover it. "I don't want to go back to being Eleanor. I want to be Mistress Nor."

"Nor?"

"Griffin hates the name 'Eleanor.' He just started calling me Nor one day and that's what he calls me. Then he called me Mistress Nor, and when he called me Mistress Nor, it was like I heard my real name for the first time."

"There is a queen named Noor. Queen of Jordan. Beautiful woman. Brilliant and accomplished. I send her roses on her birthday. It's a good name for a queen but perhaps not a dominatrix. Nor. Rhymes with *whore*. Can't have that, can we?"

"No, I guess not."

Kingsley leaned over and took her chin in his hand. He looked at her, looked into her eyes, at her face, looked like a man aiming for a target. Where was the bull's-eye?

"Nora."

The name sounded elegant with his accent. Strong, sophisticated. Not her name and yet there was her name buried inside it. Those three letters—Eleanor, Nor, Nora…it was her and yet it wasn't.

"I like it," she said.

"Mistress Nora. Yes…*parfait*."

"It is."

"Mistress Nora," he said again. "Nora, *la Maîtresse. Son Maîtresse.*"

"*Votre Maîtresse,*" she said, completing the conjugation. The Mistress. His Mistress. *Your* Mistress.

"*Oui,*" he said. "*Ma Maîtresse.*"

My Mistress.

"Mistress Nora," she said, rolling the name around her mouth and loving the way it tasted—sweet and spiked like Christmas punch.

"What's my name?" Nora asked.

"Mistress Nora."

"Who am I?

"Mistress Nora."

"Who will be Queen of the Underground?"

Kingsley smiled. "Mistress Nora."

"Fuck yes, I will," Nora said, beaming.

Nora.

That was her name.

Not Elle like her friends called her.

Not Ellie like her mother called her.

Not Eleanor, which Søren called her in public.

Not even Little One, which he called her in private.

And not Nor because that wasn't quite right.

Nora.

Mistress Nora.

"Mistress Fucking Nora," she said aloud.

"Well, Mistress Fucking Nora," Kingsley said, "if you're going to be queen, you'll need a throne room. I'll start working on your dungeon tomorrow."

"Finally."

"Go, get some rest. We'll start fresh tomorrow."

"Do I get to play with the whip?"

"You can't even flog a towel off the wall. Now go to bed.

There's a naughty Haitian submissive in my bed who will be wondering where my cock has gone to. Sleep well."

"I plan to." She stood up. When she'd sat down she'd still been Elle. When she stood up she was Nora. Mistress Nora.

She headed to Kingsley's office door.

"You really topped Griffin?" he asked.

"I did. Like a boss," she said, laughing. "But don't be too impressed. Like I said, he's a puppy."

"You were gone for a year. So was I. Tessa told me that while we were gone, Griffin became one of the most sought-after doms in the club. He's brutal when he wants to be. When we were gone, he wanted to be. Tessa had bruises for two weeks after a session with him—inside and out. He's made grown men bleed, and he's not even a sadist. He says he does it for 'shits and giggles.' If Griffin seems like a puppy to you, it's because you're a tiger."

Nora narrowed her eyes at him and raised her hand in a claw. "Rawr."

Kingsley laughed. "Go to bed."

"Yes, Master."

"Goodnight, Mistress."

"Mistress… I could get used to that."

Truth was, she was already used to it.

She walked out of his office intending to go straight to her bedroom. She'd take a long bath, sleep for twelve hours, eat all the food for breakfast…

But she didn't make it to her bedroom. She stopped at Kingsley's playroom first. Inside she turned on the light and walked around gazing at the array of BDSM toys hanging on the wall. He had ten floggers of various sizes and materials hanging on evenly spaced hooks—red floggers, blue floggers, black, brown, elk-hide, cowhide, deer-hide, vinyl and vicious rubber floggers. He had canes, too, over a dozen of them. Tiny little white ones that burned like a bee sting on sensitive skin. Large rattan canes that could put a full-grown man in the hospital if wielded with too much force.

When she came to the crops, she smiled. Oh, yes, these were her favorite. Something about a riding crop. The feel of it, the balance, the elegance. Riding crops were designed for humans to use on horses, for striking thick skin and driving a ton of pure muscle. Perhaps that's why she loved the crop so much. Kingsley had told her a dominatrix would never be physically stronger than the men she topped. It wasn't about physical strength. It was about control, about taking command over a beast bigger and stronger but with a will that could be bent, a drive that could be directed, power that could be restrained, channeled, dominated.

Nora reached out and took a particular riding crop off a brass hook. It was red, bloodred, and about two feet long. A shorter crop had less give to it. It hurt more than one with more swish in its swing. She knew this instinctively, not from her few weeks as a dominant, but her years as a submissive. She'd long been on the receiving end of a riding crop. How good and right it felt to wield it by the handle.

She spun it in her hand like a baton. She hadn't twirled a baton since she was a little girl pretending to be a majorette, but it all came back to her. Pure muscle memory. It danced lightly over her fingers as she turned it. Testing out the old skills she walked the perimeter of the room, twirling it in her hand as she walked. A few times she almost lost it, but she caught it and soon the rhythm was hers again.

Her own dungeon. She would have a room like this soon enough. All the toys she could ever want. A dream come true. A dark and decadent dream. A secret dream like playing Daddy's girl with Søren. She'd had the dream of being a domme all her life. She remembered sexual fantasies from long before she'd met Søren. When she was fourteen, she'd snuck into an R-rated movie and saw her first sex scene with a woman on top. That fantasy had given her some of her earliest orgasms.

Wasn't it strange that Søren had never picked up on those domination fantasies of hers? He could read her so well that he could sense from her fascination with the couple at the club that she had a Daddy's-girl fantasy. Why hadn't he known she'd had this side to her? He was a smart man, a brilliant man, an insightful man. There's no reason he shouldn't have known. Kingsley had known.

"Oh, you son of a bitch," she said out loud. "You knew."

"Who knew?" Kingsley asked from the doorway.

She turned and faced him.

"I came for a flogger," he said. "I thought you were going to bed. Tell me...who knew?"

"He did. He knew everything about me. The more private it was, the more personal, the more humiliating... He knew it. He could read me like a book. He knew I wanted to be a domme. He had to know."

"Of course he knew. I told him when you were sixteen that you were a dominant or a switch."

"Why didn't he tell me?"

"Did he have to?"

"It would have been nice if we could have talked about it," she said.

Kingsley gave a little scoffing laugh as he plucked a large black flogger off the wall.

"If you're looking for someone 'nice' you picked the wrong priest."

"I can't believe he knew all this time, and he never said a word."

"I can," Kingsley said. "He loved you. He didn't want to

lose you. He's a dominant and a sadist. If you were a dominant, too, he couldn't switch for you. He knew he'd lose you if you let your domme side out to play. I suppose we proved him right."

"That's why you didn't want me to tell him I topped you." Kingsley nodded.

"I didn't leave him because I have a domme side," she said. "I left him because he tried to leave the church for me, and because he ordered me to marry him like my feelings didn't matter one fucking bit to him. Oh, and he did this." She threw her riding crop against the wall. "That's what he thinks of me."

"I warned you he had this side."

"I know you did." She looked at Kingsley and shook her head. "He made me promise him forever. Did you know that? I had to obey him forever just because he got me out of going to jail when I was fifteen. Did he really think I owed him the rest of my natural life because of that? I would have gotten out of juvie at twenty-one. Maybe I shouldn't have made the deal."

"You don't believe that."

"No," she admitted. "But sometimes, I do wonder…"

"What do you wonder?" Kingsley asked, coming to stand in front of her.

"When I was with my mom at the convent, we talked one day about my dad. She told me something I didn't know, and it's been bugging me ever since she told me. Now I know why." She paused, gathered her words. She wasn't sure why Kingsley needed to know what she was going to tell him, but he did. He had to know.

"Go on," Kingsley said gently. She had his complete attention.

"I was still a baby when my parents divorced," she began. "My mom asked for full custody of me, but the judge said my dad could have me on the weekends. But then Dad got caught stealing some car parts. Spent three months in jail. But there were about four weekends I stayed with him at his place before he got arrested and my mom got full custody. Do you know where he lived back then?"

"No."

"A shitty apartment at the edge of West Harlem. Barely two miles from Riverside Drive. Two miles from this house. King." She smiled, shook her head, laughed at the mad world they lived in. "It's funny... If he hadn't gotten arrested, I would have grown up two miles from this house. Dad started jacking cars and running a chop shop full-time when I was about ten. When I was fifteen he made me help him. Remember that?"

"I do. It's what brought him to my doorstep to save you after you were arrested."

"If I lived with my dad and wanted to steal cars, my first stop would have been Riverside Drive. A Rolls-Royce two miles from my place? Very tempting target. I would have stolen your Rolls if I'd grown up with my dad instead of my mom. I know it. I know it for a fact. I don't know how I know it so don't ask. But when I go back in time in my mind I can see where that one little event changed the course of my life. I would have stolen your Rolls that night I helped my dad jack cars, and I would have gotten arrested. And what would you have done when you found out a fifteen-year-old girl had been the one who stole your Rolls?"

"I would have gone to the police station to get a look at this girl. Like I did with Mistress Irina when she was arrested for trying to poison her husband. I wouldn't have been able to resist seeing the little girl car thief."

"So you, not Søren, would have met me first. If I'd lived with my dad on the weekends, then I wouldn't ever have gone to church with my mom on Sundays, right? No Sacred Heart for me," she said. "It was like God flipped a coin and it landed on heads instead of tails, on Søren instead of you. It could have landed on tails."

"And you would have landed on me."

She nodded, not laughing. It wasn't a joke. She saw it all happening. Kingsley would have walked into the police station interrogation room and it would have been him sitting across from her when she opened her eyes. She would have said, *Who the fuck are you?* and he would have answered, *That's for you to decide,* chérie. *I'm either your best friend or your worst enemy.* He would have wanted her. Kingsley was no saint. He would have had far fewer qualms about fucking her as a teenager than Søren had. Kingsley wasn't a priest, didn't care what happened to him. Instead of at age twenty and with Søren, she would have lost her virginity at age fifteen or sixteen to Kingsley. Although it hadn't happened that way, it was as if she had the memories of her other life on that other path. Her first time with Kingsley would have been nothing like her first time with Søren. She would have been scared with Kingsley, and he wouldn't have hurt her first. No flogging, no caning. She would have been on top to minimize the pain and to remind them both what she was—a switch. Because he would have recognized her as the switch she was from day one and would have trained her accordingly—to hurt and be hurt, to dominate and to submit, to rule and to serve. And where would Søren have been in all this? At Sacred Heart, praying, working, without realizing the girl he could have owned was tied to the bed of the boy he'd once loved.

"You told me once what would have happened if you'd seen me first. But I never told you what would have happened if I'd seen you first," she said.

"What would have happened?"

She met his eyes. "I would have fallen in love with you. I still remember that night I first saw you. The night of the wedding at Sacred Heart. I thought I'd never meet a man who tempted me like Søren did. And then you waltzed in whistling and wearing those boots and your bad attitude and you threatened to lose your watch in me. The reason I didn't fall in love with you that night was because I'd already given my whole heart to him. But if I'd seen you first...and wasn't in love with him, I would have loved you."

"Yes," he said. "I believe that. And I would have fallen in love with you."

"Do you think that's what was meant to happen? You and me in love?" Nora asked. "Søren came to see you because he needed your help to get me out of jail. But if I'd stolen your car..."

"I might never have seen Søren again," Kingsley said. "I was in a bad place when he showed up here in my music room asking me to help him help you. And he helped me pull myself together. But if I'd seen you first in that police station, fifteen, scared, alone...I would have pulled myself together to take care of you."

She'd seen the way Kingsley treated his assistant, Calliope. He protected her, adored her, watched over her... He would have done the same for her had she moved in with him at age sixteen. She would have, too. A father in jail, a mother who was a religious fanatic...easy enough to get her legally emancipated. By age eighteen she would have been Kingsley's second-in-command. His second, his partner in crime, his dominant, his submissive, his lover, his everything. Kingsley had never fallen in love with her because she was always Søren's. But with Søren out of the picture...

"And it all happened because my piece-of-shit father got caught stealing a hundred bucks' worth of spare parts from a junkyard. Something he'd done a thousand times before. One choice, one mistake, one tiny twist of fate..."

"Chills the blood to think of it, doesn't it?" Kingsley asked, and she could see it did trouble him to realize how tangled was the thread that tied their three lives together.

"If he'd never met me, he would never have broken his vows. What if that's how it should have been?"

"Is that what you wish had happened?" Kingsley asked. "Do you wish we'd seen each other first?"

"All I know is that looking back I can see where the road forks. But I also see that if I'd ended up on the other path, with you…I still would have found my way to this moment. I'm saying this feels like destiny, like both paths would have brought me here, like every path would have brought me here. But I could have been here so much sooner if he…"

Her voice trailed off. Anger choked her throat, strangling her words. Her hands clenched and unclenched. She wanted to hit someone, something. Set fires, burn the old world down and rise up from the ashes. If Søren were here right now she would teach him a new pain…

Nora saw the flogger in Kingsley's hand. She took it from him and walked to the towel still pinned on the wall.

"Søren knew I was a switch the whole time, and he never said a fucking thing to me about it. If I'd never met him, I would have been doing this since I was sixteen."

With all her anger and sorrow and bitterness, she threw the flogger with a fearsome snap.

The towel went sailing to the floor. It sat limp and defeated at her feet. She wished it was Søren's heart.

Nora turned to face him.

"Well, look at that," Nora said, smiling at Kingsley.

"By George, I think she's got it."

10

Milady

KINGSLEY TOOK NORA'S HAND AND HELPED HER STEP over a naked body on the floor. The man didn't appear to be dead, merely spent. Merely *very* spent considering he didn't seem to notice the woman in the blue-and-black silk cancan dress and the man in the Regency suit and Hessian boots stepping over his panting, sweating torso to reach a set of steps behind him.

Nora didn't thank Kingsley for his gallantry. She couldn't if she wanted to. In addition to the cancan dress, seamed stockings and her black button-up ankle boots, she also wore a blue leather collar and a blue leather leash. The leash Nora clenched between her teeth. When they made it to the landing at the top of the stairs and saw no one else near, Kingsley took the leash from between her teeth.

"What is this place?" she asked. They were in a big fancy Westchester County mansion that looked like every other Westchester County mansion on the street.

"It's called the Body House," Kingsley said.

"Why haven't we ever been here before?"

Kingsley had taken her to every kink club in the city, but she'd never even heard of the Body House.

"It's not our sort of place," Kingsley said. "Now shh…" Kingsley lifted a finger to his lips to shush her, and she rolled her eyes behind her feathered masquerade mask. "Your voice is recognizable. If you have to speak, do so very quietly."

"I could speak in a French accent," Nora said, putting on her very best French accent, which she'd picked up from Kingsley. He winced at it. "That bad?"

"You sound like a drunk Brigette Bardot."

"Oh, I do not. Søren said my fake French accent is very good."

"It is," he said. Kingsley paused and it was a meaningful pause. "Too good."

"Too good?"

Kingsley didn't answer for a moment. Nora waited. When he spoke again he said, "It's not personal. But when you speak like that with the accent, you sound just like Marie-Laure."

"I sound like your sister?"

He nodded. "When she spoke English she had a strong accent. She used it to flirt with the boys at school. It's how I remember her, playing up her accent to throw herself at Søren. Your voice and the accent together… It's uncanny. Like she's back from the dead."

He gave her a look of apology, a look that asked for mercy.

"I didn't know. I'm sorry."

Kingsley had never forgiven his sister for marrying Søren, had never forgiven himself what happened after. There was no spot more raw on Kingsley's soul than the one left by his sister, Marie-Laure.

"It's not your fault. Anything can bring her back to me. The scent of Chanel No. 5. The music of *Swan Lake*. I smell it, I hear it, and it's like she's standing behind me or in the next room. And when you speak in that accent, I can hear her."

"I'll keep my mouth shut, then, and you can tell everyone I'm not allowed to talk."

"Merci." He put the leash back between her teeth which was a sign to all and sundry that she was off-limits to playing with anyone but Kingsley. If he hung the leash down where anyone could take it, anyone could play with her.

Nora was not here to play.

"That's Mistress Vee," Kingsley said, nodding toward a corner of the living room where a woman in a black leather catsuit was painstakingly tying up a middle-aged man in a corset made entirely of silk rope. "She does masterful shibari. I'm hoping she'll be willing to teach you."

Nora pulled a fan out of her blue silk reticule and unfurled it as she spat out the leash. Holding the fan in front of her mouth, she whispered, "Who is he?"

"You don't know?" Kingsley asked.

"No."

"He's the governor's son."

"King?"

"What?"

"I don't know what our own governor looks like much less his relatives."

"You'll learn what he looks like eventually."

"Why?"

"He'll be one of your clients."

Nora would have rolled her eyes at this pronouncement except it was likely true.

"Is the mayor's son going to be a client of mine, too?" she asked.

"No. He's not a submissive," Kingsley said. "But I did a

little cover-up work for the mayor's wife before the election. She owes me a favor now."

"Who doesn't?" she asked. If you were powerful in New York, Kingsley made sure you owed him a favor. She owed him a favor herself. A big one. He'd taken her in after she'd run away from the convent. She had her old bedroom back. No one had touched her things, moved her clothes, packed up her stuff and stored it all away. It had been left in place waiting for her return. Even the book she'd been reading when she left, *Villette* by Charlotte Brontë, had been left on the night-stand, her bookmark still in place on page 268. When she had returned, Kingsley had opened the door to her bedroom and said, "Welcome home."

A roof over her head, a bed to sleep in, clothes, food and books. None of which she'd have if Kingsley had turned her away. Which begged the question…

"Why did you take me in?" she whispered behind her fan.

"Why did I take you in?" Kingsley repeated. "Are you truly asking me that?"

"I wouldn't have blamed you if you'd sent me packing." His anger at her for running away and not telling him where she'd gone, not contacting him once in all those months, had been real. Terrifyingly real.

"I tried to explain you to Juliette. Explain us, I mean."

"That must have taken all night."

"It might take the rest of my life. She said you and I, we're family in a way."

"I certainly wouldn't call us friends," she said, not out of cruelty but mere honesty. Nora was a writer and she took the meaning of words seriously. This man who'd been her lover since she was twenty, who had introduced her to her domi-nant side, who'd gotten her pregnant and then run for the hills when she'd needed him most, but who had taken her in without question when she'd turned up on his doorstep in the middle of the night? To call him a "friend" seemed an insult to what they were to each other. It would be like calling Kingsley and Søren "school chums."

But family?

"I'm not sure about the 'family' here, either," she said. "No offense."

"And why ever not?" Kingsley sounded almost insulted.

"Because I've never wanted to fuck a member of my own family."

Kingsley laughed under his breath.

"You aren't, by any chance, training me to be a dominatrix to punish him, are you?"

Kingsley put his hand over his heart. "You wound me, *chérie*. Would I really do something like that?"

"Yes."

Kingsley winked and nodded toward a scene happening on the level below them.

"Showtime."

Three burly men dressed in leather entered the large living room below and started moving the furniture. Chairs were pushed to the outer perimeter and every other bit of furniture was taken to another room. Someone clearly needed a big space to play. From the other room, they brought out a large black St. Andrew's Cross and set it near the main wall.

"Her harem," Kingsley said, leaning close to her ear.

The men tested the cross and found it sturdy. They tested the ankle and wrist restraints on the cross and found them solid. They tested the distance from the cross to the nearest onlookers and found it adequate.

One of the three men disappeared again into the other room. When he returned he wasn't alone.

A blindfolded man was escorted into the play area and

made to stand in front of the cross with his back to it. From her perch on high Nora could see him well. He had a trim and sinewy frame, tall but not too tall. She could see his ribs and his muscles when he inhaled. His arms were covered from shoulder to wrist in vibrant full-sleeve tattoos. Unfortunately he had on pants, black ones that hung low on his hips so she could see the little line of hair leading from his navel down, down, a trail she'd love to follow. Although his face was that of a young man—he looked no older than thirty—he had gray hair. Gray flecked with black, but mostly gray. Kingsley's teenage assistant, Calliope, said such men were known as "silver foxes." Nora had never wanted a pet fox before. Now she reconsidered.

"He's pretty," she said to Kingsley behind her fan. "Who is he?"

"You like him?" Kingsley asked.

"Who wouldn't?"

"His name is Thorny."

"I love his ink," she said, eyeing his tattoos.

"You want him?" Kingsley asked.

"I might not say no if he offered," she readily admitted. "If he's a sub."

"Oh, he's a sub. For two thousand dollars."

"He's a pro-sub?"

Kingsley shook his head.

"Pro-dom?"

Kingsley shook his head again.

"Pro-switch?"

"He's a pro…pro. And for two thousand dollars he'll be almost anything you want him to be."

Nora's eyes widened.

"He's a prostitute?" Nora asked. Kingsley nodded. "The

Body House… Bawdy house… King, did you bring me to a brothel?"

Again he nodded.

With her mouth hidden by the fan she whispered a question to Kingsley.

"Why the hell did you bring me to a brothel? I've been arrested before, you know. I don't want to get arrested again."

She had nothing against sex workers, especially since she was training to be one herself. But kink for money was legal in New York. Sex for money wasn't.

Kingsley took the leash and put it between her teeth again. Next time they went undercover he could wear the wig and play the sub, and she would stick a leather rope in his mouth.

Nora kept her eyes on the handsome silver fox below her. She wished he could see her. She'd like to look in his eyes and take her measure of him. Even with the blindfold on, she could see he was nervous. His chest panted with quick breaths. Perhaps he was excited? Or perhaps he was scared?

Scared of whom?

That was when Nora smelled the cherry blossoms. She inhaled deeply. Such a marvelous sweet scent. The scent of a new spring.

Nora turned and behind her stood a woman. And such a woman she was. Like French royalty she wore a gown of silver silk. Over the gown she wore a hooded pelisse. Under the hood was a face, girlish and fine, wearing little makeup apart from red lipstick. She looked so young, so painfully young and innocent. She smiled and Nora knew she was in the presence of a rather cold-blooded sadist.

"Kingsley Edge?" the young woman said. "Or am I mistaken?"

Her voice was entirely without an accent, which was an accent in itself. Despite her girlish look, she had a woman's voice. And she did not smile or laugh. Nora had a feeling she'd never giggled in her life.

"At your service, Milady." Kingsley held out his hand and she slipped hers into his palm. He turned her hand up and kissed the inside of her wrist.

"A pleasure to finally make your acquaintance."

"The pleasure is all mine. I would introduce you to my submissive, but she isn't allowed to speak."

He inclined his head toward Nora, who gave a little curtsy behind her fan. It would all be so silly and ridiculous if it weren't so deadly serious. This woman knew almost as many secrets as Kingsley did, but unlike Kingsley, she was willing to tell them to serve her own purposes.

"Does she have a name?" Milady asked. "Or has she not earned one yet?"

"It's Nora," Kingsley said, grasping the back of her neck lightly, a sign of claiming. "Nora Sutherlin. And I assure you, she has earned her name."

Nora turned her head sharply toward Kingsley, who didn't even meet her eyes. Oh, he was going to get it... As soon as they were alone she would tear him up and burn him like an old love letter from a cheating lover. He'd given her the same last name as her college boyfriend. She'd warned him that if he ever called her by the name Sutherlin again she'd slap him into the next century. No doubt that's why he'd done it.

"Nora...lovely." Milady didn't glance at Nora but she kept her eyes trained on Kingsley. She looked him up and down, perusing him like a piece of merchandise that she might want to buy if the price was right. "Would you allow your submissive to assist me?"

"She's new," Kingsley said. "I'm not sure she could be of much help to you."

"Oh, but she could. Don't worry. I'll keep her out of harm's way."

Kingsley seemed reluctant to let Nora go. "Of course. I only hope she behaves."

"I'm sure she will."

Nora wasn't so sure.

Kingsley snapped his fingers and Nora obediently faced him. Since Milady watched her so closely she did her best to keep her eyes low and her attitude biddable. In the past, such a dutiful air would have been her natural state at a kink party. When around Søren she submitted because it was simply what one did in his presence. Now it felt like a costume she'd put on along with her cancan dress and mask.

Kingsley unhooked the leash from the collar and gave her a kiss on the lips, a convincing one. Even Nora was convinced that Kingsley considered her his passion and his property tonight. Then he gave her a swat on the cancan and said, "Go with Milady. Be a good girl and make me proud."

She gave Kingsley a curtsy, too, and followed Milady down the stairs.

Everyone watched them as they entered the play area although Nora noted that most eyes were on Milady. From the arched doorway emerged one of her burly trio carrying a large white velvet bag in one hand and a small flat stool in the other. He set them both a few feet back from the blindfolded man.

"Nora," Milady said, taking her by the wrist, "I want you to meet someone. This is Thorny, not his real name, of course." The reason for the name was obvious, as Thorny's tattoos on both of his arms were of vines covered in thorns. All vines. No roses. "I want you to stand behind the cross and keep an eye on Thorny. He's not very fond of whips. If he passes out, you should let me know. What's that English saying? No use beating a dead whore?"

"Horse," Nora said, her jaw clenching.

"Ah, she speaks."

"I do. And if he doesn't like whipping, why are you whipping him?"

"Because I like whipping." Milady's tone suggested Nora had asked the stupidest question in the entire world.

"Shouldn't you find someone who likes whips and whip him instead?"

"He's being well compensated for his troubles."

"Does he have a safe word?"

"I have a safe word. It's *roses*. The whips are loud. If he says my safe word I might not hear him so you'll have to find a way to let me know. It's your responsibility to keep him safe. Do you accept that?"

"I guess I will since you don't seem very interested in his safety."

"I must say...you don't behave like any submissive I've ever met."

"I'm not like any submissive you've ever met," Nora said, feeling a surge of protectiveness toward the man at the cross. Kingsley or Søren would never whip anyone who didn't like being whipped. That was serious pain and if done incorrectly, it could leave open wounds and scars.

"No...no you aren't," Milady said, looking Nora up and down this time, studying her. "Let me tell you a little secret about myself. I have a particular kink. I enjoy paying men money to do things they wouldn't ordinarily do. Like Thorny here—he hates whips with a passion. He told me it was a hard limit. I offered one thousand dollars to let me whip him. He said no. Two thousand? No. Four thousand? Yes. With enough money every hard limit becomes a soft limit. And everyone has a price. My kink is finding it. What's your price, Nora?"

"I'm not for sale."

"Everyone's for sale. What if I paid you two thousand dollars to whip our friend Thorny, would you do it?"

"No. He doesn't want to be whipped."

"You wouldn't hurt someone against their will?"

"Only to protect myself or someone else."

"Money might not be your price, then. Would you hurt someone against their will to keep a secret?"

"Depends on the secret."

Milady gave her a little smile, an impish grin that made Nora want to rip Milady's lips off.

"Would you hurt someone against their will to keep your priest's secret?"

11

White Whips Red Blood

IT WAS A GOOD THING NORA HAD SPENT NINE YEARS of her life obeying Søren's every order. Had she not been so well trained, she likely would have ripped Milady's face off and put it in a jar. Or at the very least let loose a litany of profanity to make a sailor clutch his pearls. Instead, and because she had learned a modicum of self-control as Søren's property, she kept her mouth shut while on the inside she plotted murder.

Milady ignored the stare of pure burning hatred Nora shot at her while she untied her pelisse and passed it to one of her burly trio. She took Thorny by the hand and turned him to face the cross. With her hands and not her words, Milady directed Thorny into place. She cuffed his ankles to chains and bound his wrists high on the cross. Nora knew she should be paying attention to Thorny but she spared a glance up at Kingsley. He looked at her with narrowed curious eyes. Did he sense her distress? She hoped this show didn't last long. They needed to get out of here now. Milady knew who she was and what she was and that she had been Søren's lover. And if she knew all of that, she might know Søren's real name and if she did…she could get him into a whole world of trouble.

Or…was this just a mind game designed to scare Nora off? Nora wasn't scared off but she was angry. Søren might be a hypocritical, pretentious, arrogant, insufferably possessive bastard but he was her hypocritical, pretentious, arrogant, insufferably possessive bastard.

She couldn't worry about that right now. Milady had opened the white velvet bag and pulled out two matching whips—white whips. Pure white with white crackers on the ends of the tails. Consummate show-woman that she was, Milady walked the perimeter of the room, whips extended to the side as if measuring the space. Would she miss and accidentally hit a spectator? Milady wanted the crowd to be afraid she would miss so they would be so terribly impressed when she didn't.

Nora had the worst seat in the house. She would see the tips of the whips but not the action, but this was fine by her. Thorny had to be her priority, not watching the show. A man who'd never been whipped before was about to get whipped in public by a woman wielding not one, but two single-tails.

"Scared?" Nora whispered to Thorny.

"Terrified," he said with a brash grin. She wondered how long that grin would last.

Milady finished her circuit of the room and stood six feet or so away from the cross and Thorny. Before Søren whipped her or flogged her or hurt her, he'd almost always touched her, held her or spoke a few choice whispered words to her. Sometimes he'd claim her, saying, "You're mine, Little One. Mine to hurt and mine to heal." Sometimes he'd confess, "I've been dreaming of hurting you all day." Sometimes he'd touch her inside and tease her: "As wet as you are I think you want this as much as I do." Sometimes he'd simply say, "I love you,

Little One" or *"Jeg elsker dig, min lille en"* before he brought the pain down.

Nora watched and Milady didn't whisper a single word of warning to Thorny. Instead she cracked the first whip and then the second in rapid succession. Everyone in the room jumped, everyone but Nora and Kingsley, who were accustomed to the sound. Thorny flinched although he hadn't been struck yet. Milady was merely warming up. And what a warm-up it was. She sent the whips, both of them, in graceful tandem flicking high and low and along the floor and toward the ceiling. They snapped and cracked and swirled and twirled like white smoke around her. She drew lines in the air, wrote words and made figure eights. Every turn ended with another sonic crack.

Then Milady turned her attention to Thorny. First she flicked the whip around the outline of his body, missing him on purpose to show that she could. Many of the cracks were concentrated around his head. Nora watched his face closely. He breathed heavily but his face was set in stone.

The stone broke at the first strike of the whip on his back. Nora knew that pain, like being stung by a bee. A big fucking vicious demon bee. Thorny gasped, winced, grunted, groaned…but he didn't say *roses* or *red* or *stop* so she simply stood there, monitoring his breathing, praying it would be over soon.

Milady made the whip dance and it danced all over Thorny's body. Up his arms to his wrists and down again. Over his shoulders, across his neck, down his spine and back up again. She avoided the kidneys, which was a good sign that she had a modicum of respect for the rules of safe play. Otherwise she shredded Thorny's body.

Søren had never whipped her for this long. Maybe Kingsley could have taken a beating this severe, but not someone who'd never been whipped before. Thorny had had enough. Nora could tell. Finally he uttered a desperate "roses."

"Louder," Nora said. "She didn't hear you."

"Roses!" Thorny called out, loud enough anyone in the room could hear him.

Milady didn't stop, and Nora knew she had no intention of stopping. So she did the only thing she could do.

Nora stepped under the cross and held out her arm, catching the end of one whip around her wrist. She yanked it from Milady's grasp before she realized what she'd done.

An audible gasp echoed through the room, the sound of two dozen people in shock.

Milady didn't look shocked, however. But she didn't look happy.

"What do you think you're doing?" Milady asked, her voice still light and sweet even as her eyes blazed.

"I believe your friend said his safe word," Kingsley said from the top of the stairs. Milady turned and looked up at him. "And you ignored it. Didn't you?"

No one spoke but no one contradicted him, either. Nora saw a few nods, a few nervous glances. Behind her Thorny panted loudly. He needed to be taken down immediately and tended to. Blood seeped from the wounds on his back. Shallow cuts that would heal quickly, but there were dozens of them.

"Take him down," Kingsley ordered as he descended the stairs.

"He's my toy tonight." Milady coiled her remaining white whip. "I say when he comes down."

"No, I believe he says when he wants down. Mister Thorny? Yes? No?"

"Please," Thorny said between breaths. "Take me down."

Kingsley nodded at Nora, who worked quickly, unbuckling his wrists first and then unchaining his ankles. She yanked the blindfold off him and met him eye to eye. He had startling blue eyes that almost seemed to glow in the dark. But she didn't attribute that to any supernatural powers. He'd been in so much pain his eyes were rimmed with red, which made the blue that much more vibrant in contrast.

"God, you're pretty," he said. Men. She rolled her eyes as she set him in a chair. "How bad is it?"

She looked at his back. Every square inch of skin was burning scarlet and blood seeped out from roughly two dozen tiny cuts. She chucked him under the chin and smiled.

"You'll live," she said.

"I wish." Thorny laughed at a joke she didn't get.

"My apologies, darling," Milady said. "My lovely assistant was supposed to let me know when he'd had enough."

"She did," Kingsley said. "And so did he. Are you all right?" Kingsley directed the question at Thorny, acting as though Milady were beneath his notice.

"I could use a drink."

"We'll take him home," Kingsley said. "We're leaving anyway. Thank you for an…evening."

The lack of an adjective was evidently noted.

"You didn't enjoy the show?" Milady asked, wearing a faux pout.

"I thought the finale was dazzling," Kingsley said, looking at Nora. "Are you hurt?"

She shook her head. Søren had taught her how to catch a whip on her arm and around her waist. He'd sometimes wrap her with a whip and reel her in when he was in a playful mood. Catching the whip had stung and she could have been hurt badly, but she'd acted on pure instinct.

"Of course she's not hurt," Milady said, raising her voice so the entire room heard her. "She's the property of the priest. She can take a whipping with the best of them. Can't she?"

Kingsley's eyebrow lifted a discernible millimeter.

"Oh, Kingsley," Milady said, lowering her voice. "You thought I didn't know who she was? I know everything. I know she's training to be a dominatrix, which is hilarious. The priest's little girl? The girl he used to drag through your club by her hair and publicly beat?"

Nora rolled her eyes. Søren had never dragged her by her hair through The 8th Circle. He'd dragged her by her collar, yes, but not her hair.

"You ignored a submissive's safe word," Kingsley said. "While she put herself between him and a whip. She's already a better dominatrix than you are."

"My clients would say otherwise."

"Because your clients haven't been with her yet." Kingsley held out his arm and Nora took it. "We'll be going. Shall we?" he said to Thorny.

"It's okay," he said looking up at Kingsley. "Thank you. I've got a ride."

"Of course." Kingsley reached into his breast pocket and produced his business card. He passed it to Thorny. "If you're looking for a new domme, call me."

"No offense," Thorny said. "I'd rather call her." He pointed at Nora.

"None taken," Kingsley said. "So would I."

"I'll have my whip back, please." Milady said *please* to Nora but there was no graciousness in her tone. It wasn't a request.

Nora looped it neatly in her hands but before she handed it back, she ripped off the long white cracker at the end, a four-inch nylon string. With a twist and a knot, Nora tied the nylon cord around Thorny's index finger, a reminder.

Thorny looked up at her and grinned. "Don't worry. I won't forget you. I owe you."

"I think we can dispense with the pretense that you're his silent submissive," Milady said to Nora. "After all…we all know who she is, don't we?" Milady addressed the crowd again. Before Milady could do it, Nora pulled off her mask and the wig and ran her hands through her real hair, releasing the waves.

"She speaks when she has something to say," Kingsley said.

"I'm sure she has something to say to me, doesn't she?" Milady asked.

"I do," Nora said.

"Yes?" Milady batted her eyelashes. "I'm all ears."

"If you hurt my priest, I'll drag *you* by *your* hair through the club and publicly beat you. This is between us, you, me and Kingsley. He's not a part of this."

"I heard you left him," Milady said. "That makes him fair game."

"He's not a game."

"So possessive? Really? How…illuminating. If you're threatening me over him you must think there is some sort of chance I could get him up on my cross."

"He would die before he submitted to you," Nora said. "Or me. Or anyone but God."

"I just want to hurt him a little tiny bit." Milady wrinkled her nose and smiled an elfin smile. "That arrogant blond Apollo. What a prize that would be. I'd wear a lock of his blond hair around my neck in a locket."

"You don't get to touch a hair on his head," Nora said, raising one finger and pointing it at Milady's face. "You don't get to hurt him."

"And why not?" Milady asked, putting on her best and sweetest pout.

Nora raised her chin and stared Milady down.

"That's my job."

12

The Whip Master

"I'LL KILL HER," NORA SAID.

"You can't kill her." Kingsley leaned back in his desk chair and threw his booted feet up on his desk. "You can maim her, I suppose. I wouldn't stop you from maiming her."

"You know you want to maim her, too. Don't you?" Ever since that farce of a party last night, that was all Nora had been able to think about—maiming Milady. She'd string her up by her own whips and walk around Manhattan wearing Milady's hair in a locket around her own neck. She'd need a big damn locket because she planned on scalping the woman.

"Don't encourage him, Nora, *s'il vous plaît*." Those words came from Juliette, who was poring diligently over Kingsley's files. He'd given his beautiful Haitian submissive her own small secretary's desk for his private office. Juliette looked up from her work and shook her head. "He's not allowed to kill or maim anyone unless it's unavoidable."

"The lady has spoken," Kingsley said to Nora. He put the tips of two fingers to his lips, kissed them and blew the kiss at Juliette, who casually caught it in midair and patted her neck with it. Juliette liked neck kisses, too. Nora appreciated this fact about her.

"She threatened Søren," Nora said.

"She didn't threaten him. She threatened you." Kingsley looked at her expectantly. Expecting her to deny it?

"Søren would never submit to that woman. Or any woman. Or any man."

"No, he wouldn't," Kingsley said. "Which is why it amuses me so much that you are taking her boasts so seriously."

"What I want to know is how she knew," Nora said, leaning forward in the chair. "How did she know Nora Sutherlin was Eleanor Schreiber?"

"Calliope," Kingsley said.

"No way. Not her. She loves you. She wouldn't rat us out for all the money in the world," Nora said.

"She didn't. I told her to leak the information."

"You what?"

Kingsley laughed. "I told her to spread a little gossip for me. She told two 'friends' of hers who can't keep their mouths shut and the news spread like wildfire."

"You dragged me to that party knowing she would fuck with me?"

"I knew you'd fuck back," he said. "As always, I am in control of the flow of information in and out of this house. If a secret gets out, it's because I want it out. Now that you've had your little showdown with Milady, all the Underground will know that you, the former Eleanor Schreiber, are now Mistress Nora Sutherlin. The Midsummer Night's Fling will be packed. Standing room only. Everyone in the state will be there to see you two face off again." He swept his hand at the windows behind him to indicate the city at large, before interlacing his fingers behind his head and smiling his arrogant smile.

"Oh, God, the whole fucking kink world will be there." Nora collapsed back in the chair, her hands to her forehead. She felt a sudden blinding, stabbing pain behind her eyes. "And it's your fault."

"It's your fault," Kingsley said. "You're the one who made a scene at the party last night."

"She was beating Thorny bloody. He safed out. He wanted her to stop. She ignored him on purpose."

"Of course she did. She wanted to publicly humiliate you for letting your charge get harmed. Well, you found an unusual solution, didn't you?"

"What happened?" Juliette asked.

"*La Maîtresse* over here," Kingsley said, pointing at Nora, "stepped in front of a man being whipped with not one but two stock whips. She caught the whip on her arm like a fucking rodeo clown, and she's very lucky she didn't lose an eye."

"That's very dangerous," Juliette said. "I wish I could have been there to see it."

Nora looked at Kingsley and pointed at Juliette. "I love this woman."

"So do I," Kingsley said. "But she's going to get another beating if she doesn't stop encouraging you."

"You're my responsibility, *mon amour*," Juliette said to Kingsley, sounding sensible as always. "She isn't."

Nora sunk back into the chair, stretched her legs out and let her arms flop to the sides in despair. It wasn't a terribly ladylike position for a woman wearing an A-line skirt, a silk fitted blouse and high heels. She'd had a fitting early that morning with a tailor and had attempted to dress as one would expect an off-duty dominatrix to dress. Now that the whole fucking Underground knew that she, Eleanor, was also her, Mistress Nora, she had to start dressing the part. At least the heels were spiked stilettos so she could kill someone with them if she needed to. Or just wanted to.

"Elle?" Kingsley said. Nora raised her head and frowned at him. "Nora."

"Better."

"Nora, listen. You can do this. You can beat her."

"I want to beat her. I want to beat her black-and-blue. No. Actually I don't want to beat her." Nora sat up straight and stared down Kingsley. "This is what I want to do. I want to find out who she loves. I want to find a man she owns and adores. Then I want to beat him. I want to fuck him. Then I want to send him back to her with my name carved on his back and my phone number tattooed on his cock. That's what I want."

Kingsley met her eyes across his desk.

"I told you she was a sadist," he said to Juliette.

Juliette smiled. "If I doubted you before, I don't anymore."

He looked at Juliette and nodded slightly. Juliette gathered files and rose from her desk. She bent and kissed Kingsley on both cheeks.

"I will let you two talk in private." She gave Nora a curtsy before gracefully walking out of the office and closing the door behind her.

Once they were alone Kingsley stood up and walked around the desk. He held out his hand and Nora took it. With one tug he pulled her up to stand in front of him.

"Calm down," he said.

"I can't."

"I wasn't talking to you. I was talking to my cock," Kingsley said.

"Should have known."

"Listen to me." Kingsley took her face in his hands. "You

know there is no one on earth who appreciates your passion for inflicting cruel and unusual punishments on your enemies more than I do. That is my language and you are speaking it fluently. But we have to be calm and rational if we're going to win against Milady. Going out and fucking and beating everyone she knows won't solve anything."

"Yeah, but it would be fun."

"You are drunk on freedom."

"I have to admit, I'm kind of liking not answering to a man. Last night…that guy? Thorny? He's cute."

"*Très* cute."

"Two years ago if I saw him at the club, I'd have to beg Søren's permission to even talk to him. Now if he wants and I want, we can do what we want when we want, and I don't have to ask anyone's permission. I can even do this…" Nora leaned in and kissed Kingsley on the lips. How could she not? He was so close and looked so handsome in his black trousers, black boots, gray shirt and black vest. Not a lord or a duke, but a king to the bone. He didn't hesitate to return the kiss, but he kept the passion enchained. This was a slow kiss, deep and sensual. A kiss that could and should last for hours. "I can kiss you and no one has to know. I can kiss you because I want to kiss you, not because he's sharing me with you. I'm sharing me with you."

"You always were. You never spread your legs for me just to make him happy. Even that first night when you were only twenty, we both know you did it for you."

Nora kissed him again, which was the best way she knew of admitting he was right.

"I'll do it for you now. Let's go to the playroom," Nora whispered against his lips. "I need to practice my flogging on someone."

Kingsley laughed, a low sensuous laugh. "Not yet."

"I know you want it," she said, resting her head on his shoulder.

"I want it."

"You don't think I'm ready yet?"

"You don't think you're ready yet. If you did, it would have happened already."

Nora groaned—loudly.

"You're driving me crazy, King." She collapsed into her chair in frustration.

"Believe me, the feeling is mutual." Kingsley knelt in front of her and placed his hands on her bare thighs.

"She beat the shit out of a man just to intimidate me," Nora said as Kingsley slid his hands up her legs and under her skirt. "I just... I hate her. I'm not used to hating anybody. Except him. But..."

"What?" Kingsley asked as he slid her panties down her thighs.

"I have to win, King. I can't lose to that woman."

"You won't. I'll make sure of it, Mistress." He pushed her legs open and draped them over each arm of the chair. With his fingertips he parted the folds of her vulva. He leaned close and licked her. Nora sighed with pleasure and dug her hand into Kingsley's hair, holding his head right where she needed it. She wanted to hurt him and she wanted to fuck him but she hadn't passed his stupid test yet, so she would take his tongue on her clitoris as a compromise until she figured out how to beat him at his own game.

Kingsley was a master of the French kiss and that's what he gave her now, but not on her mouth. His tongue darted in and out of her vagina, his lips sucked her lips, licked her lips, massaged her lips until everything between her legs throbbed with need. She couldn't kiss him back but she let him know with her gasps and moans he pleased her. He pushed a finger into her and rubbed along her pubic bone where a bundle of nerves came to life at his expert touch. Hooking his finger under and in, he pushed against that soft indentation inside her, creating a sensation so acute, so pleasurable, that fluid burst from her inner lips and some deep interior muscle clamped onto the aching emptiness in her. Nora inhaled and didn't exhale. Her body went stiff. Kingsley's hot tongue circled her clitoris and she came with a cry, with her hips hovering an inch off her seat, with one hand buried in his hair and the other hand clenching so hard to the chair arms her fingernails left half-moons in the leather upholstery.

Kingsley sat back, still on his knees, and pulled his gray silk handkerchief from his pocket. He used it first to wipe the wetness off his lips and then to wipe the wetness off hers. Because he was Kingsley, when finished he put it back in his breast pocket.

"Feel better?" he asked, standing up.

"I still want to kill her," Nora said, slowly closing her legs.

"If you still feel like killing anyone after what I just did to you, it's serious."

"Yes, it's fucking serious. She's so good. I've never seen whip work like that. Søren doesn't even use two whips at once. And you won't let me touch one whip, much less two. How am I going to beat a domme like that? I don't even have a whip—"

"Yes, you do."

"What?"

Kingsley grinned a devilish grin. He cocked his head to the side. Twice.

"Are you having a seizure?" Nora asked.

"On top of the filing cabinet."

"I was supposed to understand 'there's something on top of the filing cabinet' from two head nods?"

"Just go."

Nora raised her eyebrow and on slightly shaking legs walked over to Kingsley's antique wooden filing cabinets. On the very top of the one closest to his desk sat a wooden box she hadn't noticed until now. She lifted the lid and there it was.

"It's red," she said, lifting the red leather whip out of the box.

"Milady wears all white. Mistress Irina wears all black. You will wear all red."

"Bloodred," Nora said, gazing in wonder at the whip. The leather was soft, slick and supple and the handle was carved ebony wood.

"They say Mary, Queen of Scots, wore red to her own execution. The perfect color to wear if you're going to get bloody."

"Red is a Catholic color," she said, turning to face Kingsley. "She wore red because she was a Catholic and was being martyred for her faith."

Kingsley came to her and wrapped the whip around her neck.

"I won't let anyone take your head," he said.

"Thank you." She took the whip in her hands and pulled it taut. "I love it. Wish I knew how to use it."

"You will. You have your first whip lesson today." He lifted his arm and glanced at an imaginary watch. "Your whip teacher is here right now. *Allons-y.*"

"I have a whip teacher?"

"You do. If you feel strong enough. Do you?"

She felt weak from the orgasm, languid and happy.

"I feel relaxed. I mean, I want to cut that bitch, but I feel relaxed about it."

"Good enough. Just keep your focus on defeating her, and you'll be fine."

Kingsley took the whip from her hands and coiled it neatly. He took her by the arm and led her from the office.

"I've always wanted to use a whip," Nora said. "I think I saw too many *Indiana Jones* movies as a kid. Do you think he was kinky?"

"French Vanilla," Kingsley said.

"What's that?"

"Vanilla with a strong libido and a taste for anal."

"I can see that."

"Zorro, however, was kinky," Kingsley said. "And he was much better with a whip than Dr. Jones."

"Zorro was kinky? That explains the mask. You think he was a switch?" Nora asked as they reached the playroom door. Kingsley opened the door and ushered her inside. "Can I have Zorro for my whip teacher?"

"No," Kingsley said. "But you can have him."

Nora gasped. For there standing in the playroom wearing his off-duty uniform of black jeans and a long-sleeved black T-shirt was...

"Søren."

13

Reunion

SØREN UNCROSSED HIS ARMS AND RAISED ONE HAND. With his finger he carved the letter *Z* in the air.

Behind her the door closed. Kingsley had left her alone in the room with Søren.

"Søren," she said again, not quite believing her eyes. She took a shuddering breath. He was here. Søren. Standing there right by an entire wall of whips and floggers looking beautiful and handsome and poised all at once while she stood there gulping air like a fish on land.

"How are you, Eleanor?" His voice was calm and controlled, and she hated him for that. How could he be so calm at a time like this? And how could he ask that question of all questions?

How was she? *How was she?* This was what he said to her after not seeing her for a year? How was she supposed to answer that question? What was she supposed to say to him, to this man who'd been her entire life since she was fifteen years old? This man who had saved her and doomed her all at the same time? Nothing to say. Nothing she could say. So she did the only thing she could do at a moment like this when words were meaningless.

She started out walking but halfway across the room the walk turned into a run. She threw herself into his arms and kissed him.

He was shocked at first. That was obvious from the look on his face.

"I was under the impression you hated me," he said.

"I'll hate you again later."

His mouth found hers and the kiss was everything she'd forgotten she needed. He dominated her with the kiss, overwhelmed her, overpowered her. She was on her back on the bed before she knew it had happened. If she'd had any pride or any dignity or any self-control whatsoever she would have stopped it with a word. But she didn't want her pride and she didn't want her dignity and God knew she didn't want self-control. She just wanted him.

"I have to hurt you," Søren said as he dug his hands in her hair and tilted her head back. He bit and kissed and licked her neck and throat. He was all over her, his body, his hands, his knees pushing between her thighs, staking a claim on her.

"Hurt me, then. Do it fast before I change my mind." A pointless warning. There was no changing her mind. She thought about stopping this moment the way one thinks of stopping a runaway train by stepping in front of it and holding out your hands. A fine heroic fantasy but nothing ever to be attempted in the real world.

Søren rose up on his knees between her legs and ripped her blouse open and off her body. It was rare he tore her clothes. He had more self-control than that. But not today. Neither one of them did.

With rough hands and with no regard to her comfort, Søren

stripped her naked. Her clothes ended up on the floor with her shoes. As Søren pulled his own shirt off, Nora reached up to touch his chest and stomach. This body, how she had missed it. This long, lean, indomitable body that she had craved like the drowning craved air.

As her hands touched the sensitive sides of his rib cage, he grabbed her wrists and pushed them into the bed over her head. He did it hard enough to hurt her and she released a cry of true pain. Søren closed his eyes, inhaled, breathing in her pain. Her suffering. His oxygen. She bit his chest over his heart, giving pain for pain.

While he held her pinned to the mattress, he sucked her nipples. They were hard already but his hot wet mouth made them ache and throb. His knees edged her legs open wider. Blood rushed through her, pounding in her veins, in her lungs, in her hips. She begged to be allowed to touch him again, but he kept her imprisoned against the bed, unable to lift her hands held in his iron grasp. She would have bruises on her forearms.

God, she had missed this.

Søren moved down her body, kissing her sides, her stomach. Heat radiated from his mouth all through her. There would be no escape. He held her down with his hands but she stayed there because of her heart.

Without warning Søren turned her, pushing her onto her stomach. She felt the bed move. He stood at the foot, holding her ankle in his hand, tying it to the bedpost with a length of rope. He tied the other ankle to the opposite bedpost. She tried to push her legs together but couldn't. They were trapped, held open three feet wide.

She heard him undressing. He moved quickly, as impatient as she. She heard other sounds—he took a flogger off the wall and something else, too. A cane? A crop? Didn't matter. It was all the same to her.

The bed moved again. He knelt between her thighs. The first blow of the flogger fell right in the center of her back. The second blow struck the same spot. The third hit her harder than the first two combined. But between the fourth and the fifth brutal strike, Søren entered her. She was wet from Kingsley's expert ministrations, but it still burned going in. Her whimper of pain didn't stop him nor did she want it to. Søren pushed in again, all the way in, and she arched her back to receive him fully. When he was as deep as he could be in this position, he flogged her again.

It was a special torture to be flogged while being fucked. Pleasure warred with pain. One would gain ground over the other before the other took control of the field. Nora dug her fingers deep into the black sheets and rocked her hips into the bed. She felt a flood of wetness bathing him and coating her thighs. He moved easily in her now and she groaned. His every movement sent her reeling. Her vision swam. Her muscles clenched and released, clutching at him inside her. He was still flogging her, but the pleasure had won the battle against the pain. All she felt was him embedded inside her. All she wanted was for him to fuck her as if he owned her.

Nora heard another sound, the sound of a flogger landing on the floor. She felt his hands flat on her battered back and he slid them upward to her hair. He dug both hands into the waves, lifting her hair and baring the back of her neck to him. Then he bit down hard into her neck, clutching her with his teeth. No conscience, no consideration. Only brute animal fucking.

The pounding seemed to go on endlessly. Pinned down underneath him with her legs tied open, Nora could do nothing but take his merciless thrusts. She could have stopped him with a safe word, of course, but that was the last thing she wanted. Once he came and she came it would be over and then she would hate him again. Once she let herself hate him again, that would be it. They would be done. Their bodies would part and they would part and that would be it.

The end.

But it wasn't over yet. Søren slipped one hand under her body and found her clitoris. When he touched it she buried her face in the bed to mute her moans. It wasn't fair he knew how to manipulate her pleasure this well. It wasn't fair he knew her mind. It wasn't fair that he knew she wanted this against her will and took her anyway. It wasn't fair that she was glad he did. It wasn't fair that God had given him a heart to love her and a second heart to love God. And it wasn't fair he'd had to choose between the two. It wasn't fair that she knew Søren would regret leaving the church for her. It wasn't fair that the only way she could love him was by leaving him.

But whoever said life was fair?

She opened her eyes as Søren's teeth released her neck. He buried his face in her hair and inhaled.

"Jeg elsker dig, min lille en."

I love you, my Little One.

Being called that name hurt worse than anything—worse than the flogging, worse than the fucking, worse than the teeth buried in her soft skin. He said it again as his fingertips worked her clitoris in that way he knew would bring her to the edge. Why did she have to love a priest? Of all the men in the world she could have loved it had to be him. He said it a third and fourth time, letting the words match the rhythm of his thrusts. She couldn't escape the words or the name or his touch, so precise as if he could feel everything she felt. Could he also feel her anger at him? Could he feel her sorrow that he'd left her no choice but to leave? Could he feel her orgasm building and rising to the breaking point? When it broke, it broke hard, waves of pleasure radiating from her core through her entire body.

Søren must have had the same thought she had, that once this mad interlude ended it might never happen again, because he held off coming longer than he ever had before. The pounding went on ceaselessly, so long she came again as hard as the first time. Harder as she dug her teeth into his arm to muffle her own cries.

He tucked her hips up and rose over her. One hand rested on the side of her head to hold himself up while the other dug hard into her hair, holding her down and against the bed, immobile. His mouth caressed her naked shoulders, her back and her neck.

"Where's your collar?" he asked, between thrusts.

"It's gone. I threw it out."

"Liar."

He punished her lie with a vicious thrust she knew she deserved. Then he kissed her with a vicious kiss and she knew she deserved that, too.

He was lost inside her. Into her ear he whispered beautiful words. She had no idea what they were because he spoke Danish, his first language. Was he confessing his love for her? His hatred of her? His need for her? His loneliness? It could be all of that or none of it. Maybe he was asking her to come back to him. If so it was good he spoke in another language so she wouldn't have to answer. She knew how to say *never* in English.

When neither of them could take any more, when the sex had become too much for either of them, he let go at last and came inside her, filling her with his semen and pulling out to leave her empty.

"Eleanor?"

She heard her name from far away. In the distance she sensed him unbuckling her ankles from the footboard.

"Eleanor?"

"That's not my name anymore."

"Eleanor, you're bleeding."

She rolled onto her back, came up on her elbows and looked down. Her thighs were red with blood and so was Søren.

"Shit," she said, half laughing. The spell of the moment broken in an instant. "Sorry about that."

"Did you start your period?"

"I had an IUD put in a few days ago. They warned me this would happen. Sudden heavy bleeding. Thought I was wetter than usual."

The black-and-white coverlet beneath her bore a red stain the size of her hand.

Søren pushed his fingers into her, and she winced as he found a sensitive spot. His eyes widened slightly.

"Those are the strings," she said. "My doctor said you could feel them in the beginning."

When he pulled his hand out his fingers were red.

"You remember what happened the last time you bled on me?" he asked.

"Are you going to make me wash the sheets in the bathtub again?" It wouldn't surprise her in the least if he did.

"Not exactly."

As Nora ran the water in the bathtub, she had to laugh at herself. How embarrassingly easy it was to fall back into that old familiar pattern. He dominated her, she submitted to him, he hurt her, she let him. How could she ever truly break free of him when obeying him was as simple as breathing and running from him left her as breathless as choking?

He'd allowed her to clean herself off first. Then she put on the black bathrobe that hung on the back of the bathroom

door. It was a man's robe and too big for her. When she bent
to turn off the taps the robe fell down her shoulder. Søren
pushed it back into place.

"I didn't mean to do that," she said.

"What? Entice me with a show of skin? I have seen it before."

"I didn't mean to do that." She touched his chest. In a spot
right over his heart she'd left a bite mark, a deep one. Deep
enough to leave a bruise, not deep enough to make him bleed.

"I assumed you were attempting to eat my heart out," Søren
said.

"The thought had occurred to me."

"It was a fight, Eleanor. Couples fight. Apologies are made.
Hurt feelings put aside. Life goes on."

"I don't want to talk about that night. Not now or ever.
What's done is done. And life is going on. It's going on without you."

"Yes," he said, raising his hand stained with her blood.
"Obviously we're perfect strangers now."

She rolled her eyes.

"Get in the fucking bathtub, Blondie."

He gave her a cold look.

"Please and thank you? Sir?" she said, her tone mocking, but
the words were enough to appease him. He stepped into the
bathtub and sat down, stretching out his long legs so that his
feet rested on the ledge by the taps and his back at the opposite end. Nora knelt on a thick folded towel at the side of the
tub and soaked a soft bath sponge in the warm soapy water.

"I am sorry," she said, rubbing the sponge on his lower
stomach over a patch of dried blood. "I didn't plan going all
Moses on you."

"Moses?"

"You know, parting the Red Sea."

He gave her the blackest of black looks. "Are you in pain?" he asked, speaking to her like he'd speak to a child.

"From the IUD, the kink or the sex?"

"All of the above."

"A little cramping from the IUD. Normal. I have welts on the back of my knees and a bite bruise on the back of my neck. Not normal but not unheard of when one submits to a sadist." Søren gave a little smirk. "And from the sex? I'm fine."

She wasn't fine. She was far from fine. If her hands hadn't been too busy with the sponge, Søren would have seen they were shaking.

"Fine? Really?"

"A little sore. I think you fucked me a whole hour. Were you feeling a little…pent up?" she asked, casually but not.

"Is that your way of asking me if I've slept with anyone since you left me?"

"Just curious."

"No, I haven't. Relieved? Or disappointed?"

"Would you believe me if I said I didn't know how I felt?" She'd been with other people since leaving him and she could hardly hold him to a different standard than she held herself. Yet she knew they were different. She had sex for fun. It was a casual necessity, like eating lunch. For Søren sex was anything but casual. And he could go for years without it. She fucked when she wanted it. He fucked when he meant it. Long ago she'd asked him when and how he decided to break his vows—all the nights with her, that one night with Kingsley…he'd had both of them since becoming a priest, since taking a vow of chastity. If he was happy to fuck them, why not someone else?

I break my vows when I know I can justify it before God and know God will say, "I don't blame you." When God looks at you and He looks at Kingsley, something tells me that's what He would say.

When she stood before God and He asked her why she loved this priest and had given her body to him, she had a feeling God would say the same to her.

Søren exhaled, a pensive sound. "Yes, actually, I would."

"Then... I don't know. I don't know how I feel right now."

"If it's any comfort to you, neither do I."

Søren raised a wet hand from the water and caressed her cheek with it. Water ran down her face and into the water like tears.

It shouldn't have been so nerve-racking to do something as simple as scrub the blood off Søren. But he watched her every move intently and without speaking as she lathered her hands in soap and ran them gently over his lower stomach and penis. Did he see how much it affected her, being this intimate with his naked body? The first time she'd touched him in a sexual way, she'd been seventeen years old and he'd put her hand on his erection. They were at his family home for his father's funeral. She'd snuck out of her room and found him in his childhood bedroom. They'd told each other secrets in the dark, and when she couldn't wait another minute more for him to see her as a woman who wanted him and not a girl needing his protection, she'd taken her clothes off for him and offered him her body. His pleasure meant her pain. His pain meant her pleasure. He hurt her because it aroused him; when it aroused him he pleasured her. The cycle went on and on, repeating itself night after night. She'd come to crave pain like Pavlov's dog had learned to salivate at the ringing of a bell because it signaled feeding time.

She'd broken off her leash. If only she could break the bell...

Until then she could pretend. She pretended she was still his and nothing bad had ever happened. She ran the sponge over his broad shoulders, down his strong chest and flat stomach. She lathered her hands again and washed his feet, massaging the soles and ankles, digging her fingers between his toes until she forced a smile from him.

"How can such a beautiful man with an otherwise perfect body have such weird feet?" she asked.

"My feet are not 'weird.'"

"Your big toes are crooked."

"It happens to runners."

"Your toes are weird. If that's what happens to runners, it's yet another reason for me never to go running."

"You ran from me."

Nora dropped the sponge into the water.

"Run from you? That's funny." She'd been bleeding so hard she could barely walk. It had taken everything she had to stand on her two feet in front of him, and it took more than she had to walk out his door. She'd fainted in his bathroom from hunger since she couldn't keep any food down. She had literally crawled on the floor of his house when he'd broken her riding crop, and she'd had to pick up the pieces.

"I saw a nature show once when I was kid," she began, keeping her voice as low as possible. "There was a wolf caught in a trap and he gnawed his own foot off to get free. It was awful. I couldn't imagine being so desperate to be free I'd amputate a part of my own body. I couldn't understand the wolf. Now I do."

"Are you so desperate to be free of me you'd gnaw your own leg off?"

"I'm saying leaving you was as easy as gnawing my own leg off."

"My Little One…"

"It's been over a year, Søren. I'm not the same person I was. A lot can happen in a year."

"I realize this. Apparently in one year my submissive decided she was a dominatrix."

"I didn't decide I was a dominatrix. I am a dominant. I want to make money. You put the two together and you get dominatrix."

"You aren't a dominant, Eleanor."

"Then what am I, since you seem to be the expert on me?"

"You're mine. That's what you are."

She shook her head. "Not anymore, Søren. I'm doing this. I know you don't like it. I know you don't agree with it, but I'm doing it."

"There are easier ways to hurt me than by becoming a dominatrix."

"That you think I'm doing this to hurt you is all the proof I need that leaving you was the right thing to do. You know I have this part of me. You know this is who I am. You've always known. Pretending it's not there won't make it go away. If you'd let me explore my dominant side instead of ignoring it, hiding it from me...I might never have left. But you forbade me from seeing Kingsley, one of your precious three nonnegotiables. God, me and Kingsley. Have you ever considered he might be one of my nonnegotiables, too?"

"He's using you to get back at me. I'd choose your nonnegotiables more wisely."

"Fine. Then I choose me. You and Kingsley both can go fuck yourselves. Or each other. God knows you both want to bad enough."

She stood up and dropped the sponge into the bathtub.

"You're clean," she said. "You can get out whenever you want."

Søren didn't stand up like she expected him to, not at first. No, first he sank down into the water, submerging himself entirely. When he came back up, it was with a cascade of water. As he stood he ran his hands through his hair, slicking it back as water poured off and down him, licking every inch of his six-foot-four frame—his strong thighs corded with runner's muscles, his narrow hips, his taut stomach and back that seemed to go on forever when one kissed it from hip to neck and down again like she had so many nights after they finished making love. And his eyelashes, naturally dark, darkened even more when wet and his blond hair turned to shining gold. Wet and naked he was magnificent and shameless, and he was putting on this show all for her benefit. And it worked because she did want him so much it hurt, and when it hurt she wanted him, because when she wanted him it hurt. Somewhere in the distance she heard Pavlov's bell ringing. This time she ignored the sound.

"Remember when I said I would hate you again later?" Nora asked, handing him a thick white towel.

"Yes."

"Later is now."

14

Reign of Terror

NORA DRESSED IN HER OWN BEDROOM. IT TOOK AN act of will to go back to the playroom and face him. At least she had one tiny victory under her belt. He'd tempted her with his body, and she'd walked away. Miracles did happen.

When she opened the door to the playroom, she found him fully dressed again, his hair still wet but otherwise he'd returned to his neutral state of clothed and calm and clean.

"What exactly are you doing here?" she asked from the open doorway, not sure she wanted to go back inside.

"Teaching you to use a whip. I thought that was obvious." He held up the whip coiled around his hand.

"Why you?"

"Whether or not you acknowledge you're still mine, I know you are. As long as you are mine, your safety is my primary concern and responsibility. This career path you've chosen is not an easy one. We'd like to think everyone in this community is simply a pervert with a heart of gold, but there are dangerous men out there who will hire you for less than pleasant reasons. I've known hard-core masochists who are as dangerous as sadists. If you fail to give them what they want and what they've paid for, they can and will turn on you. You need to know what you're doing. Doing your job well will be your best defense. As long as your clients are afraid of you, you'll be safe. *Safer.*"

"Kingsley is trying to turn me into the Queen of the Underground," she said, taking the whip from his hands.

"Make it a reign of terror, then. For your sake and theirs."

The whip lesson started off easy. Søren demonstrated how to hold the whip and explained the different sorts of cracks—a forward crack, the sidearm crack, the coachman's crack. She'd never paid any attention to the techniques Søren had used before. She'd always been content to simply enjoy watching him in action when he beat someone else. But now she longed to understand everything—how to flick the whip in such a way to make the sonic boom, how to strike someone in such a way you didn't rip their back open, how to strike someone in such a way you did rip their back open.

When it was her turn he stood behind her to one side, helping her get comfortable with the swing of the whip and how to control it.

"Can I crack it?" she asked.

"You can. Let me leave the room first."

"What? You don't trust me?"

"Your first time with a whip? No. Absolutely not."

"That's probably smart. Okay, back off. I'm going to crack it."

"Put your safety glasses on first, or you'll put your eye out."

"Yes, Daddy."

She said it mockingly, without thinking, simply answering sarcasm with sarcasm. But this was Søren and no such remark could go unremarked.

"Are we playing that game again, Eleanor?"

"I didn't mean it like that," she said, lightly throwing the whip, doing her best to ignore him.

"I could read you a bedtime story."

She whirled and faced him. "Are you trying to make this more difficult than it already is?"

"What is 'this' you're referring to?"

"Us. Us not being an us."

"Then, yes, I am. I am trying to make it more difficult for you. It couldn't possibly be more difficult for me than it already is."

"You seem fine to me."

"Fine?" Søren laughed as if she'd said the most absurd thing in her life, as if she'd said the sky was green and two plus two equaled cat. "Eleanor, I had to take a leave of absence after you left. I couldn't work. I couldn't sleep. I couldn't eat. I couldn't pray. Everything I've gone through in my life—with my father, my sister, being separated from my mother for thirteen years—in a heartbeat, in an instant, in the twinkling of an eye I would have *happily* gone through that again before I went through the hell you put me through when you left me. I consoled a parishioner recently whose wife just died and when I told him I was a widower and could sympathize with his agony, I wasn't speaking about Marie-Laure. I meant you."

Nora swallowed. She raised her chin and met his eyes. They were blue now, not gray, and they blazed with something— rage. Against her? Himself? God?

"I'm not dead, Søren."

"You were gone. How was I to know how you were, *if* you were? It was agony, and I don't use that word lightly. They talk of Christ's agony on the cross. Now I know of agony."

Anyone who didn't know Søren as intimately as she did wouldn't have been surprised by the passion in his voice, the anguish. But she'd known him since she was fifteen. Søren was a brick wall and the mortar was made of iron, and he did not crack. He never cracked. He'd always been her wall, an impenetrable fortress, and no matter how hard she threw herself against that wall, she'd never broken it down. But when he said the word *agony* she saw a hairline fracture, and she knew the whole wall could come down any second.

She knew what he kept behind that wall. God help them all if it came tumbling down.

Last night she'd stepped in front of a man being whipped and put her body between him and the whip. Today she stepped between Søren's pain and the wall.

She reached up and touched his face. That was all she did. He closed his eyes and rested his cheek against her hand.

"I didn't leave you to hurt you," she whispered.

"But it did."

"I spent seven years on the receiving end of pain. I'm ready to be on the giving end."

"Did you have to start with me?"

"Yes."

He nodded his head, and she met his eyes. The crack remained, but the wall held. For now anyway.

Nora lowered her hand and picked up her whip.

"Will you show me the coachman's crack again? I think I'm going to like a shorter whip with a longer handle."

"If you can control a shorter whip, you can control a longer one. It's best to learn on a shorter whip," he said, his voice stronger than before, sturdier.

"Then let's get back to work."

They worked for an hour and at the end of the hour, Nora had learned the forward crack. He left for a moment and returned with a bundle of socks which he rolled into tight balls. First she tossed them up in the air for him and Søren knocked them out of the air—an impressive display of good aim. Then he threw them for her and she was able to hit one out of fifteen. A decent start.

"Unfortunately," Søren said as he gathered the socks for a second round, "there's no chance you'll master the whip in time for this party Kingsley's planning. You'd have to work ten hours a day from now until then and you'd still not be as good as I am or Kingsley is."

Or Milady.

Nora sighed. "Well, I'll figure something out. Whips aren't the only way to hurt someone. I know me. I'm creative."

"Yes, you are. You always have been."

"It's funny you say that," she said. "You know, that I'm creative."

"Why is that?"

"I..." She hesitated for a moment. "While I was away I wrote a book."

"You did?"

"I did. A whole book. A big one. Like, four hundred and fifty pages. Amazing what you can get done when you're trapped in a convent with nothing else to do. But I didn't just write it. I sent it to a literary agent, and she's representing it. Me. We're doing some final fixes on it, and then she's going to try to sell it. Crazy, right?" She laughed nervously.

"Eleanor, that's wonderful."

"It's just a dirty romance," she said, shrugging.

"So was *Lady Chatterley's Lover.*"

"I don't know if this is quite D. H. Lawrence, but...I'm really happy with it. I keep running to the library to play with it. Gotta make it perfect. I'm going to use the first money I make to buy a laptop—a really fancy one so I don't have to work at the library anymore."

"Is this why you're working for Kingsley? For money?"

"Money is the reason everybody works," she said.

"Kingsley has all the money in the world."

"I want my own money, my own house. Freedom. Money is freedom."

"I'm under a vow of poverty. Do you think I'm not free?"

"No, you aren't. You have people you have to answer to. If you want to buy a car, you have to ask permission. If you want to go on a trip, you have to beg the Jesuits or the diocese for time off and you have to find someone in your family to pay for you. If you hadn't donated so much money to the Jesuits and the diocese after your father died, they would have transferred you already five times. That doesn't seem like freedom to me."

"You think I should leave the priesthood?" he asked, a hint of dark mirth in his eyes.

"We are not having this conversation again. I will walk again, and I won't come back this time."

"You will walk the circumference of the entire globe and find yourself right where you started. Here," he said, taking her into his arms.

Søren bent his head and kissed her. She didn't return the kiss at first. Her dignity wouldn't allow it. But in a fight between her dignity and her desire, her desire won every time.

Nora heard someone clear his throat.

"Ahem. Am I interrupting the lesson?"

They pulled away from each other and found Kingsley standing in the playroom doorway.

"No, we're done for the day," Nora said.

"*Bien.* And progress? It was made?"

"I'm okay at it," Nora said. "But it'll take months to be as good as I need to be."

"We don't have that much time," Kingsley said.

"Perhaps you should have thought about that before you

decided to put Eleanor on display to the entire world before she was ready." Søren scowled at Kingsley.

"She'll be ready one way or another. I have faith in her even if you don't. Shall I show you out?" Kingsley asked, stepping into the room to leave the doorway empty and open. The air crackled between Kingsley and Søren, not with their old playful sexual tension but with true animosity. She'd wondered if they'd made peace with each other but clearly today was nothing but a temporary détente.

"I know my way out." Søren released her hand and walked toward the door. "Eleanor. I hope to see you soon. You should come back to church."

"I'm excommunicated."

"I spoke to the bishop. You're welcome to return anytime. Always."

Eleanor had no words for that. She had no idea how to feel. She'd gotten used to being an outcast and sleeping in on Sundays.

"How magnanimous," Kingsley said, almost sneering. "A priest and a bishop got together, had tea and decided you were worthy enough to attend their worthless relic of a church on Sundays. You must be so honored they're going to let you back into the Dirty Old Men Who Like to Fuck Little Boys and Tell Grown Women What to Do with Their Bodies Club."

Søren turned his attention from her to Kingsley.

"Might I have a word with you?" Søren asked.

"Bien sûr."

It happened so fast Nora could do nothing but gasp as Søren grabbed Kingsley by the neck and slammed him into the wall. With his body, Søren had Kingsley pinioned like an insect on display in a glass case. His mouth was at Kingsley's ear, close enough to kiss him.

"You go too far," Søren said, biting off each word. "You

make choices you later regret and then blame anyone but your-self for what you suffer at your own hand. You don't need me to hurt you. You do that to yourself. You can blame me and you can punish me for all my crimes, real and imagined. But you leave Eleanor out of this petty plan of yours to get your revenge on me. She is my heart. If anything happens to her because of you, I will castrate you. I know how much you want children. I will take that dream from you with my bare hands and a rusty knife. You know what I'm capable of. And you know I know how, because I have done it before. My fa-ther survived the procedure. You'll be lucky if you do."

"Søren, let him go," Nora said. "He can't breathe."

"He's probably enjoying it."

"I'm not. Goddammit, Søren, let him go," Nora ordered.

Kingsley was struggling, pushing back against Søren, his feet fighting for purchase, his lungs for air.

This wasn't a game. This wasn't kink. Søren could kill him any second.

Søren held on and held on. Kingsley struggled and strug-gled.

Finally, Søren let him go.

Kingsley inhaled hugely, his hand on his neck. Nora started over to him but he raised his hand to stop her.

"It's fine. I deserved that." Kingsley expelled the words between breaths.

"No one deserves that," Nora said, furious.

Søren looked back at her over his shoulder.

"No?" Søren asked, and punched Kingsley in the center of the stomach so hard Kingsley slid down the wall and to the floor.

Søren walked out without another word.

"King?" Nora ran to him and knelt at his side.

"Fine," he said, his head back, his eyes streaming with tears. "I'm fine."

"Are you going to tell me you deserved that, too?"

"I did, *oui*. I absolutely had that coming to me."

"Don't take this personally, but I believe that," she said. If Kingsley said he had it coming to him, then he had it coming to him. Kingsley half laughed, half grunted.

"Did that hurt as much as it looked like it did?" she asked.

"More. *Le prêtre* is in a bad mood. We'll have to get used to it."

"He usually doesn't go around choking people who piss him off." Nora shook her head. "Or punching them. I've never seen him like this before."

Kingsley sighed.

"I have." He grunted again as he moved. "God, it's like being back in high school again. If he was going to put me in the hospital, he could at least get me off first."

"You don't have an erection right now, do you?"

"Not a full one."

Nora groaned and leaned her forehead against Kingsley's.

"What are we going to do?" she asked.

"We'll figure something out. I know you...you're ten times the domme Milady is."

"I can't whip like she does, though."

"There are other ways to hurt people. As you see." He laughed a little and tried to stand, then thought better of it and slid back to the floor.

"Yes, there are, aren't there?" Nora grinned.

"That's not a good smile."

"It's the best smile, King."

"Why are you smiling when I'm down here dying?"

"Because I can't learn how to whip like she does by Midsummer. But you can teach me how to throw a punch like that, can't you?"

Kingsley smiled the same scary smile she wore.

"Milady will never know what hit her."

15

The Black Box

ONE WEEK LATER, NORA EXPERIENCED THE PARTICU-
lar torment of having good news and no one to tell it to. She
made a phone call or two and when it was time, she borrowed
Kingsley's car and drove to the club. Since returning to the
city, Nora had avoided The 8th Circle. By now everyone knew
she'd left Søren but no one knew why and she didn't want
to face those questions yet, not until she had a good answer.

Upon arriving at the club, she went to the room that would
be her new dungeon. When Kingsley had told her which dungeon was to be hers in the Hall of Masters—as someone had
dubbed it—she nearly killed the man.

"You put me right across the hall from Søren?" she'd demanded.

"I did."

"How much do you hate him, King? Seriously, answer me.
On a scale of one to ten, how much?"

"This isn't about hate. I'm angry with him, yes, but it's
not hate."

"Then what is it?"

"You are the former submissive of the most infamous sadist in our little community," Kingsley said. Little? Several
thousand people held keys to The 8th Circle. "People have
expectations. We need to subvert those."

"What expectations?"

"They expect you to go running back to him any day."

"They do?"

"They're already taking bets on when you'll show up in his
collar again. When I put you in the dungeon across from his,
it's our way of showing them we aren't afraid of him. This is
business, Mistress Nora," he said, emphasizing her new name.
"It's not personal. It's marketing."

Marketing.

Kingsley could call it that if he wanted to, but she knew
the truth. Whether he'd admit it or not, Kingsley was trying to torture Søren by putting her dungeon across from his.
Kingsley had her on his side and that gave him the upper hand
against his former lover. Calculating and merciless when he
wanted to be, Kingsley was willing to press any advantage.
Nora was his advantage. So much for being a queen. In the
game between Kingsley and Søren, she was still very much
a pawn.

Nora opened the door to her dungeon and found it abuzz
with workers and a decorator putting everything together for
her. The front room of the two-room suite would hold a bed,
a table and a sofa, plus an en suite bathroom. The back room
was her actual dungeon. Kingsley had given her a twenty-
five-thousand-dollar budget to work with, and she'd spent
every penny of that on crops, canes, floggers, whips, clamps,
sex toys, a medical bed, a St. Andrew's Cross and the pièce de
résistance…a large wooden throne perfect for bondage. The
man who'd sold it to her said it came from an ancient castle

at the foot of the Carpathian Mountains. Probably bullshit, but it was a gorgeous monstrosity and she had to have it. It put her a tad over budget, but if Kingsley wanted her to be a queen, this queen needed a throne.

While the workmen and the decorator put her dungeon together, Nora crossed the hall. With no one around and no one watching, she pulled a key out of her pocket and slipped it into the lock on a door, the door opposite her door.

Søren wasn't in his dungeon. Yet her hands shook as she turned the key and opened the door, feeling like an apostate entering a temple. She shut the door behind her, locked it and leaned back against the door.

She took a ragged breath. The scent of winter permeated the air like the rarest, lightest perfume. With her eyes closed she did nothing but inhale again and again, drinking in the scent like a recovering alcoholic sniffing the mouth of an empty bottle of wine. She walked to the bed—an iron bed with a curved iron headboard and iron bedposts. Snow-white linens covered the bed, and she lifted his pillow to her face and breathed in his scent again. She ran her hands over the downy coverlet. Glancing around she saw nothing had been changed since she'd last set foot in here. On the wall opposite the bed stood a black St. Andrew's Cross. An actual cross, small and carved of rough wood, hung over the door. A touch of blasphemy? No, although it might seem as such. Kingsley himself had designed this room to his exact specifications. Apart from the bed, which was a full-size, the room resembled the hermitage at their old school in Maine, the hermitage where Kingsley and Søren had carried on their secret affair under the noses of the Jesuit priests and other students who would never have dreamed that the cold, taciturn, no doubt heartless young Mister Stearns had it within him to love or be loved by anyone.

But he did. His aloofness and reserve were his armor. She'd seen it with her own eyes—parishioners at Sacred Heart ached to be close to him. He was their priest and they adored him for his dedication to the church, his love for God and his devotion to their spiritual well-being. But although he would regularly dine in the homes of his parishioners when invited or spend hours with them when they brought their troubles to his office, he never reciprocated by inviting them to his home at the rectory or asking them for help unless it was church-related. The one secret about his personal life he'd ever let slip was the story of his marriage to a young French ballerina when he was eighteen, and that had been a calculated maneuver so that his congregation would know he wasn't the sort of priest from whom they need hide their children.

Here, however, in this room, all the armor came off. Here he was free. He didn't hide his passions, his hungers. Hungers few outside these walls would understand. But she did. She understood because they were her desires, too.

Nora wandered the room, touching this and that. A black crop. A white set of leather cuffs that matched the collar he'd given her when she was eighteen. Handcuffs. Rope cuffs. A set of scalpels of various sizes.

On a shelf sat a black lacquer box that she feared to open for the memory she knew lurked inside it. But Nora had Pandora's self-restraint when it came to secret boxes. She opened it. Anyone who saw the box out of context of this room and its owner would likely assume it held something like jewelry or love letters or a nice set of mah-jongg tiles. They could have guessed for hours without knowing what it actually held, which was a set of surgical steel needles, a set of needle receiving tubes, small clamps of various sizes and a collection of silver rings. Not the sort of rings for fingers, however.

What few people realized about Søren was that he possessed a wicked sense of humor. Nora, when she'd still been Eleanor, awoke on a Valentine's Day years ago to find a card on the otherwise empty pillow next to her. The front of the card bore the words "The club, my room, tonight at 9:00." That was all. When she opened the card she found a simple hand-drawn heart on the inside pierced by an arrow. But on closer inspection she saw it wasn't an unfletched arrow as she'd assumed.

It was a needle.

That night she arrived at the club on time. She knew better than to keep Søren waiting. Outside his dungeon door she took off her snowy, sludgy boots and knocked once before slipping inside.

She shut the door but didn't lock it. No one would interrupt them tonight, not even Kingsley unless he was invited, and then of course it wouldn't be an interruption—Kingsley was always welcome in Søren's dungeon. In addition to all the usual furniture in the room—the bed, the cross, one chair—she found a table covered in a white sheet between the foot of the bed and the St. Andrew's Cross on the opposite wall. Next to the end of the table sat a black lacquer box, closed, lying on a small metal table with wheels, the sort she'd seen in doctor's offices to hold medical instruments.

She went to the bathroom where she found Søren at the sink, the sleeves of his white button-down shirt rolled up to his elbows while he washed his hands. Not washed, scrubbed. He scrubbed his hands with the dedication of a surgeon.

"Sir?"

He turned his face to her but kept his hands under the steaming water.

"Happy Valentine's Day, Little One." He kissed her forehead.

"You're in a good mood, my sir," she said to his bright

smile, his bright eyes. He looked almost feverish. "Should I be worried?"

"I would be if I were you," he said with a wink.

"My pussy just whimpered."

"I wondered what that sound was. Now go change. There's a shirt on the bed. Then sit on the table at the end closest to us."

The instructions were simple enough. The shirt on the bed was one of his, a black Oxford shirt he must have been wearing earlier today, as she could smell his scent on it. She might have been cold wearing nothing but his shirt, except Søren had turned the heat up in the room. Even when torturing her, he thought of her comfort.

Sitting on the end of the table as ordered, she felt like a child with her naked feet dangling, not able to reach the floor. Soon Søren came out of the bathroom, drying his hands on a small white towel.

He tossed the towel aside and stood between her knees. He kissed her.

"Nervous?" he asked between soft, gentle kisses.

"A little," she said. "What's going on, sir?"

"Do you remember a few months ago when Kingsley was reading to us from *Story of O*?"

She nodded and said nothing. Of course she remembered it. Both of them had taken their turns with her that night and when the kink and the sex were over and done with, none of them could sleep. Kingsley had offered to read a bedtime story and had procured from his library an English translation of *Histoire d'O*, the most infamous erotic novel in the history of the French language. Was there anything in the world more erotic than to be in bed with a beautiful man who'd beaten and fucked her while another beautiful man who'd also beaten

and fucked her lounged in a chair by the bed, wearing nothing but fitted trousers and reading French erotica to them?

"If I recall correctly," Søren continued, "you were particularly enamored of the scene when Sir Stephen has O pierced."

"A genital piercing seems more intimate than a collar," she
said. "Something that can't be taken off easily. Something that
you can wear in public that no one can see."

"Exactly," Søren said. "Which is why I'm going to pierce
you tonight."

"Pierce me?"

"Don't be afraid. I learned from the best. Mistress Irina took
me through all the steps. I'll do a simple clitoral hood piercing. A ring. Something you'll wear always, in public and private. Something, like you said, more intimate than a collar."

She could have asked questions. Søren often allowed her to
ask questions before he hurt her.

She could have asked, *Do I have to?* Or *Will it hurt?* But instead she asked, "Can I see the ring?"

"Of course, Little One." He opened the lacquer box and
removed a small plastic bag.

"Mistress Irina has already sterilized everything for me.
Don't touch the ring."

She looked at the ring—a silver steel circle with a ball for
a clasp. Couples exchanged wedding bands when they married. A diamond ring on her finger seemed a hollow symbol
compared to this ring. She would wear it not on her body,
but pierced into her body, and she would bleed for it. And it
would be her own lover who put it in her.

"I'm ready," she said, returning the ring to him.

"Lie back," Søren instructed.

She rolled down onto the table and heard the sound of
metal moving. From under the white sheet, Søren had pulled
out stirrups like those she'd put her feet in every trip to her

gynecologist's office. Her knees fell open wide as she moved into position. Because he was Søren he also cuffed her ankles to the stirrups. No running away now—not that she wanted to. Much. Søren angled a light at the most intimate part of her body. And yet she wasn't embarrassed, wasn't ashamed. Her body belonged to him. She wouldn't hide his own property from him.

She heard the distinctive snap of latex gloves, and felt the cold touch of the cleansing cloth that he wiped over her clitoris and vulva to disinfect the area. His fingers delicately prodded the tender flesh. He seemed to be measuring, checking position. With the tip of a pen he marked one spot and another. He pressed something small and cold up and under the hood that covered her clitoris.

"Mistress Irina suggests you blow out while I push the needle through."

She nodded, unable to speak. She was mute from fear and arousal. Around Søren they were inseparable sensations, twin strands of the same cord.

"I'll count for you. When I say three, you blow out hard. Yes?"

"Yes, sir," she said between shallow breaths.

"One…two…three," and on *three* she pushed her air out as he pushed the needle through, and felt nothing more than a quick pinch. He'd hurt her far worse before. This was nothing.

"Good girl," Søren said and she rose up and saw his blond head between her wide-open thighs and her feet in the stirrups, a sight that would linger long after that night in her most private fantasies.

Carefully, not moving the lower half of her body at all, Eleanor rose up on her hands to see him finish the piercing. He took the ring and threaded it through the hole made by the needle. With his dexterous fingers, he fastened it with the small steel ball.

"It is finished," Søren said. She looked down at the ring and into Søren's eyes. He pushed two fingers inside her and her hands clutched the edge of the table as he opened her up. He still had the gloves on. While he spread her wide they kissed again. When he pulled his fingers out of her, they were quickly replaced with his cock deep inside her. He unbuttoned his shirt, the one she wore, not the one he wore, and held her breasts in his hands, rubbing her nipples until they hardened. Unable to sit up any longer she rolled back and arched into his hands, into his penetration. Her clitoris throbbed as blood rushed to the area. She felt everything, every movement. Her clitoris had never been so sensitive or receptive. She orgasmed quickly, suddenly, before she'd steeled herself for it. A second orgasm closely followed the first. The ring throbbed like a beating heart, and her hips felt heavy and tight. She looked down at herself and saw the ring as much a part of her body as Søren's cock inside her. The piercing was an act of sadism, of course, putting a needle and a ring through her clitoral hood, but the ring itself was a symbol—not merely of his sadism and ownership of her body, but of her trust in him, her devotion. A wedding band could be yanked off the finger and tossed across the room. There would be no removing this ring in a moment of passion. It was there to stay like an arrow through a heart.

An arrow or a needle.

Or a knife.

"Eleanor?"

Nora slammed the black lacquer box shut and turned around. Søren stood in the doorway of his dungeon looking at her with a question in his eyes.

"Sorry," she said. "Lost in thought."

Søren stepped into his dungeon and locked the door behind him. He walked to her and looked down at the box in her hand.

"Good memories in this box," he said, carefully opening the lid.

"A few," she admitted. "One or two."

Søren took a sterilized needle out of its plastic, shut the box and set it aside.

"Or three." He took her much smaller hand in his large hand and pricked the tip of her index finger with the needle. He did it calmly, deliberately, but she saw his pupils dilate wildly as the needle tip sunk into her flesh. When he pulled it out, a drop of bright red blood pooled on her skin.

"Oh, no," she said. "Does this mean I'll fall into a hundred-year sleep?"

"I don't see any spinning wheels anywhere, Sleeping Beauty." He brought her hand to his mouth and kissed the blood off her finger. He bent his head to kiss her lips and she pulled away.

"That's not what I came here for," she said. "And don't flirt. I'm still furious at you for almost choking Kingsley to death."

Søren sighed. "You call it choking. He'd call it foreplay. Kingsley and I aren't your concern."

"If you do it again, I'm calling the police. You can sit in an interrogation room and explain to the cops why you assaulted your brother-in-law. Maybe if you're lucky, this time I'll come to you and offer to get *you* out of trouble in exchange for your eternal obedience to *me*."

"The police know Kingsley. I wouldn't get arrested for assaulting him. I'd likely get a medal."

"I'm serious. Don't take out your anger at me on him."

"Did you come here simply to scold me for hurting Kingsley? If so, I am duly contrite," he said without a trace of contrition. "Now, if you're not here for me, I'm afraid I'll have to ask you to leave. I'm meeting Simone in twenty minutes."

"I know. She told me. That's why I'm here. I needed to tell someone," she said, and pulled a piece of paper from her pocket. It was an email she'd printed out earlier today. Søren took it from her, unfolded it and read the words on the page, first with mere interest and then with obvious joy.

"Eleanor, is that what I think it is?"

"I sold my book."

16

Good News

"A PUBLISHER CALLED LIBRETTO IS BUYING IT. TWO-book deal. It's for almost no money, and my agent warned me I wouldn't see a penny of it for about three months, but they're a solid company with a really good track record for launching authors." The words came out fast as they'd been bottled up inside her for twenty-six whole hours. Ever since she'd gotten the phone call and the email with the details, she'd been fighting the need to scream from the rooftops.

Søren raised his hand and touched her smile. "I'm so proud of you."

"Me, too. Although I'm terrified. They want another book from me in six months, and I don't even have a laptop yet. I hope King hooks me up with a rich client soon. I need to get to work."

"I have the utmost faith in you."

"Thank you," she whispered. "I don't know if I'll ever break the habit of telling you everything."

"I hope you never do. When you start keeping secrets from me, then I'll know something's very wrong."

"I know you won't tell on me. You're good at keeping my secrets."

"It's what priests do. Should we celebrate?"

"How? You want to take me out to dinner?"

"I wish I could."

She wished he could, too. And it grated. It grated right on her heart that he, an unmarried adult man, couldn't take her, an unmarried adult woman, out to dinner without risking a scandal simply because of the collar he wore around his neck and the initials behind his name.

"We could celebrate in private," he said. "Later tonight... if you wish."

"If I wish? That's different. You used to summon me, and I came crawling."

"You never came while you were crawling. Shortly thereafter, however."

"If Simone's listening at the door then she really is going to be very jealous. She's crazy about you."

"Simone wouldn't eavesdrop on us."

"Fuck, I would."

Søren smiled. A quick smile, there and gone again like the flash of headlights in a darkened room.

"I should go," Nora said. She started for the door but Søren grabbed her hand and pulled her to him. "Søren, don't."

"Don't what? Don't do this?" He wrapped one foot around her calf to lock her against him. He put his hand under her chin and held it in place while he kissed her. Against her will, she warmed to the kiss, to the touch of his hand on her face, his body so close to hers. Every morning she woke up with a ghost in her bed in the shape of his body. His scent was long gone from her sheets. She almost wished for winter so she could smell him without being near him. Being close to him hurt. Being away from him hurt. Søren had told her years ago that to love him was to hurt. She thought that night he referred only to his sadism. Now she knew better.

Reluctantly she pulled away from him again, putting two feet between them. Breathing room.

"Don't pretend you aren't tempted, Little One. I know you too well."

"What I want to do and what I'm willing to do aren't the same thing anymore. And I can read you, too, you know. And when I look in your eyes, I read warnings. If I go back to you, you will take everything from me that I've gained by leaving you."

"We made a deal, remember? You gave me forever and I would give you everything. I fully intend to hold up my end of the deal, no matter what it costs me."

"It was a bad deal," she said. "I made it when I was fifteen. And you haven't given me everything."

"I have given you my heart, my body and every secret about me you would ever want to know. I have put my priesthood on the line for you, my work, my reputation, my happiness and quite often my own sanity. What more do you want from me?"

"An apology, for starters."

"For what? I'll put it in writing."

"I'm sure it will be quite well crafted, written with lovely penmanship and entirely insincere. For what? You order me to marry you, order me to never see Kingsley again, break my riding crop and you have to ask what for?"

"You knew what I was. You were warned. I warned you. Kingsley warned you. I will not apologize for who and what I am."

"Then let's make a new deal. I won't ask you to change what you are, and you don't ask me to change what I am."

"What are you? Tell me. I'd love to know what you think you are."

"Free."

Søren smiled at her. "Is that so? Then why are you still wearing your collar?"

"I'm not."

He paused long enough to make her nervous. Then he came to her, pressing her back against the wall with the weight of his body. She hated him for being so tall and strong. He could dominate her simply by standing in front of her. She closed her eyes as he slipped his hand down her side, down her thigh, up her thigh... Nora inhaled as he slid his hand into her panties and pressed his fingers against her clitoral ring. He grasped it and tugged lightly.

"I marked you with this, and you haven't taken it out," Søren said.

"I don't want to take it out. It feels good when I'm fucking."

"Is that the real reason?" Søren's fingertip caressed her clitoris. It swelled under his touch.

"The only reason."

"You can lie to me all you want," Søren said. "We both know the truth."

He pushed a finger inside her, and she spread her legs for him, too well trained to stop herself. She could safe out. But then he'd stop. Wait, wasn't that the point? Nora had forgotten the point. How could she remember the point when he was massaging all those little places in her that made her so wet when he touched them?

"This is what you came here for, wasn't it?" he asked.

"No, I came to ask you a favor."

"I'd hardly call this a favor," he said into her ear. "I'm more than happy to do it."

She held on to his biceps to steady herself. She could feel the tension in his muscles. Knowing him, what he most wanted to do was push her down on his bed, stick her with needles again and fuck her blind. She wasn't entirely opposed to this idea.

"I wanted to ask you…" she said between breaths, "please don't come to the Midsummer party. It'll be hard enough without you there, but if you're there…"

"If I grant you this favor, what will you give me in return?"

"Me. Right now."

Søren pulled his hand out of her panties, took her by the back of the hair and pushed her to the bed. He put her on her back near the footboard and knelt between her legs. He yanked her underwear off and tossed them aside. His black T-shirt came off next, but when she reached for the button on his pants, he grabbed her wrists and pushed them down into the bed, pinning her against the sheets. He did it quickly, with terrifying grace and strength.

"My dungeon," he said. "My rules."

Søren squeezed her wrists to the point of pain. With Kingsley she would have fought the pain and her urge to cry out. But not with Søren. He needed her pain and she gave it to him freely. His thumbs pushed into the tendon of her wrists and the pain was unbearable. She bore it anyway. The relief when he released her was almost as intense as the pain had been. He opened his pants and nudged her thighs wide-open with his knees. With a slow thrust he entered her. Once inside her, he gently wrapped his fingers around her throat. One hand on her throat…one hand over her mouth, muffling her moans. She could still safe out if she needed to by snapping her fingers in his ear. This wasn't the first time he'd used his own hand to gag her while he fucked her.

Nora lifted her hips to take him deeper. Søren's eyes were closed as he moved in her, the fingers on her neck pressing in with each thrust, relaxing with each retreat. Not once did he choke her, cut off her air supply or even push hard enough to scare her. His hand wasn't there to hurt her or choke her. No…he'd made a collar of his own fingers.

He moved slowly, every movement deliberate.

"You miss this," he said, punctuating his words with a hard sharp thrust.

She bit his hand, a signal she wanted to speak, and he uncovered her mouth.

"I can have sex whenever I want it with whoever I want."

"It wasn't sex I was talking about. You miss being dominated."

"Not enough to come back to you."

"But you will…eventually you will."

She wanted to deny it and would have, but he put his hand over her mouth again to silence her. He fucked her harder now, faster, rougher. His thrusts were possessive. He had a point to make and he was going to make it no matter how much it hurt her. And it did hurt. Beautiful pain, intimate pain, extravagant pain. She panted behind his hand, moaned even as her hips rose to meet each of his thrusts. They moved in tandem, knowing each other's bodies so well they could have danced this dance blindfolded and in the dark. No one made her feel quite like Søren did. No one filled her as he filled her. No one fucked her as he fucked her. No one loved her as he loved her. That's what made leaving him so difficult and so necessary. She would never be herself if she went back to him. She would be his and she would like it. She'd love it even as she loved him. But who wanted to be the sort of person who loved being in prison?

The pressure in her body increased. She felt it from her lungs to her knees. She had to come. She was almost there. Søren moved his hand from her mouth and slipped it between her legs. She cried out as he caressed that sensitive spot where their bodies met and joined, the pad of his thumb toying with the ring. Nora's body went still as her orgasm shot through her, setting her inner muscles to clenching, her vagina pulsing all around him. With the slightest intake of air, Søren came inside her, and she felt the warm fluid spilling into her and out onto his sheets.

Søren rested his body against hers as the last contractions came and faded. Nora laughed softly and Søren pulled up and looked down at her.

"What's so funny?" he asked.

"I would have let you fuck me even if you hadn't agreed not to come to the Midsummer party."

"I wasn't planning to come to the party anyway."

She wanted to slap him for that, for manipulating her into submitting to him. But she'd been manipulating him, as well.

"So I was right, I guess. You can't be bought," she said.

"When did I say I couldn't be bought?" Søren asked as he buttoned his pants and ran a hand through his hair. Everything back to normal now. Or at least their version of normal.

"I said it. To Milady."

"The dominatrix?"

"We had a little run-in the other night."

"You've picked a formidable enemy in her. She's fairly notorious for being exceptionally cruel. Masochists adore her."

"And she's actually more arrogant than you are. Hard to believe, right?"

"Unfathomable."

"She threatened me with you. She threatened to expose you. Is it possible she knows your real name or where you work?"

"Possible, yes. I wouldn't worry about me, however. If I have to speak to her, I will."

"Watch out, she'll try to bribe you into submitting to her.

I told her you couldn't be bought, that she'd be wasting her time. It probably turned her on."

"I can be bought, but not with money."

"Then what?"

"If it meant your happiness, Eleanor, if it meant bringing you home to me, I'd sell my own soul."

She pursed her lips at him. "We both know you don't mean that."

"Only because selling my soul wouldn't work. Not even the devil would dare cross swords with you. If he tried to drag you home to me, he'd end up on your St. Andrew's Cross."

"I'd make him like it, too."

"I'm certain you would."

"We're talking about Kingsley, aren't we?" Nora asked.

"Who else?"

Nora reached for the doorknob intending to leave, but she stopped first.

"You have a session with Simone."

"Yes, soon."

"You see her often?" Nora asked.

"Once a week. She's a wonderful masochist. Discreet. Kind. High pain tolerance. She asks for no more than I'm comfortable giving her." She didn't expect sex, in other words.

"Are you ever going to have sex with her?" Nora asked.

"Would it displease you if I did?"

"Considering I've been with other people since I've come back...it wouldn't be fair of me to begrudge you for...you know..."

"Exploiting my newfound freedom to its fullest?" He raised his eyebrow.

"That."

"I have no intention of breaking my vows with anyone but

you, Eleanor. I can't promise I won't fail in this. I've failed before, as you know."

"Kingsley doesn't count."

"Kingsley counts most of all." He said the words in such a way she could have sworn she heard an ominous rumble of thunder in the distance.

"I know. I know he does. You know what I mean. He's one of your three nonnegotiables, right?"

"Even when I want to string him up by his testicles, yes."

"It might be good for you if you did see someone else. Might calm those testicle-stringing-up urges a little."

"You don't want me waiting for you to come back to me, do you?"

"If you do, you'll be waiting a very long time."

"I can wait."

"Out of love for me, or because you're punishing me?"

"I'm not punishing you," Søren said.

"You sure about that?"

Søren smiled and it was a sort of smile she hadn't seen from him before, a smile that scared her.

"Trust me, Little One, when I decide to punish you, you'll know it."

Nora swallowed hard but kept her composure.

"I'm leaving," she said.

"You can stay and watch if you like. Simone will be here any minute."

"I'll leave you two alone," she said, unlocking the door, wanting to run from him but determined instead to simply walk away. "Søren..."

"Yes?"

"I can't come back to you, but I know what you need, and I know sometimes I'm the only person who can give it to you. So if you ever do need me, I will come to you."

"You shouldn't make such a promise, Little One."

"Why not?"

"I always need you."

Nora felt the words like a slap. She would have preferred the slap. Without another word she opened the door and stepped into the hall in time to see Simone walking toward her. A pretty girl in her midtwenties, Simone had rainbow-striped hair and a dozen or more piercings. She was also a PhD student in international relations. When Søren wasn't beating her on his St. Andrew's Cross, he was helping her with her doctoral thesis since he'd written two of his own. Kink made for strange bedfellows in their world. Even stranger friendships sometimes.

"Mistress?" Simone greeted her as she came to Søren's dungeon door. Nora still had her hand on the doorknob behind her. "Something wrong?"

"No. Don't worry, dear." Nora put on a fake smile and kissed Simone quickly on the cheek. "Have fun. I warmed him up for you."

She pulled out her keys and slipped into her own dungeon. The decorator was gone, the workmen were gone. She was alone at last in her beautiful brand-new dungeon. And it was beautiful. Everything she'd dreamed it would be. The front room looked as if it had been plucked out of the Moulin Rouge. Everything—the sheets, the pillows, the love seat, the rugs—red and gold and decadent. The dungeon itself was a beautiful nightmare—rows upon rows of crops hung on the wall in order of length, floggers were arrayed in order of weight and canes arranged by thickness. The medical bed for her medical fetishists sat in one corner. A St. Andrew's Cross stood along the far wall. And right in the center was her throne. Perfect. She could live in this room. If she had as many clients as Kingsley warned her she would, she just might

end up living here. But there was still a week to go before
the Midsummer Night's Fling and she hadn't seen one client
yet. Not even Kingsley, who'd promised to be her first. Then
again, she hadn't passed his stupid test yet. She should forget
about passing it and just jump him one night and take him
against his will. From what he'd told her about his first time
with Søren, he'd probably enjoy it.

Nora stepped out of her dungeon and back into the bedroom.

She nearly jumped out of her skin when she saw someone
standing by the bed.

"Sorry," he said. "The door was unlocked."

"You scared the shit out of me."

"I hope that wasn't a literal statement," he said.

"Figurative."

"Whew." He ran his hand over his brow.

"Thorny, right? That was your name?" she asked, recog-
nizing him as the man on Milady's cross at the Body House.

"That's me." He smiled and shoved his hands in his jeans
pockets. He wore a T-shirt with the sleeves cut off. He had
nice arms, sculpted biceps, but she imagined he'd gone sleeve-
less to show off his beautiful tattoos. She would have, too, if
she had ink like that.

"Can I help you with something?" Nora asked.

"No, but I can help you with something."

"I didn't know I needed help."

"You pissed off Milady. Trust me, you need help."

Nora gave a slight rueful laugh. "Yes, I hear I've made a
formidable enemy."

"I know one of her slaves. She's planning on fucking with
you at the Midsummer Fling. I wanted to warn you about
that. Not sure what she's going to do, but I'm guessing it'll be
some kind of challenge."

"Thank you. I appreciate the heads-up."

"You're welcome."

"Can I ask why you're telling me this? I mean, you and I barely know each other and, as you know, pissing Milady off is apparently not a good idea."

"I like pain," he said.

"Who doesn't? But what does that have to do with anything?"

"I'm getting there. I like pain, but I hate whips. My father used to whip me with a switch. Feels a lot like a single-tail. Floggers are great. A good flogging is the greatest thing ever but whips are my hard limit."

"She paid you to get over that."

"I should have asked for more money. But you…you stood up for me when she was beating me. You stepped between me and a whip and not that many people would do that for a whore, no matter how cute I am."

"You're not a whore."

"Yes, I am. It's on my business cards. See?" Thorny pulled his wallet out of his pocket and passed her a business card covered in scrolling thorned vines.

Thorny, Whore for Hire.

"Wow. It really does say *whore* on your business cards. Look, Thorny, I don't care that you're an escort. I do care that she was beating someone who had safed out."

"That's why I'm here. I owe you."

"Do you know what Milady's planning?"

"If I had to guess I'd say she'll probably do something to try to make you look weak in front of everybody."

"Every domme's nightmare."

"Don't freak out. Just do what they do in prison—find the biggest, baddest guy in the club and destroy him. You defeat the alpha and you become the alpha. That's how it works."

"Good advice, Thorny. Thank you."

"You're welcome, Mistress. Always good to get on a domme's good side. Now if you'll excuse me, my favorite client is waiting for me. She gives me wood."

"Hot, is she?"

"Yes. But she's also a lumber heiress. She's bringing me some nice high-grade maple tonight. I'm making my own bed."

"You're weird, Thorny. I like that about you."

"Thank you, Mistress." He playfully bowed to her and turned to leave.

"Thorny?" Nora called out.

"Yes, Mistress?" he said as he turned on his heel to face her.

"Is it hard?"

"Not at the moment, but if you took your clothes off that would help."

She gave him the look that would send future clients wondering if their health insurance covered dungeon-related injuries.

"Oh, you mean the job?" Thorny said. "It's a good job if you're the right person to do it. And I am. My clients are all women. Professional women who are rich, successful, busy. Too busy for a serious relationship. They call me and I give them a night or a week. Whatever they need. I give the best Boyfriend Experience in the state, and it's all the fun."

"What about you? You don't want a serious relationship?"

"I can't have one," he said with a shrug.

"Why? Just because you're an escort?"

"No," he said. "Because I'm dying."

Nora's eyes widened and Thorny laughed.

"Don't worry. I'm not going to drop dead here and now, right this second. Wait. I might actually. I have a brain aneurysm. It could burst today. It could burst ten years from now. It could never burst. But I don't know when it will, and when you live with the fear you can go any minute, the last thing you want to do is drag someone else into that nightmare. Not a wife. Definitely not kids."

"I'm… I'm very sorry."

"Don't be. I'm at peace about it. Getting the shit beat out of me regularly helps keep things in perspective."

"Is this why you and Milady were…close?"

"I was her sub for a while. Until you came along I thought all dominatrixes were like her."

"Like her how?"

"Like they did what they wanted to do to you without taking your feelings into consideration."

"Bad dominatrixes do that. The good ones are there for the client's needs, not their own."

"I get that now. Before I thought it was just the way it was, but I kept going back to her, because she was so good at giving me pain and getting me into subspace. Pain takes me out of myself, helps me forget for a while."

"Subspace is good for that. I understand."

"Choosing to be in pain helped me get to stage five of the grieving process."

"Stage five is acceptance, right?"

"Right. Acceptance and tattooing."

Nora laughed. "Getting tattoos is part of your grieving process?"

"When one part of your body is out of your control, it feels good to take control of another part. I can't do anything about my brain, but I could master my skin. With ink and kink."

"The tattoos are beautiful. I thought so the night I met you. All thorns, no roses."

He held out his arm so she could see them close up. With her fingers she traced the winding thorny vine tattoos from his shoulder to his wrist.

"'Gather ye rosebuds while ye may / Old Time is still a-flying / And this same flower that smiles today / Tomorrow will be dying.'" Nora recited the famous Robert Herrick poem.

"Exactly," Thorny said. "I want to live my life so that when I die, there's not a single rosebud left on the bush. I will have picked them all and there's nothing left on the ground but stems and thorns. Gathering rosebuds sounds much more romantic than notching the bedpost, right? And it's better for the bed, too. Seriously, I notched my bedpost so much it broke off."

"Hence the lumber heiress," she said.

He pointed at her. "Precisely. Speaking of, I'm late for a very important date."

"Here's your card back."

"Keep it," Thorny said. "Who knows? You might need the Boyfriend Experience someday."

Nora walked over to him and kissed him on the cheek.

"I just might. I've never had a real boyfriend before. Go have fun with your wood."

"I always do." In her doorway he stopped and turned back. "Oh, one more piece of advice, Mistress. You know, from one flesh peddler to another."

"I'll take all the advice I can get."

"I like my clients. I love my work. But never forget, you're not there to make friends. You're there to do a job. Don't get personally involved with your clients. And whatever you do, always get your money up front."

With that he gave her a wink and walked out of her dungeon.

And then it hit her like a slap to the face—a really sexy slap that's the precursor to hair pulling and rough and dirty sex. That kind of slap. The best kind of slap.

Always get your money up front.

Nora fished in her bag for her cell phone Kingsley had bought for her. She dialed his number and when Juliette answered, she asked for Kingsley.

"Oui, Maîtresse?" Kingsley said.

"Come to my dungeon tonight at nine."

"Why?"

"Because I have good news," she said. "I know how to pass your test."

17

A Wicked Game

NORA TOOK A SHOWER IN HER NEW DUNGEON BATH-
room and dressed in clothes from her new wardrobe—red
skirt (leather), red-and-black-striped corset (silk), black boots
(leather with red laces) and since Kingsley was the client tonight and no rule stayed unbroken for long around Kingsley,
she put nothing on under the skirt except for one dot of perfume at the top of her thighs.

Two hours before the scene was to begin, she still didn't
know exactly what to do with Kingsley. She knew how to pass
his test, yes. But after that? Her first session with her first client, it had to be good. No, not good. It had to be bad. Wicked.
She wanted to ruin Kingsley so that he never looked at another dominatrix again. Fuck that. She wanted him to look at
Søren and think him an amateur compared to her. Funny…
she almost wanted to knock on Søren's door and ask him for
advice. *Hey,* she'd say, *I'm about to top Kingsley, and I want it to
be evil. Any suggestions?* Oh, yes, that conversation would go
over well, wouldn't it? Nora laughed at the very thought of it.

But...

Maybe she didn't need to call Søren. She already knew what he would do to Kingsley.

He would strip me naked and drop all my clothes onto the floor. Then he'd walk on them. With shoes on.

I worshipped him for it.

He would sometimes pretend I wasn't there even when I spoke to him...

I worshipped him for it.

He would tell me he didn't want me anymore and then as I was ready to kill myself in agony, he'd smile to show it was all a joke...

And I worshipped him for it.

I mocked him once for what happened between him and his sister and you know what he did...

Then Nora knew what she would do to him.

He'd either love her for it or hate her for it, but the man would get his money's worth.

When nine o'clock arrived, Nora was ready. She heard a rapping on the door and opened it.

Kingsley waited outside her door looking every inch the gentleman he wasn't in his dark suit with his French cuffs and silk tie.

"Bonne nuit, Maîtresse," he said. "You summoned me?"

"I did," Nora said, putting her hands on his chest and kissing him on both cheeks before giving him a long deep kiss on the mouth. A special kiss. The kind of kiss to drive a man to distraction. "Come in."

He slipped past her into her new dungeon and she locked the door for privacy. Kingsley kept his submissive and masochistic side a secret from the rest of the Underground—only she, Søren and Juliette knew about it.

"Excellent work," he said, taking a stroll of the bedroom and the dungeon, casual as an English lord taking his morning constitutional through Hyde Park. "I like the cross. Nice selection of toys. A dungeon worthy of a queen."

"And you're my first prisoner," she said.

"Not yet." He wagged his finger at her. "You said you know how to pass my test and you haven't passed it yet. Until you do, you can't have me. Although I don't blame you for trying."

"I know how to pass your test. I figured it out with a little help from a friend."

"Well, you do look the part." He raked his eyes up and down her body. "You have the attitude." He tapped her under her chin and she raised it a millimeter higher. "But something's still missing…"

"Something is missing. Your wallet."

Kingsley slapped his hand over his breast pocket.

"You don't think I kissed you just for the fun of it?" she asked. Kingsley cocked his eyebrow at her. "Okay, it was fun. But it also distracted you while I was going through your pockets."

"I will kill Søren for teaching you how to pick pockets."

"It's a good trick," she said, opening his wallet and extracting two thousand dollars in cash. "This should more than cover tonight's session."

And even better, it would pay for her new laptop.

She tossed his wallet back to him, and tucked the wad of money into her corset between her breasts.

"King or commoner, everybody pays up front. Right?" she asked.

Kingsley bowed gallantly. "*Maîtresse*, I am yours."

"Well…it's about fucking time."

"I've been looking forward to this."

"So have I," she admitted. "You want to know how much I've wanted this?"

"How much?"

Nora slapped him.

Hard.

Kingsley clearly hadn't been expecting the slap. The look on his face was so stunned by it she laughed.

"That much," she said.

"Fuck." He already sounded breathless. The King of the Underground did not get slapped.

"Good. Because it's the first and last time I'm going to hit you tonight."

"If you aren't going to hurt me, then I want my money back."

"Oh, I'll hurt you. I'll even break you. By the time I'm done with you, you'll be begging to be inside me."

"If you can accomplish that without hitting me, I'll give you a thousand-dollar tip."

"Deal," she said, grabbing his tie. Using it like a leash, she drew him into the dungeon portion of her suite. She stood him in the center of the room, a room she'd had painted red, red as passion, red as blood.

"Stand here, and don't move." She pointed to a spot on the floor, a spot marked by a painted black X. Kingsley put his feet where she'd indicated and Nora began to undress him.

She pulled off his jacket and hung it on a hook on the wall, untied his tie and unbuttoned his shirt. Methodically and efficiently she removed his clothes, every stitch, right down to his boots.

"I know you said you liked it when Our Mutual Friend threw your clothes on the floor and stepped on them. But I'm not him. I may do such things to my other clients, but not to you. You're my king and I will accord you all due respect even as I'm beating you into the hospital."

"But not tonight?"

"No...tonight is special," she said running her hands over

his naked chest. She pushed her fingers against one of the old scars on his chest. "So many wounds. So many scars. Outside and in. Do they hurt?"

"Only the ones on the inside, *Maîtresse*."

"Those are the ones I'm interested in tonight." She touched his face, his lips, his eyelashes. Gentle touches, designed to soothe, not scare. "I'm going to blindfold you now. Do you have a safe word?"

"*Non.*"

"Do you want one?"

"*Non.*"

"I think, my King, you will regret that."

With that, she wrapped his own tie around his eyes and knotted it in the back. She picked up a lighter and flicked it in front of his covered eyes. He didn't flinch. Good. She needed total blindness for what she planned on doing to him. Once he was blindfolded completely she strapped leather cuffs to his wrists. From the ceiling she pulled down a hook and rope and secured Kingsley's wrists to the hook. She pulled the cord and hoisted his hands in the air over his head and knotted the rope. He stood naked and bound, completely and utterly vulnerable. He couldn't run, he couldn't see, he couldn't leave. Perfect.

"I have to get something in the other room," Nora said. "I'll be right back."

She walked to the bedroom and shut the door behind her. From under the bed she pulled out a cheap glass jar and a baseball bat.

Showtime.

"Who the fuck are you?" Nora yelled. "How did you get in here?"

Nora turned and threw the jar against the door so that it shattered, making a sound like a lamp breaking. She hit the door frame with the baseball bat. She screamed as if she'd been hit.

Then…silence.

"Nora?" Kingsley's voice called out through the door. He sounded terrified for her.

She smiled.

She counted to thirty. She heard Kingsley's voice again calling her name. She didn't answer him.

"Nora? Mistress?" Kingsley asked. "This isn't funny."

She reached into her corset for the tiny bottle of perfume she'd bought an hour ago.

Chanel No. 5.

She walked over to the CD player hidden under a shelf and hit Play.

The familiar strains of *Swan Lake* permeated the air.

Nora walked up behind Kingsley and put her mouth to his ear.

"Bonsoir, petit frère," Nora whispered. Good evening, little brother.

"Stop it, Nora. This isn't funny," he said.

"Did you miss me?" Nora asked, still speaking in her very best French accent.

"I know what you're doing."

Nora spritzed one spray of the perfume into the air over Kingsley's head. It settled around him like radioactive fallout.

He inhaled it deeply.

"I want this to stop," he said.

"But I just arrived…" Nora purred in her best faux French accent, the one Kingsley said made her sound exactly like his dead sister. "And I have missed you, *petit frère*, even if you haven't missed me at all."

Kingsley yanked on his bonds above his head.

"Let me out, Nora. Right now."

"Nora? Was that her name? She's sound asleep in the other room. I think she'll wake. *Peut-être.* Or not..."

"You're dead. Nora isn't."

"I'm not dead," Nora said. "You can't really die until you've finished all your business on earth. And you and I, *mon frère,* we have unfinished business, don't we? *Oui? Non?*"

Kingsley didn't answer at first. Nora held her breath. She knew he was close, almost there...so close to giving in...he didn't want to...but he did...

"Oui," he said at last.

"I thought so. Now answer my question—have you missed me?"

"Je ne sais pas."

"You don't know if you missed me or not? How could you not know?"

"I was angry with you."

"Pourquoi? What did I ever do to you?"

"You married Søren."

"It was his idea."

"You knew he didn't love you. He told you he didn't love you."

"He would love me. In time he would have loved me. Everyone loved me. *Tout le monde. Oui?* The most beautiful girl anyone has ever seen? I think you called me that once. Every boy at your school adored me."

"It was an all-boys school. You weren't special. You were just there, and they wanted to fuck you."

"Oh là là, such language." Nora walked around him, letting him hear her footsteps. "Were you jealous? Did you want to marry him? That would have been cute, you two standing at the altar."

"Don't be absurd. I didn't want to marry anyone, not then or now. But I didn't want him to marry you."

"But he did. He must have wanted to marry me if he did it. He does everything for a reason."

"You tell yourself that," Kingsley said. "He fucked me, not you."

"He respected me. He wanted us to wait until we knew each other better. That was all."

"If you believe that, you're crazier than I ever thought you were. You disgusted him. The way you threw yourself at him. The way you touched him when he slept, groping him, trying to arouse him. Not even I would ever touch him while he slept."

"Why didn't you?"

"He didn't like it," Kingsley said. "It reminded him of his sister, and he didn't want to remember her. The same way I don't want to remember you, you vile bitch."

Nora didn't speak at first, shocked by Kingsley's rancor. She had to remind herself that it wasn't her he was angry at, but his long-dead sister.

"Do I really deserve that?" Nora asked. "Your sister?"

"*Non,*" Kingsley said. "No, you don't. Forgive me."

"Why are you so angry at me? Is it because he picked me over you? He did it again, didn't he? With his little girl who is bleeding from her ear out in the bedroom? He picked her over you, *oui?*"

"*Non,*" Kingsley said.

"He didn't?"

"*Non.* She left him. Do you know why?"

"Tell me, *mon frère.*"

"She left him because he wanted to leave the priesthood for her. But you know something?"

"I'm waiting…"

"He offered to leave the priesthood for me, too."

Nora's eyes widened in shock. She almost gasped but she

controlled herself. If she broke character for one second it would all fall apart.

"Did he?" She kept her voice light and curious.

"It was years ago, not long after he came to the city. He'd met his little girl, his little virgin queen, and he'd fallen in love with her. It hurt to know he loved her so much when I wanted him still. After eleven years I wanted him. And I told him I wanted him, and he asked me if he left the church for me, could I be faithful to him. I pretended at the time he was joking, but I know he wasn't. He doesn't make jokes like that. If I had said yes, if I'd agreed to be faithful to him and her, he would have done it."

"You said no?" Nora asked, more stunned by this than anything else.

"I did."

"*Pourquoi?* Why would you say no to his offer if you loved him so much?"

"Because I'm not sixteen anymore. He can have me on my terms or he can't have me at all. And you know what else? I left him first. And it made me happy to do it. I took your broken, bloody body back to France and buried you next to our parents. And I knew he was in Maine waiting for me to come back to him. We'd pick up where we left off. He had his trust fund, all those millions of dollars were his because his wife was dead. I would go back, and we would be together, me and him. Lovers. Rich. Free. I didn't go back."

"Why not?"

"I didn't know at the time. I thought I was punishing him. But now I know I was saving myself. I wouldn't have been his lover. I would have been his slave. I'd been his slave, and I didn't want his chains anymore. But you can't be in his bed without wearing his chains."

No one knew the truth of that better than Nora.

"Do you regret it? Not going back to him?" she asked and wondered what her own answer to this question would be.

"*Non,*" Kingsley said. "I miss him, I love him, I want him. *Je ne regrette rien.*"

I regret nothing.

"Even my death? Do you regret killing me?"

"I didn't kill you. You killed yourself."

"Because you slept with my husband behind my back."

"I would have let him fuck me in front of your face if I could have talked him into it."

"I knew you hated me."

"I hated your arrogance. You thought you could have any man in the world. You didn't even love Søren. You wanted him because he didn't want you. He wasn't a man to you. He was a challenge. And you lost."

"And look at us...neither of us has him now. Poor us."

"Poor us? Do I look poor to you?" Kingsley demanded. "I'm rich. I have Juliette. She's going to have my children someday. I have my home, my life. Work I love. And you're lying in a grave in two pieces because you were so angry at your husband for wanting me instead of you, you killed yourself."

"And you don't miss me at all..." Nora put as much hurt into her voice as possible. Real hurt. Remembered hurt.

"That's not true," he said, his voice breaking—a crack, a chip in a wineglass, but still...a break.

"Isn't it?"

"I loved you before... I did. We played together on the beach as children. You buried me in sand. When you cut your foot on the rock in the water, I carried you to Papa. You were so scared. You thought a shark would bite you because you bled in the ocean." Kingsley laughed to himself. "There are no sharks off the coast of France."

"I was a child. Children think silly things."

"Why did you die?" Kingsley asked. "I didn't want you to die. I wanted you to be angry. I wanted you to throw things at me. I wanted you to scream and hit me and hit him and tell us we were sick and disgusting. I wanted you to see he loved me, not you, and to have the marriage annulled. That's all I wanted. You weren't supposed to die. You weren't supposed to run away. I know you. You were a fighter. You didn't run when you were angry. You stayed. You fought. You didn't run. Why did you run?"

"Je ne sais pas," Nora whispered, touching the tears on Kingsley's face. "I don't know why I ran that day. But I regret it. We could have worked it out, you and I. It would have taken time. It would have hurt for a long time. But we could have loved each other again. I shouldn't have died. And I'm sorry, Kingsley. *Mon frère. Petit frère.* I'm so sorry."

"I am, too," he whispered in French. *Moi, aussi.*

Nora kissed him on the cheek, both cheeks, and then she kissed his lips softly. As she kissed him, she reached behind his head and untied the blindfold. His eyes flew open and when he saw it was her, he kissed her back.

"Who am I?" Nora asked, making sure he saw her for who she really was. She dropped the French accent. The game was over.

"Nora. Mistress Nora."

"And who are you?"

"Kingsley Edge."

"And where are we?"

"Your dungeon in the club."

"Good. Just checking," she said, stroking his cheek with the back of her hand. "You did so good, King. So good."

"You…" He exhaled heavily, as if he'd been holding his breath all this time. "You sick, sadistic bitch."

"Who's your queen?" she asked, batting her eyelashes.

"You are."

"Now do I get my tip?"

"Majesty," Kingsley said between breaths, "you get more than the tip. You can have every inch."

18

Creating a Monster

NORA WRAPPED THE TIE AROUND KINGSLEY'S NECK and drew him to the throne. She pushed him down into it and with three lengths of rope, tied his hands over his head to the back of the chair and his ankles to the legs. His chest rose and fell with his heavy breaths. She could see the muscles in his stomach, tight and fluttering. Even bound to the chair he looked powerful, strong, dangerous, desirable.

"A throne fit for a king," Nora said, running her fingers over the ridges of muscle in his stomach. Her fingers traveled from his stomach over his hip. She took his cock in her hand and stroked his full length from base to tip and back down again with a firm grip, just the way he liked it. "I hope you don't mind my little game I played on you."

"Mind what? What we were talking about again?"

"Now I know how women become the power behind the throne. We just give the king a reach-around."

"A whore, a whore, my kingdom for a whore," Kingsley

said, and Nora laughed. He grinned broadly, his dark eyes shining with happiness and pleasure.

"Catharsis looks good on you, King," Nora said, dropping to her knees in front of him. "And since you're a king on a throne, I suppose I should kneel. I'd kiss your signet ring, but since you aren't wearing one, I'll have to find something else to kiss."

"I have a suggestion..."

Nora needed no suggestions and no encouragement. She licked Kingsley in his favorite spot to be licked—right under the head. With a firm hand she held and massaged the base while her tongue worked up and down him and all around. He panted and pulled against his bonds.

"No coming," she said, looking up at him. "That's an order."

"What if I do?"

"I'll get out the cock ring and force you to get hard again, and if I do that, one of us is going to have fun with your cock, and it's not going to be you."

"I was wrong about you. I thought you would be almost as bad as the priest to play with."

"And?"

"You're worse."

Such a compliment could only be rewarded with a round of passionate, thorough and vigorous cock-sucking. She stroked him as she sucked him, running her hands over his thighs and his scarred chest. It must have been the worst sort of torture to experience so much pleasure—pleasure that left him breathless and groaning—knowing he couldn't come lest he face a very unpleasant consequence. Kingsley hated cock rings almost as much as he hated collars. But they weren't a hard limit, which meant she could use one on him if he misbehaved.

She almost hoped he misbehaved.

But not yet. No coming yet. She wanted to enjoy this night for herself, for her own private reasons. Something bad had happened between her and Kingsley and she feared the rift between them would always be too vast for either of them to traverse to the other side. But here they were, baring their true selves to each other again, his masochistic side, her dominant side.

Nora saw Kingsley's fingers clench into fists. A thousand nights with him had trained her to recognize that meant he was close to coming. She stopped sucking him and sat back on her knees.

Slowly he opened his eyes.

"I hate you," Kingsley said.

"That hurts, King. That stings."

"Do you know what hurts? Having an erection and being two seconds from coming and your domme stops sucking you off."

"That is a very sad story. Tell me more."

"I've created a monster."

"You didn't create a monster," she said, leaning forward and putting both hands on either side of his head. She kissed his earlobe and bit it hard enough to make him flinch. "You just let her off her leash."

She kissed him on the mouth before he could answer. From inside the top of her right boot she pulled out a condom. Kingsley's head fell back, and he muttered a heartfelt *"Dieu merci."* Thank God.

Nora left the throne and grabbed her lube and a small vibrator that fit over her finger.

"Oh…tingly," Kingsley said as she rubbed him with the lubricant. She massaged him for a long time, long enough he started panting again. "How much longer are you going to torture me?" Kingsley asked, half smiling, half grimacing. He was brutally hard and still pulling on his wrist restraints. She wondered idly what he would do to her if he managed to escape his bonds. Probably a sex act still illegal in thirty-nine states. Too bad she'd tied him up so well.

"For the rest of your life, most likely," Nora said. "In one way or another."

"Good."

"Now sit there like a good boy while I use your cock to get off."

"Use me," Kingsley breathed. "Use all of me."

The throne was large enough for the both of them and then some. She straddled his lap, took his erection in her hand, and inch by inch, lowered herself onto him, sighing with pleasure as he filled her. He felt so good inside her, so big and hard and deep, it almost seemed like a crime to take money for this.

Not that that would stop her. She had a laptop to buy, after all.

Nora turned on the finger vibrator and pressed it to her swollen clitoris. Kingsley inhaled sharply.

"What did you feel?" she asked, as breathless now as he.

"You clenched," he said. "I could feel it all around me. Felt like being squeezed by a hand."

"You mean this?" She clamped her vaginal muscles down on him again and he gasped.

"That…is obscene," he said between breaths. "Do it again."

"What do we say when we want our Mistress to use her pussy to massage our cock?"

"*S'il vous plaît, Maîtresse?* You are the most beautiful mistress in the world and my body belongs to you for the next…" He glanced over her shoulder to the pendulum clock on the wall. "Twenty-three minutes."

"Better make the most of you, then."

She rocked her hips forward, the vibrator buzzing against

her clitoris. Beneath her, Kingsley lifted his hips, moving with her and against her in slow undulations. Every thirty seconds or so she would concentrate solely on her inner muscles and clench them tight. Every time she did it, Kingsley rewarded her with a sharp intake of air. She cupped the back of his neck and kissed him again. Locked together like this, she couldn't move much, but she didn't have to or want to. Right now she wanted to stop time, rush nothing, enjoy every inch and every second and every shuddering ragged breath.

"It's good to be in you again..." he murmured against her lips. "You stayed away too long."

"I'm back now."

"You won't leave again?"

"Of course not. Who would beat the hell out of you if I did?"

"Life," he said. And it was such an adorably cynical French thing to say that Nora laughed and kissed him.

The kiss turned passionate, then torrid. Her blood burned in her veins and she gripped Kingsley's shoulder to ride out the orgasm that tore through her, sending currents of electricity in waves and spikes and delicious tremors.

As she caught her breath, she managed to ask him, "Did you come, too?"

"*Non.*"

"You didn't?" As hard as Nora came, she assumed everyone else in the world had orgasmed, as well.

"You haven't given me permission to come."

"Oops. I knew I was forgetting something." She reached above his head and untied his hands from the top of the throne. She lifted herself off him and knelt between his knees. "I'm letting you go but only to change positions."

"I will fuck you in any position you name as long as you let me come," he said.

"Don't tempt me. I have new suspension toys to try out," she said, glancing up at the ceiling where the suspension rig awaited its first victim. "How do you want to fuck me?" she asked, as she unstrapped both his ankles. Kingsley reached down and held out his hand. She took it and he pulled her to him.

"I can have you? Any way I want?" he asked.

"I think you've earned it." She wrapped her arms around his shoulders and pressed her breasts to his chest. His skin was so hot it burned to the touch. Or was that her? Weeks ago he'd warned her that she'd never have the physical strength of a man, and he proved it by lifting her easily off her feet. She twined her legs around his back instinctively and he turned them both, pushing her back into the throne and draping her legs over each chair arm. She flinched when he penetrated again. He was so deep she felt him against her cervix. When he thrust again, however, he hit every spot she wanted him to hit. He was kneeling on the seat of the throne, pinning her to the back, pushing into her with long but fast thrusts. Nora clung to his shoulders, and he held her in place by her hips. She felt so wet and so open that she would have let him pound her like this all night if he wanted. They were both switches, her and Kingsley, and in this heated moment she thanked God for making her this way. She could be like Kingsley and have it all. Kingsley had a submissive he owned, Juliette, and could play with whomever he wanted as long as he gave his nights to her. In secret he had Nora who would be his Mistress, his Queen of Pain. And she could have that, as well. Clients to dominate, Kingsley to brutalize and use for her own private pleasure. And maybe if and when she needed it, she could ask Kingsley to hurt her and to use her just like this—pushing her back to the wall and fucking her raw. Oh, yes, it would be good to be the queen.

"Please, *Maîtresse*," Kingsley said, his voice sounding pained.

"Come," she said. "Whenever you're ready, come for me. I want it."

He increased the speed and pressure of his thrusts and Nora kissed his neck. At the instant she knew he was about to come, she sunk her teeth deep into his shoulder, hard enough to break the skin. Kingsley let out a beautiful wounded cry and shuddered in her arms. Entangled in each other's arms and legs, they eased into the seat of the throne, the king and queen, spent but united.

"Vampire," he teased, touching the bite mark on his shoulder.

"Not a vampire," she said. "A tiger, remember?"

Kingsley touched her face and pressed his lips to the top of her breasts.

"Certainly not a kitten anymore..."

When they had both come to their senses again, Nora ordered Kingsley to dress. In front of her, of course, while she watched the show.

"I'm going to enjoy being a dominatrix," she said, taking the two thousand dollars out of her corset and fanning herself with it. "Torturing men, orgasms, money—my three favorite things."

"No fucking your other clients," he reminded her. "I'm a king, not a pimp. Don't get me arrested for pandering."

"Speaking of sex for money... Thorny came to see me today."

"Did he?"

"He says Milady is planning on fucking with me."

"I could have told you that."

"What do you think she'll do to me?"

"I don't know, but if she's anything like you, she'll find your rawest wound and pour salt on it."

"Søren's my rawest wound."

"Then I think you're safe," Kingsley said. "He gave away his entire family fortune to me and his sisters. If she thinks she can buy his obedience for a few thousand dollars, she doesn't know who she's dealing with."

"Speaking of a few thousand dollars… I believe you said something about a tip if I broke you? Didn't you? I think it's fair to say I broke you."

"Because I wanted to be broken."

Nora waved her hand, beckoning him to pay up.

Kingsley sighed, pulled out his wallet and passed her ten more hundred-dollar bills.

"My best friend is named Benjamin," she said. "I do so love that man."

"Enjoy that tip. I probably won't ever tip you again. The French don't tip." He pulled on his trousers and left them open while he tucked in his shirt. Watching Kingsley get dressed was almost as erotic as watching him get undressed.

"You know I earned it."

"You earned it by being a sick, twisted mind-fucker. I'd kill anyone else who tried that trick on me, including *le prêtre*."

"It's all your fault for telling me I sound like your sister when I use a French accent. You should have known I'd use that against you in a session someday."

"Maybe I wanted you to."

"Did you?"

"Fuck, no. But I'm glad you did," he said, taking his jacket off the hook. "I wouldn't talk to anyone but you about it, but I think of her more than I want to. Especially when he and I are fighting. It brings back bad memories, and she's in many of my bad memories."

"I'm proud of you," she said, watching as he pulled on his jacket and flipped the collar and lapels into place. He looked so much younger than his forty years now, vibrant, bright-eyed and thoroughly fucked.

"For what? For surviving your little mind game?"

"For not letting Søren leave the priesthood for you when he offered."

"It wasn't me he was offering to leave the church for. It was some old idea of me he must have had. Kingsley, his sixteen-year-old slave who would have died for him. I love him," Kingsley said, pulling on his jacket. "You know it. I know it. He knows it. I was born to fall in love with him, and I lived in love with him and I will die still in love with him. But fuck him if he thinks that means I'm willing to be someone I'm not for him."

"Same here," Nora said, raising an imaginary wineglass in a toast. "He told me I wasn't allowed to see you anymore. We all have our breaking points. That was mine."

"Good girl," Kingsley said. "Maybe someday that blond prick will learn we don't exist for his pleasure."

"If he does learn...then what?"

"Then we'll need a bigger throne. One that'll hold a king, queen and a god. Or at least a man who thinks he is."

Nora laughed. "Glad I got the throne. It's nice and sturdy. Good for bondage. Good for fucking."

"Oh, speaking of the throne, Mistress Nora..."

"Yes?" Nora asked as Kingsley finished pulling on his boots.

"It cost ten thousand dollars."

"Quality isn't cheap. And Ikea does not sell thrones. I've looked."

"It put you over budget. By..." He paused as if counting in his head. "Three thousand dollars."

He snatched the money out of her hand.

"Kingsley!"

"Don't forget, *mon canard*," he said, "you aren't the only sadist in this room."

With a wink, he was his old self again, arrogant and lewd.

"Oh, you bastard."

"I am," he said without shame. "But this may cheer you up. You're ready."

"You sure about that?" she asked.

"Considering the Midsummer Night's Fling is in two nights? You better be."

"I will be. I hope."

"I'll show myself out." He strolled from the dungeon as casually as he'd entered it. He called back to her, "Sweep up this fucking glass you broke before someone gets hurt."

"Yes, boss." She sighed.

Nora looked down at her now empty hand.

Well, so much for her new laptop.

19

The Glass Locket

THE EVENING OF THE MIDSUMMER NIGHT'S FLING, Nora went to her dungeon at The 8th Circle to wait for Kingsley. Once he arrived, they would go upstairs to the elevator and make their descent into the pit where the party already raged. When Nora entered her suite, she lit a lamp on the bedside table and found a box on her bed.

A rectangular box, it was wrapped in plain brown paper and string. Warily, fearing a trick or trap from Milady, Nora pulled the little white card from the little white envelope and read the words written on it.

"Finish your Ruth and Boaz story."

It wasn't signed.

Ruth and Boaz story? Oh, yes, her Ruth and Boaz story. She'd been a senior in high school when a priest, subbing in for their AP English teacher, had given them busy work while he wrote his homily for that Sunday. "Compose a short story with characters from the Bible" was the entirety of Father Jones's assignment.

Nora, still Eleanor back then, chose to write about Ruth and Boaz from the Book of Ruth because two days earlier she and Søren had been talking about it. Eleanor had asked if there were any books of the Bible that were as sexy as the Book of Esther, and Søren replied that some interesting erotic things happened between Ruth and Boaz on the threshing floor. When Eleanor read the book, she'd walked away disappointed and gone to Søren's office to complain.

"What the fuck did I just read?" Eleanor demanded. "Was that entire book about wheat?"

Søren looked up from his work and eyed her with amusement.

"You have to read between the lines," he'd said.

"Ruth and Naomi are poor."

"Yes."

"Naomi is Ruth's mother-in-law and Ruth's husband is dead, right?"

"Correct."

"Naomi thinks Boaz, the rich farmer, has a crush on Ruth because he gave her extra wheat."

"Not quite a dozen roses but when you're nearly starving, wheat makes for a more welcome bouquet. It was Boaz's way of showing he cared about Ruth and her needs."

"So Naomi says Boaz is Ruth's closest relative so she should pretty herself up and go to Boaz and take off his shoes while he's sleeping? None of that made any sense."

"Boaz was related to Ruth's late husband, and according to the Levirate law, it was the male next of kin's duty to marry a childless widow and give her sons. Another man was a closer relative than Boaz, but it was Boaz who Naomi wanted for Ruth. She sent Ruth to seduce Boaz so Boaz would marry Ruth and not the other kinsman. If Ruth and Boaz had already been intimate, it gave Boaz an incentive to marry her quickly."

"But what about the shoes thing? Naomi told Ruth to go to the threshing floor where Boaz is sleeping and 'uncover his feet.' Feet are not sexy."

"It is if you know the word 'feet' is a euphemism in this instance."

"For what?"

"Use your imagination."

"I'd rather you demonstrate," she said. "Again."

Søren gave her a wilting glare.

"Don't look at me like that. You're the one who put your fingers in my shoe," she said. The previous weekend she'd gone to Søren's father's funeral with him and *things* had happened.

"Are you planning on mentioning that fact every day?"

"Until it happens again."

"Eleanor—"

"Better than thinking about Dad, right?" she asked. Her own father had been dead for a week. She still didn't know how to feel about it so she tried not to feel anything.

Søren's expression softened. He walked to her where she stood in the doorway of his office and faced her across the threshold.

"You and I seem to have the same coping mechanism," he said.

"What? You've been thinking about that night, too? Our night?"

"Better than thinking about my father."

Søren touched her face, and she looked up and into his eyes. She sensed him struggling to hold back, to stop himself from kissing her, touching her, doing everything they'd done together that night at his family's home and more.

"Penis," Søren said.

"Well, if you're offering…"

Søren ignored her. "Many biblical scholars believe the phrase 'uncover his feet' in the Book of Ruth is a euphemism for male genitals," Søren said. He chucked her lightly under the chin and took a small step back—breathing room for both of them.

"So Naomi told Ruth to sneak into the threshing room while Boaz was asleep and uncover his dick and wait for him to wake up and bone her?" Eleanor asked.

"A fair synopsis."

"And that worked?"

"When a man wakes up in the middle of the night with an erection and a beautiful woman lying beside him, things of a biblical nature can occur."

"Søren?"

"Yes, Eleanor?"

"Your threshing floor or mine?"

Søren put his mouth at her ear. Eleanor closed her eyes and braced for a kiss.

"Out of my office," he whispered. "Now."

The conversation was still fresh in her mind, so when Father Jones told them to spend the class period writing a story with Bible characters, she knew just what to write.

"I got it," Naomi said. "I know exactly how we can get you a meal ticket. I mean, a husband. That guy, Boaz. He's cute, right?"

"I wouldn't throw him out of bed for eating wheat crackers."

"Good. This is what I want you to do. Take a bath. Put on your best dress. Boaz is working late tonight so he'll be sleeping on the threshing floor. You sneak in after dark and uncover his feet. When he wakes up, tell him who you are and that he should marry you. Also, pick up some extra wheat while you're there. How's that for a plan?"

"Uncover his feet? Why would I uncover his feet?"

"You know, uncover his feet." Naomi winked at her.

"Am I trying to make his toes cold or something so he'll wake up?"

"No. His FEET. Uncover his FEET."

"I still don't know—"

"His penis, Ruth. I'm talking about his penis. His dick. His cock. His shaft. His lovestick. His staff of manliness."

"You could have just said that."

"Uncover his dick and cozy up to it while he's sleeping. Then when he wakes up hard as a rock and you're right next to him, he'll want you. Let him have you. Poor guy probably hasn't gotten laid in a while and he'll want it again so much that by tomorrow evening, you'll have him for a husband."

"Good plan. Great plan. But can we go back over the part where I take his dick out of his clothes while he's unconscious?"

Eleanor had so much fun with her story she'd forgotten it was a school assignment until Father Jones, called Father Bones because of his near skeletal frame, asked everyone to turn in their papers. As he was a substitute, Eleanor doubted he'd even read their stories. Typical busy work, right?

Wrong.

The next day Eleanor found herself hauled before the principal, vice principal and the school's elderly guidance counselor, Mrs. Oates. Apparently Eleanor's intimate descriptions of sexual intercourse—including a threshing-floor blow job—between a young widow and an older man had convinced the administration she was, in fact, sexually active herself. As she was an underage, unmarried Catholic high school student who'd signed the school's honor code, this didn't go over well. When they'd threatened to call her mother, Eleanor had begged them to instead call her priest.

She'd never heard a more welcome sound in her life than the roar of a Ducati motorcycle engine outside her school principal's office.

"What did she do this time?" Søren asked as he stepped into the office.

"I—" Eleanor began, but it was as far as she got.

"Not you," Søren said. "Anyone but Eleanor, please."

The principal explained the situation—the graphic story, the sexual content, the specificity of intimate detail. Søren had taken the story from the principal and sat in a chair reading it while everyone watched and waited for his verdict. Apart from her, Søren was the youngest person in the room by twenty years at least and yet he had an aura of authority about him. Everyone deferred to him. If he couldn't get her out of this, no one could.

"You didn't finish the story, Eleanor," he said at last.

"It's a good thing she didn't," Father Jones said. "It's bad enough as it is."

"Bad? I thought it was quite good."

"Good?" Father Jones nearly choked on the word. "It's sexually explicit. It's a Bible assignment, not *Penthouse* Letters."

"Did you tell students they couldn't put sexual content into their stories?" Søren had asked them.

"It's not the content so much as the implication," the guidance counselor said in her most placating voice. "No one could write sex that *descriptively* if they weren't having it. Miss Schreiber, like all students, signed an honor code. Sex outside of marriage is a violation of the code."

"I suppose Ruth wouldn't be welcome at this school, then. Neither would Queen Esther, Tamar or King David."

"Father Stearns," Mrs. Oates, the guidance counselor, said, "we all know that Eleanor's father died recently, and we were disturbed by certain elements in the story. Ruth referring to Boaz as her father during intercourse, for one."

Eleanor started to open her mouth to defend herself. Søren raised his hand to silence her.

"I believe you're referring to the dialogue exchange wherein Boaz says, 'Who's your Daddy?' and Ruth responds, 'You are, Bobo'?"

"Well...yes," Mrs. Oates said, blushing.

Søren turned to Eleanor. "Sorry," she mouthed at him and resisted the urge to call him "Bobo." Søren sighed, and looked at her guidance counselor.

"'Who's your Daddy?'" Søren repeated. "That is Eleanor's supposed cry for help?"

The guidance counselor attempted an answer but the principal interrupted.

"Writing such a story seems like odd behavior for a young woman whose father was killed last week. Our condolences, of course, but you understand our concern?"

"My father died recently, and given the chance I might have danced an Irish jig on his grave so I can hardly judge Eleanor for being relieved her criminal of a father has gone to whatever circle of hell is reserved for men who force their children to commit felonies for them. And if Eleanor were sexually abused by her father in any way, she would have told me. Correct, Eleanor?"

"Correct. He never touched me like that. I'd still be puking if he had."

"There we have it," Søren said. "Are we done?"

"Not quite," the principal said. "We still—"

"May I see the other stories the students wrote?"

Father Jones and the principal looked at each other before passing Søren a sheaf of papers. For the next hour, Søren read all twenty-one stories while everyone waited. Eleanor took her homework out and pretended to do something to it. On either side of him, Søren made two piles. When he finished reading them he held up the pile on the left.

"You have a problem," Søren said.

"What is that?" the principal asked.

"You have nine students in your AP English class who are murderers."

"What?"

"Nine stories written by Eleanor's classmates contain explicit depictions of killing human beings—three crucifixions, two decapitations and various and sundry other brutal deaths. You should call the police right now and have those students arrested."

Søren tossed the stories onto the principal's desk.

Silence reigned in the room until Father Jones spoke up.

"Father Stearns, with all due respect, there's a difference between those stories and Miss Schreiber's."

"There is, yes," Søren said. "Those stories are written by boys. Interesting that it's a female student being singled out for writing something inappropriate when none of the male students were."

"Boys like wars and violence and that sort of thing," the principal said. "It's natural."

"It's also natural for teenagers to be curious about sex. Also, consensual sex between two adults—which Ruth and Boaz were—isn't illegal," Søren said. "Killing someone is, however. Now you either give Eleanor a passing grade for her story and let her return to class, or you call the police and have those nine male students arrested."

"We are not having students arrested," her principal said. "The boys wrote Bible stories—"

"As did Eleanor."

"If she's having sex, which she clearly is if she's writing this sort of material, that's an honor code violation—"

"Forgive me for speaking bluntly," Søren said. "I was married and widowed before I joined the Jesuits. I'm well aware of the mechanics of sexual intercourse, and the act that

Eleanor describes in her story could only be accomplished if Ruth were double-jointed and Boaz's 'foot' thirteen to fifteen inches long. Writing about sex doesn't necessarily mean one is having it."

"Perhaps," the guidance counselor said gently, "if she would submit to a psychological and medical examination, then—"

Søren stood up. She'd often seen him using his height to his advantage and today he took full advantage of all six foot four inches of him.

"If anyone lays a hand on Eleanor or any other underage member of my congregation without my permission, you will have to answer to me *and* the American Civil Liberties Union." Søren looked around the room defying anyone to contradict him. No one spoke. "Eleanor, you can go back to class. Later you and I will have a talk about what sort of writing is and is not appropriate for school assignments. Yes?"

"Yes, Father Stearns." Since no one stopped her, she left the office. She didn't go back to class, however, but waited in the hall. Five minutes later Søren walked out of the principal's office with a look in his eyes that could be described as murderous.

"They're lucky Jesuits are pacifists," he said as he zipped up his motorcycle jacket over his clericals. "Why aren't you in class?"

"I wanted to thank you," she said, walking beside him to the glass double doors at the front of the school.

"You can thank me by graduating before we have to go through this nonsense again."

She laughed. "Four more months. Thanks for hauling my ass out of the fire again."

"Your ass is my ass. If it's going to get burned, I'll do the burning."

"Aww… You say the sweetest things, Blondie," she said,

standing by the double doors. "You know, if they'd made me take my clothes off for a doctor, they'd see handprint bruises on my thighs left by a certain big blond sadist we both know and love."

"The bruises haven't faded yet?" Søren didn't seem pleased to hear that.

"Not completely. They're in the gross and yellow stage."

Søren paused by the front door. "Are you still comfortable with what happened that night?"

"Comfortable with what? That I fooled around with my priest at his father's funeral a week and a half ago?"

"I admit I never intended us to be that intimate that soon. I don't regret it. But I'm still reeling a bit." It was a humble confession and it touched her heart to hear he was as affected by what happened as she was. Perhaps even more so.

"I know it's been a long time since you've been with someone...you know, like that."

"A very long time," he said quietly.

"I don't know about you, but I can't wait to do it again. I mean, the fooling around part. Not the funeral part."

Søren smiled at her. "Later. After you graduate."

"Then what?"

Søren reached into his pocket and pulled out something that looked like part of a weed.

"I intended to give you this later."

"What is it?" She looked at the pale brown plant in her hand.

"The head of a stalk of wheat," he said with a wink. "When you're ready, we can revisit my threshing floor."

Then he got on his Ducati and turned the key.

"Finish your Ruth and Boaz story," he ordered. "And it might be sooner rather than later."

Then he rode away, taking her heart with him.

★ ★ ★

With shaking hands Nora untied the cord on the box and ripped off the plain brown paper.

"Goddammit, Søren..."

It was a laptop. Of course it was. Of course he'd found a way to give her the thing she most needed, her heart's desire. But how? How had he paid for this? What had he done? Did he borrow money from his sister Claire? Or Kingsley? Did he sell some valuable Stearns family antique? Did the priest sell his fucking plasma? Nobody had that much plasma.

"Maîtresse?"

Nora turned and found Kingsley standing in her dungeon doorway. He looked resplendent tonight in Regency-era British military dress with obscenely tight white trousers and his saddle-brown Hessian boots. She appreciated how much it must have hurt the Frenchman to dress in British regimentals, but the red of his coat matched the red of her corset and boots. He looked ready to do battle. She didn't. She felt ready to surrender right into Søren's arms.

"King..." She couldn't breathe. She felt too much.

"Shall we?" he asked.

Nora looked down at the box in her hands. She nodded and set it back on the bed. Later she'd return for it. He held out his arm, and she took it.

No going back now.

"Are you ready?" Kingsley asked as they took the back way upstairs to the elevator.

"No," she said.

Kingsley looked at her with some concern. "You have five minutes to get ready."

"I..." She looked around and pulled Kingsley between the coat-check booth in the main hallway and the elevator. She pressed her head to the wall and breathed through her hands.

"What is it?"

"Kingsley, Søren gave me a laptop. A really expensive one. He took a vow of poverty. He has no money. How did he pay for it?"

"He didn't get it from me," Kingsley said with a shrug. "I suppose he could have asked his sister. Claire could have paid for it."

"Actually, I paid for it."

Nora whirled around and saw Milady standing by the elevator wearing an elegant Regency-style dress of pure white silk. It almost looked like a wedding dress. But Nora paid no attention to her clothes, her perfectly coiffed thick black hair, her perfect pouty lips or her long eyelashes. No, Nora's eyes focused on the locket around Milady's neck. A glass memento mori locket, it was designed to hold a lock of hair from someone beloved now dead. But that's not what this locket held. Nora could see right into it.

Inside was a lock of golden-blond hair.

Søren's hair.

"Oh, you bitch…" Nora said with a smile. "He wouldn't."

"He did."

"Not a chance in hell."

"I told you everyone was for sale."

Milady laughed. No, it wasn't a laugh. It was a giggle, cute and girlish. It enraged Nora. She charged forward and Kingsley grabbed her arm, stopping her.

"Not here," he said into her ear. "Save it for the game."

"It's not a game anymore," Nora said, glaring into Milady's soul. That bitch had touched Søren. Even if all she'd done was take a pair of scissors to his hair, she was still a dead woman. She should have stabbed herself in the heart with those scissors she'd used on Søren's hair. It would have saved Nora the trouble of doing it for her.

"You don't get to touch my priest," Nora said to Milady.

"It's too late for that. You fucked with me and my favorite toy. I fucked with you and your favorite toy. But if it's any consolation I consider us even now. Do you?"

"No."

"Play on, then."

Milady, still giggling, stepped into the elevator. When the doors closed behind her, Nora looked at Kingsley.

"He wouldn't…" She looked at Kingsley. "No way would he submit to that woman or any woman or anyone on earth just for money."

"You really think he did it for money?" Kingsley asked, arching his eyebrow, a look that said, *You know better than that.*

Nora leaned against the wall, resting her head on the fading red wallpaper. Why…why would Søren do this to her? Why would he give her a gift that cost more to her than buying it herself would have?

"Fucking sadist…" She exhaled the words.

"Mistress?" Kingsley said.

Nora stood up straight and took a calming breath. Søren let Milady touch him. Fine. Very well. He had his reasons. Hopefully one of his reasons was that he wanted to inspire a murderous rage in her, which she would then take out on Milady. If so, it had worked.

Like a fucking charm.

"Okay, King," she said. "Now I'm ready."

When the one elevator that led down to the pit returned to the main floor, Nora was ready. It was the three of them all alone now—Kingsley, Nora and Nora's wild beating heart. Adrenaline surged through her body, uncontrolled. The nervousness might work in her favor. She'd heard of people who'd torn doors off burning cars and lifted fallen walls off people when hit with an adrenaline rush. She had no interest in tearing off doors or lifting walls. But she wouldn't mind tearing off Milady's head and throwing it against a wall. Such a thought gave her a grin, a wicked, wonderful grin.

The elevator began its descent. Then the doors opened. The sound of the crowd hit her like a storm wind. She straightened her shoulders, raised her chin, twirled her riding crop.

"She touched Søren."

"It seems to be the case," Kingsley said. "And what will you do about it, Your Majesty?"

Nora looked at Kingsley.

"Off with her head."

20

The Red Queen

KINGSLEY STEPPED OUT INTO THE DARKNESS AND THE cacophony first. He reached back for her but she didn't take his hand. On her own, without his help and without fear, she stepped across the threshold and stood at his side. Music roared from mountain-size speakers. She recognized the song. It was one of Kingsley's favorites, a perfect score to accompany a seduction, a beating, a sin, a confession and absolution in bed.

Time slowed down as they descended the stairs into the pit below. Between flashes of blue and red she could see Kingsley's pupils dilating as they adjusted to the low light. His lips parted slightly and she could see his chest rise with a breath. His face, handsome, imposing, unsmiling, wore the expression of a veteran soldier going into battle. Alert and unafraid.

Nora looked up and saw Griffin at the ledge of the VIP bar's balcony, staring down at her, watching her every move. He blew her a kiss. Mistress Irina, Kingsley's Russian dominatrix, quietly walked away from a man at a kneeling bench and fell into step behind her and Kingsley. A sign of allegiance no one

would miss. The trio walked on, their destination the elevator
that would take them to the VIP bar. Anything that would
happen would happen in those one hundred steps between the
stairs and the elevator. She sensed everyone around her knew
this. They were waiting, all of them. Waiting for whatever
was to happen. She recognized every face in the crowd, which
meant every face in the crowd recognized her. Kingsley had
made it known far and wide that the girl called Eleanor Schreiber no longer existed and a woman name Mistress Nora had
taken her place. The faces watching her smirked and rolled
their eyes. But no one spoke to them. No one stopped them.
Kingsley pressed on and the crowd parted for him as they always did. No one would dare defy the king. He could have
anyone banished from the city's kink community with a word.
They'd be personae non gratae, denied play at any club in the
city. And that was the punishment for a first strike. If someone did dare to piss off Kingsley Edge, they never did it twice.

So there was a chance, a slim chance, they would make it
to the elevator without anyone stopping her. They were halfway there already. Fifty steps away. She'd made this journey
countless times, Søren leading her through the crowd, her
head bowed in quiet submission. Now she walked it with her
head high, next to Kingsley, not behind him. Equals. Forty
steps. Thirty five. Almost there.

Nora saw Milady in the crowd standing next to a mountain
of a man. His head bent to her ear as she whispered to him.
No one else seemed to see what was happening. No one but
Nora. She knew what it meant, what the whispers signified.
There was no way in hell Nora would make it from here to
the elevator that easily.

The man stood up straight and stepped into their path,
blocking the way between the trio and the elevator. The three
of them stopped because the three of them had to. The crowd

pressed in around them, watching. Milady stood off to the side, smiling.

The music stopped.

"Bonsoir," Kingsley said, looking up at the mountain. He was six foot six if he was an inch, taller than both Kingsley and Søren. He had the build of a professional weightlifter, a night club bouncer, a linebacker, all shoulders, no neck. Nora guessed his weight at three-fifty—pure muscle and no mercy.

"Who's the new girl?" the man nicknamed Unbreakable asked.

"Show a little respect, Trent." Mistress Irina had never lost her Russian accent and it made every word she said sound twice as intimidating. That she called him by his real name, Trent, instead of his nickname meant she'd either tried and failed to break him herself or she was jonesing for her turn.

"For who? Her?" Trent pointed at Nora.

"Yes, her and King," Mistress Irina said. "You want to get out of our way?"

"I want to know who the new girl is, is what I want," Trent said. He crossed his arms over his chest, one slab of meat over another slab of meat.

Kingsley sighed. "Mistress Nora, this is Trent, otherwise known as Unbreakable for obvious reasons. Trent, this is—"

"Mistress Nora," she said, smiling because it was in her nature to smile at dumb animals. "A pleasure to beat you."

Trent barked a laugh.

"Beat me? You, little girl?"

"Yes, if you like. What's your safe word?"

"Mommy," he said, grinning like a rabid dog.

"That's cute. You're cute."

"And you're...short," Trent said. "You have nice tits, though."

"Thank you." Nora pushed her breasts up in her bustier. "My mom gave them to me."

"You kind of look familiar." Trent bent over and pretended to examine her face. Of course he knew who she was. Who didn't?

"I have one of those faces," Nora said.

"No... I know who you are. Aren't you the priest's little slut?"

"No, but I used to be the priest's big slut."

That got a laugh out of the crowd. Good.

"I think I saw him drag you on a leash through this club once on your hands and knees, didn't I?"

"No."

"That didn't happen?"

"Oh, it happened. But it happened more than once. He did that to me a lot."

Another laugh. If she kept the crowd laughing she'd own them all with or without a collar.

"So where is he? Where's your master?"

"He's probably at church right now alphabetizing his altar boys."

"Is that like sodomizing?" Trent asked.

"This is a different thing. It involves words and reading. You wouldn't understand."

"I've never heard you talk before. I liked it better when your master wouldn't let you speak."

"Too bad I don't have a master anymore, then. But you'll like me if you get to know me. I'm a very nice dominatrix."

"You're not a dominatrix. You're a dumb little slut playing dress-up. Nobody here is afraid of you. Nobody here is impressed by you. And nobody here wants you."

"That hurts. It really does. I could have sworn somebody

here wanted me. Did anybody here want me?" she shouted
to the crowd.

"Up here," Griffin called from the balcony. "I want you,
Mistress Nora."

"Thank you, Master Griffin," Nora called back. "You want
to tag team someone later?"

"Sure. Girl or guy?"

"Griffin's choice."

"Both then. Hurry up. I have a boner, and I want to use it
before I lose it."

"On my way," Nora called back and gave Griffin a salute.
She saw uncertainty on the faces around her. Kingsley saw her
as a dominatrix. Mistress Irina did. And now Master Griffin,
too? But Trent remained unmoved and unimpressed. "Could
you excuse us? We need to get to the elevator now so Griffin
and I can fuck some people up."

"Say *please*," Trent said, glaring down at her.

"Well, I suppose I could fuck some people up down here.
But Griffin's up there. So you should move. Right now. If you
don't move, I'll break your face, smash your balls and make
you cry in front of this entire assembly of perverts."

She stood up straight and tall—as tall as a woman who was
five foot three and wearing four-inch heels could stand—and
put her hands behind her back. From under the waistband of
her tight skirt she pulled out a cold piece of metal and slipped
it over her hand.

"You talk a very good game, little girl," Trent said. "I wish
I believed you. Might be nice to find a woman around here
with real balls."

"Are you giving me permission, then, to break your face
and crush your balls? Kingsley says I can't hit anyone without
their permission. I mean, unless it's self-defense. That's okay,
right?" She looked at Kingsley.

"Bien sûr," he said. "If he tries anything with you, you can kill him for all I care."

"Oh, goodie. Would you please try something with me, Trent?" Nora asked.

"If you insist," Trent said. He leaned his head back and spit at her.

Nora ducked the spit and used Trent's moment of distraction to bring her fist around, knuckles first like Kingsley had taught her. He'd told her to aim for the cheekbone but she slightly miscalculated and instead struck Trent in the nose. She felt it go soft under her hand, like a cracker turning to crumbs. She heard a scream and saw a spurt of blood like Mount Vesuvius erupting and Trent was Pompeii. Party over. Her boots were steel-tipped and as Trent raised his hands to cup his bloody nose, Nora kicked him in the testicles. In an instant he was on his side on the floor in the fetal position. The crowd gasped and moved away. Kingsley stood watching as she put her foot on Trent's neck and started to stand on it with her full weight.

"Mommy," he said. Except he didn't say it, he screamed it.

"Well, poo," Nora said, dramatically lifting her foot off his neck. "That didn't take long. And I was just getting warmed up."

"You broke my fucking nose, you bitch." He wailed the words.

"That's 'You broke my fucking nose, Mistress Bitch,' to you."

Trent tried to get up on his hands and knees. He reached for Kingsley's foot.

"Don't scuff my leather," Kingsley said, kicking Trent's hand away.

"King, she broke my nose."

"She told you she was going to, silly boy," Kingsley said. "Did you think she was joking?"

"I think he thought I was joking," Nora said. She did a little turn and looked around, the assembly watching in stony silence. "Do you all think I'm joking?"

No one dared speak.

Nora continued. "Does that look like I'm joking?" She pointed down at Trent, who was still cradling his bloody nose on the floor.

Still…no one spoke.

"Look," Nora said, smiling at the crowd. "I know. I know. You're all saying, 'That's Eleanor, Søren's submissive.' I know a lot of you respect him and fear him. I know a lot of you know what sort of sadist he is. No one knows that better than I do. I respect him, too, of course. I learned a lot from him. And the most important thing I learned was this—if someone fucks with you, you show them the wrath of God. This is what the wrath of God looks like." Nora pointed to Trent in the fetal position at her feet. Unbreakable was thoroughly broken. "Does anyone else want to piss me off tonight? Anyone?"

No answer at all. No volunteers.

"I'm asking very little of you all," Nora said. "I'm not asking for your respect or your loyalty or your understanding. If I deserve that, then I'll earn it in time. I don't want much. All I want is to walk from here to that elevator without touching the ground. Is that too much to ask? I'd say about twenty male bodies flat on their stomachs should do it. Leave about a foot between each."

Everyone stared in silence, wide-eyed and uncertain.

"Am I speaking Greek?" Nora asked. "Human red carpet. On the floor. Right now or Kingsley and I will start choosing people at random to ban from the club for a solid year. Everyone obeys or everyone is punished. You all decide." She snapped her fingers and pointed. A young man stepped forward and lay on the ground halfway between Trent and the elevator. Another man, quite a bit older but still handsome, took his shirt off and lay down a foot away from the younger man. One by one by one, a bridge of sorts built itself between her and the elevator.

Nora stepped on Trent, who grunted under her weight on his back. From Trent she stepped onto the young man's back, careful not to hurt him. Not too much anyway. Kingsley followed behind her and so did Mistress Irina. They, too, used the human bridge Nora had built. The eleventh step on the bridge wasn't lying on his stomach but on his back. Nora recognized him as the very first person who had jumped to follow her order.

"You were very quick to obey," Nora said, looking down at the man. He had a black handkerchief tied over his hair like a pirate and he wore a black mask over his eyes and a black pirate's shirt. He lifted the shirt to his chest to offer her his stomach to stand on. "This pleases me."

"Don't forget," he said, grinning up at her. "Money up front."

Nora rolled her eyes before playfully kicking Thorny's side. "On your stomach, whore. That's an order."

He flipped over onto his stomach as ordered, wiggling his ass for her as he moved. She would deal with Thorny later— probably by fucking his brains out. But now she had to get to the elevator without anyone else stopping her. As she strolled along her human promenade, she heard grunts and gasps from beneath and behind her. Kingsley and Irina were using her walkway, as well. A much-needed reminder to the denizens of The 8th Circle where everyone stood. Kingsley, Nora and Irina stood on the denizens of The 8th Circle when they felt like it. That's where everyone stood.

They made it to the elevator and Kingsley and Irina stepped inside. But Nora stopped.

"*Maîtresse?*" Kingsley asked.

"One second. I forgot something."

Nora turned on her heel and walked back on her human body sidewalk to where Trent still lay on the floor.

"Let me see your face," Nora said. Groaning, Trent came up on his knees. She knew masochists like him, dangerous as wild horses until you broke them. But once broken, they were meek as lambs. Blood dripped from his nose. He wouldn't bleed to death. Probably.

She put her hand under his chin and smiled at him.

"Call me if you want to play again," she said. "I cost a thousand an hour."

Then, using the back of her hand, she wiped the blood off his face. She turned and saw Milady standing far off to the side, almost as if she were trying to hide.

Nora walked toward Milady and the crowd parted for her.

"Brass knuckles?" Milady asked. "That's cheating."

"It's my game. My rules." Nora wiped her bloody brass knuckles off on Milady's pristine white dress. "Look at that. The White Queen becomes the Red Queen," Nora said to her with a grin she hoped looked as maniacal as it felt. "And you have something that belongs to me."

"I do?"

"You do." Nora reached out, wrapped her fingers around the locket that contained Søren's hair and yanked it off.

"I want her removed," Kingsley said from inside the open iron elevator. "I watched her ignore a submissive's safe word during a whipping. She's henceforth banned from any of my clubs. *Au revoir*, Milady."

Two of Kingsley's bouncers, nearly the size of Trent, came forward.

"I can tell the world about your priest," Milady said. "And I will."

"You think Søren's stupid enough to come down here using his real name? What are you going to tell them anyway? That you paid two thousand dollars for a lock of his hair? Unless you fucked him, he didn't break any vows."

"He's fucked you."

"I've been gone for over a year. You've been here a year. You haven't seen him break any vows, have you?"

"Everyone here has seen you two together."

"I'm not afraid of you and neither is he," Nora said. "But you're afraid of me."

"I'm not afraid of you. You're a nobody." Milady laughed. Nora moved as if to punch her in the nose, brass knuckles bloody and shining. Milady squealed, turned and covered her face. Instinct, of course. Anyone would have done it, even Nora. But Nora hadn't done it. Milady had.

"Kidding," Nora said. "See? It pays to be an ex-submissive. We know how to take a hit without flinching."

Now the crowd around them laughed and laughed and laughed as the once-formidable dominatrix was reduced to squealing and hiding her face from Nora. From *Mistress* Nora.

Nora smiled. Milady looked afraid. Leaning in, Nora whispered a final farewell.

"Now we're even."

21

A Confession

DEFEATING MILADY HAD BEEN A BREEZE COMPARED to what Nora had to do the next day. She borrowed a car from Kingsley, drove to Wakefield, Connecticut, and walked through the heavy wooden front doors of Sacred Heart Catholic Church. She passed through the lobby—*narthex, Eleanor, it's called the narthex*—and headed to his office.

"Elle?"

Nora froze at the sound of a familiar voice. She turned and found Diane, Søren's secretary, striding down the hall toward her.

"Diane," Nora said, bracing for a hug. Diane could hug the life out of someone.

But Diane stopped three feet from her. No hugs were forthcoming.

Fuck.

"How are you, Elle? Haven't seen you in a while." Diane put her hands in her pockets. As if the lack of a hug wasn't tell enough…

"I went away for a year. Traveling."

"I see. And you're back now?"

"For a quick visit."

"I see."

"I see you see," Nora said. "You know, since that's the second time you said 'I see.'"

That tugged a small smile out of Diane.

"Something tells me you have something to say to me?" Nora waited, bracing herself.

Diane raised her hand to her head and breathed out hard.

"You were in my wedding." She said the words as if she were accusing Nora of committing a crime.

"The wedding he officiated," Nora reminded her.

"You could have told me."

"Sounds like somebody told you."

Diane took her by the arm and escorted her into the small office next to Søren's.

"He told you," Nora said in a whisper since Diane's office didn't have a door.

Diane turned to the window and nodded. She was ten years older than Nora, a wife, a mother, and so loyal to Søren that Nora already knew where this conversation would go.

"I love him," Diane said. "You know that."

"I do," Nora said. Diane had been one of Søren's first minor scandals at Sacred Heart. It was a snow-white conservative congregation and Diane was black and divorced. She'd had forty dollars in her checking account when Søren had hired her and the only thing that exceeded his loyalty to his secretary was her loyalty to him. "He loves you, too. I don't know how many times he's told me he couldn't run the church without you."

"I almost had to. Last year, he comes into the office looking like someone died, and he wouldn't tell me why. Not for a week. Not until I begged him on my knees—and that is not an exaggeration—did he tell me what happened. Twelve years I have worked for that man and I had no idea—none—that he had...you. Until you were gone."

"So are you mad at me or are you mad at him?"

"I wasn't mad at either of you. You're both adults. He said nothing much happened between the two of you until you were twenty."

"I was a virgin until I was twenty. Until him."

Diane winced.

"I'm sorry," Nora said, although she wasn't. "You probably don't want that image in your head. Look, I know you care about him and it must have been hard for you to learn he had a..."

"Mistress?"

"You wouldn't be the first person to call me that. Anyway, I know it was a shock for you, but he's—"

"Are you coming back to him?"

"What? Are you serious?"

"I am. Are you coming back to him?"

"I hadn't planned on it. Why?"

"Because he misses you. And he's not the same without you."

"Let me get this straight—you, a priest's secretary, are telling a priest's ex-lover to start sleeping with him again?"

"I don't judge him for having a relationship. The Bible says it is not good for man to be alone. But I... I don't. I don't want to see him in pain anymore."

"I don't want to be in pain anymore. Do you know how hard it is to be in love with a Catholic priest?"

"I can't imagine it's easy."

"It isn't. And before you decide I'm the bad guy for leaving him, you should know he pushed me away. He crossed a line with me, and I had no choice."

"He crossed a line with you?" Diane sounded dubious.

"He did."

"You were twenty when you slept with him the first time. A grown-ass woman. When I was twenty I was already on my first marriage. If you'd been fifteen, maybe I could sympathize here. But when it comes to talking about crossing lines, an adult woman who sleeps with a priest has no room to talk."

Nora smiled. "You know, Diane, he warned me the night of your wedding that if we ever got caught, I'd take the lion's share of the blame. Guess he was right."

"All I'm saying is that he needs you. He loves you. He says—"

"What do I say?"

Søren stood looming in the doorway.

Nora sighed. "You should let your secretary have a door to her office," Nora said.

"She doesn't want one. I've offered," Søren said.

"If I have a door, people will want to come in and close it and tell me things I don't want to hear. His job is taking care of those people and their problems. My job is taking care of him."

"Which you do admirably," Søren said to his long-suffering secretary. "Too admirably perhaps."

"Someone has to take care of you, right?" Diane asked. The question was a knife in Nora's stomach. The message was clear—Diane had to take care of him since Nora wasn't doing it anymore.

"Eleanor? I assume you're here to see me?"

"If you have a minute."

"I don't, actually. I have a date with some repentant sinners. But if you'd like to wait in my office, I'll be finished in an hour."

He turned on his heel and walked down the opposite hallway.

"He's hearing confessions now," Diane said. "Like he said, you can wait if you want."

"No. I don't want to wait. Excuse me."

She left Diane in her office and followed Søren down the hall. Sacred Heart had a traditional-style confessional booth, two doors on opposite sides and a screen in between. Once it had sat in the corner of the sanctuary but Søren had it moved to an alcove at the end of the west hallway that had once been a Chapel of Perpetual Adoration. It was a safer, quieter, more intimate spot for baring one's soul than the sanctuary. She stepped into the old chapel and shut the wooden door behind her. An engraved plaque on the door warned not to enter if the door was shut. No one would disturb them until she'd had her say.

Nora entered the side of the confessional reserved for the penitent.

"I'm here when you're ready to speak," Søren said from the other side of the booth. Although she couldn't see his face, she could tell from his voice he didn't know it was her.

"Oh, I'm ready to speak, Father."

She heard him sigh.

"Far be it from me to stop a sinner from confessing," he said.

"I'm actually here for your confession."

"Mine?"

"What happened between you and Milady?"

"Nothing you need to know about."

"She was wearing your hair in a locket around her neck, and now I have a laptop. These things are related."

"If you must know, I went to speak to her because she'd threatened us both. All of Kingsley's dominas are sane and reasonable women. I assumed I could reason with her. She said she had no intention of exposing me to anyone but was merely attempting to needle you. When I went to leave she asked me if she could have a lock of my hair. I told her no. She asked me if I would sell it to her. I remembered you were in great need of a computer so you could write your next book and that you thought it would cost two thousand dollars. I named my price. She paid it willingly."

"Did she touch you?"

"I don't believe you can cut someone's hair without touching that person."

"You know what I mean."

"Do you care if she did?"

"There are people who deserve to touch you and people who don't. She doesn't deserve to touch you."

"She kissed me. I let her."

"Did you like it?"

"I believe the standard saying is 'It was like being kissed by my sister,' but, of course, you know that means something entirely different coming from me."

"So you did like it?"

"No."

Nora closed her eyes tight. It would have almost been better if he had liked it. To imagine him sitting there, suffering through a kiss, closing his eyes and thinking of England, and all so she could have a fucking laptop which she could have bought for herself in a week or two...

"Why? Why did you do that, Søren?"

"I wanted to give you a gift."

"No, you wanted to make me jealous or make me angry or make me lose my mind. If you wanted to give me a gift you would have picked a bunch of goddamn daisies off the side of the road."

"You can't write a book with daisies," he said.

Nora wrapped her arms around her stomach, feeling sick and dizzy and torn.

"Do you like it?"

"It's perfect," she whispered. "It's exactly what I wanted."

"Diane picked it out. I'm something of a Luddite, as you know."

"Søren, I…" Nora was in an agony of indecision. "I'm not giving up my job and my life and coming back to you just because you bought me a gift or whatever that was. You know that, right?"

"Keep it. Use it. I paid dearly for it after all."

"I'll keep it," she promised. "I won't come back to you… but I will keep the gift."

"You'll come back to me when you're ready."

"I'm not going to be ready. And you have to get it out of your head that I'm the one who ran away from you because you lost your temper one night. You rejected me. I told you the truth about me, and you didn't want to hear it. If I came back to you, you would take me from me. You would take Nora from me, and I just found her. I'm not giving me up for you. I can't sacrifice so much of myself that there's nothing left to give back to you."

"You promised me forever, Eleanor."

"You can't give me everything any more than I can give you forever."

"I *can* give you everything. Whatever it takes, I will keep my promise to you."

"Call me Nora just once, and I'll believe that. Then I'll know you won't take from me everything I've worked for and fought for. Jesus, Søren, I broke a man's nose. I made a notorious dominatrix squeal like a little girl. I fucked with Kingsley's head so hard he cried. And I loved every second of it. Every single second. That's me. That's how I am now. And you want to take it from me."

"If you truly trusted me, you'd know that whatever I took from you, I would give back tenfold."

"Then you owe me a hundred years of dominance for the ten years of submission I gave you. And ten riding crops to replace the one you broke."

"Ten crops? I hope I have enough hair to sell."

"Don't even joke about that."

"Why not?"

Nora could barely get the words out. They backed up in her throat, a verbal bottleneck. She forced them through anyway.

"Because I love your hair."

"Eleanor... Little One...please..."

His words sounded as pained as her own.

Nora couldn't stand it any longer. She slipped out of her side of the booth and opened the door to his.

"Here. This belongs to you." She held out the glass locket that contained his lock of hair. Søren took it and tucked it in his pocket. He looked at her.

"So does this."

Søren took her by the wrist and yanked her to him, then shut the door behind them.

His kiss traveled to her mouth, and she opened to him. In such close quarters she had little room to move or breathe. Their bodies were pressed together, and she couldn't escape unless he let her. He seemed to have no intention of letting her.

"Come back to me," he said against her lips.

"I can't."

"Come back to me," he said, against her neck.

"I won't."

"Come back to me," he said, lifting her skirt to her hips.

"I don't..."

"You can't say it, can you?" He slipped his hands into her panties and ripped them off with one fierce tear. "You can't say you don't want to come back to me because we both know you do."

"Not enough to do it."

"Not yet. But you will."

"Arrogant pr—" Before she could finish the insult, Søren's mouth was on hers again, devouring it with kisses. She tasted his tongue, smelled the winter on his skin and surrendered. When he dug his fingers into her thighs and squeezed them hard enough to leave bruises, she knew he meant to have her. Right here. Right now. And nothing would stop him unless she said her safe word. With his tongue in her mouth she couldn't speak, nor did she try to. She let him swallow her cries of pain because it was her pain he fed on, her pain that sustained him. Oh, but it fed her, too. And every cruel and beautiful thing he did to her, the gifts he gave her at once merciless and merciful, left her starving for him.

Søren dug his fingers into her hips, finding the pressure point that made her weak with pain. A skilled sadist, he could give her agony and leave her with not a single mark, except for the marks he left on her heart. Again he hurt her. Again he swallowed the cry of pain that rose in her throat. His hand moved between her thighs and eased her wet lips open, forcing her vagina to widen enough to take him. Her inner muscles protested at first but then opened for him, growing slick and ready in seconds. He didn't so much lift her off her feet as slide her up the smooth polished wood of the confessional to bring her down onto him, impaling her. Their bodies were locked tight together, her wetness sealing him to her, their backs against the walls as the smallness of the space forced them as close as two people could be. Her booted foot on the wall behind him was all it took to hold herself in place, and his hand at the side of her head and his full length inside her was all it took to hold her to him. He moved, barely an inch, and drank the cry of pleasure from her lips. They couldn't make a sound, the two of them. Not here. Not now. She couldn't risk even a whimper, not if someone waited outside.

In heated silence Søren unbuttoned her white silk blouse and unhooked her bra in the front. Her breasts spilled out as he released the clasp, and her nipples hardened as they brushed the rough fabric of his clericals, an exquisite teasing torture.

Nora didn't know which one of them, her or Søren, moved first, but within her body she felt her vaginal muscles tightening on him, clenching him, holding him inside her. Everything seemed to happen in slow motion, as if they moved through honey or deep water. If he thrust roughly into her, the wood would creak, the sound would be overheard. All they could do was push against each other, slowly, willfully, methodically, making no noise, muting even their breaths by breathing into each other's mouths.

Her breasts felt swollen with the need to be touched and sucked. She arched her back and he took her nipple in his mouth. She bit the fabric at his shoulder to muffle her moan. Inside she burned and pulsed, burned and clenched. Her clitoris ached and throbbed, desperately needing attention. Her hips tilted upward and his cock shifted inside her, sliding in deeper. She stiffened, closed her eyes, tilted her hips again. Tiny explosions of pleasure ripped through her. She felt weightless, suspended as she was between his body and the wall behind her, dizzy with pleasure, near to bursting with the fullness of him inside her. The less she could move, the more intense every movement felt.

Søren's teeth scraped her nipple, and she flinched with pleasure. His warm mouth moved up her breast, up her chest, up her neck and to her ear.

In a whisper no one but her and God could hear, he said, "I should have fucked you when you were fifteen."

Were it any other place, any other time, Nora would have groaned at the words. But she swallowed the sound. Her head fell back against the wall, and Søren cradled it in his palm. The act, tender and protective, undid her.

Søren gathered her closer to him. They couldn't be any closer than they were now, and he pumped into her until she came with a noiseless whimper, her vagina thrumming around him in a thousand, a million little spasms. With a few final deep thrusts he came inside her.

Panting together they remained entwined until Søren finally lowered Nora to her feet. She adjusted her clothes, buttoned her blouse, felt his warm fluid on her inner thighs but didn't wipe it off. Right now, this second, she needed to leave, but she stayed because he kissed her again, she stayed because they'd just made love in the confessional, which was something she'd never dreamed they'd do because Søren was usually so careful, and if he wasn't careful today it was because, as Kingsley had warned, he was losing control of himself out of his grief over losing her. He would take every chance he could to be with her and would regret the chances he missed. She knew this because she knew him, and it was how she felt, too.

Nora pulled away from his kisses and looked into his eyes, the color of steel but not as hard. His guard was down, his eyes soft, his face open and waiting for her words. He looked young for a second, younger than she'd ever seen him. Hope made him young. Fear made him vulnerable.

"I can't be in your debt. I refuse to be in your debt," she said. "Even your gifts aren't gifts. They always come with a price." He'd sold his own hair and let a woman he didn't know, didn't desire, kiss him and all to give her a gift. The debt she owed him was so high she'd pay any price to be back in the black.

"Everything has a price," he said, his hands caressing her neck, her throat. She looked down and discovered he'd put the locket on her without her even realizing it.

"I can't wear this," she said, clutching the locket in her hand. She pulled to yank it off. This time she didn't just bend the clasp, she broke it. "I won't wear your collar. I won't be in your debt."

"Too late," he said.

"Give me an order. Order me to do anything, and I'll do it. Then we'll be even, you and I. Whatever you want. One order. I'll obey it."

She knew what he would order her to do. She knew he would order her to come back to him. Standing there with her hands on his chest and his heart beating wildly under her palm, she knew she'd do it. She would go back to him when he gave the order. Oh, she would hate herself for it and Kingsley would hate her for it…but she would be at peace again at least. The peace of the runaway convict recaptured by the guards and hauled back to prison where she belonged.

She braced herself for the order, the inevitable order to return to him and be his again and wear his collar. For she had no doubt in her mind, none at all, that he would order her back to him.

"Write another book," Søren said.

Nora's eyes flashed at him in shock. That was his order. She knew that tone. She knew that look.

"Yes, sir."

She wrote another book.

22

A Houseguest

Two Years Later

NORA'S FIRST THOUGHT UPON WAKING WAS, *THERE is a teenage boy in my house.*

She lay in bed and thought about that thought, thought about what to do with it and him. He appeared to be sound asleep and dreaming. No reason to disturb him yet, so Nora let him be.

In her kitchen she brewed a pot of coffee. While she waited she checked her hotline phone. No missed calls. No messages. So the silent treatment would continue. Fine. If that's what Kingsley wanted, who was she to argue? Without him calling her all the time and pouting until she took on this rich new client and that important new client, she'd actually gotten to spend a little time in her house.

Her house. All hers. Although she'd lived in the house for over a year, she still couldn't believe it was hers. Kingsley hated her house as much as she loved it. He'd pitched a full-blown

French fit when she'd told him she was moving out the day after she paid the down payment in cash and signed the contract. Having both his submissive and his dominant under the same roof was convenient for Kingsley but confining for her. She wanted her privacy, she'd told Kingsley. Needed it to save her sanity. And it was his own fault she'd bought the house anyway. He'd sent her all the way to Westport, Connecticut, for a session with a client, the dean of a small liberal arts college right outside of town. After her session with him, she'd taken a wrong turn and found herself in a residential neighborhood. When she saw a Catholic church on the corner, she'd stopped to ask directions. She'd done it instinctively, sought advice and help inside the church. The secretary had drawn her a map to the interstate on the back of a pamphlet with the title "You *Can* Go Home Again—A Roadmap for Lapsed Catholics." When she asked the secretary how she'd guessed Nora was a lapsed Catholic, the older woman had smiled and said, "You started to dip your fingers in the holy water when you walked in and you stopped yourself."

"An old habit," Nora had said, guilty as charged.

"He misses you, you know," the woman said as Nora started out of the office with her roadmap.

Nora froze, the words chilling her to the bone.

"He's better off without me," Nora told her. "Whether he knows that or not, he is."

"God isn't better off without any of His children in His life and His church. He wants them all home, even His prodigals. Especially His prodigals."

Nora had given her a smile, a sad smile although she hadn't planned on being sad that day.

"I wasn't talking about God."

The neighborhood St. Luke's belonged to was a quaint and lovely one, the day around her bright and shining, so Nora went for a walk. She lived most of her life at night and indoors. Sunlight had become a rare luxury, and she needed more of it. Griffin wanted her to go to Miami with him soon, and she considered the offer as she walked.

Then she'd seen the house.

A Tudor home, two-story, black beams and off-white stucco. An old New England cottage with beautiful bones and a price tag in her budget. It even had an oak tree—the biggest, greenest, oldest, most beautiful gnarled old oak tree she'd ever seen and right in the corner of the yard. An oak tree. She could have her own oak tree. So what if a Catholic church stood on the corner of the street, and if she lived here she'd be an easy forty-minute drive from Wakefield, Sacred Heart and Søren? That had nothing to do with her love for this house. It looked like a writer's house, she told herself. That was why she wanted it. She was a writer. A writer needed a writer's house.

But…there was one catch. She didn't pay a cent to live at Kingsley's. If she bought this house, this dream house of hers, she would never be able to quit working for Kingsley. Not unless a miracle happened, and she was suddenly making six or seven figures a year from her books. Buying a house meant making a commitment—not to the house as much as to the job that paid for it. Was she ready to accept she would be working as a professional domme for the next fifteen to thirty years of her life? If so, that meant she could never ever go back to Søren because he would make her quit working for Kingsley, which meant she couldn't afford the house.

She bought the house.

Therefore Mistress Nora she would remain until the house was paid off. Unless Kingsley fired her, of course. So far the silent treatment seemed to be the extent of her punishment, but that could change with the very next phone call from Kingsley—if it ever came.

She poured a cup of coffee and carried it into her office. She sat down at her computer and tried to work on her new book. When the words didn't come she gave up and tried writing something completely different.

She was going back to Him.

Nora stared at the words. Where had that come from?

She kept writing just to see where this was going.

She drove to His house and found Him at His piano. He was playing Beethoven—a good sign. It meant He'd been thinking of her.

"Why did you come here, Little One?" He asked, closing the fallboard over the keys.

"I came to give you a gift," she said. "Sir."

"Did you?"

"Hold out your hand. Close your eyes."

"I don't play this game," He said.

"Trust me, please. You can't win this game if you don't play it."

He smiled. "Just once, then. For you."

He closed His eyes and held out His hand. She laid her white collar on His palm.

"Open your eyes," she said.

He opened them and saw the collar in His hand.

"I give up. I surrender."

At first He did nothing but gaze upon her as if He'd never seen her before. Then a smile spread across a face so handsome it was hard to believe it belonged to a mortal human. He unbuckled the collar with dexterous fingers and raised it to her neck. Instinctively she pulled back, skittish as an unbroken horse afraid of the bridle.

"Trust me," He whispered. "Please."

She closed her eyes and let Him place the collar onto her neck. He locked it at the back. There it was. She was His again. That hadn't hurt too much, had it?

"Tell me I own you," He whispered in her ear.

"You own me, sir."

"Tell me your heart and your body are mine to do with whatever I please."

"I am yours, heart and body. Do with me whatever you please, sir."

"Tell me you love me."

"I love you, sir."

"I love you, too...Nora."

Her eyes flew open. He had called her Nora.

"Sir?"

"I know how much it hurt me to lose you. I wouldn't ask you to lose you, either. You can be Nora with everyone else as long as you are Eleanor, my Little One, with me."

"I can still..."

"Yes."

"Even Kingsley?"

"Yes."

"Simone? Sheridan?"

"If I can watch sometime," He said with a wink.

"Every time." She threw herself into His arms, and He gathered her to Him. "I didn't think... I thought you'd make me give it all up."

"I promised you everything, didn't I?"

"Yes, you did." She looked at up Him.

"Now you know, Little One...when I make a promise, I keep it."

Nora stared at the scene she'd just written. She highlighted it and was about to hit Delete when her hotline phone rang.

"Mistress Nora's House of Ill Repute. How may I direct your cock?"

"You aren't cute," Kingsley said.

"I beg to differ. I'm fucking precious. Are you finally speaking to me again?"

"I am, but not because I want to."

"Juliette finally wore you down, did she?" Nora asked, her hands shaking despite her jocular tone.

"She's not happy with me when I'm not happy with you."

"I knew I liked that woman for a reason."

"Are you alone?" he asked.

"Sort of. Alone in my office."

"You have company? Is it Talel?" Kingsley asked.

"I have company. It's not Talel. Did you call to yell at me again?" she asked.

"Are you done sleeping with clients?" Kingsley asked.

"I didn't sleep with a client," Nora said for possibly the one hundredth time since their fight began. "Let's review the facts of the case. Talel had a domme. He didn't like her. He went looking for a new domme. He came to you. You booked him with me. I'd never met him until I walked into his hotel suite. Since he'd had a falling-out with his last domme he wanted to talk before we played. He's handsome, he's interesting, he's a sheikh, which I didn't even know actually existed outside romance novels…so of course I fucked him. But he didn't pay me for it."

"He paid me. He paid me two thousand dollars for one hour of your time. Paid up front."

"I paid him back. Therefore net zero money was exchanged."

"You could have at least charged him for the sex," Kingsley said in a chiding tone. Was his anger finally starting to thaw?

"Don't worry. I might not have charged him for kink or sex, but he did leave me a very good tip," she said, peeking out the window blinds and looking at the car in her driveway, an inferno-red Aston Martin. "Do you forgive me?"

"I'm considering it."

"I work all the time," Nora said. "I needed a vacation."

"And it had to be a vacation with the son of a billionaire who owns Middle Eastern oil fields—plural?"

"I liked him," Nora said, smiling at the memories of her nights with Talel.

Three weeks ago he'd come to New York and made discreet inquiries with Kingsley about hiring a dominatrix to see to his personal submissive needs. Kingsley had sent her to his hotel suite, a suite that cost more a night than her entire monthly mortgage payment. She'd taken one look at him and known she couldn't take his money. She hadn't wanted Talel's money. She'd wanted him. She'd beaten him and they had sex in his hotel suite afterward. The next day they were on his private plane to Jordan where they holed up in an even more luxurious hotel suite, more luxurious than anything America had to offer. She'd used him, abused him, beaten him, fucked him and let him cater to all her sexual needs and desires. They'd spent almost seven straight days in bed, coming up for air only to eat enough food to give them the energy to fuck again. Kingsley had been livid. She'd had sex with a client, a very wealthy client who stood to inherit billions as long as his father never learned about his sexual proclivities. When Nora came back to the city, Kingsley refused to see her or speak to her. When she thought of everything she'd done to Talel and everything he'd done to her, she considered it a small price to pay.

"I liked him, too," Kingsley said. "I especially liked his bank balance."

"You saw dollar signs when you looked at him. I saw a man. I wanted him. I took him. Now he's gone home and he won't be visiting again for a good long while. So either forgive me or you fire me. I'm done being punished by you for doing something you would have done in my boots."

Kingsley didn't say anything at first. She waited, not speaking, letting him mull it over.

"You left and I didn't know where you'd gone," Kingsley finally said.

"Is that why you were so angry at me?"

"It was part of it. I don't like having to say 'I don't know' when *le prêtre* asks me where you are."

"I'm allowed to have a personal life, aren't I? Or do I need you to sign a permission slip for me every time I want to have sex?"

"I would prefer to sign a permission slip," Kingsley said.

Nora laughed softly. "So you forgive me?"

"If I must. And I must. Juliette's furious at me for not talking to you. I had to sleep in the guest room with the dogs last night. She locked me out of my own bedroom."

"Tell Juliette I owe her lunch. So are we good? You and me? King and queen back together?"

"Yes," he said. "But don't do it again. If your priest finds out I sent you to have sex with a client, I'm a dead man. I'm not a pimp. You fuck on your own time. Not company time. You do it one more time, and I will find a new queen."

"Speaking of fucking on my own time…"

"Yes?"

"I have a guest in the house, and I'd like to go check on him."

"Make it a quickie."

"Why?"

"You have an appointment in two hours."

"Oh, yeah, I forgot about that. Rabbi Friedman. Today's whipping day."

"Don't forget Judge B. and Sheridan."

"I could never forget Sheridan." Sheridan was Nora's favorite client and everyone knew it. And Judge B.'s wife always gave her cookies. A dominatrix did not forget her cookies.

"Any instructions for your Little Miss?"

"Tell her to wear pink panties—lacy ones. I want to cut them off with a knife and gag her with them."

"Why don't you ever make me wear pink panties for you anymore?"

"King?"

"*Quoi?*"

Click.

Nora dropped the phone and kicked it across the floor. Entirely unnecessary but wonderfully cathartic. She would have gone over to pick the phone up but someone beat her to it.

"Good morning, Mistress. Did you drop this?"

Nora smiled at the teenage boy standing in the doorway to her office. He was wearing boxer shorts, leather wrist cuffs and a smile. A sheepish blushing smile.

"I didn't drop it. I drop-*kicked* it, but thank you." She took the phone back from him. "How are you this morning?"

Noah, a nineteen-year-old, soon-to-be college sophomore, walked around her desk and leaned against it. She put her legs on the desk, one on each side of his hips.

"I'm..." He paused, rubbed the back of his neck and laughed. Gorgeous kid, dark reddish-brown hair, newly broad shoulders that were probably rail thin two years ago, hazel eyes that could never hide his pleasure or surprise and lips swollen from kisses and bites—her kisses, her bites. "Good."

"Good," she said. "Would you like me to take those off you?" Nora nodded at his wrist cuffs.

"I don't know. I kind of like them." He stretched out his arms and looked at the leather cuffs on his wrists, turning them this way and that.

"They look good on you. You wear sub well." She took his arm in her hands and unbuckled the right leather wrist cuff. Such a good boy. He instinctively knew he wasn't to take off his own cuffs. That was his Mistress's job. "Did you have fun last night?"

"I did." He nodded slowly, thoughtfully. "Did you?"

"I woke up sore and smiling," she said. "Always a good combination."

"Never imagined I'd lose my V-card to a...you know..."

"Woman with a whip collection?"

"That."

"If you never imagined that, then you need to be more imaginative in the future."

"I will be. And here I thought you were just a writer who liked extra whip in her coffee."

"I like extra whip in my everything." She unbuckled his left wrist cuff and tossed both cuffs down on her desk. She'd met Noah at her favorite local coffee shop where he worked as a barista and she worked on her books when she needed to get out of the house. He hung out with her on his fifteen-minute breaks and when she asked him yesterday evening if he had a girlfriend, he admitted he'd never had one. College was expensive and his parents didn't help much. He spent every free hour at work. No time to date. She'd commiserated with him. Having two jobs meant she had no time to date, either. Two hours later Noah was cuffed to her headboard and wasn't a virgin anymore.

Sometimes, Nora told Noah, you just have to make the time.

"Should I..." Noah pointed at the door.

"You can stay and take a shower with me if you want."

"You looked busy." He nodded at her open computer. "I don't want to interrupt the muse or whatever."

"The muse knows better than to interrupt me when I have company."

"Your muse sounds very understanding," Noah said as Nora slipped her hand into his boxers and started to stroke him gently. He was hard already. Teenage boys—God's gift to older women. "Very...very...nice muse."

"Have you ever fucked anyone on a desk, Noah?"

"Until last night I hadn't even fucked anyone in a bed."

"Would you like to fuck someone on a desk?"

"If someone would let me."

"Someone might let you. If you ask nicely."

Nora stood up, still stroking Noah. He bent his head and kissed her, his eyes closed and his hands nervous and reticent as he reached for her.

"You can touch me," she said against his lips. She appreciated his reticence, his desire to do what she told him to do, no more and no less.

"I don't want to screw up," he said, sliding his hand under her little black slip she'd put on when she'd woken up. "I still have no idea what I'm doing."

"Me," she said. "That's what you're doing. Now put me on the desk and touch me any way and anywhere you like."

Nora could tell he was doing his very best to be strong and suave as he cupped her ass and lifted her onto the desk.

"If I drop you do we still get to have sex?" Noah asked.

"Yes, but we'd have to play it as it lays."

"I think that's golf," Noah said.

"Same rules apply."

He laughed, which was exactly what she wanted him to do. He relaxed and kissed her now with enthusiasm, all nervousness gone. His hands wandered under her slip, massaged her thighs, pushed them wider. He penetrated her with one finger and rubbed inside her. Last night she'd given him a thorough introduction to locating the clitoris and the G-spot and what to do when he found himself in contact with one or the other. The lessons seemed to have stuck because she was soon very, very wet and he was very, very hard and if they didn't fuck very, very soon she would be very, very put out.

She pushed his boxers down his hips until they pooled at his ankles where they belonged, grasped his cock and guided him inside her. He lifted her slip up and off her and Nora lay back on her desk, naked and happy. When he bent over her to kiss her breasts she twined her hands into his hair, holding him right where she wanted him, pumping her hips against him as he pushed into her.

"This is so much more fun than writing," she said. "I should tell my muse to fuck off more often."

Noah laughed as he glanced over at her still-open laptop.

"What were you writing?" he asked, taking her breasts in his hands.

Nora turned her head and glanced at her screen, the blinking cursor, the highlighted text.

You can be Nora with everyone else as long as you are Eleanor, my Little One, with me.

She slammed her laptop closed.

"Fiction."

23

Theology

NORA GRACIOUSLY ALLOWED NOAH TO JOIN HER IN the shower. She also graciously allowed him to wash her body inside and out with his bare hands. Afterward Nora put on her black silk bathrobe and kissed him goodbye at the front door. She didn't mind if the neighbors saw them. They seemed like nice people and she enjoyed giving them something to talk about at dinner.

He turned to leave but turned back around again.

"This was a one-night thing, right?" he asked.

Nora cupped his face. No scruff. No five-o'clock shadow. Not even a two-o'clock shadow.

"And one morning."

"So I guess I shouldn't call you later?"

"It's sweet of you to offer. If I weren't me, and you weren't so young..."

"I'm not that young. I'll be a sophomore at Yorke this year."

"You're young. My life is complicated enough without adding a very sweet, very handsome, very young complication to it. Plus...we have to work, remember?"

"I get it." He gave her a shy smile in return. "See you at the coffee shop sometime?"

"You're the only one who gets my order right."

"Extra whip," he said.

"Story of my life."

Noah kissed her one last time and walked out her front door to his car. He hadn't been the first male virgin she'd deflowered since becoming a dominatrix, and she knew he wouldn't be her last. Since she was making something of a habit of it, she'd developed a personal philosophy regarding her encounters with inexperienced younger men. She would show them the world of sex had more flavors to it than vanilla, and say goodbye the next morning leaving her boys better off than when she found them. Wiser, more experienced and grinning like idiots.

But Noah hadn't been grinning like an idiot when he left. Neither had she. She nearly called him back. A terrible idea, of course. He was nineteen. She was thirty. He was sweet and innocent. Nora was, well... Nora.

And yet...it might be nice to have someone in her life who didn't come to her house just for the kink and sex and leave after the shower. Who was she kidding? She worked two jobs. She was rarely at home. Last thing she had time for was a pet.

Nora watched Noah drive away. Maybe she should find a new coffee shop. For Noah's sake, of course. Not hers. She was fine.

With less enthusiasm than usual, Nora put her day together. She packed clothes for her various clients—Sheridan wanted suits, Judge B loved her stiletto heels, and Rabbi Friedman couldn't care less what she wore as long as she used the stock whip on him until he had to crawl from her dungeon—

literally. Once dressed and packed, Nora headed into the city. She blamed her lassitude on the August heat. The city sweltered at the melting point. She could imagine the sidewalks bubbling like molten lava. The sun beat down on her as if it had something to prove. She couldn't get into the air-conditioned car fast enough.

On the way to the city her hotline phone rang again.

"King, I'm busy here. I have three sessions today. I don't have time to give the mayor's baby brother an OTK spanking. Again."

She heard a laugh on the other end. Juliette's laugh, warm and honeyed and endlessly amused by her lover's top domme.

"Sorry, Juliette. I thought it was King."

"What does OTK mean?"

"Over the knee."

"Ah, I'm learning all the terms. Monsieur asked me to call you. His hands are full."

"I don't want to know what his hands are full of, do I?"

"He's giving Max a bath. The puppy got out and played in the garbage before we could catch him."

Nora heard the plaintive cry of a miserable beast in the background, a full-grown Rottweiler that only Juliette would call a "puppy." She heard something else, too—it sounded like every swear word in the French language coming out in one long, blue sentence.

"King knows he can pay people to give his dogs baths, right?"

"He's having too much fun to delegate."

"What, pray tell, does His Royal Dog Groomer want from me now?"

"Your Sheridan called. She can't make her appointment tonight. Her agent called her in for an audition. She'd like to reschedule for tomorrow at nine."

"That's fine."

"Also, I needed to know if you had room in your schedule tonight for a session with a new client."

"New client? Tonight?"

"He wants your earliest appointment."

Nora dug her red leather appointment book out of her bag.

"Thursday afternoon," Nora said. "I have Troy at two. Put him at 3:30."

"Done. *Merci.*"

"No problem. Who's the new guy anyway?"

"He's—"

Nora heard a *"Merde!"* followed by the sound of wet feet running rampant.

"I have to go," Juliette said.

"Let me guess—Max ran away from King and is running around the entire house dripping water?"

"One of them will not survive this day," Juliette said. "Both, *j'espère.*"

"Bonne chance," Nora said and hung up the phone.

She had a lovely session with Judge B, a brutal session with Rabbi Friedman. She had dinner in the city with Griffin before heading back home. But when she arrived back at her house that evening, Nora couldn't bring herself to open the front door of her house. Once the key was in the lock, she realized the last place she wanted to be was alone in her own house with her own thoughts and her empty bed. Instead of going home, she walked across the street and down the block.

When she stepped through the side door of St. Luke's she almost stumbled from pure sensory overload. She could smell the faint memory of incense in the air, a scent she'd recognize anywhere. And there was no light quite like the light of evening through stained-glass saints and angels and no sound quite like the sound of high heels on church floors. She climbed up the choir loft steps and took a seat in one of the pews. Inside her day planner she jotted down her appointment for Thursday. Usually she wrote down the initials of her client so she could better prepare for the scene but she didn't know who it was. Not that it mattered much. She'd beaten every sort of masochist there was. Whatever he wanted, she could give it to him.

When she'd finished updating her schedule, she pulled her laptop out of her bag. She should have been thinking of Noah. She'd spent the night with him, and the morning. But as always it was Søren who consumed her thoughts. She started writing a memory simply to have some mastery over it. When she put Søren on paper he became hers again. If only for a little while.

He sat at the table in the bar of the club drinking a glass of red wine with their king. They spoke in French too rapidly for her to understand more than a few words here and there. It didn't matter what they spoke of, however. Nothing mattered except His thigh under her chin and His left hand on the back of her neck, caressing the tender skin under her collar. She sat on the floor at His feet, a white pillow between her knees and the floor.

He didn't speak to her, but He did tap her under the chin. She lifted her head and met His eyes. He dipped two fingers into His red wine and brought them to her lips, and she drank the wine off His hand.

Their king said something followed by the word "parfait." Perfect. He was speaking of her, their king was, speaking of her submission to Him. A perfect submissive. Not true although she was flattered. It was not she who was perfect, but Him. Don't call the painting perfect even if you see it that way. The painting didn't create itself. Call the artist perfect. If she was perfect it was only because He was perfect first.

He rose to His feet and she waited. She would not rise until He bid her to rise. She would stay there all night if she must waiting for the order.

"Come, Little One," He said, brushing her cheek with His fingertips.

He didn't tell her where they were going, because it didn't matter. As long as she never lost sight of Him, she would never lose her way.

She followed Him to His dungeon, which was a terrible word to describe a beautiful room. In the olden days, prisoners were kept and tortured in dungeons. But long before that the word held a different meaning. It came from Latin, from the word "dominus," which meant lord or master. The master's keep, that's what a dungeon was. The place where the castle's lord kept his precious things, not a dank, dark hole for prisoners.

He was the master, and she was that which He kept.

Once safely inside His keep He kissed her with a claiming kiss, a conquering kiss, a master's kiss. He called her by name and the name He called her was "Mine." He stripped her of her white shoes, her white dress, her white stockings, until she wore nothing for Him but her white collar. He ran a bath of warm water and set her into it. As she sat in the water He rolled up the sleeves of His black shirt, revealing strong forearms, strong wrists, a pale dusting of hair and a small white scar left by His father.

"Don't look at the scar, Little One," He said, lathering his hands with gentle soap.

"I hate to think of you hurt, sir. I wish I could have been there for you."

He pushed her onto her hands and knees. Her nipples hardened as the water kissed them.

"You weren't even born yet," He said, spreading her thighs with His hands and washing inside of her. He had told her what would happen tonight so she braced herself as two wet fingers entered her anally.

"I wasn't even born when I was born."

"When were you born?" He asked her as He opened His two fingers inside of her, widening her. The muscles inside her protested against the penetration and she bit her lip to stifle a cry of discomfort.

"The first time I saw you."

His lips touched her hair as He inserted something into her body, something hard and thick, something to open her and keep her open. He washed His hands in her bathwater and helped her to her feet. She felt strange with the object inside her. Tense. Full. There was no pain, however. Not like last time when He'd taken her without warning. Then He'd swooped down on her like a god in the form of man, taking her with force if not by it. It had left her shaken, afraid of Him. Burned. Burned like someone who'd stared at the sun. Those who kept a safe distance could bask in the glow of the sun, see by its light, glory in its warmth. Those who came too close were burned.

She did love to burn.

With a soft white towel He dried her. He led her to the bed and she sat on the edge. The bed was soft. Sitting felt strange but didn't hurt. She'd worn her hair pinned up as He'd requested, and now He took the pins out one by one and set them aside before taking a silver hairbrush and running it through the black waves of her hair. The act was soothing, soporific. She was naked and deeply penetrated and yet she could have fallen asleep with her head against His stomach. He wanted her like this…at peace, limp, open. She heard the sound of Him setting the hairbrush aside and she opened her heavy eyes. Gently He wrapped a white silk sash around her wrists and used it as a lead, guiding her to the center of the bed. He put her on her stomach and tied her wrists loosely to the headboard. The light in the room was low so it didn't surprise her when He produced three small tea candles. It did surprise her, however, when He laid the three flat round candles on her spine. They formed a line, the three of them. One on the back of her neck. One between her shoulder blades. One at the small of her back. Then He lit them. As small as they were it didn't take long before she felt the wax heating and melting onto her skin. The candles burned without searing her. It was His touch that seared her instead. As the wax melted onto her naked spine, His hands roved over her body, her legs and her arms, between her thighs and inside her vagina. He pushed a fingertip against her cervix, a test to see if she would flinch or jump, which wasn't allowed when she had candles on her body. She inhaled sharply but didn't move. She'd passed the test.

The wax turned to liquid and slid over her back, creating paraffin wings over her rib cage and sides. She barely felt the thick hard object inside her anymore. It had become a part of her. All her attention was focused on the burning wax. What happened inside her was beneath her notice.

As the three flames of the three candles reached her skin, He licked the tips of His fingers and snuffed them out. The wax congealed almost instantly, and He peeled it from her body. Although she couldn't see her own back she knew the wax had left a bright red mark wherever it had touched. His lips caressed her burns, bringing fresh pain to her and fresh pleasure to Him.

The bed shifted under His weight, and she heard the rustle of fabric as He undressed. Naked He covered her body with His, pressing His chest into her back and renewing the pain of the burns with His own heat. He pulled back and drew the object out of her. She missed it immediately, felt the emptiness like a wound and when He entered her with His own body, she was healed.

Carefully He lowered Himself onto her. Carefully He thrust into her. She felt no pain. She was far too slick and open for pain. Not quite pleasure either but for the pleasure of being penetrated by Him, used by Him. That was its own pleasure far removed from the physical manifestation of it.

He pulled out of her but only to order her onto her back. With her ankles resting on His shoulders He entered her again. His fingers found her clitoris and stroked it. She shivered and gasped and the muscles inside her clenched in pleasure. Turning His hand, He pushed two fingers into her vagina and she felt him filling both holes. Yes… she closed her eyes and her head fell back against the sheets. Yes… this was what she'd always wanted, to have Him inside every part of her, to keep nothing of her from Him. Submission had become synonymous with surrender to her. Willing surrender. The Lord of the Castle had come to invade her world. If she fought Him, she would lose everything. But if she surrendered to Him, He would carry her off like a spoil of war. When she entered His keep she would find riches beyond her wildest dreams waiting for her if she were only brave enough to surrender.

She surrendered.

Three fingers penetrated her vagina. Four. Both holes were filled and she could take nothing more. Like a wine chalice she was made to be filled. It was her purpose, her raison d'être. He knew it and so He filled her. Filled her to the brim and more and she overflowed with Him, the sheets wet beneath her. She came silently and hard, her clitoris throbbing against His fingers and the deep muscles of her pelvis contracting around the cock in her ass. This was a new pleasure she'd never before experienced. The contractions were deeper and harder. Nerves she didn't know she had went wild. She felt the orgasm all the way up her spine and into her thighs and calves and down to her toes. When He came inside her, she felt that, too. She felt everything everywhere. It was blinding pleasure, obliterating, like staring into the sun. But she didn't blink, didn't turn away. Once one saw the sun, what was there left to see anyway?

The ecstasy pulsed and faded at last. He untied her wrists from the headboard and pulled her to Him, her chest to His chest, her leg over His thigh, His fingers gentle probing inside her wet holes.

"Better?" He asked and she knew He meant was it better than last time. It couldn't possibly have been any worse.

"Perfect, sir." Everything was perfect now—He was perfect, the sex had been perfect...a perfect evening...

"Parfait," He said and she remembered His conversation with their king and asked Him about it.

"What did he say to you about me? I heard him say 'parfait.'"

"He said you were the perfect submissive."

*"What else did he say?" she asked because she knew there was
more to it.*

He didn't answer at first.

"Sir?"

*Her sir smiled, but it wasn't a happy smile. Still, she had asked
and He would answer.*

"He said...'Enjoy it while it lasts.'"

She heard footsteps on the choir loft stairs and looked up
from her writing.

"Well, if it isn't my favorite lapsarian. How are you, Miss
Nora?"

"Hello, Father Mike. You do know *lapsarian* is an adjective referring to the fall of man, right? Not a noun meaning
a lapsed Catholic."

"Well, it should mean a lapsed Catholic. It sounds like a
lapsed Catholic. I've been wanting to ask you something," he
said as he lugged what appeared to be a heavy box of something over the back of a pew. "How does a young lady who
writes dirty books know so much about theology?"

"Osmosis."

Father Mike O'Dowell, the priest of St. Luke's, cocked a
white and bushy eyebrow right at her.

"I used to 'date' someone who had a PhD in theology," she
explained. "It was a dirty joke."

"I'm a priest, not a child. You don't have to put *date* in
quotes. I assume you used to sleep with someone who had a
PhD in theology?"

"I did."

"Osmosis. I get it." He tapped the side of his nose and
pointed at her. "Clever."

"Did I shock you?"

"No, ma'am."

"One of these days I'm going to shock you, Father Mike. It's my top goal in life."

"Good luck with that, my dear. I used to minister to men on death row. I'd be more shocked if you'd never 'dated' someone."

"I 'dated' a nineteen-year-old boy this morning."

Father Mike sighed wistfully. "God, I miss nineteen."

Nora laughed. Father Mike looked like an old-school priest, and talked like it with his faded Irish accent, but he didn't scare her one bit. He had a mighty scowl but it turned to a smile too quickly to intimidate her.

"Do you need some help there, Father?"

"Please. Unless I'm interrupting your prayers."

"Not praying," she said as she took a stack of brand-new shiny blue hymnals from the box and helped Father Mike place them in the back of each pew. "Just thinking."

"Thinking? Sounds dangerous."

"It is."

"Boy trouble?" he asked.

"Always."

"Somebody break your heart?"

"No. I broke someone's heart."

"Feeling guilty?" Father Mike asked. "There's hope for you yet if you haven't lost your Catholic guilt."

"Sorry. No guilt. Not where he's concerned. It's just… we were very happy together right up until the moment we weren't."

"What happened?"

"I changed," she said. "There was something I needed to do with my life, and he wouldn't let me do it. I had to choose between staying with him and not being the real me, and being the real me and leaving him. Does that make sense?"

"Oh, yes. I've been there, lass. My own brother wouldn't speak to me for five years after I left home to join the church."

"Five years? But you're Irish. Aren't you all supposed to send one child in the family to a convent or a seminary?"

Father Mike stood up straight and stared at a wrought-iron cross hanging on the wall at the back of the choir loft.

"Our priest growing up…he mistreated my oldest brother."

"Mike," she said, reaching out to squeeze his arm. "I'm sorry."

"We put that bastard in jail after my father beat him with a golf club. Ten years later when I told the family I was joining the church, Seamus said it was like the husband of a Jewish girl joining the Nazi party."

"The path I took, it hurt my…ex–whatever he was. What I wanted to do with my life, the person I needed to be, he couldn't be a part of it," Nora said.

"It scared Seamus when I became a priest. First time he saw me in the collar he swore he didn't even know me anymore. I looked the same but he couldn't see me. Took a while before his eyes adjusted."

"My gentleman has very good eyes. But he still can't see me for me."

"Any regrets about leaving him?"

"If I had to do it over again, I'd do the same thing. And," she said, glancing down at her closed laptop in her bag, "we certainly enjoyed it while it lasted."

"Then what's the problem, lass?"

Nora shrugged as she sorted the hymnals in her hand.

"I miss him."

Father Mike gave her a look of compassion and the kindness almost undid her.

"That is a problem, isn't it?"

"Yes," Nora said, swallowing. "Yes, it is."

"You think he'll come around?" Father Mike asked as he gathered up the old, crumbling hymnals and started placing them in the box.

"I keep hoping he will. No luck yet."

"Is he a good man?"

"He…" Nora paused, trying to figure out the best way to answer the question. "He sold a very precious possession of his once in order to buy me something I needed and couldn't afford at the time."

"What did he buy you?"

"A laptop so I could write my dirty books."

"What did he sell?"

"His dignity."

"Sounds like a very good man then."

"He's the best man alive," Nora said and realized as she said the words, she meant them.

"Sounds like you're still in love with him."

"I am. He knows I am."

"He's still in love with you?"

"He was last time I checked. Seems like it should be easy, right? He loves me. I love him. But it never is that easy."

"God said 'Love is patient. Love is kind.' He never said 'Love is easy.'"

"Love is patient," Nora repeated. "You think if I'm patient he'll eventually come around and love me for me instead of waiting for me to be someone I'm not?"

"I've been screwing up mightily for sixty-eight years. God's still patiently waiting for me to get it right, and He hasn't given up on me yet."

"Fine. I'll give him sixty-five more years to come to his senses. Then I'm moving on with my life. But after that I'm finding a new priest to be in love with."

Father Mike's eyes went round as Communion wafers.

"Did I finally shock you?" she asked, handing over a stack of hymnals.

He shook his head again, and his eyes returned to their normal size. "You'll have to do better than that. I know too many priests. Anyone I know?"

"I'm kidding," she lied. "I wouldn't sleep with a priest. That would be a sin."

"For your sake, I hope you're kidding."

"Why is that?"

"You're a sweet girl, even if you do correct my theology. Involved with a priest? I wouldn't wish that on my worst enemy."

"That bad, is it?" Nora asked, keeping her voice neutral as she sorted hymnals into the box.

"Priest I went to seminary with had a lover for years. Fifteen, if you can believe it, before it was over."

"Over? Did they get caught?"

"One dark night she washed down a bottle of sleeping pills with a bottle of vodka. Never woke up."

Father Mike said the words casually, but Nora felt them like a punch in the gut. She wanted to ask the woman's name, what church she attended. Nora wanted to know if her priest called her by a pet name that made her melt, if he told her he needed her, if he told her she was his heart.

"And him?" she asked, keeping her tone neutral as she slipped a hymnal into the box. "What happened to him?"

"They transferred him to a church five hundred miles away. They sent him packing so fast he didn't even get the chance to pay his last respects to her family."

"That's awful," Nora said not meeting his eyes.

"It's shameful, is what it is. She thought she was giving him the best years of her life. Turned out they were the only years. Suicide is a mortal sin, but I'd put it on his head, not hers."

"Do you honestly think God wants a celibate clergy?"

"Doesn't matter if God wants it or not. The church wants it and the church sets the dress code. God doesn't want all men to shave their heads and march in formation either, but the army certainly does. You want to join the army, be prepared to march. Don't want to march, don't join the army. If you do join the army, for God's sake, don't marry a pacifist."

"You can't help who you fall in love with sometimes."

"The heart wants what the heart wants," Father Mike said. "Which is why God gave us hearts and common sense, and He put them in different places."

"We're Catholics, Father Mike. We believe in the Sacred Heart, remember? No one ever talks about the Sacred Common Sense."

"True. But still, my heart breaks for the girl."

"What about you?" she asked. "Any regrets about being a priest? Anything to repent?"

"Being a priest has been my North Star on this journey. But I wonder sometimes about the children I didn't have. You get called Father all you life, you can't help but wonder…"

Nora looked at the iron cross on the wall.

"My old priest would have made a wonderful father." She remembered a long-ago visit to Denmark, and seeing Søren holding his baby niece Gitte in his arms. For hours he walked with her, trying to comfort and quiet her colicky cries. He was so patient, so endlessly patient. Nora didn't want to have children herself and she had no regrets about that at all. But Søren never holding his son or daughter? That hurt her. That she regretted. And she hated to think about it, but Søren was fourteen years her senior and women lived longer than men. Wouldn't it be something to have part of Søren live on after he was gone?

"Breaks my heart to know he'll never have children," Nora said. "And you, too. I wish they'd let priests get married. Don't you think it's a little weird, priests preaching about love when they're not allowed to feel it?"

"Oh, priests know everything there is to know about love."

"You do, do you?" she asked with a smile.

"Don't confuse love with romance, young lady. Romance is beautiful, it's a gesture, it's a walk in a park with a pretty girl. Love is ugly sometimes. It's a crawl into a war zone to save a friend. Romance whispers sweet nothings. Love tells painful truths. Romance gives an engagement ring. Love takes a bullet. I gave up marriage and children and sex and the comforts of family, because I love my Lord, and I would take a bullet for anyone in this church, including you, young lady. Now you tell me I don't know what love is."

Nora couldn't tell him that because she couldn't say a word. She leaned over the pew and took Father Mike in her arms.

"You're flirting," he said in a teasing tone. "My heart belongs to another."

"I'm not flirting," she said, her head on his shoulder. "Sometimes even a lapsed Catholic needs a hug from a priest."

Father Mike chuckled and patted her on the back, kindly as a grandfather. Her phone buzzed in her pocket and she rolled her eyes.

"Sorry," she said. "That was me."

"Good. Afraid it was my pacemaker."

Nora glanced at her phone. "Well. Speak of the devil," she said.

"Is it him?" Father Mike whispered, grinning at her like a teenage girl at a sleepover.

"It is."

"Answer it, lass. Maybe he's finally coming around. I would if I were him."

Nora leaned over the pew, kissed Father Mike on the cheek and hit the answer button.

"This better be good," she said.

"Define *good*," came a sonorous voice over the line.

"I'm very busy," she said. "I'm at St. Luke's helping a priest friend of mine organize his hymnals."

"If I didn't know Mike O'Dowell, I would assume 'organize his hymnals' was a euphemism."

"Not a euphemism unless you're calling to ask me to organize your hymnals."

"My hymnals are in perfect order already, but thank you." His voice was cool, tempered, even. Yet she sensed something not right, a fissure in his composure.

"Then to what do I owe the pleasure of this phone call?"

"I need you."

"Should I bring wine and wear lingerie?" she asked. "Or bring lingerie and wear wine?"

"Not necessary. I'm afraid this won't be a particularly romantic evening."

"What's wrong?" she asked, slipping out the side door of St. Luke's and into the parking lot.

"There was an accident."

"What happened?" Nora asked, her stomach sinking to the asphalt. "Was someone hurt?"

"We can discuss it tonight. I should go."

"Søren—wait. Was anyone hurt?"

"Yes," he said, sounding resigned and tired.

"Who?"

"We can talk about it tonight."

"Søren," she said again. "Please, you're scaring me. Who was hurt?"

He sighed and Nora's heart died a little in the sigh. That he didn't want to tell her who was hurt meant she didn't want to know.

"I was."

24

Cleaning Wounds

NORA DROVE TO SACRED HEART AS FAST AS SHE could praying the entire way she'd find Søren alone in the house. She parked her car behind the house in the grove that ringed the rectory. When Nora reached the side door of the rectory she found a sign taped to the window. It read "No visitors allowed. Leave Father Stearns alone. This is an order." It was signed "Diane, Who Means Business."

Thank God for Diane. At least she knew no one would bother her and Søren tonight.

"Søren?" she called out when she slipped through the side door and into the kitchen. No one answered. The kitchen counters were bursting with small elegant arrangements in various pots and vases of the sort one received after the death of a loved one or during a long illness. Unapologetically nosy, she peeked at a card in the nearest arrangement, a single orchid in a pale blue pot, and read the note—"Heal fast, Father S. We need you to crush First Presbyterian with us. Love, Your Sacred Heart Soccer Team."

"Søren?" She called his name louder and raced through the house, seeking him out in every room. He wasn't downstairs so she rushed upstairs, the soles of her navy blue sandals slapping loudly against the wood stairs.

"In here, Eleanor," he called back. She ran to the bathroom and found him standing in front of the sink. He had a gauze bandage wrapped around his right forearm and right hand. "I could use your assistance if you don't mind the sight of blood, which we both know you don't."

"Please tell me what happened," she demanded, her heart galloping as if she'd run a four-minute mile. It hadn't stopped since his phone call. "Are you all right?"

"I'm fine. Sprained wrist. A few lacerations. Nothing that won't heal."

She stepped into the bathroom and washed her hands brusquely.

"If you could remove the gauze and then replace it, I would be in your debt," Søren said. "It's not easy to do with one hand."

"How did you of all people manage to sprain your wrist?" She took his arm into her hands and started peeling back the layers of gauze. "And why couldn't you just tell me you had a sprained wrist over the phone? You were fighting with King again, weren't you?" If he was, she'd sprain his other wrist.

"A drunk driver ran me off the road."

"On your motorcycle?" Nora could scarcely breathe.

"I'm afraid so. But like me, it only suffered cosmetic damage. I'm quite lucky. As a priest I should say I'm blessed, but let's be honest, sometimes it's nothing but luck that keeps one out of the morgue."

"Oh, my God." Nora could barely speak for the shock and fury. "A drunk driver ran you off the road? Who is he? I'll kill him."

"*She*, not he. She was a twenty-year-old college student, and she is already dead so I wouldn't worry about exacting any revenge. She's in God's hands."

"Jesus…you were involved in a fatal car accident, and you didn't tell me?"

"I just told you."

"You told me on the phone you'd been in an accident. You didn't tell me it was a fatal car accident."

"I know how you drive under the best of circumstances. I didn't want you in an accident on your way to see me."

"You would be furious at me if I'd been in a serious car accident and didn't tell you."

"I'm a priest, Eleanor. I can hardly call you from the hospital, can I? I do rounds there and every doctor and nurse knows me. The nurse called Diane, and as soon as the church had word of the accident, I had a dozen parishioners at the ER offering their comfort, prayers and food. Don't take offense. I would have much preferred your company."

"When did this happen?"

"Two nights ago."

"Two nights?"

Søren exhaled heavily. He'd always hated having to explain himself. He did everything for a reason, he'd said time and time again. Couldn't she simply trust that?

"I've had visitors all yesterday checking on me. The bishop, half a dozen Jesuits, Diane and her family, Dr. Sutton, Dr. Keighley and, of course, Claire insisted on staying the night last night. My sister is, as you know, overprotective of me."

"Did Diane bring you home?"

"Claire did. And she's also taking care of repairs to the Ducati. I knew you'd be worried about it."

She couldn't have cared less about the fucking motorcycle.

"That's good." Nora nodded. "I'm glad Claire was here. And you… I'm glad you're okay."

"I will be once the bandage is changed."

"Right." She took the hint and got back to work. "Sorry. I'm not used to this."

Her hands shook as she finished unwrapping the bandage from his arm. When she peeled back the gauze pads she found road rash, raw and red but healing.

"Dealing with minor wounds? I would think the most infamous dominatrix in the state would be an expert by now."

"I'm not used to being the last person to know when something's happened to you."

"You aren't the last to know. I haven't told Kingsley. You know how he feels about doctors and hospitals."

"I'll tell him. He won't yell at me as much as he'll yell at you."

"Tell him not to send flowers. He sent so many flowers when my mother died, I could have started my own nursery."

"I'll request booze instead."

"A much better gift."

Nora held his arm over the sink and washed the wounds with antiseptic. Anyone else would have flinched and winced at the discomfort, but Søren remained stoic, expressionless.

Pink fluid, blood and water, filled the sink. As gently as she could, she scrubbed at the lacerations. Bits of rock came out, black flecks on the white porcelain.

"Fuck," she said. "You still have pavement in your arm."

"They warned me at the hospital it would take time for it all to work its way out."

Nora blinked back tears, her throat too tight to speak. Visions of the accident wormed their way unbidden into her mind—screaming tires, twisting metal, Søren's precious blood drying on the asphalt.

"I wanted to do this to you," Søren said, his head bent over hers as she worked. "The first day I ever saw you."

"You wanted to wash my arm in your sink? That's a weird kink."

Søren laughed softly. "Your knees. You had the ugliest scrapes on them, remember? Someone had pushed you at school, and your knees looked like they had half the sidewalk embedded in them."

"They healed eventually."

"I was worried you were being neglected. The day I met you... You dressed like a street urchin and appeared injured and unwashed."

"Mom worked two jobs. If there was neglect it was benign neglect."

"There is no such thing. Still, I thought it a promising sign, the scrapes on your knees. You were clearly a young lady not afraid of pain or bothered by blood. Sadists don't play well with the squeamish."

Nora grinned. "You can't be squeamish and be a dominatrix, either. The shit I have seen in the last couple years could turn your hair blond." She looked up at him. "Oops. Too late."

"That bad?" he asked.

"That good. I wasn't complaining. I love my job. Most of the time."

"What about the rest of the time?"

"Do you love your job all the time?" she asked him.

"Point taken."

In silence she finished cleaning the wounds on his arm. He must not have been wearing his gloves because the heel of his palm had received the brunt of the impact.

"Did they give you any painkillers?" she asked.

"Vicodin. I'm trying not to take any."

"Stop being a martyr. If you don't take them, I will. Those bad boys are serious fun."

Søren glared at her. "It isn't martyrdom. The pain is... calming. And distracting. A college student with her entire life ahead of her had a little too much fun at a friend's birthday party and died two nights ago, almost taking me with her. I'd rather focus on my pain than her family's."

"Can I talk you into taking two ibuprofen and a glass of wine?"

"I could be persuaded. But first... I need your assistance with one more injury."

"You cut up somewhere else?"

"My back," he said.

Nora pursed her lips and raised her hands to his shirt buttons.

"This better not be a ploy just to get me to undress you," she said, carefully easing his black clerical shirt off him and dropping it onto the floor.

"If it were such a ploy I would have said I had a groin injury."

"Good point. Turn around." She picked up the bottle of antiseptic as Søren turned his back to her. She nearly dropped it into the sink. "Oh, my God..."

From his shoulder to his hip he was nothing but one solid purple bruise, with a few patches of road rash by his waist.

"I landed hard and skidded," Søren explained far too calmly for someone who'd looked death in the eye two nights ago. "On my back, as you see."

"I see," she said, swallowing a sudden hard lump in her throat. She could barely look at him and she couldn't bear to look away. Apart from one night he'd been with Kingsley a decade ago, she'd been Søren's only lover since he was eighteen years old. She felt protective of his body and terrible violence had been done unto it. Anger burned bright but she had nowhere to direct it.

"That can't be comfortable," Nora said, raising her hand to touch his wounds but lowering her hand again, afraid to hurt him.

"I wouldn't recommend the sensation. But you know more about bruises than I do," he said, and the levity in his voice sounded forced.

"Not this bad," she said. "Have you seen your back?"

"I've had worse."

"That will heal, won't it?"

"The doctor said it's mostly first-degree road rash with a few patches of second-degree road rash. As long as it stays clean it shouldn't scar. The bruise will heal in a month."

"Good. As long as you're okay."

"I haven't been 'okay' since you left me."

"You start a fight with me tonight, and I'll pour lemon juice all over your cuts."

"Truce." He held up his hands.

"Truce," she said, almost wanting to fight. It would make her feel better, as if things were normal between them. "At least until you heal. Then the war's back on."

Nora looked down at the small gauze pads. She'd go through an entire box of them trying to clean up the laceration under his rib cage.

"Something wrong?" he asked.

"Hold on. I have a better idea."

Søren turned around as she yanked her shirt off.

"Eleanor?"

She opened the shower door and turned on the water.

"It'll be easier to do it in the shower." She unzipped her pants and kicked off her shoes. In seconds she was naked as the bathroom filled with steam.

Søren raised his eyebrow.

"We'll clean your back off in the shower," she said, enunciating every word. "That is what I mean by 'do it.'"

"Little One, I don't think this is necessary—"

"Have you seen your back?"

"Not all of it."

"It's necessary."

He undressed and stepped into the shower, and she followed him inside and adjusted the flow of the water onto his back. Funny—that morning she'd had a teenage boy in her shower for purposes entirely erotic. Tonight she stood under the steaming water in a different shower for reasons that couldn't be less erotic. She lathered her hands with soap and Søren braced himself against the tiled wall as she worked the lather and hot water into his wounds. Although she worked as gently as she could and Søren made no sound, she knew she was hurting him. His forehead rested on his uninjured left wrist, and he shut his eyes tight. He breathed shallow breaths, his body unnaturally still. How many thousands of times had he inflicted pain upon her with floggers, with whips, with canes, with his own brutal bare hands…and yet here she stood silently weeping as she hurt him with nothing more than soap and water on his raw and wounded flesh?

"I know it hurts," she said, feeling a terrible tenderness toward him as she dug tiny bits of pavement from his bleeding back with her fingernails. His blood was on her hands, red and mortal. He could have died two nights ago. She knew doctors and nurses in the ER called motorcycles "donor-cycles" because of the high fatality rate in motorcycle crashes. She could have lost Søren forever. And what would her last words have been to him? She didn't even remember what she'd last said to him, it had been so long since she'd seen him. They'd probably fought about something, about her leaving him and refusing to come back unless he accepted her for who she was now, not who she'd been. Father Mike had asked her today if she'd had any regrets about Søren. If he'd died without her getting to tell him one last time how much she loved him? She would regret that the rest of her life.

"I'm so sorry, sir," she said, apologizing for who knew what. For leaving him? For hurting him? For knowing how close she'd come to losing him two nights ago and still not being willing to give up her new life to go back to him?

"I'm considering this a learning experience. I now have a new appreciation for the concept of scourging."

"Scourging?"

"Christ was scourged before he was crucified. Pontius Pilate hoped to mollify the crowd who wished to see Jesus executed by sentencing him to a scourging. Scourging involved a near fatal beating with a whip that had glass and bone and rocks embedded in the lashes."

"Or pavement?"

"Or pavement," he said and finally heard a crack in that infuriating male stoicism of his.

"This wasn't your fault. She was drunk."

"After the wreck, I spoke to the police officer working the scene. I asked him who had died but they hadn't identified her yet. All he knew was that she was a young woman in a black Lexus."

A black Lexus? That was Nora's car.

"I had to see her," Søren said. "I didn't want to but I had to see her body. I had to because I was… I thought it might be you. A wildly irrational fear. I don't have wildly irrational fears, Eleanor. That's not me. But those two hundred steps between the wreck of my bike and the ambulance where they had her…it was the longest walk of my life. And there she was, this young woman broken and bloody and already dead. And

I was relieved... I looked at a dead girl, and I was relieved. I could barely stand up I was so relieved it wasn't you. I should go to confession and repent of that."

"It's human. It's normal. No one would blame you for being relieved you didn't know the victim, not even God."

"I'd never survive it if something happened to you."

"Søren... I'm here. It was someone else. It wasn't me."

"Of course not. You only come over when I tell you I need you. It wouldn't have been you on that road."

"Søren, please. You know I—"

"It's fine, Eleanor. I'm fine."

"No, you're not," she said, grateful for the water masking her tears.

"No," he said. "I'm not."

"Don't feel bad," she said softly, kissing him on his naked shoulder. "Neither am I."

25

News

AFTER THEIR SHOWER, NORA PUT HER CLOTHES BACK on and helped Søren as he pulled on a clean black T-shirt, which was by far the strangest moment in their relationship. After her trip to the hospital at age nineteen when she'd drunk herself into a minor bout of alcohol poisoning, it was Søren helping her out of the shower, Søren helping her dress. But now...

"Stop, Eleanor."

"What?"

"Stop crying."

"I'm not crying," she said while crying.

He bent and kissed her on the lips. "I have minor injuries, and I'm not an invalid. I've had much worse."

"When your father broke your arm?" she asked as she wound a clean ACE bandage around his arm.

"At St. Ignatius actually. I think I was...thirteen?"

"What happened?" she asked. Søren never spoke of his days at St. Ignatius, the Catholic boarding school he attended in

Maine from age eleven to seventeen, and she knew he spoke of it now to simply distract her from her tears.

"We had a cat at school named Jezebel. A vicious little feral thing. Hated all humans and would claw anyone who tried to pet her. Except me for some reason. She tolerated me. No idea why. I can only assume she felt sorry for me as I was the only creature on campus more despised by the other students than she was."

"Aww…you had a pet kitty," Nora said as she adjusted the bandage on Søren's wrist.

Søren grinned. "I suppose I did." The grin faded. "One night a student yanked her tail, and she attacked him. He retaliated by locking her in a bathroom. Then he and his friends gathered a huge box of rocks. They were planning on stoning her to death with them. They were older, about to graduate, didn't care about consequences. I held her against my chest with my back to them as they threw the stones."

"Couldn't you have let her escape?"

"And let them catch her and kill her another time? No, this was better. They could have gotten away with killing a feral cat but stoning a student? Every last one of them were expelled. Meanwhile I had bruises on my backside from my thighs to my shoulders and claw marks all over my chest. And not the nice sort you leave on me."

Nora shook her head. "Little ingrate. And here you were protecting her."

"Jezebel didn't understand I was trying to protect her by holding her so close to me. She thought she was being smothered. I don't blame her for scratching me."

Nora paused a moment, took a breath, picked up the silver fastener that would hold the bandage in place.

"You," she said. She felt as if she had a stone in her throat and no matter how hard she swallowed it wouldn't go down.

"What, Little One?"

"You make it very hard for me to hate you sometimes."

"Don't worry. You'll find a reason to hate me again soon enough. You always do."

Nora hated to leave him alone but his refrigerator had nothing in it but the most disgustingly healthy-looking vegetarian casseroles and fruit trays, gifts from well-meaning parishioners. She pretended it wasn't there and went for Indian takeout, the best in the city. The only in the city, too. As she pulled out plates from the kitchen cabinets and opened a bottle of wine, she felt something unexpected, something like homesickness. Once upon a time this place had been her second home. She and Søren had made love on that kitchen table a dozen times at least, a hundred times in the living room/library, a thousand times in the bedroom. But they'd also talked together here in this kitchen, read together in the living room, taken long Tuesday-afternoon naps together on the sofa, Søren on his back and her stretched out on top of him. Since she left him, she only came back to the rectory when he needed her for kink and sex. They hadn't had a meal under this roof together in years.

"You're quiet," Søren said from the kitchen doorway.

"I was wondering if Diane's warning notes are going to keep everyone away."

"They will. She's told everyone my sister is staying with me. If they see the car they'll assume it's hers. And they'll see the notes and run for their lives. Diane is not to be trifled with."

"She knows I'm here tonight, doesn't she?"

"She does."

"I guess a sign from a church secretary works as well as a tie on the door."

"Why would she put a tie on the door?" he asked, peeking his nose inside the bag of takeout.

"You do it in college with your roommates. Tie on the door means 'I'm fucking someone right now so don't come in.'"

"As you can imagine, this was not a system we employed in seminary."

She shooed him away from the food as she filled two plates and sat on top of the kitchen table.

"None for me?" he asked.

"This is for you. Sit. I'll feed you."

"I told you I wasn't an invalid," he said.

"You're right-handed, and you've sprained your right wrist."

"I'm also a pianist who is fairly close to being ambidextrous. I can manage a fork with my left hand. It's eating, not surgery."

She held up her fork with a bite of paneer on the end.

"Open up for the choo-choo train," she said. He gave her a look of disgust to end all looks of disgust.

"Fine," she said. "More for me then. I'll eat the choo-choo." She ate the piece of paneer and moaned in exaggerated food pleasure.

"You're ridiculous," Søren said as he prepared his own food. "I hope you know that."

"I have a client who's an adult baby. He likes being fed choo-choo and airplane style. When I started working as a dominatrix I went out and bought riding crops and floggers and handcuffs...never occurred to me I'd also have to stock up on baby food and adult diapers."

"Human sexuality is as varied as the colors of the rainbow," Søren said. "Sadly it's not always a pot of gold at the end."

"Sometimes it's a pot of sh—"

"Eleanor, we're eating."

"Sorry, sir." She took a huge bite of food to cover her giggles.

"You are an endlessly unusual woman." Søren sat in a chair opposite her, his big bare feet up on the table next to her hip.

"Whenever I think I've explored every corner of you, I turn another corner and find a new wing."

"Says the Danish Catholic polyglot sadist priest. My weirdness has nothing on you."

"You chose to be a dominatrix as an adult. My mother was Danish. I converted to Catholicism at age fourteen because I was sent, against my will, to a Catholic school and had a conversion experience. I learn languages because it helps my work as a priest and a translator of religious documents, and the sadism is, as you know, nothing I asked for."

"If you could give it back, would you?"

"Yes."

"Really?" She hadn't expected him to answer so quickly and so easily.

"Would you choose to be what I am if you had a choice?" he asked.

"A sadist? I did choose it, remember? I beat up more people in one day than you do in one month."

"It's not the same. I can't even become aroused without inflicting pain or humiliation. You don't need it the way I do. Don't confuse wanting with needing."

"Why not? If I want it as much as you need it, isn't it the same?"

"Very well then. Same question to you. If you could make yourself stop wanting it, would you?"

"I guess I have to say no. Being a sadist pays for my house."

"And if money were no object?"

"You're asking me if I would be vanilla if I could be vanilla?"

"I am."

"I do think about it sometimes," she said. "It might make life easier."

"Easier isn't necessarily more rewarding."

"But infinitely less complicated." She paused to eat and pull her thoughts together. "I had sex with a virgin last night."

"You found one?" he asked.

"Right under my nose. Third one I've found. I even have a punch card—if I fuck two more virgins I get a free frozen yogurt on my birthday."

"Virgins don't seem your particular cup of tea. What's the appeal?"

"I don't know. Untapped potential maybe. Being someone's first is a power trip, especially when you're not just introducing them to sex but kink, too. And they're not us," she admitted.

"What do you mean?"

"I mean, they're not one of us. I don't meet these guys at kink clubs. I meet them out in the real world. I met Noah at a coffee shop where I write."

"You mean you meet them in your other life. Not the life you share with Kingsley and me and your clients."

She nodded.

"Right. He's a normal college kid. Sweet. Sexy. Nice. No baggage. I let him spend the night and this morning… I was glad he was still there. I felt very vanilla."

"Juliette sleeps with Kingsley almost every night. Their relationship is anything but vanilla."

"Juliette is fine sleeping with a man who routinely fucks other people. That's harder to find for a woman. Noah doesn't know I do kink for money. I didn't tell him that today I got paid five hundred dollars from a judge to let him jack off on my feet. Or that I routinely stick a dildo in the ass of the mayor's baby brother. Or that the bed he lost his virginity in was paid for by me carving my name with a needle into the dick of the man who owns the largest furniture store chain on the Eastern Seaboard. I mean, look at you. You're a sadist. You're practically worshipped in the Underground as a god of pain, and yet you don't even like what I do for a living."

"If I weren't in love with you, I'd have no qualms whatsoever with your line of work."

"I want to be in a relationship with someone who doesn't have a problem with it and who is also in love with me. If a man as kinky as you can't accept it...who can?"

She stabbed her fork into her food.

"You're lonely," Søren said.

She shrugged. "Just overworked."

"You never say no to me when I tell you I need you. I have trouble believing you're here out of pure concern for my well-being."

"Why not?"

"You're not that nice." He pointed his fork at her before resuming his dinner.

Nora scowled at him. "This is why I can't be vanilla," Nora said. "I'm enjoying the fantasy of stabbing you in the neck with my fork too much. I'd miss being kinky."

"You would miss me."

"Yes," she admitted. "And my riding crops. And being treated like a queen all the time. No vanilla guys for me."

"For the best," Søren said. "I was briefly married to someone who didn't have any idea who or what she'd married. A fate best to be avoided."

"That's not going to happen. What vanilla guy would fall in love with a dominatrix anyway?"

"If we're talking about you specifically?" Søren said, learning forward to offer her a bite of curry. Because he'd had such a rough couple of days, she let him feed her. "All of them."

After dinner she washed the dishes and stored the leftovers in the refrigerator. When she finished, she found him in the living room in his big armchair with a book in his uninjured hand. She stood in front of him with her arms crossed over her chest.

"Don't interrupt me," Søren said, giving her the barest glance over the top of the book. "I'm reading."

She plucked the book out of his hand.

The Red by Nora Sutherlin.

"You can't read this book," she said.

"Why ever not?"

"It's pornographic."

"I'm a grown man. I can read anything I like, and I like this book." He took it back from her.

"You are also a Catholic priest. You fucking priests burned Sappho's poetry in the third century and now we have almost nothing left of it. Catholic priests don't deserve good porn," she said, taking the book out of his hand.

"The Catholic Church also created the convent which was the sole sanctuary for lesbians and other women and girls who wanted to avoid marriage. It was also the only place women were allowed to live without men, and where they were allowed to learn how to read and write. The Western Canon exists because of the Catholic Church." He attempted to pluck the book out of her hand. Nora pulled it out of reach.

"Fine," he said and reached between the cushion of his chair and the arm. He pulled out another book. *The Lotus-Eaters* by Nora Sutherlin.

Nora laughed as she sunk to the floor and rested her chin on Søren's knee.

"The Lotus-Eaters," she said. "Of course you'd have a copy of my book about temple prostitution."

"I'm thinking the Catholic Church should bring back sacred prostitution. It would improve attendance," he said, flipping casually through the pages.

"Do I want to know how you keep getting copies of my books? You aren't shoplifting from a bookstore, are you?"

"Juliette smuggles them to me. She's quite a fan of your work. She thought I would like this one since it seems to be dedicated to me. Then again, they're all dedicated to me." He opened the book to the dedication page where the words "As Always, Beloved, Your Eleanor" were printed.

"It's not dedicated to you. It's an acrostic. Aabye was Søren Kierkegaard's middle name."

"I'm well aware of this, as are you."

"Obviously, it's dedicated to Søren Kierkegaard."

"I didn't realize you were such a fan of early nineteenth-century Protestant Danish theologians."

"Christian existentialism makes me wet."

"Speaking of…" He took *The Red* back from her and turned the pages. "Yes. Yes." He flipped through a few more pages. "Yes. Twice."

"What are you talking about?"

"I'm seeing which love scenes in your book I inspired." He held the book open to a certain page, and Nora saw it was a scene that involved the enigmatic hero challenging his younger lover to a contest of sorts. She had to hold a full glass of wine in her hand while he fucked her and if she didn't spill any, she won and if she did spill the wine, he won. And when he won, they both won.

"I changed the names to protect the not-so-innocent. And it's hardly autobiographical," she said, a half-truth. "She's an art gallery owner. He's a mysterious rich guy who says he'll pay to keep her gallery open if she agrees to do everything he tells her to do for a year."

"I remember you and I making a similar sort of bargain."

"You asked for 'forever' from me. Mister Mysterious only

asks for one year. *And* he put out immediately. You made me wait until I was twenty before you fucked me."

"Believe it or not, I do have a conscience, Eleanor. You were a very attractive fifteen-year-old, but you were too young for me, and I had no intention of going to prison for statutory rape."

"You fucked a sixteen-year-old."

"When I was seventeen."

"You should have taken me to Denmark and fucked me there. Age of consent is fifteen in your motherland."

"I won't ask why you committed that fact to memory."

"I don't think you thought I was too young for you. I think you got off on stringing me along and making me beg for it. Admit it."

"You're punishing me for that by making me wait for you to come back to me. Admit it."

Nora only stared at him.

"Isn't that your plan?" Søren asked, his eyebrow lifted in a question. "I made you wait for over four years. You'll make me wait just as long or more?"

"You think this is some insidious plan of mine? I'm building this new life for myself without you just because you didn't fuck me when I was fifteen like I asked you to?"

"Aren't you?"

"Søren, I swear if you get any more smug you'll turn into Kingsley."

She pushed in closer, and buried her head in his lap. His hand resting on the back of her neck felt as comforting as a collar, as confining as a noose.

"No," she said. "I'm not punishing you. I'm just… I'm trying to live my life."

"Without me."

"That was your choice, not mine," she said. "You chose

to be a priest, which was the last thing in the world Claire wanted you to do. Or Kingsley. Or your mother. So don't sit there and judge me for going down a path you can't follow when you walked away from everyone you loved when you put on your collar."

"You have no intention of coming back to me?" he asked.

"Let me answer your question with a question—will you let me keep working for Kingsley?"

"You enjoy the work that much?"

"I enjoy being a domme that much. I enjoy being able to afford my house that much. So what's your answer?"

"My answer is…no," he said. "I can't support this choice you've made. The work you do is too dangerous, and I love you too much to allow you to do it. If you were mine again, I would order you to quit."

Nora already knew that was his answer, but hearing it reopened the wound she'd been trying to ignore for three years since she left him.

"So we're at a stalemate," she said, glancing over at Søren's chessboard sitting on the bookshelf.

"Perhaps it's time to break the stalemate," Søren said.

"How?" Nora looked up at him.

Søren didn't speak for a moment. He was weighing his words.

"I told you when I had my accident, I was on my way home from dinner with someone. That someone was the superior of my province."

"Hot date?"

"Not quite. I've been asked to take my Final Vows."

Nora's brow furrowed in confusion.

"I thought you told them no years ago."

"The last time they asked me was shortly after you left me."

Nora sat very still and felt the weight of his decision heavy

on her. She understood what it meant if he were to say yes.
Final Vows were a big deal for a Jesuit. Jesuits usually took
them twenty or more years after entering the order. When a
priest's life and ministry was examined by his peers and su-
periors and found worthy, he was invited to take his Final
Vows. Søren had told her once that it was similar to a teacher
being offered tenure.

If Søren took his Final Vows, he would be committing to
remaining in the priesthood until he died. She understood it
meant he would never again ask and/or order her to marry
him. She understood it meant he had made his mind up about
the rest of his life, and it didn't include marriage or children,
which she couldn't blame him for as she didn't want those
things, either. But she wanted to make no more vows ever,
no more promises she couldn't keep. A vow was the opposite
of freedom and she shrank from the very thought of it.

"The ceremony's one week from Sunday."

"So you're going to do it?" she asked.

"Give me a reason to say no," he said.

"I can't."

"Then I'll tell them yes."

Nora couldn't look at him. She turned her head and stared
at the chessboard again. Søren had taught her the game years
ago. They'd often play when she'd spent the night with him
after the kink and the sex were out of their systems. Although
she always considered chess with Søren a sort of kink. He always beat her when they played. Except that one time she
punished him for making her play by swallowing a pawn.

"Little One? Where are you?"

"Here," she said. "I'm here with you."

He pinched her nose. This time she couldn't give him the
smile he wanted.

"I want you to be there. Will you do that for me?"

"I don't know if I can," she said, her head still in his lap, his hand still on the back of her neck.

"Are you worried things will change between us after I take the vows?"

"Won't they?" she asked.

"Yes."

"You'll start keeping your vow of chastity, won't you?"

"You left me, Eleanor, and you said yourself you're not coming back."

"That's a yes, isn't it?"

The pause between her question and his answer was the longest pause she'd ever lived through but if that thrumming empty air, that painful fermata, had gone on forever, it still wouldn't have been long enough for her. She could have lived her entire life quite happily without hearing his answer. Someday she would learn never to ask questions she didn't want the answer to.

"Yes."

26

NORA TURNED ON THE LIGHT IN SØREN'S BEDROOM and pulled down the covers on the bed.

"You're staying the night," Søren said. Not a question, a statement of fact.

"I'd stay until you were healed completely if I could. You know that, right?" she said, resting her head on his chest. He wrapped his good arm around her.

"A fool's errand, Little One. If you waited until all my wounds were healed, you would be here forever."

She didn't tell him that was the point. She merely turned her face up to his and let him kiss her.

"I have something to show you," he said.

"If it's what I think it is, I've seen it before."

"Behave, Eleanor. It was a gift from Laila," Søren said. "It's on the bedside table."

The table in question sat between the bed and the wall of his upstairs bedroom. On it sat a little metal contraption. It appeared to be some sort of mobile no bigger than his hand.

Tiny silver snowflakes dangled off fan blades suspended over a votive candle.

"It's a spinner," Søren explained. "You light the candle on the base. When the heat from the wick rises, the blades turn. Try it."

Nora took a lighter from the bedside table and lit the candle. In only seconds the fan blades started to turn and the silver snowflakes rotated like a carousel. Søren reached past her and turned off the lamp.

She glanced around the darkened bedroom and smiled, delighted as a child as the light danced in the dark room.

"It looks like it's snowing," she said. "Indoors. In August."

"A little Scandinavian magic," he said. "Laila collects the spinners. At Christmas the house is full of them. A fire hazard but quite pretty at night."

"It's beautiful," she said, as she slipped into bed to lie next to him. Together they watched the magic of snow indoors in August. But it wasn't magic, merely an illusion. But if that were true, why did she smell snow?

Søren slid his bare leg over her hip and she said, "Stop."

"Why?"

"You'll hurt yourself," she said as he ignored her *stop*. He rose up on his uninjured left arm, his right arm at her side. Even in the dark she could see his eyes watching her.

"I'm already hurt." He dipped his head and kissed her. She didn't say *stop* again.

She felt a thousand things as he kissed her—the fear of hurting him was first and foremost. Whenever she started to put her arms around his back she remembered his injuries and stopped herself. She placed her hands over her head and clung to the headboard instead of him. She felt other fears, as well. The fear of hurting herself. Kissing like this, deep kissing in bed at night, was the province of lovers, not ex-lovers.

Ex-lovers could fuck on occasion without it meaning much of anything. But this was nothing but kissing and nothing but kissing was so much more than sex.

"Come back to me…" Søren whispered the words against her lips.

"I can't."

"It can't snow indoors in August either, can it?" he asked as the magic snowflakes flickered and twinkled across the bed and over the ceiling and walls. He didn't wait for an answer before kissing her again.

She pushed her hips against him. He wasn't aroused. Of course not. Kissing wouldn't arouse him unless he also hurt her. She only wished he knew that kissing her like this, as if she was the only woman in the world, hurt worse than a beating.

"If I come back to you, wearing your collar, submitting to you again, what's to stop you from ordering me to give up everything I worked for—my name, my freedom, my job, my house, my whole life…?"

Søren ran the tip of his tongue from the base of her throat, up her neck and to her lips. Against them he whispered one word…

"Nothing."

They were at an impasse. An impossible impasse not even General Hannibal and all the elephants in the world could traverse. She would not go back to him unless he let her be Nora. He would not take her back unless she became Eleanor again. They both wanted each other but apparently not enough to cede any ground to the other. Nothing left to do so Nora attempted retreat. Søren wouldn't let her go, however. He twined their legs together, pressed his chest to her back. There would be no eluding his arms tonight, not that she wanted to. Tonight she was his prisoner. Tomorrow morning she would escape him again.

She slept fitfully, plagued by dreams of death, hers and his. She woke once with a start, disoriented in the darkness. The candle had burned itself out. The magic show was over. Next to her Søren slept, his eerily dark eyelashes resting lightly on his pale skin. He didn't like being touched in his sleep but she couldn't resist one small kiss on his slightly parted lips. He made the smallest sound in the back of his throat and she felt his erection against her thigh. She laughed softly, almost soundlessly, and laid her head back on the pillow. He couldn't get hard from making out with her for half an hour, but let him fall asleep for a few hours and there it was…boys will be boys. Now she knew how Ruth felt lying next to Boaz on the threshing floor.

Her body vibrated with laughter as she remembered a better time. Søren's eyelashes fluttered and opened. He moved on top of her and without thinking, Nora opened her legs to him. She was still slick and wet inside from her earlier arousal. Being near him, naked and in his bed, was the source of her aching arousal and when he penetrated her fully she cried out as much in surprise as pleasure. Nora took all of him she could into her. When it wasn't enough she begged for more.

"Hurt me," she murmured against his skin. "Please?"

"No."

"Please…"

"No." He kept thrusting, thrusting hard but not hard enough to hurt her. This must have tortured him as much as it tortured her. He needed pain, craved it, thrived on it. To deny her pain was to deny his pleasure.

He'd woken up hard. It happened sometimes, especially in the morning. But without more pain he might not be able to come. She feared he intended to punish her as she'd punished Kingsley—sex but no orgasm, coupling with no consummation.

"You slapped me our first night together." She was so wet she felt it dripping onto the sheets beneath her, could hear it when he pulled back and pushed in. "You did it before you took my virginity."

"I'll do it again when you come back to me. Not before."

"You're only punishing yourself."

"And yet it's you who is begging…"

Nora shifted beneath him, tilting her hips so that his cock was in the deepest part of her, hitting her cervix painfully. Better. Her head fell back and she moaned. Yes…this is what she wanted from him…to be used, hurt, taken, ravished, impaled, invaded, breached and violated. She let herself be weak because he was so strong and to fight it would be futile. She didn't want to fight it. She'd broken a teenage boy last night, taken his virginity, and she submitted to Søren as her penance. It was no great punishment to watch him fuck her, all the hardness of his body, his arms and stomach and long thighs, against and inside the softness of her. She couldn't lose this… she needed it…she was so close…

"Please hurt me, sir…"

"No," he said again. If there were a crueler word in the world than that one she'd never heard it.

Maybe his own pain was enough. It had to be hurting him, moving like this when half his back was black and purple. She lifted her hips again and again into his, seeking release. But it was too late. It was over. Søren pulled out of her, his erection already gone.

Nora lay panting, overwhelmed with the realization of what had just happened, what they'd just attempted. The failure hung over the bed like a poison cloud.

"You're punishing me," she said. The words sounded hollow in the room. They rang off the walls and back against the bed.

"I am."

"Because I left you? Or because I won't come back?"

"Because I can."

"And you wonder why I left you…"

"Don't lie to yourself, Eleanor. And don't lie to me. The pain wasn't why you left. The pain was why you stayed."

She didn't argue with him because she couldn't. He turned his back to her and once more became a wall of silence, a wall of stone. Closing her eyes, Nora slipped her hand down her body and against her clitoris. He'd left her slick and sore and empty, and she had to come or she wouldn't be able to sleep. She dipped her fingertip into her own wetness and touched herself until the pleasure hit its peak and her muscles contracted around the nothing inside her.

Spent now, she considered leaving. Leaving tonight, this minute. Getting up, getting dressed and walking out without another word. He'd fucked her and hadn't finished to prove a point. When he was inside her it wasn't his come or his cock she begged for but his pain. If she were to do something so foolish as to fall in love with someone vanilla, this was what she could expect…endless frustration. It would leave her as unfulfilled as her body was right now. It would leave her always wanting more.

She could leave. She should leave.

Or she could go back to sleep and leave him in the cold light of morning. That would hurt him more so that's what she did.

When she woke again it was to sunlight in an otherwise empty bed. Not an empty house, however. She heard Søren's voice but not only his voice.

In a panic she grabbed the nearest clothes she could find, one of his shirts, and threw it on. She crept over to Søren's closet, shutting herself in as silently as she could.

Through an air duct she could hear the voices. Søren's she recognized. The other she didn't. It was a male voice, however. It could be another priest. Oh, that would be bad. Or the bishop. Worst-case scenario.

The voices stopped. Nora heard footsteps approaching. The closet door swung open.

Søren looked at her with a cocked eyebrow.

"Is he gone?" she whispered.

"If only I had a camera," he said. "Kingsley's Red Queen hiding in my closet between a cassock and a garment bag."

"Oh, shut up. Is he gone?"

"He is. He was delivering a plant."

"A plant? I had a panic attack over a goddamn fern?"

"It was a ficus."

"If we're going to destroy your career in the church, I hope it's over something better than a ficus."

"It's a very nice ficus."

"Can I come out of your closet now?" she asked.

"No. For one thing…is this really the best you could do?" Søren asked. "The closet?"

"I assumed under the bed was the first place they'd look."

"Yes, considering these were on top of the bed." He held up a pair of underwear. Hers.

She grabbed them out of his hand.

"Sorry. I'm a little out of practice," she said. "I used to be better at this."

"Better at what?"

"Leaving before sunrise. I'll go now before anyone else shows up with another fern."

"Ficus."

Nora pushed past him and found her jeans over the back of the armchair and her shirt hanging on the doorknob. When she was still Søren's sub, she knew better than this. She'd put her clothes right next to her side of the bed so she could find them in an instant and dress. They'd had a couple close calls before. Diane had come to Søren's with church emergencies while she and Søren were in bed together. Once while Søren was inside her. They'd both stayed calm. Nora had dressed as quickly and quietly as she could while Søren went downstairs. Then she'd sunk to the floor between the bed and the wall, out of sight. Rule number one was "leave the bedroom door open." If the door was closed, it would raise suspicion. An open door meant he had nothing to hide. If someone came into the bedroom she could slip under the bed. But that wouldn't happen because no one would suspect a priest of hiding a lover in a room with the door wide-open, right?

Søren walked over to her and took her clothes out of her hands.

"What?" she demanded.

"I need your help."

"After that stunt you pulled last night? You're on your own, Blondie."

"It involves putting a knife to my throat."

She narrowed her eyes at him.

"Now you're talking."

Five minutes later Nora sat on the bathroom counter with Søren standing between her knees. She held a straight razor in her hand and she ran it carefully down Søren's cheek, wet with shaving soap.

"I thought you were Mister Ambidextrous," she said, rinsing the shaving soap of the blade.

"I trust my left hand for eating, not for shaving with a straight razor."

"You could use a normal razor like a normal person. I'm kinky and I love playing with knives as much as the next dominatrix, but you don't catch me shaving my legs with a straight razor."

"Sentimental value. It belonged to my grandfather."

"Which one?"

"My mother's father. I never met my paternal grandfather. He died before I was born."

She tilted Søren's chin up to shave along his throat.

"Do you know anything about him?"

"He was an English baron and a raging alcoholic who very likely abused my father as much as my father abused my sister."

Nora rinsed off the straight razor again and turned Søren's head to the left.

"Does that change how you feel about him at all?"

"I've met dozens of people who were abused as children who did not turn into abusers themselves as adults. Elizabeth didn't."

"You didn't."

"Some would disagree." He gave her a pointed look.

"I don't and only my opinion counts in this instance. What you and I did and what happened between your father and your sister are worlds apart. I wouldn't blame you if you'd given your father the Holofernes treatment."

Nora mimed slicing her head off with the razor.

"Don't cut yourself. I'd have enough trouble explaining a half-naked woman in my closet. I don't need a headless corpse in my bathroom."

"No decapitation? You're getting so vanilla in your old age," she said.

He cocked his eyebrow at her. "Is that so?"

"We had about one minute of vanilla sex last night."

"Only to prove a point. The point being you need, want and desire pain, and wouldn't enjoy being with someone who couldn't give that to you."

"I give it to other people."

"You know it's not the same. I can torture my own body

and it takes the edge off the need, but it doesn't take it away. Do you even submit to Kingsley anymore?"

"I can't talk to you about what Kingsley and I do together."

"Why not? You always told me in delightfully exacting detail what you two had done in my absence."

"He's a client," she said. "I don't gossip about clients."

"Kingsley pays you for pain and sex?"

"No, don't be silly. He pays me for pain. I give him the sex for free."

"You know you miss it, Eleanor. The way you were begging me to hurt you last night? That wasn't pillow talk."

"Doesn't matter. You're injured and can't even shave your own face. Now shut up before I accidentally give you the Holofernes treatment."

He shut up and so did she while she finished shaving his face. She knew his sudden good behavior wasn't due to any desire of his to actually submit to her. He simply didn't want her nicking him. He stared placidly past her, letting her move his chin this way and that while she scraped off the last of his stubble. When she finished, she soaked a hand towel under the hot water and used it to wipe the last of the soap off his cheeks and chin and throat. She might have taken longer than necessary doing this. She did love his face, the sharp planes of his chin and jaw, the sculpted lips, the gunmetal-gray eyes that saw everything and revealed nothing.

She kissed him.

Søren returned the kiss, but only for a moment before pulling back.

"What was that for?" His tone was skeptical.

"You're very handsome and when there's a very handsome man standing between my knees, I kiss him."

"I should spend more time between your knees then."

"That is not the sentiment of a priest about to take Final Vows."

"Not true. Half the priests taking Final Vows with me would say the same to you if they knew you."

"What about the other half?"

"Gay."

"Right," she said, laughing. "Forgot."

"Please be there with me," he said. "Will you?"

She rested her forehead on the center of his bare chest. He kissed her hair.

"Just because I didn't want you leaving the church for me, doesn't mean I can sit there and watch you give away the rest of your life to the church. Your life and your body." This body that she'd thought of as hers for so long would now be the sole property of the church. "Are you sure this is what you want?"

"Do you know the Danish fairy tale *Den Lille Havfrue*?"

"In English?"

"The Little Mermaid."

"Of course I know it."

"The real story? Not the sanitized modern version?" Søren took his razor from her hand and washed it under scalding water in the sink.

"I think so. Mermaid falls in love with a prince and gets herself turned into a human being so they can be together, right?"

"The little mermaid's fins are rent in two as if a sword has passed through her body. But since she was never meant to walk on land, with every step she takes, she feels something like knives cutting into her feet and her body bleeding from the wounds."

"How cheerful."

"Danes are known for many virtues—cheerfulness is not chief among them."

Søren took Nora's ankle in his left hand and lifted her foot. With the razor tip held between two fingers on his injured right hand, Søren carefully placed a small cut on the heel of her foot—a small wound, yes, but she knew until it healed in a day or two, she'd feel it with every step she took.

"The little mermaid fails to win her prince's heart and returns to the ocean," Søren continued. "When she dies she finds she has a soul, a reward for all her suffering."

"But she doesn't get her prince?"

"No. Being transformed into something she isn't fails to win the prince. A good moral. Very Danish. Don't try to be something you aren't."

"And what are you?" she asked.

"I am a priest," he said. "Which I always knew I was. I knew I belonged in the church when I fell in love with you. I knew I was born to be a priest whether I wanted to be one or not. If I'd left the church to marry you, I would have felt the pain of it with every step I took…" He made a second small cut in the heel of her other foot.

"Yes, we could have been together on land," he continued, "but at what price? You didn't let me leave the ocean I belong in and in a way, I'm grateful to you. Especially since you're here now."

"Of course I'm here," she said, reaching down to take the razor from his hand. She set it on the counter and placed her hands on either side of his strong neck. "I know how to swim."

Søren kissed her, kissed the words on her lips that she knew had comforted him even more than a promise of attending his Final Vows would. She kissed him back with equal ardor, brushing her lips over his now smooth chin. Cutting her feet had aroused him. She slipped her hand into his pants and wrapped her fingers around his erection.

"Eleanor," he said breathlessly, "what are you doing?"

"Solving the crisis in the priesthood," she said. "I met a nun once who said the secret was giving priests daily hand jobs. It's not intercourse—not anal, not vaginal, not oral—but it can get a priest off. I might join a religious order if I were guaranteed daily orgasms hand-delivered by a handsome oblate."

"I should run that idea by the superior of the Paraclete order."

"What are they?"

"An order of priests and sisters dedicated to helping and comforting other priests." Søren wrapped his left arm around her back and pressed closer to her.

"Then consider me your Paraclete."

"I always have."

He bit her earlobe while she continued to stroke him. She loved hearing his labored breathing in her ear. His left hand, the uninjured once, dug hard into the small of her back. Nora didn't mind. The pain he gave her stoked his pleasure. He was brutally hard. Hard and soft, aroused and yet putty in her hand. But that's how men worked. Even dominant sadists like Søren. He'd teased her that morning that their little kingdom would be aghast to see their fearsome Red Queen hiding in a closet from a ficus-delivery boy. Well, wouldn't they be equally amused to see their god of pain melting against her, at once tense and loose, over nothing more than a well-timed hand job?

Nora wet her hand under the tap. Søren gasped a little against her neck as she took him in her grasp again, rubbing him with warm wet fingers. His hips moved, but only just into her grip, tiny pulses that were more erotic to her than hard thrusts because she knew how badly he wanted to stay in control and he couldn't entirely master himself. But he could master her.

"Don't stop," he ordered.

"No, sir." She could tell Søren hadn't come in some time. Fluid dripped from the tip onto her hand and she massaged it back into the frenulum. His chest rose in sharp breaths. It pleased her to be able to distract him from his own pain for a few minutes. It soothed her aching conscience. She knew leaving him had been the right thing to do, and she knew going back to him would be a mistake. But Kingsley had trained her well as a dominatrix. It went against her nature to hurt someone who didn't ask for pain. Søren not only hadn't asked for the pain she'd given him, he hadn't paid for it up front.

"I love touching you," she said. "I didn't get to do this very often when I was in your collar. You always tied me up and touched me while I lay there dying to touch you."

"You should have begged a little more, and I might have let you." Of course he would tell her this now, years after it mattered. Such a talented sadist, he could torment her in the past by giving her secrets in the present.

"If I stopped touching you now, would you beg?"

"No."

"What would you do?"

"Finish with my left hand."

She laughed and felt his smile against her skin. She wrapped her foot around his left leg for no reason other than she wanted to be closer to him while she touched him. Now she concentrated on the head, the thick tip, rubbing her thumb over the little slick indentation at the top. Her hand roved down against him, clasping him firmly at the base before dragging her hand all the way to the head again. She did it again, pulling harder this time, making Søren shudder slightly. She gripped him tightly but moved slowly. He wasn't the only sadist in the room.

And because he wasn't the only sadist in the room, right

when she had him, when she knew he'd come any second, she stopped.

She stopped and smiled at him, leaning back on the bathroom counter onto her hands.

"Okay," she said, "finish with your left hand."

He narrowed his eyes at her.

"If you insist."

With his left hand he grabbed her by the arm and drew her roughly to him. Even with his right arm remaining mostly out of commission, he was still stronger than Nora. In an instant he had her turned around. He grabbed the back of her neck, pushed her onto the counter and held her there. She heard the sound of fabric moving only seconds before she felt him inside her. Touching him had made her wet, and he entered her easily. With cruel thrusts he slammed into her as she lay helpless, pinned to the tile countertop by his left hand on the back of her neck.

Nora should have known better than to think she could get the upper hand with him. As roughly as he held her down, there was no chance for escaping. Unless she said her safe word. But then he'd stop and where was the fun in that? His thrusts were deep and long and in this position she felt exposed, open, helpless. She loved it. She hated it. She hated that she loved it and loved that she hated it because hating it meant she wasn't completely his yet. There was still hope she could escape him completely. Someday. Eventually. But not yet. Not while he felt this good.

Delicious tremors passed through her hips and up into her back and down her thighs as he fucked her. She felt filled by him, stretched open, owned and mastered. When she came she did so silently, a final last rebellion against him. When he came in her, she sighed, grateful for the warm wet heat she'd missed so much. She made her other lovers wear condoms.

Not Søren, though. She could never be with him with something between them.

Søren pulled out of her and let her up. The back of her neck ached where his hands had gripped her. Without a word to him she walked out of the bathroom, heading to the bedroom to put on her clothes leaving bloody footprints behind her.

"Where are you going?" Søren demanded.

"Getting out of the ocean," she said. "I'm done swimming."

27

A New Client

MISTRESS NORA'S DUNGEON IS A HAPPY DUNGEON. That was her motto. Men came to her broken in all the wrong ways and she sent them home smiling, broken in all the right ways. But in the days after Søren told her his news, Mistress Nora's dungeon wasn't a happy dungeon because Mistress Nora wasn't happy. She told Kingsley to send her masochists that week and only masochists. With a scalpel she carved her name into the back of a handsome world-famous violinist, her penmanship careful and elegant as she knew her name would remain in his skin for months before it healed and faded. In an upstate home that was more fortress than house, Nora whipped a retired four-star general into near-unconsciousness. He tipped her a thousand dollars for being the first woman to beat him as hard as he'd dreamed of being beaten. The next day Kingsley sent her to a hotel suite, all gilt and red and velvet, a Rococo monstrosity from a Sacher-Masoch fever dream. In the suite she presided over a rite in which the client was tied to the bed on his back spread-eagle and branded with

a branding iron on his biceps and inner thighs. Four dominatrixes. Four brands. Permanent scars. He wept with gratitude
after the scene as Nora cleaned the deep wounds. In the absence of pain, the client was impotent and he'd had his first
orgasm in a year when they'd branded him. The client was
the wealthy twenty-five-year-old son of Hungary's ambassa-
dor to the United Nations. Nora had kissed his forehead and
called him a sweet little boy. He kissed the soles of her boots
and called her his queen for life.

After four days Nora was spent. She had no more pain to
give and still no peace in her heart. She lay on her back on the
bed in her dungeon, her black-and-white braided riding crop
in her hand. Lazily she twirled it like a majorette with a baton.
If her hands went idle for a single second she knew the devil
would use them for playthings. He'd use them to make her call
Søren or worse, go to Søren. She had no right to ask him not
to take his Final Vows. None. She'd left him. She'd also told
him to stop waiting for her time and time again. She'd begged
him to find someone new to love, someone new to fuck. *Go
back to Kingsley*, she'd said to him on more than one occasion.
Sleep with Simone, she adores you, she'd said on another. *Find
someone else to fuck. Stop playing martyr, waiting for me to come
back to you.* It was a selfish request on her part, wanting him
to move on. She couldn't move on completely until he did.
When they were together they'd been like a couple holding
hands, tightly clinging to each other in a viselike grip. She'd
left him but his hand still held hers even as she struggled to
pull away from his fingers. At last he was letting her hand go
and as soon as he let go, she'd realized his hand was the only
thing holding her up.

Søren had found a new love and it was his oldest love—
older than his love for her, even older than his love for King-

sley. He was leaving them both for God. And how on earth or how in the hell was she supposed to compete with God?

Nora's hotline phone rang but she didn't answer it. Either it was Kingsley calling about scheduling another client or it was Søren, the only person other than Juliette who had her hotline number. She didn't have the mental energy to talk to Kingsley right now.

Had Søren told Kingsley he was taking Final Vows yet? Possibly. The minute after Kingsley learned of Søren's accident and injuries, he'd hired a private nurse to tend to their wounded priest twice a day. A relief for Nora. It gave her an excuse to keep her distance from him, gave her time to recover.

When near Søren, she felt too much. He exhausted her the way she imagined the people who lived at the foot of a sleeping volcano were exhausted from pretending they didn't live at the foot of a sleeping volcano. She'd seen a volcano once, long ago, during a trip out West. At first she thought it nothing more than a snow-capped mountain until someone had called it what it was, and she knew the fear of it then for it was as fearsome as it was beautiful. Finally she understood why Søren's skin smelled of snow and yet his touch was warm. At the volcano's core lurked a buried sleeping fire, a channel direct from the molten center of the earth that rose to the coldest corners of the sky. When the volcano erupted—and it would someday—not all the ice and snow in the world would be able to contain the conflagration.

But the snow had to try.

And yet Nora would rather go on living in fear at the foot of that volcano than live in safety anywhere else in the wide world.

Reluctantly Nora glanced at her phone. It had been Kingsley calling. She'd call him back in a few minutes. Or maybe she'd go over to the town house and crawl into bed with him.

Not for sex. She just couldn't stand the thought of spending the night alone in her house with this news, this news hanging over her like a poison cloud. She'd sleep at Griffin's tonight. Or King's. Or a total stranger's. She wished Talel would show up on her doorstep to take her away from her life for a day or two. Or anyone…

With a heavy sigh, Nora walked over to a coffin sitting on the floor of her dungeon. She unlocked the brass latches and opened the lid.

"Time's up, Troy," she said.

"Already?" the man in the coffin said. He was naked apart from his black socks and the smile on his face.

"Already. I even gave you five bonus minutes." She held out her hand and helped him from the coffin. "No charge."

"You're wonderful, Mistress. I feel like a million bucks."

"I wish lying in a coffin for an hour made me feel better," she said. "I'd sleep in one every night."

"Nothing like being locked in a coffin and facing your own mortality to make you feel alive." Troy pulled on his jeans and T-shirt and slipped on his shoes. He did look annoyingly refreshed and happy. "Thank you very much."

"I still can't figure out why you pay me for this," she said as Troy handed over a two-hundred-dollar tip. He was a Wall Street hotshot who regularly made six- and seven-figure commissions. He'd told her once that sensory deprivation helped with his focus and he credited his success at the brokerage to his sessions in his closed and locked coffin. "All I do is lock you in and let you out an hour later. Can't you get your own coffin and do it at home?"

"I can't lock myself in. It doesn't work unless I'm actually locked in and can't get out. My last domme would open the box every ten minutes to make sure I was still breathing. Ruined my focus. Killed my Zen. Killed my boner, too. Horrible. You leave me alone in there and that's all I ask. Same time next week?"

"You're welcome to pseudo-kill yourself in my coffin anytime. Or actually kill yourself."

"See? This is why you're the best domme," Troy said. "You can pull off the whole 'I don't care if you actually die' routine so well. That's part of the release, the excitement, knowing I could literally die and you'd let me. I face death and conquer it. Then I hit the trading floor like Godzilla, totally immune to fear."

"Of all the Wall Street guys I know, you are by far the most Wall Street," she said, opening the dungeon door for him.

"Mistress, I will take that as a compliment," he said, grinning.

"Troy?"

"Yes, Mistress?"

"It wasn't a compliment." She slammed the door in his face.

Through the door she heard a muffled "Love you, Mistress."

She picked up her red leather day planner off the side table and flipped through it. She thought she had another appointment today but couldn't remember who it was with or where it was. Juliette had taken over scheduling Nora's clients while Kingsley was giving her the silent treatment. Juliette was so much better at it Nora almost wished Kingsley hadn't forgiven her for Talel. Juliette actually scheduled her days off and other wonderful things like that. And whenever scheduling a new client, Juliette would work up something like an intake form for Nora so she would be better prepared for the session.

Inside her planner Nora found the envelope Juliette had clipped to today's date. She opened and read the form.

White male, American, age 29.
Client requests a one-hour weekly session for pain and release.

Release? Basic code for "beat him until he comes." And if he didn't come from the beating he would be, if he earned it, allowed to masturbate while she watched and made commentary.

Client has a strong tolerance for pain but requests no broken skin. A sustained beating is preferred as client wishes to achieve and remain in subspace for the duration of the session. He has been to several dominas before. His experience level is high.

Okay. No whippings. Whips did too much damage. The flogger then, the thick elk-skin one. Those marks healed fast. And candle wax, too. The wax left red marks, but they faded within a day.

One hour of flogging? Easy money.

Nora kept reading.

Medical warning: client has an inoperable brain aneurysm. In case of confusion, strange behavior, fainting, stroke or sudden illness, cease play immediately and call 911. Client has no immediate family with whom he is in contact.

"Knock, knock."

Nora turned and saw none other than Thorny himself standing in the doorway to her dungeon. He held what looked like at least two dozen red and white roses in his hand.

"You," she said.

"Me?" He pointed at himself.

"You're my new client?" she asked, pleasantly surprised. She'd had enough bad surprises lately. She was due for a good surprise.

"Is that a problem?" he asked as he stepped inside.

"Not a problem. Just unexpected. I haven't seen you in two years."

"Been busy," he said. "Busy bee with busy beavers. These are for you, Mistress."

"Thank you, they're beautiful."

"Watch out. I ordered roses with extra thorns."

"You would, wouldn't you?" Smiling she set the roses on her nightstand. "Thorny, what are you doing here?"

He looked good, healthy despite the aneurysm. He had on tight black jeans and an artfully torn T-shirt, no sleeves to show off his elegant full sleeve tattoos.

"The usual reason—I need to be flogged, often and by someone who knows how."

"I haven't seen you in two years and you all of sudden need a flogging from me?"

He crossed his arms over his chest and leaned back against her bedpost.

"Bad week," he admitted.

"What happened?"

"Consult with a hotshot surgeon who was convinced he could take care of this," he said, tapping his forehead. "Long story short, he can't. My fault for getting my hopes up."

"Oh, Thorny, I'm so sorry," she said.

He shrugged and didn't meet her eyes. He looked defeated, scared, almost feverish. Bad week. She knew how he felt.

"I needed a pick-me-up. You're the best domme in town, so the story goes. I wanted the best."

"I don't know," she said. "I don't feel comfortable taking money from you."

"Please, I don't want pity. Anything but that from you."

"It's not pity, I promise. I have a client with terminal cancer and another with chronic pain, and I take their money without batting an eyelash. But you… I knew you before you were a client. And I liked you. Plus you warned me about Milady, which you didn't have to do."

"You stepped in front of a whip to protect me from a beating. You didn't have to do that, either."

"I wish you hadn't booked me. I would flog you for free, for the fun of it. I like you and I'm not allowed to be intimate friends with a client."

"Or more than friends?" he asked, giving her a look—that look. That more-than-friends look.

"Or more than friends," she said, remembering how much she wanted him the night she saw him at the Body House. Her heart broke for him. She couldn't imagine what he lived with day in and day out. It would be like being locked in a coffin every single day and not knowing if anyone would come along and open the lid. "We already have a prior existing relationship. If Juliette had known that she never would have booked you with me. She would have scheduled you with Mistress Irina or somebody else."

"I don't want somebody else. I want you."

"Yeah, that's the problem. Dominatrixes and clients are supposed to have distance. Boundaries. I sort of crossed a line with a client a few weeks ago and Kingsley nearly fired me over it."

"Damn."

"Don't get me wrong. I'd love to flog you."

Thorny sat on her bed. He looked good there.

"Well…maybe we could arrange a trade then," he said. "I can call and cancel my appointment, right? Tell Juliette that I chickened out. She'll give me my money back, right?"

"Of course. I just have to tell her we didn't have the session."

"Then I'm not a client anymore. And you can give me a flogging. And I can give you…well, anything you want, Mistress."

"Anything I want?"

He batted his eyelashes at her.

"You want me to beat you and top you in exchange for you fucking me?"

"Not just fucking," Thorny said. "Women don't pay me two grand a night for a vanilla fuck. I give the whole shebang."

"What is the whole shebang?"

"It's when I bang she hole."

Nora narrowed her eyes at him. Thorny laughed and took her hand into his and kissed the back of it.

"Mistress, I have a gift. And so do you. You give me your gift and I'll give you my gift. I'm clean. I've been tested. I'm a condom maniac. There is no escort on the planet who gives a better Boyfriend Experience than I do."

Nora sat back against the bedpost. Boyfriend? Wasn't she just wishing the other day for a boyfriend? A real boyfriend. Not an owner like Søren. Not a slave, either. An actual boyfriend. Someone to share her life with, not just her bed.

"When we're done will you help me strip the sheets and fold them after they're dry?" she asked.

"Absolutely. I can never get my sheets folded right without someone helping me. I like to help around the house. It's fun playing normal sometimes. You wanna play with me?"

"It's very hard to say no to a sexy silver fox with a brain tumor."

"It's not a—"

She slapped her hand over his mouth. "No quoting dumb movies in my dungeon. I get enough of that from Griffin."

"Mess, Mus-muss."

She lowered her hand.

"What was that?"

"Yes, Mistress."

"Do you really want to have sex with me or are you just

trying to distract yourself from this?" Now she tapped his forehead.

"Yeah, I want to have sex with you because I have an aneurysm. That's the only reason. Or maybe I want to have sex with you because you're the most famous dominatrix in town, I love being flogged, oh, and you're so hot 'Wicked Game' plays spontaneously when you walk into a room."

Nora gave him credit. He knew how to hit on a woman.

"How about this..." she said. "We'll go to my house. I'll give you the flogging of your dreams. If we end up having sex, great. If not, no harm, no foul. We still had a nice evening together. Good enough?"

"More than good enough. I want to seduce you, however. So, you know, watch your back."

"Ass man, are you?"

"I'm every kind of man."

Nora smiled. Every kind of man was her kind of guy.

"Let's go to my place."

"So it's a yes?"

Nora leaned in and kissed him. He kissed her back and as they kissed she saw a volcano in the rearview mirror of her mind, receding into the distance. She felt safer already.

"Yes," she said against his lips. "Why not?"

"Yes, excellent," he said. He seemed more than happy. More like...relieved. Did he need a flogging from her that bad?

"Don't die in my house," Nora said as she found her keys to lock up the dungeon. "My neighbors think I'm weird enough as it is without a bunch of ambulances showing up to cart your beautiful corpse out of my house."

"I'd rather come in your bed than go in your bed. You know I'm hypersexual, right? I can get off about eight times a day."

"Eight?"

"My cock isn't huge but it's tenacious."

"I've never met a tenacious cock before. I look forward to making its acquaintance."

"You're going to beat me up first, right?"

"Oh, Thorny," she said as she locked the dungeon behind them and they walked down the hall arm in arm. "I'm going to do such things to you..."

"Good things? Bad things?"

Nora smiled at him.

"Good bad things."

Thorny kissed her again right in the hallway.

"My favorite things."

He abruptly stopped kissing her and took a step back.

"Wait," he said.

"What?"

"You're not going to get in trouble with Kingsley for this, are you?"

"No, of course not. As long as he doesn't find out."

"Good. Just checking."

"I'll tell you what Kingsley told me once when he and I did something we weren't supposed to do—what he doesn't know won't hurt us."

"What if he finds out?"

"He'll hurt us."

"Can I ask one more question, Mistress?" Thorny said as they headed to the exit.

"Sure thing. What's the question?"

"Why do you have a coffin in your dungeon?"

28

A Mirror Image

NORA PICKED UP HER LEXUS AT KINGSLEY'S AND drove her and Thorny to her house in Connecticut. The dog days of August were earning their bad reputation today. The clouds hung in the sky heavy, dark and low and the air simmered with heat. The electricity in the atmosphere made the hair stand up on her arms. Her clothes clung to her skin and it seemed everyone, herself included, wanted nothing more than to be naked inside an air-conditioned room. A few drops of rain fell presaging the coming summer storm, the sky heady and swollen but waiting to burst open. Even the sidewalks steamed.

When they arrived at Nora's house, Thorny whistled his appreciation while Nora turned off her cell phone. Last thing she wanted was Kingsley calling and interrupting her night off.

"Looks like the kink trade pays better than the flesh trade," Thorny said.

"You know what they say—if you want to afford a house in New York City, you move out of New York City."

She let him in and took him up to her bedroom. Luckily her cleaning lady came on Fridays and the house looked
and smelled clean and pleasant. Thorny looked around ap-
preciatively. She liked this, bringing guys home to her place.
It would be a crime to have such a nice house and no one to
share it with.

"This is my bedroom," Nora said. Sunlight streamed in
through the sides of Roman blinds against the window.

"Sexy," Thorny said. "Nice bed."

Nora patted the iron footboard. The bed was a bit medieval-
looking, and anyone who'd been in Søren's dungeon would
see it looked a bit like his. She had such good memories of
that bed...

"You're not the first client who offered me something in
trade for my kink. One of my boys owns the largest furniture
store on the Eastern Seaboard. He told me if I could beat him
until he passed out, he'd let me have the pick of his show-
room. *Voilà.*"

"Passed out? Jesus," Thorny said, tugging off his jacket.
"That's too rough for my blood."

"Don't worry. I only hit as hard as my boys want to be hit.
You like floggings, right, but hate whips? They feel too much
like switches?"

"You remember that?" He grinned, obviously pleased.

"That's why they pay me the big bucks." She walked to
him where he stood at the foot of her bed, leaning against the
post. She put her hands on his chest and kissed him again. He
wasn't nearly as tall as Søren. She guessed his height at about
five-ten. In her three-inch heels she could easily reach his lips.
His kisses were sweet and gentle, affectionate, but with a hint
of the passion she knew he hid within him. She could taste
it on her tongue. Copper. The same taste as the electricity in
the humid August air.

"So you're going to give me the Boyfriend Experience?" Nora asked.

"I am."

"Then I will give you the Submissive Experience. How does that sound?"

"Does it involve you putting me into subspace and getting me off so hard I can taste music and smell stars?"

"Yes."

"That sounds perfect. But...we're doing this in here?" he asked.

"Why not?"

"Well...it's a bedroom. Just a bedroom." He glanced around the room and she saw what he saw—a spacious bedroom with a recessed sitting area, an iron bed, a few novels on the night-stand and a lamp, and not much else but an ornately carved cheval mirror standing in the corner. Apart from two potted plants hanging from the ceiling by the mirror, there was not much else...

Or was there?

"Looks, my boy, can be deceiving." She winked at him and pulled away. On her way to her closet she glanced back over her shoulder. "You should be taking your clothes off right now. In case you didn't know."

"Yes, Mistress." He yanked his shirt off and she saw both of his nipples were pierced with silver hoops. Lovely. She did her best to ignore his body while she set up the room. From her closet she took out a black step stool and two lengths of rope. She threw a two-foot chrome spreader bar on the bed and found her favorite fawn-colored wrist and ankle cuffs. They were padded with soft faux fur on the inside. She wanted Thorny to feel coddled and comfortable, even in bondage.

"I'm only going to flog you, but you'll be cuffed so you won't be able to move much until I let you out. I'll monitor your pain. If it's good you say green. If you need me to back off a notch or slow down, say yellow. If it's bad say red. Red won't stop the scene. It'll just stop the flogging until you're ready again. Your safe word will end everything. What's your safe word?"

"Her Royal Majesty Queen Elizabeth the Second."

Nora looked at him with a raised eyebrow. Thorny aimed at her one of the sexier grins that had ever been aimed at a woman in the history of sexy grinning.

"I don't safe out often," he said.

"Queen Liz it is then."

From the top of her closet, Nora pulled out a black bag. She tossed it onto the bed and unzipped it. Thorny wasn't naked yet. He still wore black boxer briefs but she didn't scold him. His interest in stripping had no doubt been diverted by what Nora took out of her bag.

"Suede," Nora said, pulling out the first flogger. It had fourteen-inch scarlet-red tails. "Very soft and sensual. The bright blue is next. It's deer-hide. The leather is buttery. Feel?"

She held it out and Thorny ran his fingers over the tails.

"Nice. Very smooth," he said.

"This black one is bull-hide. Much sharper edges. The yellow-and-black one is rubber. It's stingy like a bee so we'll leave that one alone. It would feel a little like a whipping. But this one..." She held up a hunter-green-and-black flogger. "This one's elk. Heavy and thuddy."

"I like thuddy."

"I thought you would." She pulled out one last flogger but didn't remove it from its red leather case. "This one's special. I'll save it for last."

She lined them up on the bed in order of lightest and softest to heaviest and hardest. Thorny gazed at them with heat in his eyes.

"Why do you like floggings?" Nora came to him and ran her hands over his chest, shoulders and arms.

"Floggers are beautiful. They can feel soft one second and hard as steel the next. Takes an expert to wield one the right way. And you can get hit with them all over your body. Arms, legs, feet, anywhere, without doing real damage. I don't know. They're just sexy and scary and sensual all at the same time. Just like you."

Nora kissed him again, slipping her tongue between his lips slowly as she eased her hands into his underwear and pushed them down. Her lips left his reluctantly, but she continued her downward trajectory as she dragged the boxers to the floor and bade Thorny step out of them. She stood up and took a step back.

"Very nice," she said of his body. He was hard already. All of him and not just his cock. He had a hard flat stomach, a hard V of muscle on each side of his torso, hard hipbones that jutted out, and two vertical hard lines of muscles in his thighs. "You run."

"How did you know?"

"Even blindfolded I could recognize runner quads. You have a lovely body, Thorny. I can't wait to use it and abuse it for my amusement and pleasure."

"That's what it's here for, Mistress."

"Yes. Yes, it is. And now to show you the secret of my bedroom. Go stand facing the mirror."

He did as ordered. Nora picked up her ropes and her step stool and carried them over to Thorny. Now there were two Thornys—the real one and the mirror one.

She put the step stool by his left foot and climbed it.

"Excuse me whilst I put my ferns away."

"I don't think you get enough light in here for ferns, Mistress."

"It's okay. They're fake," she said. "I had to tell the contractor something to get him to install two hooks in the ceiling of my bedroom, didn't I?"

Thorny glanced up at the J-shaped hooks screwed into the plaster above them.

"I told the contractor I needed two hooks for my plants and that he should make sure they could hold two hundred pounds each."

"Those would be some big fucking plants, Mistress."

"That's what the contractor said."

"What did you say?"

"I said I like my plants the way I like my men—hanging from hooks on my bedroom ceiling. He didn't ask any more questions after that."

Nora looped her rope over the hooks and came down from the stool. First, she buckled the padded cuffs on Thorny's wrists, then she hoisted them above his head and secured them with the rope. Next she cuffed his ankles and bound them to the two-foot spreader bar. When she finished, Thorny stood immobile, naked and hard three feet from her mirror with his arms tied to the hooks on the ceiling and his feet rooted firmly to the floor.

"Relax for me," Nora ordered as she made a circuit around his body, dragging her fingernails lightly over his stomach, sides and the small of his back. "Go as limp as you can."

He closed his eyes, and she saw him sagging in the bonds.

"This is as limp as I'm going to get," he said and Nora paused in front of him, looking meaningfully at his erection. Only looking. Not touching. That would come later.

"Excellent." Even going limp, Thorny had barely moved. The spreader bar, rope, hooks and cuffs held him firmly and safely in place. Nora touched his face and let their eyes meet.

"The name Thorny suits you. Like a hawthorn bush you're

a little dangerous to be around, but you are very lovely to look at."

"Thank you, Mistress."

"Are you blushing?" she asked, smiling at him. "Did I make a whore blush?"

"You did. Can't wait to make a domme beg."

"Wait your turn," she teased. "You're all mine now. You must spend a lot of time taking care of your clients. It's good you're taking some time to let someone else take care of you."

"Is that what you're doing? Taking care of me?"

He pushed his hips forward, but she didn't scold him for it.

"I want to take very good care of you," she said, slipping a blindfold over his eyes. The mirror in front of him was for her, so she could watch his face and his reactions. She wanted him utterly lost in sensation, seeing nothing, feeling everything. "You're in my hands now, in my bedroom. This is the safest room in the world right now. Nothing and no one will harm you here. Your body will be honored. Your desires will be honored. Your trust in me will be honored. Do you believe me?"

"Yes, Mistress." He whispered the words. Good. The spell was already taking effect. She ran her thumbs over the arch of his cheekbones, over his lips. She outlined his ears and caressed his collarbone with her fingertips.

"I'm going to enjoy flogging you very much," she said, running her hands up and down his sides, over and around his rib cage. "I love flogging beautiful men. Worse ways to spend a hot August afternoon, right?"

"I can't think of a better way, Mistress."

She took her suede flogger off the bed and combed her fingers through the velvety tails.

"You're with Mistress Nora now. Nothing bad ever happens when you're with Mistress Nora. Only good things. Wonder-

ful things. Things like this." She brushed the tips of the flogger tails over the tops of his bare feet and toes. Thorny smiled.
With a light back-and-forth motion, Nora brushed the flogger across his shins. She worked her way up his legs, gently
caressing him with the flogger, letting the tails lap and lick at
his skin. Holding the flogger high over him, she ran the tips
of the tails over the full length of his penis.

As she swept the flogger over his erection, Thorny's hips
undulated in rhythm with it, a sight she found terribly erotic.
She looked forward to when it was his turn showing off his
special skill set. But now all she wanted was to give him the
flogging of his dreams. Nothing else mattered.

When Thorny's breathing grew heavier, Nora moved to
his backside, not wanting him to come until after the beating.
She whisked the flogger over the back of his legs now and between them, licking at his inner thighs and testicles. She did
nothing that hurt, nothing that caused pain. She wanted only
to wake up his body, put his nerves on notice.

"Best ass I've seen in a long time," Nora said, gently slapping the ass in question with her flogger.

"Thank you, Mistress." Thorny gave her a little wiggle.

Nora stepped back and used a wide swing now on Thorny's
back and arms. She was careful to keep the pressure as light
as possible. Nothing would jar him out of the safe space in
his mind faster than a hard hit when he wasn't prepared for it.
No…this moment was all about pleasure…teasing…tickling…
caressing…the soft stroke of suede on bare skin. Thorny was
a vocal submissive. His sighs and gasps of pleasure filled the
room. When she'd touched every part of his body with the
flogger, even running the tips of the tails over his face, she
stopped and tossed it on the bed. She came back to Thorny
and put her hands on his hips, rubbing them to bring more
blood into his pelvic region.

"On a scale of one to ten in the realm of impact play," she said, "that was about a one. A whip can get you to a ten. I'll take you to about a six or a seven and bring you back down again. We'll go there together. You won't be alone." She spoke in a low voice and kissed the back of his neck between sentences.

When she returned to Thorny, she had the second-lightest flogger in her hand. She tickled his back with the tails and she saw a shiver pass over his body.

"You like that? It's the deerskin. I'm going to start easy, at a two, but I'll move up to a three quickly. Thighs, ass, middle and upper back and shoulders. No kidneys, no head, no neck. You will enjoy this, Thorny...almost as much as I will."

Once again she started slow, lightly brushing, lightly sweeping the flogger over the back of his body. She caught the tips of the tails and released them in her first real strike. It wasn't a hard hit but hard enough that Thorny stood up straight at the impact. She struck again across his back, spacing out the hits so he could brace himself for the next one. Soon his skin started to turn pink, then red.

"What color?" she asked. "Green means keep going. Yellow means we take a break. Red means we stop."

"Green."

"My favorite color."

With the elk flogger she concentrated her efforts on Thorny's back, hitting the same spot over and over and over again, raising the level of pain from a four to a five to a six and back down to a four again. Up again to a six and back down to a four. She teased him with a minute of easy light flogging and brought him to attention with a series of sharp hard raps that had him gasping with each hit. With the bull-hide flogger she gave him the roughest treatment yet. She aimed high then low, high then low, striking the back of his thighs and the center of his shoulders in quick succession. The sound the flogger made was a heavy thudding sound, not sharp but thick and powerful. Thorny's back gleamed a bright fire-engine red. She did love the color red.

She loved the red, she loved the scene, she loved all of it. When she had a flogger in her hand she felt like herself, like her real self. There were days she wanted to quit working for Kingsley. The more clients she took on, the more money he made, and she would rather top for pleasure than for money most days...but even if she did quit being a professional someday, she would always be a dominant. How could she give this up? She couldn't. She couldn't stop being a dominant any more than she could quit being a writer, quit being Nora.

After a long series of rapid-fire strikes to Thorny's middle back, Nora stopped and dropped the flogger on the floor. She let him take a moment to catch his breath. When she put her bare hands flat on his back he inhaled sharply. In the mirror she watched him, watched his skin ripple as she caressed him, watched his lips part as she pushed her fingers into his fresh welts.

"Lovely welts," she said, pleased with her work. "Here and here and a big one right here. Does it hurt when I touch them?"

"A little. Don't stop."

"No chance of that." She picked up her elk-hide flogger again and gave his back another once-over followed by one hell of a twice-over. Then she started pulling back, bringing the pain level down. She switched from the elk to the bull-hide and then down to the velvety deer-hide. Instead of finishing with the suede, she brought out her very special little flogger.

"This flogger will hurt but in a fun way," she said, making a few practice throws that didn't connect with Thorny's body. "I haven't used it on anyone yet, but you seemed to be the perfect person for a trial run."

"I'm all yours, Mistress," Thorny said, his breathing slower now as he came down off the rush.

She hit him square in the back and he flinched. She struck him there a few more times, but his back wasn't her primary target. Once the flogger felt completely comfortable in her hands she aimed at his upper arms, the left and the right, the left and the right, until both arms were dotted with round red welts. When she finished Thorny was panting again. Short lovely breaths, the sounds of a man lost in sensation, lost to the world. She walked around his body and stood in front of him.

"I'm taking the blindfold off," she said, wanting him prepared for the touch of her hands on his face. She lifted the blindfold and Thorny blinked. His eyes were heavy-lidded and his pupils wide as dimes.

"What was that?" he asked between breaths.

"Rosebuds," she said, holding up the flogger. The tails were tipped with red leather rosebuds. Thorny grinned. "'Gather ye rosebuds…'"

"You're amazing, Mistress."

"And you're hard." She looked down at his cock, harder now than even before the flogging. "Would you like to come?"

"Please, Mistress."

She reached into her toy bag and produced a bottle of the finest olive oil on the market, which she poured into the palm of her hand. With her slick fingers she gripped his penis and stroked it, covering it with oil.

"Olive oil was used as lube for centuries before actual lube was invented," Nora said, pulling on Thorny's cock slowly and gently as his hips undulated in time with her strokes. He was a rod of iron in her fingers, so hard she wondered if it hurt to be that stiff for so long. "It still has one massive advantage over modern lubrication."

"What is that?" Thorny was swaying on his feet, his head falling against his arm.

"It tastes a lot better." Nora went down on her knees in front of him and took his cock in her mouth. Thorny cried out as she took him deep in her throat. As hard as he was, he didn't come immediately, which pleased her. Pausing only to kiss and nibble at his hipbones, she went to work on him, licking from the base to the tip, swirling her tongue around the head, using her hand to pump the shaft as she sucked him with her mouth. He made the loveliest sounds while she licked and sucked him. Whimpers and gasps, whimpers and moans, whimpers and inarticulate pleas for something...release, mercy, more of this, more of that.

"Warn me when you're about to come," she said.

"A gentleman always does."

"I must not know many gentlemen then," Nora said before putting her mouth back on him and taking him deep again. Holding him by the hips, she moved her mouth all over every straining inch of him. As she sucked him, he fucked her mouth, pumping his hips faster as his breaths grew shorter and shallower. She tasted a few drops of salt on her tongue and drew him completely into her throat. Thorny said her name as a warning and Nora pulled back. She took him in her hand again, gripped him firmly and rubbed hard. He went silent and tense and came in a series of spurts all over the cheval mirror in front of him.

Nora stood up and wiped her mouth off on a towel. Thorny had gone slack.

"Thorny? How are we doing?"

"We are so happy right now we could cry."

Laughing, Nora unhooked his feet from the spreader bar

and removed the ankle cuffs before standing and unhooking him from the ceiling. His arms fell down to his sides and she steadied him to keep him from falling. With an arm around his waist, she guided him to her bed and put him on his stomach. She picked up her olive oil and massaged it into Thorny's muscles and welts as he groaned with pleasure.

"I have never felt so gooey," Thorny said. "I'm a noodle."

"Happy?"

"Blissed. You are so good at that."

"The flogging or the blowing?"

"All of the above. Thank you, Mistress. I wish they had a Zagat guide for dominatrixes. I would give you five stars."

"Would you like some water?"

"I would like some food and water." He slowly rolled to his side making no attempt to hide his flaccid cock from her gaze. He seemed wonderfully comfortable being completely naked in front of her. "Can I take you out to dinner? I need to carbo-load if I'm going to fuck you all night long. Pasta is sex fuel."

Nora grinned. "You shower the olive oil off your welts while I clean the semen off the mirror, and then we'll go out for some sex fuel."

"That's the weirdest sentence I've ever heard. And I'm a prostitute so you know that's saying something."

"Really?" Nora asked. "If that's the weirdest sentence anyone's ever said to you, you're clearly not spending enough time with me. You should fix that."

Thorny leaned in and kissed her, a slow wet deep kiss.

"How about I spend all night with you?" he asked.

"I do want the Boyfriend Experience at some point," she said.

"Mistress...me buying you dinner so I can get in your pants? That is the Boyfriend Experience."

29

The Boyfriend Experience

ON THE WAY HOME FROM THE BEST LITTLE ITALIAN place in Westport, the sky finally broke and hot summer rain exploded all over the streets. They ran, laughing and slipping, from the car and into her house. Once inside the door the both of them shook out their hair and shoes like dogs.

"Finally," Nora said. "The humidity was hell on my hair."

"Your hair looks very sexy when wet." Thorny ran his hands through the wet waves and smiled. "You should be wet all the time."

"Maybe I am," she said as he kissed her.

"Can't wait to find out." He tugged his jacket off and hung it on the coatrack.

"Should we go upstairs?"

"Do you have any wine in the house?"

"I was raised Catholic. Of course I do. Red or white?"

"Red."

"It is my color."

Thorny followed her into the kitchen and opened a bottle

of Pinot while she pulled down two wineglasses. He sat on the kitchen table and she stood between his thighs. They sipped from their glasses until Thorny took hers from her hand and set it down next to him.

"What is it?" she asked as he took her hands in his.

"Nothing. I just wanted to do this." He put her hands on his shoulders and placed his hands on her waist. A perfect position for kissing. So they did.

"Now tell me if I'm wrong…" Thorny said, kissing along her jawline to her ear, "but something tells me I'm not the only one in the room with something on the brain. What's on your mind?"

"Nothing. Everything. The usual."

"What's the usual?"

Nora sighed. "My ex."

"Ex-priest?"

"Ex-priest. Ex-lover. Ex-everything."

"You're thinking about him?"

"I think about him a lot."

"When did you two break up?"

"Over three years ago."

"That's a long time to be hung up on someone."

"Tell me about it."

"Is there a little of the proverbial Catholic guilt happening here?" He wound his fingers into her hair, caressed her cheekbone with his thumb.

"There's an old Zen saying," Nora said. "'To her lover, a woman is a delight. To a monk she is a distraction. To a mosquito she is a good meal.' With him, my priest, I was all of the above—a delight, a distraction and dinner. He lost a lot when he lost me."

"I didn't hear 'girlfriend' in there."

"I was his property, not his girlfriend. He was my owner,

not my boyfriend. I am thirty years old and have never had a real boyfriend in my life."

"Would you like one?" he asked, kissing her ear. Nora closed her eyes and wrapped her arms around his shoulders again.

"Yes," she said. "For a night. If you're offering."

He kissed the tendon of her shoulder and moved his mouth to her ear again.

"I'm offering."

His hand slipped under her fitted black T-shirt and tickled her stomach. Nora laughed, already feeling better.

"Do you, by any chance, have any sexy lingerie in your house?" Thorny asked.

"I might," she said as he pulled back to meet her eyes. "Why do you ask?"

"I happen to have a camera with me," he said. "Takes pics and videos. We could do a little fashion show maybe? Maybe film ourselves having sex? One of my many perversions."

Nora stepped back and looked at him. Then she crooked her finger at him and walked out of the kitchen.

"Oh…the crooking finger," Thorny said, picking up the wineglasses. "I will follow that finger wherever it goes."

In her bedroom, Thorny made himself comfortable on her bed. Shoes and socks off, jacket off, lying on his side with one of her fluffiest red pillows under him while she dug through her closet.

Thorny opened his overnight bag and took out a camera.

"You're actually taking pics?" Nora asked.

"We can erase everything when we're done. I won't even pick out a favorite and ask you to send it to me. Unless you want to."

"You fuck me all night like you promised, and I'll consider it."

"Start considering it…"

She kept her kinky clothes in her closet but the lingerie had its own drawer in her bathroom dresser. She chose three pairs of shoes—her red stilettos, her vintage black-and-beige Mary Janes, and a pair of good old-fashioned saddle shoes.

"Saddle shoes?" He sounded dubious.

"You'll see," she said and disappeared into the bathroom. She dug through her dresser drawers and found three outfits. The first one was a red-and-black merry widow that she paired with black stockings and the stilettos. She piled her still-damp mass of hair onto her head and pinned it in place, pulled down a few pieces to frame her face and applied some dark red lipstick.

She stuck one leg out the bathroom door and heard a whistle. She threw the door open dramatically and Thorny collapsed backward onto the bed.

"You look like Sophia Loren," he said, pretending to croak. "I've always wanted to go back in time and fuck Sophia Loren."

"She's still alive."

Thorny sat up straight. "There's hope for us yet," Thorny said, addressing his crotch. "Goddamn, you look beautiful. Pose for me." He flicked the camera on and aimed it at her.

"How do you want me?"

"Every way I can have you. But for now, stand with your hands behind your back and look left. Lift your chin a little and think of something sexy and elegant."

Nora did as instructed. Thorny snapped the pic. It was a digital camera so he turned it to her so she could see the shot.

"Beautiful, aren't you?" he said, grinning at the picture. "You photograph well."

"Take it again. I need to change leg positions."

She adjusted her stance and Thorny got off a few shots.

"I totally lied," Thorny said, flipping through the pictures. "I'm taking every single one of these pics with me."

"Well, if that's the case…we better take some better ones."

"What's better than this?"

She didn't answer, only gave him a look—that look—and slipped back into the bathroom to change. This time she slipped into her bustier that hooked in the front and had a bow right under her breasts. She pulled on the matching panties, the matching elbow gloves, the matching stockings, slipped her feet into her Mary Janes and buckled the straps around her ankles.

"What do you think?" she asked when she emerged again from the bathroom into the soft glow of the bedside lamp.

"Hmm…" Thorny stood up and walked over to her with the camera in his hand. "Not bad…but let's try this." He lifted her hands and put them on the back of her head. With the slightest pressure he tipped her hips to the side "Better." He took a few steps back and took a picture. When he looked at it he didn't seem pleased.

"What's wrong?" she asked.

"It's still not quite right." He set the camera down and stood in front of her. Nora tried not to laugh as he looked her up and down, his chin in his hand, his eyes narrowed like an auteur trying to see his subject in a new light. "I know what's wrong with the picture."

"What?"

"This." Thorny untied the bow on her bustier and opened it hook by hook. He paused and met her eyes as if giving her a chance to tell him no. She didn't. He pulled the bustier off her and let it fall to the floor.

"Better?" she asked.

"Almost there…" He took both her naked breasts in his hands and squeezed them. He rubbed his thumbs over her nipples, tugging and pinching them. Nora closed her eyes as he touched her. She felt blood rushing to her breasts. Her nipples hardened in his fingers and the warm delicious sensation of it suffused her entire body. She felt her vagina growing wet, and her clitoris swelling as he devoted his full attention to her nipples. When he lifted her breast in the palm of his hand and clamped his lips on the nipple to suck it, a jolt like lightning traveled down her spine. He gave her other nipple equal attention, sucking it eagerly and deeply while she held herself in place, back arched, breasts high, hands clasped on the back of her head. A soundless sigh escaped her lips. Thorny kissed his way from her breasts to her neck. He held her nipples between his fingers as he bit lightly into her throat, playfully feeding on her flesh as he teased the tips of her breasts.

Finally he stepped back.

"Now..." he said looking at her with his critical eye, "that's the look I wanted. Don't move."

He took a few pictures of her in that pose before moving her into a new pose, leaning against the wall on her forearms, her breasts thrust forward and her back arched. A classic burlesque stance. Thorny took his pictures from several angles. Then he put her against the wall and she lifted her arms over her head again, clasping her elbows.

"Beautiful," he said and she could tell from the obvious bulge in his jeans he wasn't simply flattering her.

"One more outfit. Ready?" she asked.

"I don't know. Am I?"

"With this outfit? Probably not. Brace yourself." She went back into the bathroom and quickly changed clothes. She pulled the pins out of her hair, brushed her hair into pigtails and braided them.

"It's not exactly lingerie," Nora said as she emerged from the bathroom. "But I thought you'd like it anyway."

Thorny's baby blue eyes went wide as she stepped into the light.

"Jesus, Mary and Britney..." Thorny breathed at the sight of her.

"It's the real deal," she said. "I went to Catholic school kindergarten through high school. I shortened the skirt, obviously..." Nora turned her back to Thorny and bent over slightly. The navy blue pleated skirt lifted to reveal her white cotton panties she wore underneath. She had on a white blouse—barely buttoned—the navy pleated skirt, white-navy-and-gray argyle knee socks and her black-and-white saddle shoes.

"I have never wanted to be Catholic so much in my life."

"What are you?"

"I'm from Utah originally if that gives you a hint."

Nora laughed. "One of those, eh? What's that old saying that applies to Mormons? When they're good they're very, very good, but when they're bad they're—"

"Male prostitutes?"

"Something like that. So I take it you approve of the outfit?"

"I approve. My cock approves. I don't think we have to worry about my brain killing me. My dick is going to do me in first if it doesn't get inside you soon," he said, stroking her clitoris through the fabric of her panties.

"How should I pose?"

Thorny nodded toward the bed. She sat on the edge of the bed as Thorny set the camera down by the pillow.

"I want you..." he said, reaching under her skirt and tugging her underwear down and off her. Then he pushed her knees open wide and lifted her skirt to her stomach. "Just like that."

Nora leaned back on her elbows. Thorny looked at her but without touching.

"You like it?" she asked, opening her legs wider so that her labia parted to reveal the entrance to her vagina.

"*Like* is not the word I would use right now."

"What word would you use?"

"*Lick*," he said and buried his head between her legs. She gasped as his tongue went into her vagina, a good gasp and one of pleasant surprise. Thorny sat on his knees and pulled her hips to the edge of the bed. He thrust his tongue in and out of her. Nora placed her hand gently on the back of his head as she pushed her pelvis against his mouth in small quick pulses. The pressure coiled inside her like a spring twisting and tightening. Thorny's head lowered and rose as he licked every part of her, her vulva and labia, her clitoris, passing his tongue over and into her with incredible skill and enthusiasm. The man clearly loved his work as much as she loved hers. He didn't let her come, however. He stopped and kissed her inner thigh as he reached out and picked up the camera.

"You wouldn't," she said.

"Oh, yes I would." He grinned at her over her thigh. "Touch yourself."

"Is that an order?"

"Absolutely."

"Should I call you 'sir'?"

"I had to call my dad 'sir.' How about you call me... *Mister* Thorny?"

"Yes, Mister Thorny." She winked at him as she moved her hand between her legs. "Any special requests, Mister Thorny?"

"Spread wider."

"If I spread any wider you'll be able to read my thoughts."

"Like an open book," he said, using his elbows to nudge her thighs wider.

"Pull back your clit hood. Your ring is obstructing my view," Thorny said as he adjusted the settings on the camera.

"That ring was a Valentine's Day gift, I'll have you know."

"Gift or not, it's in the way of your clit and my pictures."

Nora laughed and lightly tugged on the ring to retract the hood of skin over the swollen bud of her clitoris.

"Beautiful," Thorny said, snapping a very intimate close-up. "Now the labia nice and wide. Use both hands."

"Are we sending these pics to *Hustler* or the *American Medical Journal of Gynecology*?"

"Pretty sure they're the same thing." With the comfort of a man who made his money having sex with rich women for a living, he stripped out of his clothes without any further ado. Everything he did was a pleasure to watch—rolling on the condom, covering himself with a layer of lube, sliding his slick fingers into her and opening her up with his hand. Even wiping his hands clean on a tissue he did with a certain sexual aplomb. His casual confidence in the bedroom reminded her of someone. Oh, yes. It reminded her of her.

Thorny positioned himself at the entrance of her body and paused long enough to pick up the camera.

"Now what are you doing, Mister Thorny?" she asked with a raised eyebrow.

"This camera has a video setting. Let's make some porn." He aimed the camera down and eased inside her. Nora's head fell back as he entered her completely. She'd been wet and wanting him for hours.

"Feel good?" Thorny asked as he moved in her with long sure stokes.

"So good…"

"You like being fucked, don't you?"

"Who doesn't?"

Thorny chuckled softly. "Good answer to a stupid question."

"I usually do the fucking," she said. "Nice to let someone else be in charge every now and then."

"Who do you fuck?" Thorny asked as he moved the camera closer to her face and then back to their joined bodies.

"I fucked a college sophomore recently. Last week."

"Boy or girl?"

"Boy."

"Ever fuck an underage boy?"

"Yes."

"Do you ever fuck girls?"

"I have. I do."

"Client?"

"One is. The only client I fuck. I mean, other than you," she said, smiling up at him. A lie. She fucked Kingsley, too, but Thorny didn't need to know that.

"Do you fuck her with her strap-on?"

"Sometimes," Nora said. "Sometimes a vibrator. Sometimes just my fingers. Sometimes I tie her up and have men fuck her while I supervise."

"I shouldn't ask these questions," Thorny said.

"It's not a breach of confidentiality if I don't tell you who the client is." She put her hands behind her head and relaxed as Thorny used his free hand to unbutton her blouse, unhook her bra in the front and bare her breasts.

"No, I mean I'm going to come immediately if you don't stop talking about fucking girls."

"Do you always talk this much when you fuck?"

"I do when I'm trying to keep myself from coming. I want to stay hard inside you for a very long time."

"We could talk about the men I fuck."

"Boring."

Nora laughed. "Not to me..."

"Fine," Thorny said, setting the camera on the nightstand and angling it to record the two of them together. "Who's the most interesting person you ever fucked? I mean, other than the Catholic priest. You are still fucking him, aren't you?"

"Occasionally. What about you? Who's the most interesting person you've fucked?"

"A green-eyed dominatrix switch with the sexiest tits on the planet."

Thorny bent low and sucked her nipples again. Her breasts felt heavy and full in his hands, sensitive in his mouth. She started to put her arms around him but he stopped her, grabbing her wrists and pushing them into the bed by her head.

"Told you—I'm in charge," Thorny said. "I better tie your hands down. Otherwise you're going to keep trying to take over."

"Switches are known to do that," she admitted.

Thorny pulled out of her and grabbed the discarded wrist cuffs off the floor. He found a snap hook in her toy bag, and Nora allowed Thorny to put the cuffs on her wrists and hook her to one of the metal slats.

"There. That's better." He mounted her again and entered her, pausing once he'd fully penetrated her to adjust the camera. "How does my cock feel in you?"

"Wonderful. You should keep it in me all night, Mister Thorny. Or is that not part of the Boyfriend Experience?"

"Fucking you all night is part of the Boyfriend Experience. If you want me to fuck you only once and then fall asleep five seconds after, that's the Husband Experience."

Thorny lowered himself onto her and kissed her mouth, hard and deep, before sitting up on his knees again between her thighs. Her body temperature rose inside and out. Thorny bore down on her, his hands on her waist, working her body up and down on his cock. No wonder women paid him thousands for a night with him. They paid him for the same reason they paid their hairstylists hundreds of dollars for a cut and color and their interior decorators thousands of dollars to give their home panache—they knew they deserved the best and they were more than happy to pay to get it. And Thorny was the best money could buy.

Thorny grasped her breasts in both hands and drove into her. The breath went out of her as he rammed into her almost cruelly.

"Yes…" She sighed.

"You give all the time," he said, fucking her wildly. "Time to take."

And she took it, every inch of him, hard and brutal, deep and punishing. The sex had turned to animal rutting where both of them were past the point of controlling what they did and said. Nora lifted her hips up and against him, digging her heels into the bed, so wet and open she felt fluid rushing out of her onto her thighs. And Thorny pounded her to the point of pain and beyond which was where she wanted to be. She felt her body rising off the bed, her head swimming, her vagina pulsing and clenching and contracting, and then the final explosion as every muscle quivered and every nerve fired. Her back bowed from the force of the orgasm and when she came down from the high she heard Thorny give a quiet grunt before he collapsed on top of her. She wrapped her legs around his back, needing to feel closer to him. He nuzzled her ear, gave her a few gentle kisses and unhooked her hands.

"So that was the Boyfriend Experience?" Nora sat up and winced. He'd fucked her so hard and deep she probably needed an hour or two before they went at it again. Not that she was complaining.

"That was…" Thorny paused and looked at the clock. "Shit."

"What?"

"Pull yourself together. It's almost time."

"Time for what?" Nora asked as Thorny disposed of the condom and pulled his jeans on. He grabbed her hand and led her out of the bedroom.

"It's almost nine. *House* is on."

"What is on?"

"You don't watch *House*? Who doesn't watch *House*?"

"What's *House*?"

"You like men who are arrogant imperious assholes, right?"

"Right," she said.

"Trust me. You'll love *House*." He half pushed, half tossed her onto her sofa. He picked up her remote control and flipped through a few channels. The theme music had only just started. Thorny sat on the couch and hauled her into his arms. He put a pillow on his lap. She rested her head on it and him.

"Comfortable?" he asked.

"Very." She was lying on her sofa curled up with her head in the lap of a male escort while a TV show that was apparently about the rudest doctor on earth played on her television. Thorny wore only jeans. She had on nothing but her panties and Thorny's T-shirt she'd thrown on. And she liked it.

"By the way," Thorny said as the show went to commercial, "this right now…this is the Boyfriend Experience."

Nora smiled up at him.

"I need a boyfriend."

30

A Thorny Problem

THORNY SPENT THE NIGHT.

Not only did he spend the night he stayed the next morning and helped her cook breakfast. Together they stripped the stained sheets off the bed and Thorny helped her put on fresh ones. They took separate showers and since yesterday's summer storm had broken the heat wave, they went for a walk in her neighborhood. She showed him all her favorite houses, all her favorite haunts. The coffee shop where she'd written her last book, the little historic library where she did most of her research, the pond where she went to feed the ducks when she'd worked so much the bread she'd bought had gone stale before she could eat it.

Arm in arm they walked back to her house. She knew Thorny would leave her soon. His own life waited for him back in the city, but he seemed in no hurry. Was this still part of the Boyfriend Experience? Or did he really want to be with her?

"So…" he said as they turned the corner onto her street. "Do I get to see you again?"

"You get to… Fuck."

"That goes without saying."

"No. I mean, fuck." She pointed at a car in her driveway, a silver Rolls-Royce. "Kingsley is here."

"Oh, fuck," he said.

"Can you give us a few minutes? I'll get rid of him," she said.

"Half an hour? You'll be okay?"

"I'm Mistress Fucking Nora, right?" she said, forcing a smile. "I'm always okay."

He kissed her on the cheek and set off walking. Nora steeled herself for whatever it was that brought Kingsley over to her house. Whatever it was, it probably wasn't good. Kingsley hated leaving the city for the "wilderness," as he called Connecticut, and only did so under duress.

"King?" she called out as she shut the front door behind her. "You here?"

"In your bedroom, *Maîtresse*," he called back. *"S'il vous plait."*

Nora sighed and marched upstairs. As she neared her bedroom she heard someone speaking. Her.

"Ever fuck an underage boy?"

"Yes."

"Do you ever fuck girls?"

"I have. I do."

"Client?"

"One is. The only client I fuck. I mean, other than you…"

Nora rushed into her bedroom and ripped the camera out of Kingsley's hand.

Then she slapped him so hard her hand rang like a bell and five finger marks glowed bright red on his olive skin. His eyes blazed momentarily with fury as he raised his hand to his cheek and faced her.

"What the fuck do you think you're doing?" she demanded.

"You didn't answer your phone," Kingsley said.

"That's why you're here? That's why you're in my house without invitation going through my personal things? All without my consent?"

"You gave me the key to your house."

"For emergencies. Not so you can come in and go through my stuff." She hit the button and erased the tape before Kingsley could look at another single frame of it.

"When you fuck a client it's my business."

"I did not fuck a client."

"Alec Thornberry, aka Thorny, paid me one thousand dollars for one hour of your time. And on that tape you call him your client."

"That was a joke and it doesn't matter. You should never have looked at that."

"I've seen you fucking before, remember?"

"Fine. I'll put a camera in your bedroom and secretly film you and Juliette. How much would she like that?"

"That's entirely different."

"Right. Because you respect Juliette and you clearly have no respect for me."

"This has nothing to do with respect. I can't trust you with your clients anymore. Not after Talel. And certainly not after this."

"I had no appointments after Thorny, and I didn't have to work this morning. I have a personal connection with Thorny that made it awkward to take money from him."

"You gave him pity sex because he has a brain tumor?"

"It's not a— Kingsley." She pressed the heels of her palms against her eyes. She almost never had headaches but it felt as if she were about to have an aneurysm herself. She took two deep breaths and met Kingsley's eyes. "I like Thorny."

"I can tell," he said. "You promised me you'd never sleep with a client again."

"He canceled his session with me."

"So you could fuck him with a clear conscience?"

"I decide who is and is not a client. I didn't want him as a client. That is my right."

"Fine. Fuck him then. But do you realize he could have taken that tape and blackmailed you with it? The Red Queen getting fucked by a notorious male escort while admitting she fucks her clients." Kingsley pointed at the camera. "Do you mention Søren on the tape?"

"Not by name."

"So you did?"

"I'm not having this conversation with you. I know you think you're protecting me. I know you think this is your job. But you don't seem to realize what a gross violation of my privacy this is. I am disgusted with you right now. You could have at least waited until I came home and asked me what was on the tape. I would have told you."

"No, you wouldn't have. You don't even answer the phone when I call you, and I've called you two dozen times in the past twelve hours."

"I turned off my phone since it was my night off, and I didn't want to be interrupted because I was on a date."

"A date? You don't date."

"Of course I don't date. When I try to date anybody, you and this fucking job get in the way of it. I have to fuck clients because they're the only men I ever see."

"You want more free time?"

"I'd love it," she said.

"Fine. You're fired."

Nora was speechless.

For all of one second.

"Fuck you."

"Fuck me all you want. I'm calling Detective Cooper on your friend Thorny."

"You're having Thorny arrested? By one of my own clients?"

"I am."

"I spent the night with him so you're having *him* arrested? You can't punish Thorny to punish me."

"If it's the only way I can punish you, then so be it."

"You're as sanctimonious as Søren, and he gets paid to be holier-than-thou. Have you forgotten you have no room to talk? Who have you not fucked in this city? Or blackmailed for that matter? At least what Thorny does is consensual. You have fucked many a person over without asking permission first."

"I swore to Søren I would protect you. You're not making that job very easy, *Maîtresse*."

"You fired me and you're having Thorny arrested and for no reason other than I slept with him without asking your permission first. Kingsley, you are out of control. You came into my house without permission and violated my privacy and Thorny's in a way that is borderline unforgivable. I love you. You are now and always my King and I would step in front of a bullet for you. But if you ever do anything like this again, it won't be Søren you'll have to worry about. I will castrate you and hang your balls on the rearview mirror of my Aston Martin and take everyone in the tri-state area for a ride. Do you understand that?"

Kingsley lifted his chin and looked into her eyes.

"Do you even care why I came over here?" he asked. "Do you want to know why I called you twenty times?"

"Do I?" she asked, caring but not wanting to, not when Kingsley was acting like a madman.

"Our priest takes his Final Vows in a few days."

"I know."

"He asked me to go," Kingsley said.

"He asked me to go, too. Is that why you freaked out? Because he's taking Final Vows?"

"No, it's not," he said, biting off the words. "I don't want him staying in the church but that's the least of our worries now."

"Why?"

"Because he's leaving after he takes his vows."

"Leaving? What do you mean he's leaving?"

"He came by yesterday and asked me if I would send someone to pick up his steamer trunk. I asked him why. He told me he's been offered a new church assignment, helping troubled youth who live on the streets."

"What youth?" Nora asked. "What streets?"

"The troubled youth of Syria. Syria—one of the most dangerous countries in the world. A few days after he takes his Final Vows he's going. That's why he wants us there. Because it's the last time we might ever see him."

"No." She raised her hands as if to push away his words. "No way. He paid them a massive amount of his father's money so they'd keep him at Sacred Heart. He would never let them send him away."

"He's not letting them send him away. He volunteered," Kingsley said. "He's leaving, and he's not coming back."

Nora's legs couldn't support her anymore. Her knees shook, her heart pounded, her head swam and she sat down on the ottoman by the foot of the armchair.

"He's leaving us," she said, looking up at Kingsley.

"I suppose it's only fair considering you and I both left him."

"He wouldn't leave us only to punish us. He might leave a week or two to punish us but not…not forever."

"Keep telling yourself that," Kingsley said.

"He said…"

"What? What did he say?"

"I asked him if things would change if he took his Final Vows," Nora said. "He said yes, he'd keep his vow of chastity from now on. I never thought… I never thought he'd leave me. Us." She looked at Kingsley, her hand over her mouth. "Why didn't he tell me?"

"Possibly for the same reason you didn't tell him when you left for a year without a word to either of us."

Nora winced but didn't defend herself. She had no defense.

"What do we do?" she asked. "How do we make him stay?"

"I don't think we can. I'm sending someone to his house Sunday evening to pick up the trunk."

The steamer trunk stood at the foot of Søren's bed. Underneath one layer of innocent-looking linens and quilts was a black leather toy bag that contained the finest collection of canes, whips, floggers and spreader bars in Connecticut. The second-finest collection was in her closet upstairs.

"He'll go nuts without someone around to play with," Nora said. "Even when he was in seminary he had his friend Magdalena."

"I imagine he'll be going on a lot of long runs. Probably dodging bullets the entire time."

"I'll stop him from going," Nora said, standing up. "I'll talk to him."

"*Bonne chance.* I already tried every argument I could think of to talk him out of it. Unless you're willing to go back to him…"

Nora didn't answer.

"Are you?" Kingsley asked.

"Not to manipulate him into staying," she said.

"Then I suggest you see him today and kiss him goodbye. I doubt you'll have another chance for a very long time."

Kingsley put his hand on the doorknob and turned it. But he didn't open the door.

"I was wrong to have gone through your things," Kingsley said. "I was angry. Juliette is visiting her mother, and I needed you. I had no one to talk to about it, no one who would understand. I panicked. I overreacted. I apologize. I've lost him twice before, and I can't lose him again. I won't survive it."

"You don't mean that."

"If he were to die over there… I wouldn't be able to live without him. I'd last three days without him before I put a bullet in my brain."

"Kingsley, you—"

"You're stronger than I am. You can make it without him. I can't. That place they're sending him is a war zone. He's a fucking pacifist. What's he going to do? Pray his way out of a bullet to the back of the head? I prayed when they pulled guns on me and that didn't stop the bullets from ripping me open. God won't save him, either."

"I'll save him," Nora said.

"You will? How?"

"I don't know. But I'll figure something out."

"You stop him from going, and I'll give you your job back."

"What if I don't want it back?"

"Then have fun paying for this little house of yours without a paycheck."

With that, Kingsley walked out the door, slamming it behind him and leaving her alone and aghast and in shock.

Nora was at a loss. She couldn't think, couldn't act, could barely breathe. Kingsley had fired her like he'd threatened he would and she couldn't care less. She'd care later, but not now.

Not yet. Søren had accepted a new church assignment. And not in New York or Massachusetts or Maine or even fucking Florida. Syria? An ocean away from her in a country on the brink of civil war. How like the Jesuits to send priests there—God's soldiers, God's marines, God's fools, in Nora's estimation. Arrogant men who thought they could save the world out of sheer faith and willpower. Years ago she'd thought Søren's sister Claire crazy when she said she worried every single day that her big brother would meet his end like the Jesuits in El Salvador, slaughtered by guerrilla soldiers in 1989. Was this suicide? Did Søren want to die? Was this PTSD from his motorcycle accident? Was he punishing her for leaving him by leaving her? Was he punishing himself for his own sins he couldn't forgive? Why?

She flagellated herself with these questions for ten minutes or more to no avail. Her phone—where was it? She needed to call Søren and hear it from him. Or she should go to him, look him in the eyes, make him look her in the eyes and say it to her face, say that he was leaving her forever. Dare him to say it to her.

But she didn't dare to dare him. She knew he would.

A knock on the door interrupted her near hysteria. She ran downstairs, opened it and found Thorny on her porch.

"The coast is clear?" he asked.

"Yeah. King's gone." She held the door open for him.

"Nora? You okay?" Thorny asked as he tried to take her in his arms. She pulled back, her hand pressed to her stomach to quell the rising panic.

"King's pissed."

"I expected that."

"And he's..."

"What?"

"Nothing."

"Can you talk about it?"

"Give me a minute."

"Sure thing," he said. "Let me run up and get my stuff. Sit. We'll talk when you can. Or I can go and give you some alone time if you need it."

"I don't know," she said, shaking her head. "I don't what I need."

Thorny said nothing. He kissed her cheek and squeezed her hand.

"Be right back," he said.

He came right back downstairs with his jacket slung over his shoulder and his overnight bag in his hand.

"I got a call. Client emergency. Do you mind?"

"No, you should go. King and I are having our own little emergency."

She walked over to the door and opened it for him.

"We'll hang out again. Right?" he asked.

"I'm sure we'll be seeing each other again." Nora leaned in and kissed him, kissed him hard, hard enough it seemed to surprise him but he kissed her back just as hard.

"Later, Mistress," he said and walked out of her door. She watched him go, watched him slip his hand into the back pocket of his jeans, watched him pause in confusion.

"Looking for this?" she asked as Thorny turned back, an expression of unmistakable guilt on his face. She held the flash card in her hand, the tape that they'd made last night, the tape he'd tried to leave with.

"How—"

"I stole it while I was kissing you," she said. "My priest taught me that trick. He's one helluva pickpocket. Not that it mattered—I'd already erased it."

Nora snapped the card in half, then raised her finger to him, the crooking finger, and he followed it back into the house. She pointed at the couch and he sat, obedient and contrite.

"Nora, I—"

"I wasn't born yesterday," she said. "You can't be a good dominatrix and also be gullible. I defended you to King, by the way. He said you could blackmail me with such a tape, and I convinced him it was just a sex tape. I didn't tell him he was right. I'd thank me for that if I were you. You don't want to know what he would have done with you if I told him the truth. I promise you that."

She waited for him to say something, anything.

"What gave me away?" he asked.

"Your questions you asked me while you were fucking me. You got me on tape admitting that I slept with a priest, that I slept with clients. As my priest said to me recently—that's not pillow talk. What I want to know is why? I've had a very bad day and this isn't making it any better. A good reason why might help. Money?"

"No." He turned and stared at the window, unable to meet her eyes.

"Some sort of coup? Trying to pull one over on Kingsley? I wouldn't recommend that, by the way. He has killed people before. He'll do it again."

"It's not... I didn't want to do it. I had to do it."

"Ah. So someone forced you to do this. You're being black-mailed to blackmail me. Why you and why me?"

"I warned you two years ago about this."

"About what?"

"Not about what," Thorny said, finally meeting her eyes. "About who."

"Who?"

"Who have we both pissed off?" Thorny asked and Nora knew the answer immediately.

"Milady."

31

Picking Pockets

"I WISH I KNEW HOW TO PICK POCKETS," THORNY SAID as Nora handed him a cup of coffee.

"My priest taught me. He went to seminary in Rome and those days the streets were full of pickpockets. Poor kids. Orphans. Not even priests were safe. He has a friend in Rome who taught him all the tricks so he knew how to outsmart them."

"Nice. You outsmarted me."

"Not that hard, Thorny. Good thing you're gorgeous and good in bed because you aren't too bright."

"That hurts. But I deserve it."

"You do. Now tell me…what brings Milady back into our lives again?"

She was more curious than angry. For now. But the anger would show up if Thorny's answers were unsatisfactory.

"First of all, she's never forgiven you for humiliating her at the club that night."

"That was two years ago," she reminded Thorny as she took

a seat in the kitchen chair. Thorny sat on her kitchen counter, the coffee cup balanced on his thigh.

"She has a long memory for people who piss her off. But it's not just that. The sheikh."

"The sheikh?" she repeated, pretending she'd never heard of any such man.

"I know all about him, Nora. Talel was her client," Thorny said. "When he came to the city a few weeks ago he was supposed to see her. But they fought. Someone in the scene told him about you. He made the appointment with you out of curiosity, and you and he hit it off."

"That's one way of putting it," she said.

"He was her richest client, and her favorite. She knew I warned you about her two summers ago. She knew I helped you the night of the Fling. She thought you'd trust me because I'd helped you out."

"I did trust you. But that doesn't explain why you agreed to blackmail me."

Thorny shifted and his coffee spilled on his jeans. He laughed at himself, a sad self-deprecating sound.

"You and me, we're both flesh peddlers, right? In one way or another? You sell the pain and I sell the pleasure."

"Very true," she said.

"I came to you for a flogging and you wouldn't take my money. Why?"

"Because of what you told me two years ago," Nora said. "You don't get personally involved with clients."

Thorny nodded.

"You got involved with a client, didn't you?" she asked.

"More than involved." He met her eyes. "I fell in love with one."

"Who is she?"

"A doctor," Thorny said. "A very famous neurologist. She's

from Pakistan, and she supports her entire family who still live back there. If it got out she hires male escorts..."

"Were you her patient?"

Thorny nodded again.

"Fuck," Nora said.

"My sentiments exactly. A doctor fucking a patient can ruin her career. A doctor from a conservative religious family who fucks a patient who she hired after he told her he was a male escort could ruin her life."

"What's her name?"

"Nadia."

"Pretty name."

"Pretty lady."

"She loves you, too?" Nora asked.

"She does. She didn't even ask me to stop working. She doesn't care about my other clients. But I care. I had this crazy idea I could make enough money to quit working. I took every job I could and banked every penny I could. New York's expensive. I wanted to save up enough I wouldn't have to work for a few years while I figured out what to do with my life. Fuck, I just really wanted to spend as much time with her as I could before my brain blows its fuse. I took any job anybody offered me."

"Milady hired you?"

"Milady hired someone to hire me," he said. "Five grand for two hours of work. How could I say no to that? That's a month's rent in Manhattan."

"What did she do?" Nora asked, sipping her coffee. She already had an idea what happened.

"We had sex. Lots of it. She wanted to take a shower with me afterward—standard request. I get in first while she's looking through her purse for a hair clip. Next thing I know she's long gone and so is my phone with all my clients' numbers in it plus a few pictures of me and Nadia together in bed. Next day Milady shows up at my door telling me she has my phone. I hate to admit that I was a little relieved when she told me that she wasn't really after me. She just wanted to use me to get to you."

"You got to me."

"I thought I did."

"You spend as much time with Kingsley Edge as I do and you get contact paranoia. He thinks the worst of people and nine times out of ten he's right."

"He was right about me."

"If someone tried to hurt Søren like she's trying to hurt Nadia, I'd do the same thing you did. I just wouldn't have gotten caught."

"I'm kind of happy you killed the tape. I would have felt like shit for the rest of my life knowing I'd ruined yours. I don't know what to do now, though."

"It would take more than that tape to ruin my life. But you could have gotten Søren into big fucking trouble if Milady knows who he really is."

"Would you believe me if I said I was sorry?"

"I believe it. But that doesn't change the fact that Milady's out to get the both of us."

"She's got nothing on you now."

"It's only a matter of time before she catches me doing something I shouldn't with someone I shouldn't. Who knows? You might not be the only client of mine working for her."

"I'll have to tell Nadia. You should warn your priest, I guess."

"Want to know something?" Nora asked and Thorny raised his chin. "This isn't even the worst thing that's happened to me today."

"That bad, eh?" he asked.

"That bad."

Nora put her coffee cup on the table and stood up.

"Go home," she said, patting Thorny on the knee. "I'll handle this."

Thorny stopped before leaving.

"Nora, I am sorry."

"Me, too," she said.

"I started doing this job because I love women and I love sex and it seemed to be the best way to get both without getting involved with someone. Nadia's the best thing that ever happened to me. She's the only good thing that's happened to me in years. I didn't plan on falling in love with my own doctor."

"I never planned on falling in love with my priest, either. Love is a game of Russian roulette. You and I both lost."

"Funny," Thorny said.

"What is?"

"Funny how much losing can feel like winning."

Thorny grinned the grin of a man madly in love and she knew now why it was called "madly" in love. You'd have to be crazy to do it. Call her crazy.

She shut the door behind him, locked it and leaned back against it.

Maybe it was for the best Søren was leaving. If Milady, whoever she was, wanted to hurt Nora, then out of the country might be the best place for Søren. Milady couldn't catch her going in and out of his house at night if Søren wasn't there. She couldn't take a picture of them kissing, couldn't film them fucking. God, she was getting as paranoid as Kingsley if she was imagining a woman sneaking into the woods by the rectory to watch them together. Then again, she'd never expected Thorny of all people, the man who'd helped her beat Milady two summers ago, to turn against her. She'd walked right into it, too. Gorgeous tattooed guy with a sexy grin and a bad reputation brings her two dozen roses and offers a trade—his gift for pleasure in exchange for her gift of pain. As if she needed further proof she was lonely—she'd known the second he turned up in her dungeon something wasn't right, and she hadn't wanted to believe it. She'd gone against her instincts and only by the grace of God and Kingsley had she figured it out before it was too late.

So yes, maybe it was for the best Søren went away while she dealt with Milady.

And maybe the world was flat, Kingsley was vanilla and Nora did calculus for the fun of it.

Fuck Milady and fuck Søren for thinking she would let him go without a fight. Both of them were on her shit list today and she wasn't about to let either of them beat her. She was Mistress Nora and Mistress Nora did not get beaten. Mistress Nora did the beating.

Nora grabbed her car keys and headed out.

Without knocking she'd let herself in and although she knew he'd heard the door open and close, he didn't look at her as she walked over to the piano and set a small potted tree on top of it.

"Ficus delivery," she said.

"Lovely." He glanced at the plant as his hands stilled on the keys. "I'll add it to my collection."

He resumed playing his piece and she let him, comforted to know he had healed enough to use his right wrist again. While he played she lifted his shirt to examine his back, an act of casual intimacy only she and Kingsley could have gotten away with. The bruise was healing well as was the road rash. His back still wasn't a pretty sight, but she knew the truth about pain—the healing often hurt as much as the wounding.

Nora lowered his shirt and sat next to him on the bench, her back to the piano, and looked around the living room.

Two black trunks sat next to the sofa. One leather overnight bag sat on top. One garment bag that likely contained his two secular suits and his Jesuit cassock lay across the arm of the sofa.

And one steamer trunk packed with floggers, whips, bondage cuffs and spreader bars sat by the cold empty fireplace waiting for someone from Kingsley's household to pick it up and store it.

"What were you playing?"

"Ravel's *Jeux d'eau.*"

"Play my song."

"No."

"Please? Please, *sir*? It's a Swedish song. That's practically Danish, right?"

"I don't know who would be more insulted by that comparison—the Danes or the Swedes."

"Oh, just play it. Please?"

Søren sighed heavily. "One of these days I will learn how to tell you no."

"But not today," Nora said.

And with that he launched into eighties Swedish pop sensation A-ha's "Take On Me."

He stopped after the famous keyboard riff and turned to her.

"Oh, dear," he said. "It appears I've reinjured my wrist."

"Big liar. Scoot over," she said. Søren shifted to the left giving her more room on the small bench. "What's going to happen to your piano after you leave?"

"Elizabeth gave it to me. She'll take it back if she wants it, but most likely she'll simply donate it to the church."

"And your trunk of toys?"

"If you want them, you're welcome to them. Otherwise Kingsley will store them for me."

She turned and faced him. He was dressed casually, jeans and a white T-shirt. Of course he would look more handsome than usual today. Was his hair always that touchable? Were his lips always this kissable? Were his eyelashes always that dark?

Or was he so desirable today because he was leaving her and it was human nature—the worst part of human nature—to want what you can't have?

"You really are leaving?" she asked.

Søren reached into his back pocket, pulled out his wallet and from his wallet took out an airline ticket with his name on it. A one-way trip from JFK to Jordan to Damascus. He left next Wednesday.

"Why?" she breathed, shaking her head as he put the ticket and his wallet back in his jeans pocket.

"Priests are like doctors. We have to be where the wounded are. Some doctors work in hospitals. Some doctors work on the battlefield. I've been in the hospital long enough. Time to get back out on the field."

"There are wounded people who need you right here in this town."

"They'll find another priest."

"They need you, not some other priest."

"They need me?"

"They need you."

"What about you?" he asked, looking at her face. "Do you need me?"

"No," she said. "But I want you."

"You'll survive without me. You've been surviving without me for over three years."

"Kingsley might not."

"Kingsley survived without me for ten years."

"He would have died without you, and you know it."

"He won't die without me now. He has Juliette. He loves her. She loves him."

"He loves her. He *needs* you."

"He shouldn't need me."

"That doesn't change the fact that he does."

"Did Kingsley put you up to this?"

"Kingsley screamed at me today, and he did so after he entered my house without permission and watched a sex tape
I'd made with a friend—also without permission. So as you
can imagine, he's not my favorite person today. And yet, here
I am, begging you to stay. For his sake and mine." She didn't
tell him Kingsley fired her. She didn't tell him the tape was a
blackmail tape. She didn't tell him a lot of things she wanted
to tell him including the words *I do need you, whether I want
to or not.*

"What about my sake?"

"You really want to go to Syria?"

"Why is it so hard for you to believe that I want to do what
Jesuits do? Eleanor, I was never supposed to be a parish priest.
If that had been the case I hardly would have joined the Jesuits. I could have skipped five years of seminary and been a
diocesan priest instead. I was sent to Sacred Heart because it
was their way of slapping me on the wrist for informing on
a sex offender priest. I stayed here this long because of you.
And then you left. Why should I stay?"

"If you want a new assignment, fine. Ask them to transfer
you to the Jesuit mission in the city or go teach at your old
school in Maine or one of the eight million Jesuit schools in
New England. Go somewhere we can at least see you every
now and then."

"Do you know how few Jesuit priests speak Arabic?"

"If I truly believed you were doing this because you wanted
to do it and not for any ulterior motive, I would kiss you right
now and give you my blessing. But I can't. I don't."

She shook her head in consternation.

"I have to tell something, Eleanor, and you're not going to like it."

"What?"

Søren leaned in and whispered in her ear.

"I didn't ask for your blessing."

Nora growled at him. Søren laughed. He took her hand in his, kissed the back of it.

"I need time," Søren said finally.

"Time for what?"

"Time to simply be a priest. That's all. No distractions. No complications. Being both Father Marcus Stearns and Søren is…"

"What?"

"In a word—exhausting. I want to be Father Stearns for a while. Only Father Stearns."

"I'll miss Søren."

"I wish you missed Father Stearns. I admit I was jealous hearing you were talking to Father Mike O'Dowell instead of me."

"Just talking. No flirting. Speaking of flirting with priests, who's taking over for you when you leave? And is he cute?"

"The associate pastor at Immaculate Conception is the interim replacement. You'll have to decide for yourself if he's cute. And he's stopping by any minute now to talk about the transition so you should go. I'd rather not have to explain your presence on my piano bench."

"Then take me to bed."

"That would be even harder to explain. But if you want to come back tonight, I'd like to give you a proper goodbye."

"We'll see," she said. "I might be in jail by tonight."

"Again? What did you do this time?"

"It's nothing I've done. It's something I'm going to do."

"That sounds foreboding."

"You remember Milady?"

"I've never forgotten her."

"I inadvertently stole her favorite client out from under her. This apparently was the last straw. She's blackmailing a friend of mine, stole his phone with pics of him and his doctor girlfriend on it."

"She's his doctor?"

"She is. Almost as bad as a priest sleeping with a parishioner, right? Milady's blackmailing him to force him to blackmail me. So I'm going to kill her."

"We aren't under the seal of the confessional. I can report you for threatening someone's life."

"I'll kill you, too, then. That's one way to keep you from leaving."

"We both know you're not going to kill Milady."

"I might if I knew her real name or where she lives. But I don't think anybody does. I have to do something, though. She's trying to hurt me. She's already hurt a friend of mine. She could probably hurt my client, too, the one who was her client once. Oh, and she cut your hair and wore it in a locket around her neck just to fuck with me. If that isn't a capital crime worthy of the death penalty, I don't know what is."

"You're still angry about that?" he asked. She could tell her displeasure pleased him.

"A skosh."

"I'm going to tell you something again, Little One. This time you might like it."

"Please. I could use a little good news today."

Søren stood up and walked over to his steamer trunk. He pulled keys from his pocket and unlocked it. On his knees he pushed this and that aside until he seemingly found what he was looking for.

He stood back up and walked over to her with a white envelope in his hand.

"I realize this might tarnish the romantic aura around the memory of me selling a lock of my hair to buy you a laptop," he said. "But you did tell me she'd threatened you. While in her presence I made, well, let's call it a preemptive strike."

Nora opened the envelope and inside it was a driver's license. She didn't recognize the name on the license, but she did recognize the photograph.

She couldn't get a word out at first. Her heart swelled and warmth radiated from the center of her chest out into the world, as if her heart was a cymbal and someone had struck it with a mallet. Her eyes filled with tears and her throat closed.

"Eleanor?"

She raised her hand, needing a moment's silence.

"You let her kiss you so you could steal her driver's license," she said when she could finally speak again. "For me."

Nora came to him and wrapped her arms around him.

"For you," he said, kissing the top of her head. "You said she wanted to hurt you."

"That's your job," she said. And hurting him was her job. They were too good at their jobs.

Nora laughed against his chest, wiped her tears on his T-shirt.

"How?"

"She has a phone number clients use to make appointments. I called her. I told her I'd heard she'd threatened you. She said we should meet and talk about it. I agreed as long as we met in public and she wore vanilla attire in case one of my parishioners saw me. It was like stealing candy from a baby. People trust the clergy. Too much perhaps."

She stared at him, incredulous. "I'm speechless."

"The words you're looking for are 'thank you.'"

"Thank you."

"You're welcome."

Søren bent to kiss her as she rose up on her toes to kiss him. Their mouths met in passion and sorrow. Passion for it was a powerful kiss of hunger and need. Sorrow as it might be their last kiss if she failed.

"I'm giving you her license so you can protect yourself, not so you can hurt her. Try to remember we're on the side of the angels," he said.

"So I can't kill her?"

He shook his head.

"Fine. I'll talk to her. I might talk to her loudly. But I'll only talk to her."

"That's my good girl."

"Am I? You're leaving. Am I still your girl?"

"Forever," he said. "My love for you isn't going anywhere, I promise. Only my body."

"Your body's my favorite part."

"I'd be hurt if I actually believed that."

"You know…" she said, putting her hand flat on his chest. "You know I love you, too."

"I do."

"So you know I'll find a way to make you stay. I will. I promise you I will."

Søren caressed her cheek, rubbed his thumb over her bottom lip.

"Little One, you won't succeed, but I will enjoy watching you try."

She turned to leave him but stopped when he called her name.

"Eleanor?"

"What?" She didn't turn back around.

"I'll take my keys back now."

With a sigh Nora tossed his keys over her shoulder, the keys she'd stolen from his pocket while they were kissing. She didn't have to look back to know he caught them.

"And my wallet."

Nora surrendered his wallet.

So much for that plan.

32

Milady

NORA DROVE TO A HOUSE ON LONG ISLAND, A SMALL
house, pale yellow and gabled, a bit run-down. She knocked
on the front door and waited. An elderly woman in linen pants
and a faded blue cardigan answered the door.

"Yes?" asked the white-haired woman with a slight smile.
"Can I help you?"

"Is Kimberly home?" Nora asked. "I'm an old friend of
hers."

"Grandma? Who's at the door?"

And there she was, Milady herself, standing at the top of
a hardwood staircase in a plain navy skirt and white blouse
staring down at Nora with murder in her eyes. Nora grinned.

"Hi, Kim," Nora said. "I was in the neighborhood. Want
to go for a walk?"

"Sure," Milady/Kim said. "Let me put on my shoes."

"Nice to meet you. Mrs. Matsui, right?"

"That's right. Have a nice walk," she said as Milady stepped
past her and onto the porch.

"Pretty neighborhood," Nora said as she started down the porch stairs. "Where should we go? Is there a park nearby?"

"I'm not going anywhere with you. Not until you tell me how you found me."

Milady's hands were tight fists and her lips a hard line of extreme displeasure.

"Did you really think my priest would let you kiss him for money? A man who took a vow of poverty selling kisses for money?"

Milady glanced to the left and nodded. "We met in a bad neighborhood. I assumed I'd been robbed on the street."

"That priest. Drives me crazy most of the time and I've thought about killing him a time or two but he's damn pretty and insane in the sheets so what are you going to do?"

"What are you going to do to me?" Milady asked.

"Haven't decided yet," Nora said. "Before you get any ideas, let me clarify the situation. I know who you are—Kimberly Matsui. I know where you live—this cute little house in the burbs. I know your family—your grandfather owned a sushi restaurant that you worked in growing up, which is how you know Japanese. You are not, in fact, the daughter of a geisha. You didn't attend Harvard or any college, much less get kicked out of one. You are the widow of a wealthy man, but you haven't inherited any money from him yet because the will's being contested by his children, who claim you seduced and abused their father. I know your whole life, so does Kingsley, his secretary and a few other people who will remain nameless. If anything happens to me, they will destroy you."

"I don't deserve that. I didn't abuse my husband."

"Did you fuck your last husband to death? His kids seem to think so."

"My last husband died of cancer. Cancer I nursed him

through. We didn't have sex once the last year of his life—he was too sick."

"Maybe if you didn't marry a rich man thirty-five years older than you, you would have gotten a little more sympathy from his kids—his kids who are older than you, I noticed."

"His children are vultures who hated him for divorcing their poor sainted mother. They only wanted his money. I was his wife, his lover, his nurse and his domme. Of course he changed his will to give me everything when he died."

"That's a very sweet, sad story. Should I call the Orange County Sheriff's Department now and tell them where you're living so the process server can finally deliver that subpoena you've been hiding from? Your late husband's children would like their day in court over the will."

"I'd prefer it if you didn't."

"You might win the case. Sounds like it's a stalemate right now. The estate's in limbo until you turn up."

"I won't win. Doesn't matter that I was his wife, that I took care of him while he was dying. We met at a kink club. I was his dominatrix. I will be laughed out of that courtroom and you know it. True, I can't get his money while I'm hiding, but neither can his kids, and that's good enough for me."

"I could tell them where you are."

"Are you going to?"

"You have Thorny's phone so I'm willing to make a trade. My silence for his secrets? And my secrets. And my priest's secrets."

"I don't even know your priest's real name. You have me at a disadvantage."

"It wouldn't take long to find out the real name of the one and only six-foot-four blond priest in the area. There aren't that many priests to go around anymore. His personal life's never been exposed because Kingsley protects him, I protect him and our community protects him. We keep each other's secrets out of respect for each other. You have no respect for our community."

"I have to take care of myself. I have to take care of my grandmother. There's no one else to do it for me. And when my best customer leaves me for you, I have to take care of business."

"Talel has every right to see who he wants to see. If his father found out he was a submissive who paid women to dominate him, he'd be cut off and exiled. You think a domme who regularly blackmails her clients is the right domme for someone in that position?"

"I have to take care of me."

"Then it's your decision. I leave it up to you. You ruin Thorny's life or mine or my priest's, and I ruin yours. Or you can give me back Thorny's phone and shut down your fear factory. We all walk away with our secrets still safe. Fair enough?"

Milady rubbed her temple with two fingers. In her vanilla clothes in this vanilla setting she looked nothing like the fierce whip master Nora had seen that night at the Body House. She looked weary and scared, human. Nora almost pitied her.

"You have it so easy," Milady said, dropping her hands to her sides. "You have no idea how hard I had to work to get where I was. And you show up out of nowhere with the King of the Underground at your side. You punch a man in the nose like a fucking brute and suddenly you're the queen? I spent two years learning how to work whips in tandem. I apprenticed at a dungeon cleaning cum stains off carpet and blood off needles to learn my trade and you just waltz right in and take it all. You're not even a domme. You're a switch. A spoiled switch. Your priest sold his hair to buy you a gift. What have you ever sold for anyone?"

"I certainly never sold my clients' secrets to save my own ass."

Milady gave her a threatening look. She took a step forward but Nora didn't step back. She held her ground. She hoped and prayed this wouldn't turn into a fight. But if it did...well, it was a good thing Nora kept those brass knuckles on her. She might need them.

"Wait," Milady said, raising her hand. Nora waited.

Milady walked back into her house and came back out with a padded envelope. She passed it to Nora.

"Thorny's phone. I will forget everything I know about him, you and your priest, as long as you conveniently forget everything you know about me. The minute a process server shows up at my door, I'm making phone calls. Deal?"

"Deal," Nora said taking the envelope from her. "Have a lovely day. I'd say I'll see you around but you're banned from King's clubs."

"Your 'king' can go fuck himself."

"He probably would if he could figure out how. You could try being a little nicer. You know, not blackmailing your clients. I like my clients even when I'm beating them and calling them pathetic little boys. I respect them, and they respect me."

"I loved my husband. I respected him. Every other man is just a paycheck."

"Now you know."

"Now I know what?"

"Now you know why your clients keep coming to me. They're not paychecks. They're people."

"I might believe you if you didn't charge two thousand dollars an hour. Go top somebody for free and then lecture me about treating clients like people."

"I did top somebody for free," Nora said with a grin. "Today even."

"Who?"

"You," Nora said. "Now behave. I wouldn't want to have to punish you. But I will if I have to. Say 'Yes, Mistress' if you understand."

Milady's entire small frame vibrated with barely concealed fury.

"Yes, Mistress," she said.

"Good girl." Nora winked. Then she turned and started toward her car.

"What's it like?" Milady called out after her. Nora turned around.

"What is what like?"

"Being loved like you are."

"I told you. I take care of my clients and they—"

"Not your fucking clients. Him. Your priest. He sold his hair to me to buy you a gift. My husband had a fetish, and I was the embodiment of it. But he didn't really love me. He respected me, cared about me. But it wasn't love. What's it like being loved like that?"

Nora answered in a word.

"Exhausting."

Once in her car, Nora called Juliette and had her dig up Thorny's address. She arrived a little after nine and prayed he was home and not out on a job with a client. She tried not to think about how much it hurt knowing he'd fucked her solely to blackmail her. He'd used her and Nora wasn't a fan of getting used. Not like this anyway. She did the using, not the other way around. It wouldn't have hurt nearly so much except she'd enjoyed it, enjoyed having a boyfriend for a day, enjoyed waking up with someone in her bed and cooking breakfast together and changing the sheets and watching TV on the couch. It had all been an act, but it had been a good act and maybe she was just angry at herself for wanting something she couldn't have so much she'd fallen for the act.

She knocked on the door to Thorny's apartment and waited. He opened it and she saw the fear on his face when he looked at her.

"Crisis averted," she said, and handed him his phone.

"Oh, thank fuck." He kissed his phone and shoved it into his pocket. "Thank you."

"Take this, too," she said. "It's Milady's driver's license. It's expired but that's still her address. Don't use it to hurt her. She's agreed to back off all of us. But it's insurance."

"You're a goddess, Mistress."

"Tell me something I don't know."

"I'm leaving? That's something you don't know."

"Leaving?"

"I told Nadia what happened. She was freaked out but not angry. She said that the big hospital out in Seattle offered her a job a while back. They still want her. She's going to take it so we're moving out there. Fresh start where nobody knows who I am."

"Good idea. Seattle's beautiful. Just watch out for volcanoes."

"I already have this waiting to erupt in my head," he said, tapping his temple. "What's one more volcano?"

"I'm glad you're going with her. Gather ye rosebuds, right?"

"Well, you know that old Bible verse—I go where she goes—or whatever it is. I haven't been to church in a long time so don't quote me on that."

"You're butchering the poor Book of Ruth. She and Naomi deserve better than that."

"Were they fucking?"

Nora pursed her lips at him. "No. Ruth was Naomi's

daughter-in-law. Naomi's husband died, and both her sons. She told her two daughters-in-law, Ruth and Orpah—"

"Oprah?"

"Orpah. She was a Moabite, not a talk-show host. Anyway, Naomi told Ruth and Orpah to go back to their families and find new husbands and start new lives. Orpah went away but Ruth refused to leave Naomi. What she said to Naomi was, 'Do not ask me to leave you or forsake you / For wherever you go, I go...'"

"What?"

Nora stopped. She cocked her head. She laughed.

"That's it," she said.

"What's it?"

"Nothing." She looked at Thorny and grinned. "I mean, everything. I just figured something out. Thank you. Couldn't have done it without you, Thorny."

"Couldn't have done what?"

"I hope you and Nadia have a very long and sexy life together. I have to go."

"Don't go. I owe you...so much. I owe you a ton. I can pay you or something?"

"You just helped me figure out how to save my priest." She patted him on the cheek and resisted the urge to slap it just once to punish him for fucking her over. Considering how many men she'd used for sex the past couple of years, she gave him a pass. It had been very good sex after all.

Nora left Thorny and ran to her car. Tomorrow Søren was taking his Final Vows. The day after he'd leave her for Syria and for the rest of his life.

She turned on her car but she didn't drive home.

Søren had told her two years ago to finish her Ruth story.

Tomorrow she would finally write the ending.

33

Final Vows

ON THE MORNING OF THE LAST SUNDAY IN AUGUST, Nora stepped into the two-hundred-year-old Jesuit church in Harlem where Søren and fourteen other veteran Jesuits would take their Final Vows that day. Half an hour before the service began the pews already creaked with the weight of friends and family packed shoulder to shoulder waiting to watch their priests take the last vows they'd ever take in their lives. If they made it this far, they weren't likely to leave the order. They'd been in it for twenty years at least, each and every one of them, and they'd decided to stay in the Jesuits until the end. Søren would die a Jesuit. That was what she wanted for him, because that's what he wanted for himself. But he could be a Jesuit here, close to her and Kingsley. He didn't have to go across the world to a war zone to do it. She'd give everything to keep him here, keep him safe.

And if everything was what he asked, everything was what she'd give him.

Nora walked nervously down the center aisle, the red carpet runner beneath her feet muffling the sound of her kitten heels on the hardwood. She looked for a seat somewhere close but not too close, where she could see but not be seen. Too late. A hand snaked out from a pew on the right and grabbed her wrist. Nora started and looked into the eyes of a young woman with dark hair cut in a stylish bob and a wearing a dress that cost more than Nora's monthly mortgage payment.

"Don't you dare act like you don't remember me," the woman said, her voice stern and imperious—exactly like her brother's.

"Claire." Nora felt the profoundest sense of relief when Claire wrapped her in a near painful embrace.

"Elle," Claire breathed. "Too long."

"Way too long," Nora agreed, swallowing hard.

"You have to help me." Claire sounded scared, desperate.

"I will," Nora said.

"You will?"

Nora nodded against Claire's shoulder.

"I do love him," Nora said. "I didn't leave him because I stopped loving him."

"I know," Claire said. "No could stop loving him once they start."

Claire released her from the crushing hug, but held on to Nora's hand. She didn't seem ready or willing to let it go and Nora was grateful to her.

"I'm so glad you're here," Claire said. She had tears on her face. "I can't do this alone."

"I didn't want to come."

"Neither did I," Claire said. "But I can't tell him no."

"Did you ask him not to leave?" Nora asked.

"I didn't ask, I begged." Claire stared straight ahead. She and Søren both had similar profiles—the same ears, the same cheekbones, the same ironic tilt to the mouth when they smiled. But Claire wasn't smiling.

"Did he tell you anything about why he's going?"

"One of the priests who visited him after his motorcycle accident is going, too. He's the one who asked him to go. I can't believe he said yes." Claire squeezed Nora's hand harder.

"I can," Nora said. She didn't want to believe it, but she could. She'd left him. Kingsley had staked his claim on her. She'd refused to return to him. What was keeping him here? Nothing.

"What are we going to do?" Claire asked.

"Pray."

"Will it help?" Claire asked.

"It won't hurt."

The music started, a hymn Nora recognized. "Be Thou My Vision."

All at once the entire assembly rose to their feet. Nora glanced around as everyone sang the hymn looking for any familiar faces. At last she found a row of them standing in the balcony.

"Did he pick the music?" Nora asked Claire.

"I don't know. Why?"

"This is his favorite hymn."

"His church seems to know it well." Claire turned her head and looked up to the balcony. "I can hear them up there singing it."

"Who?"

"Sacred Heart," Claire said. "They're all in the balcony. Over a hundred of them came."

Nora looked back and up and saw faces she recognized including Diane's and Diane's family. She should be up there, Nora thought. She should be with Søren's church. But she couldn't be. She hadn't just left him, she'd left them, too.

"That's a third of the entire church," she whispered to Claire.

"See?" Claire said. "Told you. Once you start loving him, you can never stop."

Nora did love him and she would never stop loving him, which was why when he and the other fourteen Jesuits walked down the aisle and he turned his head to look at her, she smiled for him. He didn't smile back, but she could tell he wanted to. She wished Kingsley were here to hold her other hand, but she didn't blame him for not coming. He'd had to stand idly by and watch Søren marry Kingsley's sister years ago. He couldn't and wouldn't stand idly by and watch the only man he'd ever loved pledge himself to yet another rival.

The Final Vows ceremony involved a full Mass and all fifteen priests assisted. They looked almost angelic in their off-white vestments lined up side by side. They were a motley crew from all over the world—Africa, Asia, South America, Mexico and the United States. Søren was one of the younger ones but not the youngest. Most definitely the handsomest. At least her in opinion.

When it came time for Communion, Nora went forward. She hadn't taken Communion since before she left Søren. So it was fitting that she walked to his line and when he held up the wafer that was the Body of Christ, she let him place it on her tongue. When she swallowed it she felt an old wound she'd forgotten about. Then the old wound was gone, healed. The fissure in her heart sealed itself up and scarred over. The church sang a new hymn and the words spoke to her heart— *Come home, come home...ye who are weary come home.*

Old words. Trite words. And yet they cut Nora's soul to the quick.

Nora was weary. And Nora did want to go home.

One by one each of the fifteen priests made their vows.

When Søren knelt to speak his vows, Nora breathed in at the sight—the rare sight—of Søren, penitent and humble. When he spoke the vows, his voice was strong and clear and unwavering. His words carried throughout the church like an updraft and if Nora had wings she would have been able to fly.

"I, Marcus Lennox Stearns, make my profession, and I promise to Almighty God, in the presence of the Virgin Mother, the whole heavenly court and all those here present, and to you, Reverend Father Haas, representing the Superior General of the Society of Jesus and his successor and holding the place of God, perpetual poverty, chastity and obedience..."

The vow recitation continued until every last priest had said his final commitment. The rest of the Mass passed in a haze. In the heat and the humidity and the fear she would fail at her task, Nora could barely concentrate on the words. Not that it mattered. She knew the Catholic Mass by heart. The words were tattooed on her mind and branded on her soul. She rattled them off without thinking.

When the final hymn was sung and the time came for everyone to leave, Claire put her arm around Nora's waist and together they walked down the aisle. A few minutes later the fifteen priests who'd taken their public and private vows appeared on the street to be greeted by their loved ones.

"Go," Nora said to Claire. "You're the only family he has here. He'll want you to meet his church."

"Can I see you again?" Claire asked. "He's leaving and I don't..." She stopped and swallowed hard, catching her breath. "I'd like to be around someone who knows him and loves him. I know it's not the best idea but would you consider it?"

"Maybe lunch?"

"I'd like that." Claire smiled and Nora could see her fighting tears.

"So would I."

"Are you going to talk to him?" Claire asked, desperation in her eyes and hope in her voice.

"I'll wait until he's alone. Go. He needs you."

"He needs you," Claire said. "But I'll go tackle-hug him in my own special way. He probably needs that, too, even if he won't admit it."

"But be gentle. He's still recovering from the accident."

"I'll tackle-hug him gently," Claire said and squeezed Nora's hand one more time before releasing her. She ran to Søren, and Nora laughed as she saw Claire, now a grown woman of twenty-nine, throw herself into her big brother's arms the way she had all those years ago when Nora had gone with him to his father's funeral. Nora was grateful for Claire's presence in his life. She was Søren's solid ground, and she had a gift for taking that pompous priest and turning him back into a human being with one tackle-hug and a playful insult.

"Frater!" Claire said, clinging to him as if she'd die the second she let go of him.

"Behave yourself, Soror," Søren said, patting her on top of her head. "Don't scare my congregation. They're under the impression you're the normal one in the family, and we wouldn't want to disillusion them."

From a distance of about twenty feet, Nora watched as Søren introduced Claire to every member of Sacred Heart who'd come to his profession of Final Vows. Nora could see from their faces and hear from their words that none of them knew yet Søren was leaving forever that week. Knowing Søren he'd decided to depart without a long drawn-out goodbye. No going-away parties. No fanfare. Only an announcement from the pulpit made by the interim priest that Father Marcus Stearns had been called to the mission field. He sends his love and asks for your prayers.

With any help from God and a little luck, no one would be making that announcement.

When at last the final parishioner had give Søren a handshake or a hug or a kiss on the cheek, Nora stepped out of the shadows and walked to him. Claire said something in his ear and walked away after throwing Nora one last pleading look.

An eerie calm came over Nora. A calm and a focus that seemed to come from outside herself. She was a woman on a mission and the mission was all that mattered.

She reached into the pocket of her jacket and pulled out a folded rectangle of paper.

"I'm glad you came, Eleanor," Søren said. "It's good to see you in church again."

They were in public. The chance of being overheard was too great to speak the truth to each other. They'd hide behind platitudes and code words. But she didn't have to hide, not with what she wanted to say to him.

"It was good to be in church again. Maybe I'm not so lapsed after all."

"I could have told you that," he said. "Claire's taking me to dinner this evening if you'd like to join us. I think you two would get along swimmingly."

"I have other plans. Just wanted to stop by and give you something."

"You don't give a gift to a priest upon taking Final Vows," he said. "It's not like a First Communion."

"What I want to give you is a Bible verse. I memorized it for you. Is that an acceptable gift?"

"Always," he said. "What's the verse?"

"The Book of Ruth, chapter one, verses sixteen and seventeen." Nora took a breath and recited by heart. "'Do not ask me to leave you or forsake you for wherever you go I will go, wherever you stay I will stay, your people shall be my people and your God my God. Wherever you die, there I will be buried. May the Lord do so and more beside if anything but death separates us.'"

Then she handed him the folded piece of paper from her pocket, the one she'd acquired on her very special errand.

"Eleanor, this is an airplane ticket in your name."

"Destination Syria," she said. "Where you go, I go. If you go to Syria, I go with you. And I won't come home until you come home. I will not leave you. I will not forsake you. Where you die, I will be buried. And those are my Final Vows."

Then she took her ticket out of his hand, turned and walked away.

She meant every word of her vow. If he was going into a war zone, she would go, too. Nothing could stop her. Going with him to Syria was the one trump card left in her hand. She'd made the largest bet of her life, and she wasn't bluffing.

Nora went to Kingsley's town house and found him sitting in his office, staring out the window at nothing, nothing at all.

Kingsley glanced over his shoulder at her and then turned back to the windows.

Nora sat on the desk behind him and waited. A moment later Kingsley turned in his chair and rested his head in her lap. He'd fired her two days ago but none of that mattered now. She combed her fingers through his dark hair as if he were a sick child who needed a mother's touch.

"How long have you been sitting here brooding?" she asked.

"For hours."

"I'm sorry I wasn't there for you when you needed me," she said, tugging his earlobe.

"I forget sometimes you need a life outside of work."

"I do. But you'll be happy to know I will never ever be seeing Thorny again during work or after hours."

Kingsley took a heavy breath. She felt his chest moving against her knees.

"That doesn't make me happy. Relieved, yes. But not happy. I do want you to be happy." He looked up at her with wounded eyes, open and vulnerable, and she caught a glimpse of the teenage boy he'd been when Søren had first loved him.

"By going back to Søren?"

"Yes," he said.

"Why?" Nora touched Kingsley's face, brushing her fingers over his cheek.

"It'll keep him here."

Nora tilted his chin up to meet her eyes, dominant talking to submissive now.

"Is that the only reason?"

"I miss him," Kingsley said, whispering the words like a confession. "I miss how things used to be with the three of us. And I know how much he loves you. I wish I could imagine you with someone other than him, but I can't. I wish I could imagine the three of us moving on and having our own lives without each other, but I can't. Fuck, I even miss getting shitfaced with him at the rectory. We ended up on the roof once, and I still don't remember how we got down. I miss him, Elle. It's not even the sex. We haven't had sex in over ten years. It's him. It's us. It's our friendship. No, not that." Kingsley looked up at her with sorrow in his eyes. "He's all the family I have. If he leaves, he'll take my family away from me."

Nora's heart broke for him. He lowered his head to her lap again and she swiped at a tear on her cheek. Nora didn't tell Kingsley what she'd done or said to Søren. She didn't tell him about her plane ticket and her vows. He was already grieving Søren's loss. Kingsley didn't need one more thing to mourn.

"Why does it always have to hurt so much?" Kingsley asked.

"What?"

"Life."

Nora smiled. "God's a sadist. That's why."

"You think so?"

"Oh, I know so," Nora said. "I'm a writer. I do what God does in miniature every time I write a book. I create worlds and people out of nothing—*ex nihilo*—and I torture the fuck out of them for four hundred pages."

"Because you're a sadist?"

"Partly that. Plus...if I didn't torture them it would be a real fucking short book. And trust me on this, King, there is *no* money in short stories."

Kingsley laughed and buried his head into her lap again, seeking her comfort and safety and the shelter of someone stronger.

"You've solved the oldest theological conundrum of all time," Kingsley said. "Why does God allow suffering? Because there's no money in short stories."

"I'll tell you one more little secret about being a god. Even though I torture them for four hundred pages, it hurts me to do it."

"They aren't real. Why does it hurt?"

"I created them. They're mine. I love them. God loves us, too, even when He hurts us. Especially when He hurts us, I imagine."

"Søren created me," Kingsley said. "I owe my life to him, my world, my kingdom. Even Juliette. I never would have met her if he and I hadn't fought. I can't live without him any more than you can live without God."

"If I thought going back to him would fix everything for you and me and him, I would do it."

"Forgive me," Kingsley said. "I'm being selfish."

"You're scared. So am I."

"What do we do?" Kingsley looked up at her again awaiting her answer.

"What we always do."

"What's that?"

Nora bent over and kissed him. Against his lips she whispered one word.

"Fuck."

"Now, that is the best idea I've heard all day."

34

The Endgame

NORA GATHERED TOYS FROM THE PLAYROOM AND took them to Kingsley's bedroom where he waited for her. She locked the door behind her. The house was empty. No one was home but the two of them, which meant she could destroy Kingsley if she wanted to.

And she wanted to.

"Since I fired you, does this mean I don't have to pay you?" Kingsley asked as she started to undress him. She pushed his jacket off his shoulders and unbuttoned his vest.

"I don't want your money tonight. Just you. Just us."

"You can have your job back. Tomorrow," he said. "Tonight—"

She covered his lips with one finger. No more talking necessary. She knew what he meant to say, that tonight they wanted nothing between them. They needed this, needed the comfort of each other. Nora and Kingsley were a secret society of two. The two acolytes of Søren. His acolytes, his lovers, his twin children whether they liked it or not. They had to grieve together because only they knew what they could be losing. So tonight wasn't a job, it wasn't an appointment and Kingsley wasn't a client.

Without another word, Nora stripped Kingsley naked. She drew him to the end of the bed and bound his hands high on the bedpost. A long slant of evening sunlight snuck into the room between and under the heavy damask curtains. She'd rarely seen Kingsley like this, naked in sunlight. She'd taken an art class in college and recalled being taught that all visual images were a combination of light, color, line, texture, mass and motion. The dappling light cast shadows on his body. His thick eyelashes looked dipped in gold. The color of his skin was olive and his hair was as dark as his eyes and his eyes were as dark as the wick of a candle after the fire had gone out. His body was composed of the straight line of his back, the curve of powerful shoulders, the V of his hips and the ridge of muscles in his legs and arms. His smooth warm skin was interrupted with whorls of old scars that would never fully heal. The mass of him was dense with muscle, hard with desire. And the motion of him was stillness, but active stillness, waiting stillness, strength in repose, power enchained. A work of art.

Nora kissed him in the center of his back between his shoulder blades. A kiss like a blessing.

"Je vous honore," she whispered. She might be his domme, but he was still her King.

From her case of toys she'd brought in from the playroom, she pulled out one whip. Then she pulled out a second one.

She brought them over to Kingsley.

"Two?" he asked.

"Don't worry. I've gotten much better at tandem whipping in two years."

"But two?"

"Trust me," she said. She lifted the handle of each whip to

his lips and Kingsley kissed the knots. "How much pain do you want?"

"Hurt me until I forget how much I hurt," he whispered.

Nora kissed his lips and whispered a "With pleasure" in return.

She stood back from him and made a few practice cracks with the whips. The whips were in her thrall and danced at her every command. For the past two years she'd practiced her whip work, wanting to be better than Søren, as good as Milady. But not to show off or impress anyone. She learned how to use two whips in tandem so she could do this—hurt Kingsley until he forgot how much he hurt.

Nora hurt him.

She focused her attentions on the sides of his body, striking him over and over again from the back and outside of his thighs to the sides of his hips. She struck his back along the sides as well, leaving the spine alone while she ravaged him along his rib cage all the way to his shoulders and down to his hips again. She dropped the second whip and used the one in her right hand to pinpoint her strikes. By the time she finished Kingsley had tiger stripes on both sides of his body, wrapping around his rib cage to his chest. Shallow wounds but bleeding. Nora could have taken him down then but she didn't. He needed to feel pain and she needed to give it. With a heavy flogger she flogged the welts from the whip, stacking pain upon pain, layering welts on top of whip wounds. Kingsley had been quiet at first but now his gasps and cries of pain flowed freely. She gave him more pain than she gave to anyone else because he wanted it and because he could take it. What was the old saying—that which does not kill us only makes us stronger? If that was true, then Kingsley might be the strongest man alive.

Finally Nora dropped the bloodstained flogger. She unbound Kingsley and he dropped to his knees, unable to stand.

"I want you," she said, stroking his hair.

"You have me."

She bade him to stand, bade him to pull the covers and sheets back. Because it would hurt the most, she ordered him to lie on his back in the center of the bed. She cuffed his wrists to the headboard and undressed. Now naked, she sat on his stomach, lowered her mouth to his mouth and kissed him. He was hard and she felt his thick erection against her wet labia. Unable to resist, she pushed down and against his cock and his head fell back with the pleasure of it.

"Please…" he said.

"Are you sure?"

Nora couldn't deny him this simple request. She wanted it as much as he did. She pushed down and against him again and he lifted his hips up and into her. Slowly he worked his bare cock inside her. It would be fine. She had her IUD now. They were clean and there was nothing to be afraid of. Having nothing between them as he entered her felt like a step down a path they'd been afraid to take together. A path that might eventually lead them to where they could forgive each other and love each other and let the past go entirely.

Nora pressed her hands into Kingsley's lacerated sides as she rode him. His pain stoked his pleasure and he inhaled sharply, his head falling back against the black sheets again. She kissed the hollow of his throat, bit at his ears, bit at his chest and clavicle. Her body throbbed around his cock, clenching at it, squeezing it, holding it, caressing it with her inner muscles that wanted to take all of him into her as deep as she could, so deep it hurt. He pushed his heels into the bed and thrust into her from below hard enough to lift her off the bed. She clung to the headboard to steady herself as their bodies rocked together wildly, urgently. Wetness dripped out of her and coated his hips. Her teeth scored his shoulders. The pounding intensified into something animal, something blinding, something raw and fierce with need as naked and hungry as they were. Nora held off from coming as long as she could. She wanted to wait for him and he for her. When they came at last they came together, the orgasm obliterating sight and breath and even the world as it rocked through them, a shuddering that went on forever until it ended and Nora collapsed onto Kingsley's chest.

With him still inside her, she reached over his arms and unlocked the cuffs from the headboard. He rolled her onto her back and pulled out. Exhaustion hit her then and she remembered she'd barely slept the night before and the night before that. Fear had kept her awake but she wasn't afraid now, not in this bed with this man who could and would kill to protect her if it ever came to that. She opened her legs for him and he slid two fingers into her, caressing his own semen in her body. When she fell asleep moments later, he was still inside her.

When Nora woke it was full night. A sound had woken her, something like a knock or a bell. The bed was empty. She was alone. She slipped from the bed and found Juliette's silk robe on the back of the bathroom door and put it on, cinching the cord around her waist. When she left Kingsley's bedroom she heard something. Whispering voices that carried down the empty halls.

She walked down the main staircase and stopped on the landing. Søren stood in the foyer, a streetlight from outside turning his blond hair white. He had Kingsley in his arms.

Nora said nothing. Since she'd gone to work for Kingsley, a rift had formed between him and Søren. This was the first time she'd seen them this close in three years. Oh, they joked, they teased, they drank together on occasion. But it wasn't like this. It wasn't honest like this. Kingsley clutched Søren's lapels in his fists and his head rested on Søren's shoulder. Søren had his arms around Kingsley, stroking his back with one hand while the other twined tight in Kingsley's hair, holding him close. Blood had seeped through Kingsley's white shirt and she knew Søren could feel the deep welts on Kingsley's body through the fabric. Søren was whispering something in Kingsley's ear, something that shook Kingsley to his soul. The way Kingsley's back moved she could tell he was either weeping or trying not to. She'd seen Kingsley and Søren in bed together and it still hadn't been half as intimate as seeing them like this, seeing Kingsley like a scared child seeking love and safety in his father's arms.

Nora turned to go, to give them their privacy, but Søren said her name.

She turned back around and looked down at them.

Kingsley released Søren first and stood up straight. He and Søren locked eyes before Kingsley nodded at something Søren didn't have to say. When Søren brushed his lips across Kingsley's forehead, Kingsley closed his eyes, wincing as if the kiss burned. With his composure regained, Kingsley headed up the stairs, stopping to kiss her on the cheek as he passed. When she and Søren were alone, she continued downstairs and stopped on the final step meeting Søren eye to eye.

"Four months?" Søren asked, his hands on her waist.

"What's four months?"

"Can you spare me for four months? Kingsley says he can as long as I'm home by New Year's."

"You'll go to Syria, but only for four months?"

"Yes." Søren clasped his hands in front of him. Although he didn't have his collar on, he looked like a priest. Light from a street lamp streamed through the windows and surrounded

him like a ghostly halo. All she had to do was take a step forward and she would be inside his circle of light.

"If Kingsley can spare you four months, so can I," she said,
sticking to the shadows where she felt safest. She didn't want
him to see the look of relief on her face, the tears in her eyes.

"You'll tear up your ticket?"

"It's refundable," she said, her voice hoarse and sticking in
her throat.

"You were really going to follow me to Syria if I moved
there permanently?"

"Søren," she said, shaking her head. "I already hired a house
sitter."

"I'm touched. Truly." His words could have been sarcas-
tic, and she wouldn't have blamed him, but they weren't. He
was touched. Truly.

"I can't come back to you, but I won't live without you,
either. One is purgatory. The other would be hell."

Søren stepped closer, brought his mouth to hers. Nora
pulled back.

"What about your vows?" she asked.

"They can start tomorrow."

Nora laughed and took him in her arms, kissing him and
being kissed with abandon. His hands slipped into the robe,
found her breasts and held them as his tongue tasted her mouth
and she tasted his. He slid his hand between her legs.

"Kingsley?" he asked. She knew he could feel the wetness
inside her.

"He needed it. So did I," she said as his fingers slipped in
deeper. "Do you need it?"

"No," he said, and she did her best to hide her disappoint-
ment. His hands left her body and she tightened the robe
about her again.

"So you're really going to try this whole chastity/celibacy thing?" she asked.

"I was celibate for fourteen years before you. I could make it another fourteen years."

"You'll miss me."

"I already do."

"What if I said I'd come to you?"

"I'd take you back to me."

"Vows be damned?"

"Not damned," he said. "Merely dented."

"You should come up and stay the night with us. For old time's sake."

"Didn't we just have the chastity discussion ten seconds ago?"

"Remind me—was that before or after your fingers were inside me?"

"Touché." He kissed her again but quickly before taking a step back. "I should go. Eight o'clock Mass tomorrow morning."

"You leave Wednesday?"

"Wednesday. We should say our goodbyes now," he said. "I don't know if we'll have another chance before I go."

"I could take you to the airport. Or King will. Or we both will."

"Diane's taking me. If either of you do..."

"What?"

"I might not get on the plane."

Nora smiled. Søren could be cold and cruel at times but other times it seemed he was born to say the words she most needed to hear.

"Goodbye then," she said. "Be safe. I don't know what I'll do without you."

"If I know you—and I do—you'll find something to occupy yourself," he said. He kissed her cheek and turned to leave. She wanted to be strong enough to let him go without another word. But she wasn't so she ran to him, ran into the light, and let him take her in his arms. The tears flowed freely, and he rocked her against him.

"My love." He sighed as he held her. "My Little One…"

She inhaled deeply, breathing in the scent of snow on his skin and hair, the eternal winter that he carried inside him. He smelled like Christmas Eve, the one night of the year even grown-ups could believe in magic.

"You weren't really going to leave forever, were you? Leave us forever?" she asked. "You know I love you. You know I'll always love you. Even if I can't…if we can't make this work, it doesn't mean I don't love you. You're…"

"What?"

"You're my everything," she said. "I know you could leave me. I've given you every reason to. But Kingsley?"

"I would have stayed away as long as I needed to," he whispered against her hair.

"For what?"

"Winning, of course," he said. "The endgame."

He pulled up and brushed her hair from her face, brushed the tears from her cheeks.

"I should have known this was part of some strategy of yours. What is your endgame, Blondie? Tell me so I know how to beat you."

"My endgame is the same endgame as in every game of chess."

"Which is?"

Søren glanced at the stairs that led up to Kingsley's inner sanctum.

"Protect your king."

Of course. So that's why it had to be this way, why Søren

had to leave or why he had to at least try to leave. Leaving was the only move that could force Kingsley into forgiving Søren, force them into a long-overdue reconciliation. Kingsley needed Søren and Søren needed Kingsley, but they were so damn stubborn the rift between them might never have healed if Søren hadn't taken this assignment. This game wasn't chess. It was poker, and Søren held all the aces. Tonight, for the first time in three years, she'd seen Kingsley in Søren's arms, clinging to him with need and love and everything he had and felt for Søren. Søren hadn't been bluffing by packing his bags to leave. But he had gotten her and Kingsley to finally show him the cards in their hands—all hearts.

She pulled Søren tighter to herself, rested her chin on his shoulder. She felt the strength of him against her, his impressive height, his broad shoulders. And yet he felt fragile to her, too.

Into his ear she prayed her first true prayer since she'd left him.

"'Because you have made the Lord your refuge / the Most High your dwelling place / no evil shall befall you, no scourge come near your tent. / For he will command his angels concerning you, to guard you in all your ways / On their hands they will bear you up...'"

Nora paused and swallowed. "I'm sorry," she whispered. "I don't remember the rest."

"'On their hands they will bear you up / So that you will not dash your foot against a stone...'"

"Or crash your motorcycle," Nora said. "Or get shot or stabbed or beaten up by mean priests or juvenile delinquents."

"I don't recall those verses in Psalm 91."

"It's my own translation," she said, digging her fingers into the back of his neck to hold him as close as she could. There was nothing she wouldn't give right there and then in exchange for a promise from God that Søren would come back to her in one piece. But God wasn't offering her that deal so she could do nothing but let Søren go.

"I'll come home," Søren said. "I promise."

"Please," she said. "You take my heart with you."

He kissed her forehead. "Little One, you are my heart."

After one last kiss, there was no more to say. By the time she heard the roar of his Ducati's engine starting, she was already on her way back to Kingsley's bed. She found Kingsley awake and waiting for her, sitting on the edge of the bed.

Nora stood in front of him and he rested his head against her breast, wrapped his arms around her waist and she kissed the top of his head.

"You saved me," Kingsley said, clinging to her as tightly as he'd clung to Søren. "You found a way to keep him here. Four months is nothing next to forever. You were going to go with him?"

"If that's what I had to do," she said softly.

"I was wrong."

"About what, my King?" she asked in a gentle tone. The time for pain was over. Now was an hour for solace.

"I told you there were three ways to be a queen. There are four."

"What's the fourth way?"

"You can be born a queen." He looked up at her. "That's why you are a queen. Not because I made you one or you stole a throne or a crown. You were born to be the queen and you are."

"You know, in chess the queen is the strongest piece on the board."

Kingsley chuckled softly. He pushed the robe aside to kiss her nipples.

"I know. And the king is the most vulnerable."

"There is one person stronger than the queen or the king combined," she said.

"Who?"

"The man who moves the pieces."

35

The Call

NORA WOKE UP WITH A HANGOVER AND A BODY IN her bed.

The hangover was from drinking with Kingsley last night. The body was Griffin's.

How the two had converged was a bit murkier.

Nora considered crawling out of bed but Griffin chose that moment to put his heavy arm over her lower back, pinning her against his sleeping form. His naked sleeping form. That didn't necessarily mean they'd had sex. Griffin always slept naked. She wasn't naked. And she was in her own bed in a too-large black shirt still wearing panties. Through the dark she could see her shoes on the floor by the chair, her skirt and bra over the back. Griffin must have undressed her for bed because as drunk as she'd been last night, there was no way her clothes would have ended up laid out that neatly. The shirt she wore felt expensive. Must be Griffin's.

Nora settled in against Griffin's chest and tried to remember what he was doing here. She searched the stormy recesses of her mind and found a memory—she and Kingsley at his town house and several empty bottles of wine. It looked like a party but it wasn't. They weren't celebrating anything. They drank to forget and she woke up remembering. Griffin had shown up at some point and had driven her home. Knowing her she'd asked him to stay. Knowing Griffin, he would have stayed anyway just to keep an eye on her.

Finally, Griffin shifted in his sleep, allowing her to move. She crawled out of bed and went to the bathroom, drank a glass of water, brushed her teeth. When she walked back into her bedroom, Griffin was still asleep. She took his watch off the nightstand and squinted at the face in the dark. Almost 6:00 a.m.

Six o'clock Tuesday morning. Søren's plane left for Damascus in twenty-four hours. She couldn't let him go somewhere so far away and so dangerous without taking her heart with him. Her heart and her collar.

Nora opened her closet door as quietly as she could. In the back on the floor inside a rosewood box was her collar, the one he'd given her when she was eighteen, the one that marked his ownership of her. She unlocked it with the key and held the collar in her hand.

If Nora could lie to herself, she'd say that it was last night she made her decision, sometime between her third and fourth glass of wine. But it was actually Sunday night when she held Søren in her arms and prayed God would keep him safe in Syria…that's when she made her decision. As soon as she was certain to find Søren alone at the rectory, she would go to him and give him her collar, and she would tell him he could put it on her again when he returned from Syria. It would give him a reason to stay safe for her. Because she could never do this again. It would take everything she had to let Søren leave even for four months. What was she going to do for four months? How would she sleep at night knowing she couldn't see him when she needed him? When he needed her? No, she was done. She was done running because she knew all this time, for three years, she'd been running on a treadmill, exhausting herself and getting nowhere. She loved him as much as ever. She wanted him more than ever. And she had looked into a future without Søren and knew she couldn't live in that world. She wouldn't be Mistress Nora anymore. She would have to give up that part of herself. But better to sacrifice part of herself than lose all of Søren.

Wasn't it?

So today she'd go back to Søren and give him her collar. Then she'd have nearly four months—September, October, November, a couple weeks in December—to put her house up for sale and find a day job. She could go on the freelance circuit or teach writing to the aspiring. One of her clients, a big shot computer company CEO, had just lost his personal assistant of ten years to her new baby. He'd already asked Nora to come work for him and keep him in line. Maybe she would take the job. Babysitting a billionaire could have its perks. She'd take the three and a half months to find her clients new dommes. She could downsize her life and rent a small house in Wakefield so she could be close to Søren, at his beck and call once more.

Wings clipped. The bird safely back in a cage.

But it was such a beautiful cage...

"Nora?"

Nora placed her collar back in the box and closed her closet door.

"Sorry," she said. "I was trying to be quiet." She slid in next to him, and he rolled onto his side facing her.

"You feel okay?" he asked in a sleepy voice. He reached for her and pulled her close.

"Sure. Why wouldn't I?"

"You don't remember last night, do you?"

"What did I say?"

"You said I should say goodbye to Mistress Nora, because she was going away tomorrow."

"That was melodramatic of me, wasn't it?"

"To say the least."

"It wasn't a cry for help, I promise. I'm not committing suicide or anything like that."

"No, you're going back to Søren."

"I told you that, too?"

"You didn't have to. I knew what you meant."

Nora nodded.

"Did we have sex?" she asked, lifting the cover playfully, hoping to change the subject.

"I don't fuck drunk girls," Griffin said, lightly rubbing her back. "So…you sober yet?"

Nora held up two fingers in front of her face and saw three.

"Give me a minute."

Griffin took her in his arms and she stretched out on top of him.

"Sorry to give you a scare," she said. "King and I were drinking last night. And the night before. And the night before…"

"You've been partying too much lately," Griffin said. "When I say that, you know there's a problem."

"There's a problem," she said. "I thought Søren was leaving us—forever. Turns out it's just a few months. And the relief I felt when he said he would come back by New Year's…" Nora paused and searched her mind for just the right word to describe the sensation. She was a writer. The right word was everything. Finally, she found it.

"Humiliating."

"Humiliating? How is that humiliating?" Griffin asked.

"I left him. I shouldn't care if he leaves for four months or forty years. I'm supposed to his ex-lover, his ex-submissive, his ex-everything, and I swear to God, Griffin, most days I feel like I'm his wife and not his ex-anything. We're not even divorced. Just separated. This isn't how I want to live my life, in this constant struggle to get free. It's not fair to me, and it's not fair to him, either."

"Don't give up, Mistress," Griffin said, cupping the side of her neck. "Please?"

"King interferes every time I try to get involved with someone else."

"Find someone to be with that he can't fuck with then. Someone with money and power of his own. Someone he can't blackmail."

"Good idea. I'll just run out and find someone with money, power and no dirty secrets. Dime a dozen, right?" Nora rolled her eyes. Griffin laughed and kissed her. Nora let it happen. Whenever her heart was in turmoil, she let her body take over. Griffin's kisses were familiar, comfortable, warm and getting warmer, hot and getting hotter.

"My days of freedom may be numbered," she said. "Want to help me go out with a bang?"

"I'll give you all the bangs you want…"

Nora pushed Griffin onto his back, and he surrendered control to her. He surrendered and let her put the condom on him. He surrendered and let her guide him in. She felt the penetration of his cock inside her like a puncture wound. In her bitterness and defeat, she'd closed herself off and it hurt to let someone inside her. Despite the pain she let him sink into her depths, and she grew more aroused, more herself as she moved on top of him.

"Mistress Nora…" he whispered into her ear as he brushed her hair back and kissed her throat. "Queen Nora…"

"You're trying to seduce me," she said.

"You're on top of me, and I'm inside you." He yanked her shirt off her and threw it on the floor. "I think I succeeded."

Nora leaned over him, put her hands on his shoulders and arched her back, offering him her breasts to suck. His tongue swirled around her nipples, his fingers pinched and teased them. He lifted his head and latched on to her nipple, drawing it deep into his hot mouth. Nora sighed as she felt the pleasurable sensation of pulling, of tugging, of heat on her breast. All the while she rocked her hips into him, grinding her swollen clitoris against the base of his penis.

"You're trying to seduce me into not going back to him."

"I am, Mistress," he admitted shamelessly, which was how Griffin did everything. He took her breasts in his hands and massaged them. "He won't let you play with me anymore if you go back to him."

"I admit, it's a compelling argument."

"You know you'd miss me, Mistress."

"I would miss you…"

She'd miss Griffin. She'd miss freedom. She'd miss her house and her life.

And she'd miss being Mistress Nora. She'd grown so accustomed to being called Mistress or Mistress Nora it felt like her real name and Eleanor had become the name of an old friend she'd lost touch with.

She lay on top of Griffin, pressed her breasts to his chest, and he whispered her name in her ear over and over again— *Nora… Mistress Nora…my Nora…*

On top of Griffin, Nora came with a cry. Griffin kept pushing up and into her even as she lay immobile and panting on top of his chest. It felt wonderful; sex with Griffin always did.

But it wasn't enough. With Søren she had the opposite problem. He was more than enough, almost too much for her. Between not enough and too much, she'd choose too much any day.

"See?" Griffin asked as he wrapped his arms around her. "Won't you miss that?"

"I would," she said. Because she loved Griffin as a friend and a lover she didn't tell him the whole truth. Yes, she would miss him.

But she missed Søren so much more.

Thus it was decided. She would go back to Søren today. She would give him her collar today. She would tell him she would be his again today and forever, without conditions or constants and if he told her to quit her job she would and she would be his property again as soon as he came home. And she would never look back.

Nora was at peace.

Eleanor was at peace.

The phone rang.

She answered it, hoping for nothing from the call except that it would put an end to her conversation with Griffin.

"This better be good," she said as she answered the phone.

"I have a little job for you," Kingsley said.

"It's six in the morning." Nora groaned, rolled off Griffin and onto her back. "What sick sadistic pervert needs me at six in the morning?"

"A sick sadistic pervert doesn't need you. Twelve sick sadistic perverts need you."

"Twelve?" Nora sat up in bed. "I don't do group sex. Wait. How much does it pay? Forget it. I don't do groups."

"Do you want to hear this or not?" Kingsley asked. He sounded as sleepy and irritated as she felt.

"Will I like it?" she asked.

"I think you will. It's a job uniquely suited to your particular talents."

Without any hope whatsoever that she would like what Kingsley had to say to her, she told him two words. Two words she'd said before the night her life changed. She said those two words again not realizing it was about to change one more time.

"Tell me."

36

Professor Nora

ONE HOUR LATER, NORA KISSED GRIFFIN GOODBYE and told him to sleep as late as he wanted. She had on a black pencil skirt, a white blouse, and her black hair was wrapped in a loose bun. She wore her favorite high heels, not the stilettos but the retro pumps with the strap around the ankle. The woman looking back at her from the mirror looked like every man's exaggerated fantasy of a sexy librarian or schoolteacher.

Fitting as today she would be a schoolteacher.

Twenty minutes from her house, thirty minutes in traffic, was a small liberal arts school called Yorke College. She knew of it through Noah. He was about to start his sophomore year there. Today. Noah started school today and so did she.

But not as a student.

She'd had to apologize to Kingsley for being so rude to him on the phone. Instead of calling and asking her to go meet a very special client at his hotel room or to fly to another state or another country to woo a rich and infamous pervert into

Kingsley's coterie, he'd asked her if she'd be willing to teach a writing class for a few weeks.

"A what?" she'd asked him.

"Our friend Dean Howell, who is, as you know, related to the Newport Howells, has a little problem," Kingsley had explained when Nora finally started listening. "Every semester they hire a professional writer to teach a freshman creative writing course. The teacher they hired is an older man, and he's had a heart attack. Our friend the dean knows you live near the school and was wondering if you'd step in until they can find a permanent replacement."

"King, I write erotica."

"It's a college, not a high school. They'll find you eccentric. Liberal arts colleges love eccentrics."

"I've never taught a class before."

"They're students. You're a teacher. They'll do what you tell them to do."

"So you mean I should top them?"

"Young people respond well to authority. Either they submit to it or rebel against it. Sounds like a win-win, *non*?"

"You realize this is the worst idea you've ever had," Nora had said. "Me teaching college freshmen how to write. You understand this is insane."

"It's only a writing class," he said. "Not even you could get yourself in trouble teaching grammar to terrified teenagers."

"Have you met me?"

"Don't fuck any of them."

"You forget who you're talking to."

"Fine. Don't fuck *all* of them."

She'd agreed to teach the class and save Dean Howell's ass on the one condition—no new clients. She hadn't told Kingsley she was quitting yet. She'd talk to Søren first and let him know that while he was in Syria, she'd be slowly dismantling her new life so she could go back to her old one. Going back to Søren was something Kingsley would understand. He'd be happy for them. Happy for himself, too. She knew he missed the old days of their friendship and their threesomes and their late-night drinking binges as much as she missed the old days of their romance. It was all up to her. She could do it. She should do it.

And she would do it.

Today. Right after she finished up this class she'd agreed to teach.

Right after.

The second after.

She wouldn't dally one minute. She would go to the rectory and hand Søren her collar, the collar that she'd put in her handbag that very morning before she'd left. Then she'd call Kingsley and put in her four months' notice. The day Søren came back from Syria would be the day Mistress Nora died once and for all.

Story over.

The end.

Nora parked her car in the faculty lot and with help from a student, she found her building. Five minutes late—her students would have to get used to that—she walked into the classroom.

"Hello," she said as she strode through the door. "My name is Nora Sutherlin, and I'm a *New York Times* bestselling author of lots of dirty books. I know you were expecting a nature writer to be teaching this class, but I'm afraid he's had a medical emergency. I realize I'm not what you signed up for, but in my defense, my books are full of natural behavior. And quite a bit of unnatural behavior so I wouldn't recommend reading them unless you actually want to learn something. If you have a problem with me teaching your class, there's the door.

I'm sure you can find an Add/Drop form in the registrar's office. Also, I'm hungover so if I behave oddly, please forgive me. Why does this class meet so fucking early in the day?"

She rubbed her forehead.

"It's one in the afternoon," an intrepid student said.

"What's your point?" Nora asked. No one answered. "You're all college students so if at least half of you aren't hungover by our next class, I'll be very disappointed in today's new breed of college freshmen. Bad behavior is not only allowed in this class, it is encouraged. Your final grade may depend on it."

She ignored the stares of her students as she walked to the marker board, picked up a black marker and wrote on the board, "Did Oedipus overreact?"

"Professor Sutherlin?" came a girl's tentative voice.

Nora spun around with the marker in her hand.

"Ms. Sutherlin," Nora said. "I'm not really a professor, and I would feel weird about being called that. I also answer to Nora or Mistress Nora. I might even answer to Professor Nora, but I'm not sure. Did you have a question?"

"Are you going to take attendance or anything?"

"Do I look like the sort of woman who takes attendance?"

The girl opened her mouth but nothing came out.

"If you're supposed to be here and you're not, say 'I'm not here.' Anyone?" Nora asked.

No one said anything.

"There," Nora said. "Attendance taken. What's your name?"

"Geri."

"Great. Geri. You're in charge of reminding me I have to do something right after class. Before class is over say 'Ms. Sutherlin, go do the thing you have to do and don't be a pussy.' Can you do that?"

"I can do that."

"Wonderful. Grand. Fabulous. Now, I suppose you all should introduce yourselves. I don't really care about your names, however. As hungover as I am, I probably won't remember them. So instead go around the circle," she said, waving her marker to draw a circle in the air. "Tell me your favorite story. Of the written fiction variety. I'll start. As I said, I'm Nora Sutherlin. My favorite book is *Venus in Furs* by Leopold von Sacher-Masoch. It's the book from whence we receive the word *masochism*, which is what me agreeing to teach this class is a prime example of. Now your turn."

Nora rested her head on the podium. Her head pounded. Her eyes ached. The bright fluorescent lighting wasn't doing her any favors.

And her students were so…fucking…boring…

"I'm Katie from Long Island. I loved *The Awakening* by Kate Chopin."

"Ah, yes," Nora said, not raising her head from the podium. "The book where a woman forced to choose between a shitty boyfriend and a shitty husband picks suicide by drowning because for adult women there's only three viable paths in life to chose from—be a wife and mother, be a whore, or be dead. Try *A Doll's House* by Ibsen instead. Much more cheerful. Next?"

"I'm Ahmed from Brooklyn. I loved *Lord of the Rings*."

"That's better," Nora said. "Who needs books with fully formed female characters in them? Or, well, any female characters in them, for that matter. Women just drag a book down, don't they? All that talking talking feelings feelings. Boring, right? Next."

"My name's Raquel, with a Q. I'm from Cambridge, you know, outside of Boston."

"We know," Nora said.

"Um… I loved *Crime & Punishment* by Dostoyevsky."

"No, you didn't."

"What?"

"That's not your favorite book. That's no one's favorite book. Down in his cold Russian grave, Dostoyevsky just rolled what's left of his eyes. Stop trying to impress us. Tell the truth, Raquel with a Q."

"Okay, well… I really like *The Bridges of Madison Country*."

"That I can believe. Next."

The next student spoke.

"I guess if I had to pick it would be 'The Gift of the Magi' by O. Henry."

Nora looked up from her podium and scanned the faces of her students.

"Who said that?"

She saw a tentative hand go up and she looked at the hand. Then she looked at whom the hand belonged to and found herself unable to stop looking at the face that belonged to the hand that belonged to the student who had said 'The Gift of the Magi' was his favorite story.

Mister Magi had the proverbial big brown eyes, but as she looked into them she saw tiny flecks of warm yellow surrounding the irises. Looking into his eyes was a treasure hunt and she'd struck gold. His hair gleamed a warm blond in the morning summer sunlight. The kid needed a haircut. Yet she felt this nearly irrepressible urge to put her nose to his hair and smell it. He looked like summer with his bright face and bright smile and tan skin. Did he smell like it, too?

His was a handsome face, sweetly handsome, the sort of handsome that drew people in instead of scaring people off. A strong jaw, strong nose, strong neck, broad shoulders in his royal blue T-shirt that said Kentucky across the front in white letters. Around his neck he wore a cluster of hemp necklaces, a little silver cross hanging off one and lying in the hollow of this throat. He looked innocent, as if she'd shocked him and he'd just discovered he liked being shocked.

"Your favorite story is 'The Gift of the Magi'?" she asked once she'd recovered her powers of speech.

"Well…yeah," he said with a touch of Southern drawl. "It's the most beautiful love story I've ever read."

"Have you ever been in love?" she asked him.

"Not really," he said, blushing slightly.

"Have you ever had to sacrifice something of great value for someone you love?"

"No." He shook his head.

"Have you ever had someone sell their own hair to buy you your heart's desire?"

"I can't say that I have."

"I can tell. Let me tell you something about that story. It's a horror story. The husband gives up his most valuable possession, his gold watch, to buy his wife combs for her beautiful long hair. The wife sells her hair to buy her husband a chain for his watch. At the end of the day they gave up everything they had of value and ended up with nothing. How is that a love story?"

The young man shrugged, looking confused and flustered, and she knew she had him. She'd stumped him. He'd fold. He'd give up. He was cute and she liked looking at him but if he wasn't going to fight back, she'd lose interest in him in five seconds.

Five.

Four.

Three.

Two.

"They have each other," the young man finally said. "That's the point of the story. Who needs gold or hair when you have each other? Love isn't about appearances, and it isn't about money. It's not a horror story. Only a cynic would say that, and I don't think you're a cynic."

"I might be a cynic."

"A cynic is someone motivated by self-interest. Teaching a class is the act of an optimist or at least someone motived by the public interest."

"You talk like a college freshman. Anyone ever told you that?" Nora asked.

"It's my first day as a college freshman. You're my first time."

She raised her eyebrow at him and was rewarded by seeing him blush.

"I'm just saying," he said quickly, covering his embarrassment, "I don't believe you're a cynic. I do believe you're trying to mess with us."

Tryin' he said. No *g* at the end. Nora liked the way he talked. The way he talked, the way he smiled, the way he looked at her as if he'd never seen anything like her before in his life and knew he wouldn't see anything like her ever again so he better not look away in case he missed something.

"Little ole me? Mess with little ole you? Would I do something like that?"

"Yes," the young man said nodding. "I think you would. Ma'am."

In the back of her mind she heard Kingsley's voice—*This is a woman who can walk into any room, find the most handsome face in the crowd, look him in the eyes and know she will take him home with her on a leash.*

Where was her leash when she needed it?

"What's your name?" she asked Mr. Kentucky Blue with the gold flecks in his brown eyes and the summer in his hair.

"Wesley Railey. Everyone calls me Wes."

"Stay after class," she said to him.

"Am I in trouble?"

Nora smiled at him.

"Yes, Wes. Yes, you are."

"Ms. Sutherlin?"

"What is it... Gary?"

"Geri. I'm a girl."

"I don't judge. What were you saying, Geri?" Nora asked, still not taking her eyes off Wesley. It was unreal how much she liked looking at him. She felt a little dizzy, a little wobbly, even happy. The hangover was long gone and something like the opposite of a hangover had taken its place. Somewhere in the distance she heard something. It sounded like a door opening. A door she hadn't even known was there. She could walk through it and she'd find herself on a path in the country with rolling green hills to the left and a silver singing stream to the right and a yellow summer sun in the bright blue sky. She wondered where this path ended. Didn't matter. No matter where it ended she knew she had to follow it.

"Ms. Sutherlin—you told me to remind you that you had something to do after class, and you shouldn't be a pussy."

"Forget it."

"What?" Geri asked.

"Don't worry about it," Nora said to Geri.

"But Ms. Sutherlin—"

She smiled at Wesley. Wesley smiled back at her. Then for some reason he laughed. He laughed as if he could read her thoughts and knew the kind of trouble he was in was exactly the kind of trouble he wanted to be in.

As for whatever it was she was going to do after class...

"It can wait."

37

Forever

Scotland
2015

"IT CAN'T WAIT," SØREN SAID.

The sun had fled the chapel entirely. Halfway through her story she'd had to find candles and matches and light them against the dark.

"What can't wait?" she asked, studying Søren's face. The anguish was still there. If only she knew how to ease it.

"You've told me your confession. Here is mine. While I was in Syria those four months, I was a 'good' priest. Chaste. Celibate. Exactly what the church wanted me to be. And, as I'd feared, it didn't help. I might have been a 'good' priest but it didn't make me a better priest. I thought of you and Kingsley constantly. The early church never intended for clergy to be celibate. Even that pompous ass Saint Paul said it was better to marry than to burn. While apart from you and Kingsley, I burned."

Søren met her eyes and she saw cold fire blazing in them, a reflection of the candles against his steel-colored irises.

"I had a choice to make. Continue down this path, the path of chastity like the church demanded, and let my priesthood suffer. Or accept that the rule of celibacy was not something God wanted for us and break the vow. I am a better priest because of you and because of Kingsley. You both keep me humble."

"We're miracle workers then."

"You are," he said with a smile, quickly there, quickly gone. "In Syria, I had a revelation. I was angry at you. And not because you left me, not because you'd taken a path I didn't approve of or gone somewhere I couldn't follow. That you had topped Kingsley and hurt him behind my back..."

"You were mad at me because I was doing the very thing with Kingsley you wanted to do."

"The very thing I wanted to do but I couldn't let myself do it. I was terrified of hurting him like I did when we were in school together, terrified of ruining his life again like I'd done before. I was angry at you. I resented your freedom, your fearlessness. I resented your nights with Kingsley. They should have been my nights with Kingsley. I know I shut the door on being with him, but you two locked it from the inside."

She knew he wasn't speaking figuratively. The night of his Final Vows he'd come to Kingsley's house. She'd heard something, something that had woken her up. Søren had come to Kingsley's bedroom that night seeking them out and the door had been locked from the inside.

"You didn't know. I didn't even know how much I wanted to be with him again until I came home that night and you showed me the riding crop he'd given you to beat him with. It was my own fault. I was afraid of hurting Kingsley, and I hurt him far worse in the process of trying to protect him.

All of this I realized while I was in Syria. And that's when I made my decision."

"What did you decide?" she asked, feeling the foundations of her world shiver at the revelation.

"I decided two things—I would ask you to come back to me and be mine again. And you could still be Mistress Nora and you could still work for Kingsley as long as you would give me your blessing, give *us* your blessing."

"You wanted to be with Kingsley again."

Søren nodded.

"My plane landed the day after Christmas. It hadn't snowed, so I rode over and parked my motorcycle at the church on the corner of your street. I went into St. Luke's and prayed that you would say yes and come back to me. I believed you would. I knew you would. I left my motorcycle in the church parking lot—I even locked it so you wouldn't think I was an idiot."

Nora remembered her first words she'd ever spoken aloud to him—"You're kind of an idiot. You know that, right?" And all because he'd been too arrogant to put a lock on his motorcycle.

"I walked from St. Luke's down your street," Søren continued. "It was dark. Kingsley kept tabs on you as well as he could and while we were apart he fed me bits of information to keep me going. You were safe. You were happy. That's all he told me. I sensed he was keeping something from me. When I went to see you and ask you to come back to me, I found out what that was. *Who* that was."

"Wesley."

Søren paused before nodding solemnly.

"As I walked from St. Luke's to your home, my heart swelled with hope and happiness. I knew you loved me. I knew it like I knew my own name. But there he was. Eighteen years old. Innocent. Untouched. And he was moving into your house.

I watched from the shadows under an oak tree and saw you two carrying in boxes and talking. Laughing. Finally you'd brought all the boxes in. You stood by his car and asked him, 'Did we get everything?' And Wesley said—"

"He said, 'Only one more thing.' He made me hop on his back, and he gave me a piggyback ride into the house." Details of that day had gone hazy in her memory. She hadn't recalled that it was the day after Christmas that Wesley moved in, but what she did remember was the happiness she'd felt, the optimism, the joy of having someone to share her life and her home with for once.

"You smiled and bit Wesley's neck to make him laugh. I know what you look like when you're in love. You were in love with him. You might not have known it yet, but I knew. I saw it."

Nora buried her face in her hands before looking up at him.

"And I had never known such pain," Søren said, his face a blank mask. "Even the day you left me could not compete with the agony of seeing you so happy as he moved into your house and into your life and into your heart. Standing there watching you two together was pure masochism. Yet I couldn't stop looking at you and him. It was my penance. I'd waited too long. I'd lost my Little One. St. John of the Cross spoke of the 'Dark Night of the Soul.' Then, finally, that moment, I knew what he meant."

Nora lowered her head. Her eyes were watering. She felt shame and sorrow and regret—foreign feelings to a woman like her.

"I've always wondered what changed…" she said. "After that year with my mother, I came back and you and I fought. But it never felt like a real fight. At the club you always gave me a hard time, but it was a joke, a role we played for the sake of everyone watching. Two gunslingers facing off at the OK

Corral but when I was alone with you, you were you. Loving. Caring. Someone I could go to when I wanted to talk. Someone I wanted to go to when you needed me. But after you came back from Syria, I waited for you to call me and you didn't. And when I saw you again, you weren't you anymore. You were someone I didn't know. Someone who scared me."

"Kingsley enjoyed accusing me of making decisions solely to punish him—I became a priest to punish him for leaving me after his sister died, I chose you over him to punish him, I went to Syria to punish him. None of that was true. But when I came home and found Wesley moving in with you and Kingsley had known the whole time and not told me... then I punished you both."

Nora shivered at the winter in his voice.

"You barely spoke to Kingsley after you came back unless it was to threaten him. And that night I went to you for our anniversary, you were brutal. So much more brutal than you'd ever been with me. You left bruises on my face that night..." He'd held her face in his hand hard enough to leave bruises on her cheeks, kissed her hard enough to leave bruises on her lips. Bruises she couldn't hide under long sleeves and jeans. Wesley had seen those bruises and nearly left her when she defended herself, defended Søren. "You diabolical priest, you did it on purpose. You left bruises on my face and neck to scare Wes away."

"It almost worked, didn't it?"

It had almost worked. In fact, it had almost worked so well she knew if she ever needed to truly send Wesley away, that was the way to do it.

"Yes. But he didn't scare as easy as you thought he would."

"Much to his credit. I know I was unbearable that year."

"You were an asshole."

Søren gave her a tight smile. "I won't argue with that assessment. I was punishing you for having the audacity to move on when I'd finally come around to the idea of you being Nora, punishing Kingsley for hiding your relationship with Wesley from me because he was afraid I wouldn't come back from Syria if I knew." Søren paused to laugh a cold mirthless laugh. "Wesley was everything I wasn't—young and innocent and untouched. I couldn't accept that he was what you truly wanted. I refused to accept it. I used every trick in the book I could on you, Little One. Every mind game I had in my arsenal."

"And it worked," she said. "Because here I am." She stood up but only long enough to stand in front of him and kneel on the floor at his feet. "I came back. Finally."

"You did. And the night you came back to me was the first night I ever called you Nora."

"And the last night," she reminded him with a smile. She remembered waking in his bed in that familiar darkness and Søren's words, *We'll talk when it's time.* When she woke, he told her he would let her keep the clients she wanted to keep if she wanted to keep them. If she wanted to be Mistress Nora still, she could be. He wouldn't stop her being Nora with everyone else as long as she was always his Eleanor, his Little One, when she was with him.

Nora put her head in his lap and felt the comforting touch of his hand on her hair.

"Will you forgive me?" he asked. "Kingsley knows all this. I've told him and he's forgiven me. But will you forgive me?"

"Do you really need me to tell you I forgive you?"

"No, but it would comfort me to hear it."

"I can do something better than forgiving you."

Søren raised his eyebrow at her. Nora lifted her hands and unclasped the necklace she always wore that held the two wedding bands Søren had given her as a Christmas gift four years ago and the pendant her lover and submissive Nico had given her to wear when they were apart. She slipped the necklace and pendant into the pocket of her dress. Looking up at Søren she took his left hand in hers and slid the band onto his ring finger.

"Forever." She whispered her vow to him, the vow written on the band, a promise made, a promise she would keep.

Søren gazed down at his hand as if seeing it for the first time. Then he took the other ring—the one engraved with the word *everything*—and slipped it over the fourth finger on her left hand.

"Everything," he said.

No other words necessary. No other vows. They wouldn't bother vowing to forsake all others because they both loved others. Kingsley was Søren's heart as much as she was, as much as God was. She would no more ask him to give up his nights with Kingsley than she would ask him to stop giving his days to God. He would no more ask her to give up Nico than he would ask her to give up writing. This was how they were faithful to each other, by letting each other be faithful to their own hearts.

"What therefore God hath joined together, let no man put asunder."

"Amen," Nora replied.

Amen.

So be it.

She rose up on her knees and they kissed in the chapel, they kissed to seal these, their true Final Vows.

Never before had he kissed her so tenderly, so gently, as if she were fifteen again and this the only kiss he could trust himself to give her.

"Make love to me," she whispered into the kiss.

Søren smiled against her lips. "Here? In the chapel?"

"Roomier than a confessional booth, right? Please, sir?"

He cupped her chin in his hand and brushed his thumb across her bottom lip.

"Yes, Your Majesty."

Søren stood and pulled her off her knees and into his arms. With his hands in her hair, he pulled her head back to expose her neck to his kisses. His lips were gentle on her skin, gentle enough to make her shiver and sigh. He sat down in the first pew and tugged her down into his lap. She went willingly, straddling his thighs with her knees as his hands slipped under the skirts of her dress, her Scottish wedding dress she'd worn on this night, her wedding night.

His hands sought out the soft naked flesh of her thighs where her stockings and garters met her skin. Søren dug his fingers hard into her hips, hard enough that she gasped. His teeth found her earlobe and bit down. Pain. Blessed pain. The dead feel no pain, and Nora had never felt more alive than she did at this moment with her heart in her throat and her eyes shedding tears. Nora pushed his kilt up and he positioned himself at the entrance of her body. He brought her down onto him, joining them into one. Union. Communion. Love incarnate.

Nora wrapped her arms around his neck and rested her cheek against his shoulder. His strong hand cupped the back of her head like a father holding a child to his chest.

"I promised to give you everything," Søren whispered into her ear. "When you left me, I knew I could never keep my promise because I could never give you everything you needed. I couldn't be all things to you and it hurt because I wanted to be. I wanted to keep my promise."

"You are my everything."

"Perhaps we made the wrong promises. I should have promised you forever. And you should have promised me everything. You've given me everything I ever wanted. You didn't let me leave the church. You were right in that I would have regretted it. You gave me Kingsley back," he said. "When I almost lost you to Marie-Laure I found him again. And you sent Grace to me and gave me—"

"I did that for me," she said. "I'm not that selfless. I wanted..."

"What did you want?"

"I couldn't do it myself. But I thought...maybe...with her..." She stopped and smiled. "Was that wrong of me?"

"No," Søren said. "I would never have betrayed you if I thought you would have counted it as a betrayal."

"I wanted a part of you to live on after you were gone."

"Eleanor, I will never truly be gone from you. I will never leave you or forsake you."

"Where you go I will go. Your God will be my God," Nora continued the verse. "Where you die, there I will be buried."

"And we will have each other forever. In this life and the next."

"Promise?" she asked.

"Anything for you, Little One," he said. "*Everything* for you."

Søren kissed her hair as she tilted her hips against him, taking him deeper into her, holding him there, pulsing around him with her inner muscles even as her fingertips lightly played with his hair and her lips feathered soft kisses along his collar. She closed her eyes tight and gasped when he came into her, filling her depths and breathing her name.

When it was over and done with she stayed on his lap with her arms around him, holding him and being held. She heard footsteps approaching and felt Søren's body tense. She didn't let him go.

"I'm here," she whispered. "I'm always here."

She looked up and saw Kingsley standing in the doorway to the chapel. She met his eyes and he nodded.

Søren turned back and looked at Kingsley, who said the words they'd been waiting three hours to hear.

"Søren, your son is here."

38

Everything

NORA GAVE SØREN ONE LAST KISS ON THE FOREHEAD.

"It's time," she whispered. "I'll wait for you in the hallway with Kingsley if you need a minute to pray."

"Thank you."

Nora rose from his lap and straightened her skirts. Kingsley held out his hand, and she took it in hers. Together they stood in the darkened hallway, her head against his chest, his arms around her.

"How are you?" he asked.

"Scared. Happy," she said. "Scared by how happy I am."

"I know that feeling. I felt the same way the day you introduced me to my son. Now you can introduce him to his."

Nora looked into Kingsley's eyes. "You do it."

Kingsley narrowed his eyes at her.

"Elle… I speak from experience when I say this moment will be the most important moment of his life," Kingsley said. "The first time I held Céleste? The first time I met Nico?

Those were the two best days of my life. Nothing will ever be the same for him again after today."

"That's why you should do it. Because you've been through this before. And because if it's the most important moment in his life, he should share it with the most important person in the world to him. That's you."

Kingsley's eyes filled with tears and he smiled. In a hoarse voice and with a hand over his heart he answered, "It would be my honor."

"*Merci,*" she said, smiling and shaking all at once. She stepped into Kingsley's arms again and relaxed against him. Now there was nothing between them, no secrets, no shame, no bitterness, no sorrow. She loved Kingsley and Kingsley loved her and nothing would ever tear the three of them apart again. Because God had joined them together, all three of them, and what God has joined together no one would tear asunder.

Søren emerged from the chapel.

"Would you like to meet your son now, *mon ami*?" Kingsley asked.

"Yes," Søren said. "I would like that very much."

"I'll introduce you to him. Don't be upset if he likes me better than he likes you," Kingsley said. "I've already met him. And everyone likes me better."

"Eleanor, is Nico as arrogant as his father?"

"No one is as arrogant as his father. Except his father's best friend."

"That's unfair," Søren said as the three of them, side by side by side, walked down the hall and toward the castle's vestibule. "It's not arrogance. It's self-awareness."

"How have I put up with this for twenty-three years?" Nora sighed. "And where do I sign up for twenty-three years more?"

"I believe you did in the chapel," Søren said, reaching out to squeeze her left hand.

The way brightened as they reached the end of the hallway. Nora stopped and stayed in the shadows. She let go of Søren's hand.

"Give my godson a kiss for me," Nora said, kissing Søren on the lips.

Søren didn't speak. He simply touched her cheek and looked into her eyes.

"Go," she said. "It's an order."

"Yes, Mistress," Søren said with a wink.

"Shall we?" Kingsley said. With a gallant bow he ushered Søren from the hallway into the vestibule. Nora looked across the room filled to bursting with blue and gold tapestries and knights in armor and gray stone walls and mullioned windows and saw none of it. A scene far more arresting captured her gaze. A red-haired woman in a blue dress and a dark-haired man in a black suit holding the hands of a blond-haired three-year-old boy dressed in a jacket, tiny tie and short pants.

Søren took a few steps forward and stopped. Kingsley continued toward the trio and shook hands with the man, kissed the woman and knelt on the floor to greet the boy. Words were exchanged but Nora couldn't hear them. But she did see the little boy grin. Kingsley had that effect on children. He laughed when Kingsley stood up and swept him off his small feet and dropped him onto his broad shoulders. Kingsley carried the boy on his shoulders across the room. When he reached Søren, Kingsley went down onto his knees, a knight before a king, a king before his god. And the little boy, Fionn Easton, was now at eye level with Søren. Nora could barely breathe as she watched them, as she saw them looking at each other, trying to figure each other out. Fionn had intelligent eyes that were forever watching, seeking, taking the measure of everyone and everything he saw. But he had a smiling face, too, and an infectious giggle. He was a good boy and Nora loved him. How could she not? She'd dreamed of him and there he was with his father at last. Today was an embarrassment of miracles.

Søren said something to Fionn and held out his hand. Fionn took the large hand in his and shook it. Søren lifted Fionn off Kingsley's shoulders and Kingsley came to his feet again. The three of them—Kingsley, Søren and Søren's son—walked over to his mother, to Grace Easton. Zach Easton, Grace's husband and Nora's editor, walked over to her.

Nora held out her arms and Zach stepped into her embrace, lifting her off her feet.

"Hi, handsome," she said, kissing his cheek. "How much have you missed me?"

"I didn't realize how much until right now," he said. She squeezed him harder, held him closer.

"How are you handling all of this?" she asked into her ear.

"Better now that it's over with," Zach said. "I'm sorry we couldn't be here any sooner. Had to work this morning."

"You could always quit," she said. "Kingsley set you all up very nicely, I hear."

"That's all Fionn's. And I wouldn't know what to do with myself if I didn't work. God knows I couldn't leave you in anyone else's hands."

"I can't take charity, either. Kingsley would have given me a fortune if I'd asked for it. But then I wouldn't have had much incentive to write the books that have been driving you insane for the past five years, right?"

"Quite so. I hope Fionn finds something that makes him as happy as my work has made me."

"I'm sure he will. He's his father's son—smart, determined, and has a good heart."

"Took me a while to see it, but I would agree with you about Søren."

"I meant you," she said. "He's your son."

He kissed her forehead. "Thank you. You always know the right thing to say."

"You look so hot in your suit I want to drag you out of here and blow you."

"Case in point."

Nora laughed and playfully attempted to pull him back into the hallway.

"None of that," Zach said. "No blowing. Grace and I have sown all the wild oats we intend to ever sow. Back to monogamy."

"Ugh," Nora said, shuddering. "Don't say the M-word around me."

"Forgive me. When he's old enough, you can explain the facts of life to Fionn then. I'll sit in the back with popcorn and watch you attempt to explain to a twelve-year-old boy why his godmother is romantically involved with a Catholic priest *and* a French vintner. Any why she doesn't own any horses and yet always has a riding crop with her..."

"I'll start preparing the Venn diagrams and flow charts for when that blessed day comes. And speaking of my beautiful blond godson...do you have the item I requested?"

"I do. He had his haircut Thursday last. Saved a scrap for you," he said, pulling an envelope from his pocket to pass to her.

"Perfect." She took a glass locket from the pocket of her dress and opened it.

"Lovely locket. Where did you get that? Family heirloom?"

"Actually, I ripped it off the neck of an evil dominatrix who Søren sold a lock of his hair to in order to buy me a computer.

I gave it back to him, but then I stole it out of his pocket again after we'd fucked in the confessional at our church."

"That was my second guess."

The glass locket still contained the lock of Søren's hair. She added a few strands of Fionn's to it, shut it and slipped it on her necklace. Now that she and Søren wore their wedding bands, the necklace needed something new on it to go with the pendant from her Nico.

Zach pulled her in front of him and helped her clasp the necklace.

"Now it's your turn. I gave you something. You give me something. Your autograph please."

Nora sighed. She'd been waiting for this moment. From the inside pocket of his suit jacket, Zach pulled out a tri-folded bundle of legal documents.

"You sure about this?" she asked, her hands slightly shaking. "You've met me, right?"

Zach handed her the documents and an ink pen.

"If something happens to us, Grace and I want you to raise our son. And yes, I've met you. That's why we chose you." He turned his back to her so she could use him as a desk.

"Last time I signed a piece of paper on your back, it changed my life," she said. "Let's hope history doesn't repeat itself."

"Last time you signed a piece of paper on my back, we had sex all night long right afterward," Zach reminded her.

"Okay, maybe history can repeat itself."

Nora had to wait for Zach to stop laughing so she could properly sign her name without smearing the ink.

"I promise you, Grace and I have no intention of getting ourselves killed anytime soon. But if we do, Fionn's yours. Please don't raise him Catholic."

"No promises, Easton."

Nora flipped to the last page and signed her name on the

line——Eleanor Schreiber. She folded up the papers that made her guardian of Fionn Easton and his trust fund in the event of his parents' death and gave them back to Zach. He tucked them back in his pocket and kissed her forehead.

"Thank you," he whispered.

It was done.

The comforting weight of Zach's arms settled around her stomach. The two of them, the outsiders in this little play, held each other tight and watched as Søren, Kingsley, Grace and Fionn chatted about everything and nothing.

"You and I have made some beautiful book babies together, Zach," Nora said, her throat contracting as Søren brushed his hand over Fionn's head, smoothing down a wayward strand of baby-soft hair.

Zach snorted. "Book babies? We're talking about your books. More like Rosemary's Babies."

"You mean that as an insult, and yet I'm taking it as a compliment."

"This does not surprise me." Zach pulled her closer to him and she relaxed into his arms. "What's going to happen?" he asked her as they both watched Grace, Kingsley, Søren and Fionn talking.

"I don't know," she said. "But you have nothing to worry about. He'd never do anything to hurt you or Grace or Fionn. He's a good sadist."

"Will he be all right?"

"He will be. He has me and Kingsley no matter what."

"You all are a strange little coven, aren't you?" Zach asked, shaking his head in amusement.

"We prefer the term *family*. And guess what? You're in it, too." She playfully slapped her hand on the center of his chest. He covered it with his own hand before lifting it to his lips for a kiss. "For life."

Nora leaned against him, took comfort in his warmth, his solidity and their friendship, which had meant so much to her. Søren had Fionn's tiny hand in his and seemed to be examining his fingers. Long strong fingers. A future pianist's fingers perhaps? Søren kissed Fionn's fingers and Nora knew she had never been this happy in her life.

"Will he leave the priesthood?" Zach asked.

"No. But he's expecting them to kick him out once he tells his provincial about Fionn. He doesn't feel right keeping Fionn a secret. Me? Kingsley? We knew what we were getting into. A child shouldn't worry his biological father considered him a dirty little secret."

"Are you scared? There might be a scandal."

"My whole life's a scandal. But no, I'm not scared. He's been in the Jesuits thirty-four years. I think he's earned his retirement. What about you? Are you scared?"

"I worry about Fionn, that's all. He's my son. And his."

"And he's my godson. He has me to thank for his existence, after all. I won't let anything happen to him."

"So you're the one I have to blame for my life being turned upside down?"

"My doing," she said. "I'm the one who sent Grace to Søren. I didn't know Fionn would be the result but well, Grace saved us all. One new life for our three lives sounds like a good deal to me." Grace had run her guts out to get to Kingsley in time. If she hadn't, Nora and Søren would have died and she knew Kingsley was joking when he said he'd last three days in a world without Søren. Giving Grace the child her heart longed for seemed like the least they could do in repayment.

"Then I say thank you. Also..." Zach pointed at her nose. "Don't do it again."

Nora started to scold him for being so vanilla, but then she heard her favorite song.

"Do devilishly handsome Jewish book editors dance?"

"Only when asked to by impossibly sexy Catholic writers."

She took his hand and dragged him away into the not-a-real wedding reception that was still in full swing. All around them people laughed and talked and drank and danced to her favorite song by The Police, the one band she and Søren had ever agreed on. Zach spun her once and pulled her close to him.

"Are you really mad at me for turning your life upside down?" she asked.

"It needed turning upside down," he said. "Funny, though. Once it was turned upside down I realized it was finally right-side up. What about you? Your life's been turned a bit sideways. Still standing?"

"I'm always standing," she said. "Except when I'm on my back. You know Søren never told me what you said to him when you called him that day and told him about Fionn."

"I believe I said something to the effect of 'Happy Birthday. Merry Christmas. Oh, and Happy Father's Day.' I enjoyed the stunned silence that followed."

"It's not easy to shock that man. Trust me, I've made doing it my life's work."

"I love my son and I love my wife and I love my work. And I have you to thank for them all. I would be divorced, childless and living in LA right now if it weren't for you. I don't know which of the three prospects horrifies me the most."

Nora laughed and kissed Zach on the mouth, full tilt with tongue and everything. She kissed him for two reasons, the only two reasons that ever mattered to Nora—because she wanted to and because she could.

"Happy now?" he asked, as she pulled back and saw Søren, Kingsley and Grace walking into the reception, Fionn in

Kingsley's arms but his hand in Søren's. "My wife just saw you kiss me."

"Oh, no, are we in trouble?"

"She's glaring and laughing at the same time," Zach said. "I think we're safe."

"Good. Now slow dance with me. It's not a wedding reception until I've drunkenly made out with a wedding guest while slow dancing."

"That's going to be a problem," Zach said as he led her in a slow dance. "We're not drunk."

Nora grabbed a glass of wine off a passing tray.

"We can fix that," she said.

Zach took her in his arms again.

"Behave," he said. "I'm a ridiculously happily married man and father, and I'm enjoying it believe it or not."

"Vanilla," she said.

"Not quite. I did learn a thing or two from you."

"That's what I like to hear."

"What about you, Nora?" he asked. "Happy?"

"How could I not be happy?" she asked, smiling so hard it hurt. "Look around...look at all of this...this happiness."

She took her own advice and looked around as she and Zach moved lightly across the dance floor.

Zach in her arms. Her editor and her dearest friend. He had changed her life when he signed her contract for the book she thought she'd never finish. But she had finished it, with a little help from a certain blond monster she knew and loved.

Finish the book, Søren had ordered. *Not for me or for Zachary or for Wesley or even for God. Finish it for you.*

And there were Michael and Griffin talking to Alfred and smiling. All of them smiling, even Alfred, and she was fairly certain that was the first time she'd ever seen him smile.

You are formally invited to attend the collaring of Griffin Fiske and Michael Dimir.

You knew? Nora had asked Søren.

Of course I knew...

And there was Juliette standing with Kingsley, speaking to Fionn and smiling as she introduced Kingsley's daughter to Søren's son.

That was the year I met Juliette, almost killed a man over her, came home and got everything back I'd lost and then some, Kingsley had said last night about the year he'd left Søren and found Juliette, the woman he loved and the mother of his children.

Nora clutched the pendant Nico had given her, which hung next to the glass locket on the chain. Nico, Kingsley's son. Nico, her lover, her submissive, who never would have existed if Søren hadn't let Kingsley go...

And Fionn, who she'd wished for in secret and had told no one ever, not Kingsley or Søren...

He was fourteen years her senior and women lived longer than men. Wouldn't it be something to have part of Søren live on after he was gone?

In fact, all that she had and all that she loved—her writing career, Zach, Grace, Fionn, Céleste, Juliette, Kingsley, Nico, Michael and Griffin...she had Søren to thank for all of it. In one way or another he'd brought them to her and to each other by paths both straight and broken.

She wanted for nothing.

She had it all.

"Oh, that son of a bitch," Nora said as she clung to Zach's hand even as she took a step toward where Søren stood speaking softly to his beautiful son. "He did it."

"Did what?" Zach asked.

"Søren promised to give me something and he kept his promise."

"What did he give you?"
Nora laughed.
"Everything."

★ ★ ★ ★ ★